Close
to the
Bone

Stuart MacBride is the No.1 bestselling author of the DS Logan McRae series and *Birthdays for the Dead*.

His novels have won him the CWA Dagger in the Library, the Barry Award for Best Debut Novel, and Best Breakthrough Author at the ITV3 Crime Thriller awards. In 2012 Stuart was inducted into the ITV3 Crime Thriller Hall of Fame.

Stuart's other works include *Halfhead*, a near-future thriller, *Sawbones*, a novella aimed at adult emergent readers, and several short stories.

He lives in the north-east of Scotland with his wife, Fiona, and cat, Grendel.

For more information visit StuartMacBride.com

By Stuart MacBride

The Logan McRae Novels
Cold Granite
Dying Light
Broken Skin
Flesh House
Blind Eye
Dark Blood
Shatter the Bones
Close to the Bone

Other Works
Birthdays for the Dead
Sawbones – a novella
12 Days of Winter (short stories)

Writing as Stuart B. MacBride
Halfhead

STUART MACBRIDE

Close to the Bone

HARPER

This is a work of fiction. Any references to real people, living or dead, real events, businesses, organizations and localities are intended only to give the fiction a sense of reality and authenticity. All names, characters, places and incidents are either the product of the author's imagination or are used fictitiously, and their resemblance, if any, to real-life counterparts is entirely coincidental. The only exceptions to this are the characters Alex (Zander) Clark, Ian Falconer, April Logan/Graham, and Emma Sim, who have given their express permission to be fictionalized in this volume. All behaviour, history, and character traits assigned to these individuals have been designed to serve the needs of the narrative and do not necessarily bear any resemblance to the real people.

Harper

HarperCollins*Publishers*
77–85 Fulham Palace Road,
Hammersmith, London W6 8JB

www.harpercollins.co.uk

This paperback edition 2013
3

First published in Great Britain by HarperCollins*Publishers* 2013

Copyright © Stuart MacBride 2013

Stuart MacBride asserts the moral right to
be identified as the author of this work

A catalogue record for this book
is available from the British Library

ISBN: 978-0-00-734429-1

Set in Meridien 10.25/13.5 pt
Typeset by Palimpsest Book Production Limited, Falkirk, Stirlingshire

Printed and bound in Great Britain by
Clays Ltd, St Ives plc

MIX
Paper from
responsible sources
FSC www.fsc.org   FSC™ C007454

For Ishbel

Without Whom

Books like this would be a nightmare to write without access to a bunch of very clever people who don't mind me picking their brains and asking stupid questions. As usual, anything I've got right is down to them and anything I've got wrong is down to me.

So a big thank you is due to all of my forensic experts: Ishbel Gall, Dr Lorna Dawson, Prof. Dave Barclay, Dr James Grieve, and Prof. Sue Black.

More go to Dave Reilly, and Jon Lloyd for hints and tips and tricks of the trade.

Then there's the excellently historical Chris Croly, and Fiona Musk. (If you're in Aberdeen – go see the archives. They're great, and they're free!)

As always HarperCollins deserves a big shout out, especially those ninjas of publishy goodness Sarah Hodgson, Kate Elton, Jane Johnson, Julia Wisdom, Laura Mell, Oliver Malcolm, Laura Fletcher, Roger Cazalet, Lucy Upton, Damon Greeney, Catherine Friis, Emad Akhtar, Kate Stephenson, Anne O'Brien, Marie Goldie, and the DC Bishopbriggs Wild Brigade.

The same's true of Phil Patterson, Isabella Floris, Luke Speed, and everyone at Marjacq Scripts.

A number of people have helped raise a lot of money for charity by bidding to have a character named after them in this book: Peter and Emma Sim, April Logan, and Ian Falconer. Thanks, guys.

And saving the best for last – as always – Fiona and Grendel.

Like it or not, you're still alive.

Saturday

1

She holds up the book of matches. Licks her lips. She's practised the words a dozen times till they're perfect. 'Do you have anything to say before I carry out sentence?'

The man kneeling on the floor of the warehouse stares up at her. He's trembling, moaning behind the mask hiding his face. 'Oh God, oh Jesus, oh God, oh Jesus. . .' The chains around his wrists and ankles rattle against the metal stake. A waft of accelerant curls through the air from the tyre wedged over his head and shoulders. Black rubber and paraffin.

'Too late for that.' She smiles. 'Thomas Leis, you—'

'Please, you don't have to do this!'

The smile slips. He's spoiling it. 'Thomas Leis, you have been found *guilty* of witchcraft—'

'I'm not a witch, it's a mistake!'

'—condemned to burn at the stake until you be dead.'

'I didn't do *anything*!'

'Coward.' The lights are hot on her back as she strikes the first match, then sets fire to the rest. They hiss and flare, bright and shining. Pure. Glorious.

'PLEASE!'

'Burn. Like you'll burn in hell.' She drags the smile back on. 'It'll be good practice for you.' She drops the blazing matchbook onto the tyre and the accelerant catches. Whoosh – blue and yellow flames race around the rubber.

Thomas Leis *screams*.

He jerks against his chains. Thick black smoke wreaths his face, hiding the mask from view as the fire takes hold. He pleads and screams and begs. . .

She throws her head back and laughs at the heavens. Spreads her arms wide. Eyes glittering like diamonds.

The voice of God crackles through the air, making the very world vibrate: *'And . . . cut. Well done, everyone – break for lunch and we'll go for scene two thirty-six at half one.'*

A round of applause.

Then a man in a fluorescent-yellow waistcoat rushes into shot with a fire extinguisher. FWOOOSH – the flames disappear in a puff of carbon dioxide as the cameraman backs away, shielding his lens.

The runner peels off the bright green mask with the yellow crosses on it from the stuntman doubling for Thomas Leis. The stuntman's grinning, even though he knows they're going to digitally replace his face in post. Even though he *barged* over her line.

God save us from stuntmen who think they're actors.

She puts her head on one side and frowns. 'I don't know. . . It felt a bit over the top at the end there. Really hammy. Wouldn't she be more . . . you know, suppressed? Maybe even a bit sexual? Can I do it again?'

2

'I'm on my way. Tell everyone to—' Something under his foot went *crunch*. Logan froze on the doorstep, mobile phone clamped to his ear. He slid his shoe to one side and curled his top lip. 'Not *again*.'

Three little bones lay on the concrete slab, tied together with a tatty piece of red ribbon.

A hissing whisper came from the other end of the phone. *'Seriously, Guv, Pukey Pete's having ferrets up here, it's—'*

'I *said* I'm on my way.'

Logan stuck the phone against his chest and scowled out at the caravan park in the growing gloom. Bulky static caravans, the size of shipping containers, all painted a uniform institution green. A patrol car idled on the square of tarmac that acted as a turning circle, its blue-and-whites strobing in the warm late-evening air. The driver hunched forward in his seat, peering out through the windscreen at Logan, working his hands back and forth along the steering wheel – as if he was trying to feel it up.

No sign of the little buggers.

Logan kicked the broken bones off the step into the straggly ivy growing up the side of his home. Then took a deep breath and bellowed it out: 'I KNOW WHERE YOU LIVE, YOU WEE SHITES!'

Back to the phone.

'I mean, he's gone off on one before, but no' like this. He's—'

'If he's screwing up the scene, arrest him. If not, just hold his bloody hand till I get there.' Logan stomped over to the patrol car and threw himself into the passenger seat. Hauled on the belt. 'Drive.'

The PC put his foot down.

The sun was a scarlet smear across the horizon, filling the patch of rough ground with blood and shadow. Trees loomed around the periphery, their branches filled with clacks and caws as the rooks settled in for the night.

Grey and black hulks dotted the clearing: burned-out cars, their paint stripped away, seats a sagging framework of rusty wire, the tyres turned into gritty vitrified puddles.

A cordon of blue-and-white 'POLICE' tape was strung between the vehicles, making a twenty-foot no-man's-land around the Scenes Examination Branch's inner cordon of 'CRIME SCENE' yellow-and-black. Three SEB technicians knelt in the dirt, poking at something, their white Tyvek oversuits glowing pink in the twilight.

Logan wrinkled his nose. The rancid stench of vomit fought against the greasy scent of burned meat and rendered fat. Like a barbecue with food poisoning. 'Where's the pathologist?'

One of the techs – a shortarse with fogged-up safety goggles – finished scraping something dark and sticky into an evidence bag, then pointed her gloved finger at the other side of the 'CRIME SCENE' tape. There was another figure in the full Smurf outfit, hunched over a bucket, making retching noises, his back convulsing with every stomach-wrenching heave.

The short tech peeled her facemask off, exposing a circle of shiny pink skin and a thin-lipped mouth. 'Poor wee bugger. Can't blame him, really. Nearly lost a white-pudding supper myself.' She puffed out a breath, hauled at the elasticated hood of her suit. 'Christ it's *hot* in here. . .'

'You call for backup?'

A nod. 'The Ice Queen's en route as we speak.' The tech pinged her facemask back into place. 'You want to take a sneak peek? We've got as much as we're going to before they move the body.'

'How bad is it?'

She peeled off her gloves and snapped on a fresh pair. 'What, and spoil the thrill of finding out for yourself?' Then she set off across an elevated walkway – metallic stepping stones, like upturned tea trays on tiny legs, keeping their blue plastic booties from contaminating the scene. It led away between a couple of burned-out hatchbacks, disappearing behind the blackened skeletal remains of a Renault Clio. A dark curl of smoke twisted up into the sky on the other side.

Logan adjusted his safety goggles, zipped up his oversuit, and zwip-zwopped after her. The walkway clanged beneath his feet. The rancid barbecue smell got worse. And then they were there.

Christ. . .

His stomach lurched two steps to the right, then crashed back again. He swallowed, hard. Blinked. Cleared his throat. 'What do we know?'

'Not much: victim's male, we think.' Another shrug. 'He's been chained to what looks like a section of that modular metal shelving stuff – the kind you get in your garage? Been hammered into the ground like a stake.'

The victim was kneeling on the hard-packed earth, his legs tucked under his bum. His bright-orange overalls were stained around the legs and waist, blackened across his chest and flecked with little glittering tears of vitrified rubber. Someone had forced his head and right arm through the middle of a tyre – so it sat across his body like a sash – then set fire to it. It was still burning: a small tongue of greasy flame licked up the side of the rubber.

The SEB tech groaned. 'Bloody hell. . .' She hauled a fire extinguisher from a blue plastic crate, pointed the nozzle, and squeezed the handle. A whoosh of white hid the poor bastard's face from view for a moment, but when the CO_2 cleared he appeared again in all his tortured glory.

His skin was swollen and blistered, scorched crimson; the eyes cooked to an opaque white; teeth bared, yellowed and cracked. Hair gone. Patches of skull and cheekbone poking through charred flesh. . .

Don't be sick. Don't be sick.

Logan cleared his throat. Looked out over the graveyard of burned-out cars. Deep breaths. The long corrugated metal roof of Thainstone Mart was just visible between the trees in the distance, what sounded like Tom Jones belting out 'It's Not Unusual' at a disco or corporate bash, dancing and boozing it up into the wee small hours. And when they were gone some poor sod would be up all night, clearing up all the spent party poppers and empty bottles before the next livestock auction.

The SEB tech thumped the fire extinguisher back into the crate. 'It's the rubber in the tyre – once it gets up to temperature it's almost impossible to stop the damn thing from catching again.'

'Get it off him.'

'The tyre?' She gave a wee spluttering laugh. 'Before the Ice Queen gets here?'

'Doctor Forsyth—'

'Pukey Pete won't even look at the poor sod.' She sagged a bit. 'Shame. It was nice having a pathologist you could actually *talk* to. . .'

10

Now the tyre wasn't burning any more, other smells elbowed their way through Logan's facemask: excrement, urine. He took a step back.

The tech nodded. 'Stinks, doesn't he? Mind you, if it was me – if someone did *that* to me? I'd shit myself too. Must've been terrified.'

A voice cut through the still evening air: one of those singsong Highlands-and-Islands accents. 'Inspector McRae? Hello?'

Logan turned.

A woman stood behind the outer cordon of blue-and-white 'POLICE' tape, her grey linen suit creased like an elephant's scrotum. 'Inspector?' She was waving at him, as if he was headed off somewhere nice on a train, not standing on a little metal walkway beside a man who'd burned to death.

Logan picked his way along the clanking tea trays until he was in the blue-and-white area again. Peeled back his hood, took off his safety goggles, then crumpled up his facemask and stuck it in a pocket.

The woman squinted at him, pulled a pair of glasses from a big leather handbag and slipped them on, tucking a nest of brown curls behind her ears. 'Inspector McRae?'

'I'm sorry, miss, we're not giving interviews to the press right now, so—'

'I was First Attending Officer.' She stuck her hand out for shaking. 'Detective Sergeant Lorna Chalmers.' A smile. 'Just transferred down from Northern? I'm investigating that off-licence ram-raid in Inverurie yesterday, looking for the Range Rover they nicked to do the job?'

Nope, no idea. But it explained the accent. Logan snapped off his purple nitrile gloves. 'You get the cordon set up?'

'And the duty doctor, the SEB – or whatever it is they're called this week – and the pathologist too: original *and* replacement.'

Cocky.

Logan struggled out of the top half of his oversuit, then leaned back against the remains of a VW Polo. The bonnet wasn't just warm beneath his bum, it was hot.

DS Chalmers pulled out a police-issue notebook and flipped it open. 'Call came in at eight twenty, anonymous – well, mobile phone, but it's a pay-as-you-go disposable. Unidentified male said there was a "bloke on fire with a tyre round his neck and that" out by Thainstone Mart.'

Frown. 'Why didn't the local station take it?'

She grinned, showing off sharp little teeth. 'You snooze, you lose.'

Cocky and ambitious with it. Well, if that's the way she wanted to play it: he swept an arm out at the collection of burned-out vehicles. 'I need you to get every car here identified. I want names, addresses, and criminal records of the owners on my desk first thing tomorrow morning.'

She gave him a stiff-lipped smile and a nod. I am determined, nothing will stop me. 'I'm on it, Guv.'

'Good.' Logan pushed himself off the VW Polo. 'And you can start with this one. Or didn't you notice it was still warm?'

The smile slipped. 'It is? Ah, it's—'

'Was it burning when you got here?'

'I don't—'

'Details, Sergeant, they're important.'

'Only I was. . . I thought the dead man. . . I was getting everything sorted and. . .' A blush pricked across her cheeks. 'Sorry, sir.'

'Get the SEB to give it a once-over before they go. Probably won't find anything, but it's worth a try.' He struggled out of the oversuit's lower half, then swore as a tinny rendition of the 'Imperial March' from *Star Wars* blared out of his phone. Didn't even need to check the caller ID to know who it was.

Logan hit the button. 'What *now*?'

A pause, then Detective Chief Inspector Steel's smoky voice rumbled in his ear. *'Have you still got me ringing up as Darth Sodding Vader, 'cos that's no' funny!'*

Logan pressed mute. 'Sergeant, I thought I asked you to get those vehicle IDs.'

She kept her eyes on her shoes. 'Yes, sir.'

He smiled. Well, it wouldn't kill him to throw her a bone. 'You made a good FAO: keep it up.' He pressed the mute button again. 'Now bugger off.'

Spluttering burst from the phone. *'Don't you dare tell me to bugger off! I'm head of sodding CID, no' some—'*

'Not you – DS Chalmers.' He shooed her away, then shifted his mobile to the other side, pinning it in place with his shoulder while he unzipped the rest of his oversuit. 'What do you want?'

'Oh. . .' A cough. *'Right. Where's that bloody paperwork?'*

'Your in-tray. Did you even bother checking? Or did you just—'

'No' the overtime report, you divot, the budget analysis.'

'Oh, I thought you meant where was *my* paperwork. You know, the paperwork *I'm* actually supposed to do, as opposed to *your* paperwork.'

'Bad enough I've got all this shite to sort out without you throwing a strop every time you're asked to do a simple wee task—'

'Look, I'm at a murder scene, so can we skip through all the bollocks to the actual reason you called? Was it just to give me a hard time? Because if it was, you can—'

'And what about those bloody missing teenage lovebirds? When are you planning on finding them, eh? Or are you too busy swanning about with—'

'Which part of "I'm at a murder scene" do you not get?'

'—poor parents worried to death!'

'For God's sake, they're both eighteen – they're not

13

teenagers, they're *adults*.' He shuffled his way out of the blue plastic booties. 'They'll be shacked up together in an Edinburgh squat by now. Bet you any money they're at it like rabbits on a manky futon.'

'That's no excuse for dragging your heels – bloody woman's mother's been on the phone again. *Do I look like I've no' got anything better to do than run around after your scarred backside all day?'* A loud sniff rattled down the phone. *'Pull your sodding socks up: you've done bugger all on that jewellery heist last night, there's a stack of outstanding hate crimes. . . And while we're on the subject: your sodding mother!'*

'Ah, right: here we go. The *real* reason.' Logan scrunched the protective gear up into a ball and dumped it in the bin-bag taped to the remains of an Audi. 'I'm not her keeper, OK?'

'You tell that bloody woman to—'

'I said don't invite her to Jasmine's dance recital, but would you listen to me? Noooooo.'

'—sodding paisley patterned Attila the Hun! And another thing—'

A huge mud-spattered Porsche Cayenne four-by-four growled to a halt on the rutted track, behind the SEB Transit van. *Clunk* and the headlights went off, leaving the driver illuminated in the glow of the dashboard. Mouth a thin grim line, nostrils flared, eyes screwed into slits. Brilliant, it was going to be one of *those* evenings.

'—in the ear with a stick!'

Logan held up a hand and waved at the Porsche. 'Got to go, Pathologist number two's up.'

'Laz, I'm warning you, either—'

He hung up.

Dr Isobel MacAllister stuck both hands against the base of her spine and puffed. Her SOC suit swelled in front, as if she was shoplifting a floor cushion. She hauled back the elasticated hood, showing off a puffy, rose-coloured face framed by a droopy bobbed haircut that looked a lot more functional than glamorous. 'Did you *really* just ask for a time of death?'

DS Chalmers nodded, biro hovering over a blank page in her notebook.

Isobel turned to Logan. 'She's new, isn't she?'

'Just transferred down from Northern.'

'Lord preserve us from the Tartan Bunnet Brigade.' Isobel unzipped the front of her suit. 'The body appears to have been necklaced – rubber tyre placed over the head and one arm, making it impossible for the victim to remove, then the outer surface is doused with paraffin and set alight. Death is usually caused by heat and smoke inhalation, leading to shock and heart failure. That can take up to twenty minutes.' She wiped a hand across her shiny forehead. 'It's a popular method of summary execution in some African states.'

DS Chalmers scribbled something in her pad. Then looked up. 'And Colombia too. I saw this documentary where the cartels would chain the guy up on an overpass, fill the tyre with petrol and light it. Everyone driving home would see them hanging there, burning, so they knew what would happen if they screwed with. . .' She cleared her throat. 'Why are you all staring at me?'

Isobel shook her head. 'Anyway, I've—'

A car horn blared across the clearing.

She stared at the sky for a moment. Gritted her teeth. Tried again: 'As I was saying, I've—'

Breeeeeeeeeeeeeeeeeeeeeeeeeeeeeeeeeep!

'Oh, for God's sake, I can't get five minutes to myself, can I? Not even five minutes.' She jabbed a finger in the direction of her Porsche four-by-four, took a deep trembling

15

breath, and let rip. 'SEAN JOSHUA MILLER-MACALLISTER, YOU STOP THAT THIS INSTANT!'

Silence.

A wee face peered over the dashboard, big eyes and dirty blond hair. Then a flashing grin.

Breeeep! Breep! Breeeeeeeeeeeeeeeeeeeeeeeeeeeeeeeeeep!

Isobel hauled off her gloves and hurled them onto the ground. 'You see what happens? Do you? And will Ulrika get deported for it? Of course not: we'll be lucky if she even gets a slap on the wrist.' Isobel stomped off towards the car. 'YOU'RE IN BIG TROUBLE, MISTER!' Shedding the layers of SOC gear as she went.

DS Chalmers shuffled her feet. 'Well, that was. . .?'

'They caught the au pair nicking things.' Logan pulled out his phone. 'And consider yourself lucky – the last person who asked for a time of death? She made them help her take the victim's temperature. And the thermometer doesn't go in the front end.'

3

Midges bobbed and weaved in the glow of a SEB spotlight, shining like tiny blood-thirsty diamonds. In the middle distance, Tom Jones had given way to ABBA's 'Dancing Queen'. Logan stuck a finger in his ear and shifted a couple of paces further away from the grumbling diesel generators. 'What? I can't hear you.'

On the other end of the phone, DCI Steel got a notch louder. *'I said, what makes you think it's drugs?'*

'Might not be, but it looks like an execution. We'll know more when we get an ID on the body: my money's on a scheemie drug runner from Manchester or Birmingham.'

'Sodding hell, that's all I need: some flash bastard knocking off rival dealers like it's a performance art.' Silence. Then a plastic sooking sound. *'No way I'm carrying the bucket on this one.'*

'Thought that was the point of being in charge of CID?'

'Sometimes shite flows uphill, Laz, and this one's got "Assistant Chief Constable's Oversight" written all over it in black magic marker. Let him deal with the members of the press.'

The SEB tech who'd taken him to see the body shuffled into view, holding one corner of what looked like a crate wrapped in miles of thick blue plastic. It was big enough to

17

take a kneeling man chained to a metal stake. She grimaced at him. 'Budge over a bit, eh? This is bloody heavy. . .'

'And by "members" I mean—'

'Got to go, the Procurator Fiscal wants a word.' Which was a lie – she'd left nearly half an hour ago.

'Oh no you don't: you're no' going nowhere till you tell me where we are with that bloody jewellery heist. You think you get to dump all your other cases just because you've got a juicy wee gangland execution on the cards?'

'Investigations are ongoing, and—'

'You've done sod all, haven't you?'

'I've been at a bloody murder scene!'

The SEB hauled their blue plastic parcel through the graveyard of burned-out cars, swearing and grunting all the way, feet kicking up a cloud of pale dust from the parched earth.

'Well, whose fault is that? You're a DI now: act like it! Park your arse behind your desk and organize things – send some other bugger off to play at the scene.'

Rotten, stinky, wrinkled, bastarding. . . 'You're the one who told me to come out here! I wasn't even on duty, I was having my tea.' He pulled the mobile from his ear and glared at it. Concentrate hard enough and her head would explode like an overripe pluke on the other end of the phone. BANG! Brains and wee bits of skull all over the walls.

'Er. . . Guv?' DS Chalmers tapped him on the shoulder, a frown pulling one side of her face down. 'Are you OK? Only you've gone kinda purple. . .'

Logan gritted his teeth, put the phone back to his ear. 'You and I are going to have words about this tomorrow.'

'Sodding right we will. I'm no'—'

He hung up. Glowered at his phone for a beat, then jabbed the 'OFF' button. Leave it on and she'd just call back, again and again, until he finally snapped and murdered someone.

Logan took a deep breath and hissed it out through his nose. 'I swear to God. . .'

Chalmers held up her notebook, like a small shield. 'We got chassis numbers off all the cars, and guess what: I found my Range Rover.' Pause. 'The Range Rover on the CCTV? The one that ram-raided the off-licence?'

'What about the Golf?'

'Reported stolen at half ten this morning. According to Control: the registered keeper says he drove down the Kintore chippy for his tea Friday evening, came back and parked outside his mum's house, and when he woke up it was gone.' She checked her notes. 'The car, not his mum's house.'

'Go see him. Tell him sod all, just rattle his cage and see what flies out.'

'Yes, sir.' Chalmers wrote something in her notebook, then stashed it away in her jacket. 'I was right about the Colombian drug cartel thing, by the way. Had a boyfriend who downloaded videos of them hanging there, on fire like they were these. . . *horrible* Christmas decorations. He always got really horny after watching them too.' She wiped her hands down the front of her jacket, then rubbed the fingertips together, as if they were dirty. 'I broke it off: *way* too creepy.'

Logan just stared at her.

'Ah. . . Too much information from the new girl. Right.' Chalmers backed away a couple of steps. 'I'll go chase up that . . . yes.' And she was gone.

'I know, I know, I'm sorry.' Logan shifted the mobile from one side to the other, pinning it between his ear and his shoulder as he took the battered Fiat Punto around the Clinterty roundabout, heading back along the dual carriageway towards Aberdeen. 'You know what she's like.'

Samantha sighed. '*Logan McRae, you're not supposed to let*

her walk all over you any more. You know *that. We talked about this.'*

He changed gear and put his foot down. The Punto's diesel engine coughed and rattled, struggling to haul the car up the hill. 'I'm going to be a little late.'

'Pfff. . . I'll forgive you this time.'

'Good. I'll even—'

'On one condition: you wash the dishes.'

'Why's it *always* my turn to wash the dishes?'

'Because you're too cheap to buy a dishwasher.' There was a pause. *'Or a decent car.'*

A Toyota iQ wheeched past in the outside lane. One-litre engine, and it was *still* faster than the bloody Punto.

'I'm not cheap, I'm just—'

'"Prudent" is another way of saying "cheap". Why I put up with you, I have no idea.' But it sounded as if she was smiling as she said it. *'Don't be too late. And stand up for yourself next time!'*

'Promise.' Logan hung up and fumbled with the buttons until the words 'DS RENNIE' appeared on the screen.

Ringing. . . Ringing. . . Ringing. . . Then, *'Mmmph, nnnng. . .'* A yawn. A groan. *'Time is it?'*

Logan checked. 'Just gone ten.'

'Urgh. . .' Scuffing noises. *'I'm not on till midnight.'*

'Yeah, well I was supposed to be off at five, so I think I'm winning the "Who Gets To Whinge About Their Day" game, don't you? Jewellery heist.'

'Hold on. . .' A clunk, followed by what sounded like someone pouring a bottle of lemonade into a half-filled bath. *'Unnnng. . .'*

For God's sake.

Logan grimaced. 'You better not be in the toilet!'

A long, suspicious-sounding pause. *'I'm not in the toilet, I'm . . . in the kitchen . . . making a cup of tea.'*

Disgusting little sod.

'I want a list of suspects for that jewellery heist before you clock off, understand? Go round the pawnshops, the resetters, and every other scumbag we've ever done for accepting stolen goods.'

'But it's the middle of the—'

'I don't care if you have to drag them out of their beds: you get me that list. Or better yet, an arrest!'

'But I'm—'

'And while we're at it, what's happening with those hate crimes?'

'It's not. . .I. . .' His voice broke into a full-on whine. 'What am I supposed to do? I'm on night shift!'

'Rennie, you're. . .' Logan closed his mouth. Sagged a little in his seat as the Punto finally made it over the crest of the hill. It wasn't really fair, was it: passing on the bollocking, just because Steel had had a go at him? 'Sorry. I know. Just . . . tell me where we are with it.'

'No one's talking. All the victims say they fell down the stairs and stuff. Even the guy with two broken ankles won't blab.'

'Still all Chinese?'

'Latest one's Korean. Makes it four Oriental males in the last month and a half.'

'Well . . . do what you can.'

'You heading back to the ranch?'

'Going to see a man about a drugs war.'

'Yeah.' Another yawn. Then a whoosing gurgle. 'Oops. I just. . . Emma must've . . . em . . . flushed the washing machine?'

The young woman in the nurse's uniform scowled up at him, one hand on the door knob. 'I don't like this. It's late. You shouldn't be here.' Her eyebrows met in the middle, drawing a thick dark line through her curdled-porridge face, as if trying to emphasize the razor-straight fringe of her bottle-blonde hair. Small, but wide with it, arms like Popeye

21

on steroids. Hard. Shoulders brushing the tastefully striped wallpaper of the hallway.

Logan shrugged. 'He said it was OK, didn't he?'

'I don't like it.' She swung the door open, then stood to the side, face puckered around two big green eyes. Her finger waved an inch from Logan's nose. 'I'm warning you: if you upset Mr Mowat. . .'

A thin, shaky voice came from inside: a mix of public school and Aberdonian brogue, rough as gravel. 'Chloe, is that Logan?'

The waggling finger poked Logan in the chest, her voice a low growl. 'Just watch it.' Then she turned on a smile. It would have been nice to say it transformed her face, but it didn't. 'He's just arrived, Mr Mowat.'

'Well, don't just stand there, show him in.'

The room must have been at least thirty foot long. A wall of glass looked out on a garden lurking in the darkness, the occasional bush and tree picked out by coloured spotlights. Wee Hamish Mowat nudged the joystick on the arm of his wheelchair and rolled across the huge Indian rug. His pale skin was mottled with liver spots and looked half a size too big for his skeletal frame, the hair on his head so fine that every inch of scalp was visible through the grey wisps. An IV drip was hooked onto the chair, the plastic tube disappearing into the back of his wrist. It wobbled as he reached out a trembling hand.

Logan took it and shook. It was hot, as if something burned deep beneath the skin. 'Hamish, how have you been?'

'Like a buggered dog. You?'

'Getting there.'

A nod, setting the flaps of skin hanging under his chin rippling. Then he dug a handkerchief from the pocket of his grey cardigan and dabbed at the corner of his mouth. 'Are you on duty, or will you take a wee dram?' He pointed at a big glass display case, full of bottles. 'Chloe, be a dear and fetch the Dalmore. . . No, the other one: the Astrum. Yes, that's it.'

She thumped it down on the coffee table and gave Logan another glare. 'It's late, and you need your sleep, Mr Mowat.'

Wee Hamish smiled at her. 'Now you run along, and I'll call if I need you.'

'But, Mr Mowat, I—'

'Chloe.' A glint of the old steel sharpened his voice. 'I *said*, run along.'

She nodded. Sniffed at Logan. Then turned and lumbered from the room, thumping the door behind her.

Wee Hamish shook his head. 'My cousin Tam's little girl. Well, I say "little". . . Her heart's in the right place.'

Logan took two crystal tumblers from the display case. 'Not Tam "The Man" Slessor?'

'I promised I'd look after her when he was done for that container of counterfeit cigarettes.' Wee Hamish fumbled with the top of the whisky bottle. 'If you want water, there's a bottle in the fridge.'

'So how *is* Tam the Man doing these days?'

'Not too good: we buried him a month ago.' A sigh. 'Look, can you get the top off this? My fingers. . .'

Logan did. 'Do you know anything about the body we found out by Thainstone today?' He poured out one generous measure and another small enough to drive after. Passed the huge one to Wee Hamish.

'Thank you.' He raised the glass, the dark-amber liquid shivering in time with his hand. 'Here's tae us.'

Logan clinked his tumbler against Wee Hamish's. 'Fa's like us?'

A sigh. 'Gie few . . . and they're a' deid.' He took a sip. 'Unidentified male, chained to a stake and, I believe the term is: "necklaced".'

'We think it might be drug-related.'

23

'Hmm. . . What do you make of the whisky? Forty years old, nearly a grand and a half a bottle.' A little smile pulled at the corner of his pale lips. 'Can't take it with you.'

Logan took a sip. Rolled it around his mouth until his gums went numb and everything tasted of cloves and nutmeg and burned toffee. 'Is there another turf war kicking off?'

'I've been thinking about it a lot. Well, one does, doesn't one: when time's running out? What's going to be my legacy? What am I going to leave behind when I go?'

'We need this to stop before it gets even worse.'

'Don't get me wrong: I'm not ashamed of the things I've done, the things I've had other people do, but . . . I want . . . something. Got my lawyers to set up bursaries at Aberdeen University and RGU, helped people become doctors and nurses, sponsored vaccination programmes in the Third World, paid for wells to be drilled, mosquito nets for orphans. . . But I don't *feel* any different.'

He sipped at his drink. Then frowned up at the ceiling. 'Perhaps I should try a big public works project? Like Ian Wood and his Union Terrace Gardens thing, or the boy Trump and his golf course? Leave the city something to remember me by. . .' A grin. 'Other than the horror stories your colleagues tell.'

'Do you know who did it? Can you find out? Because as soon as the media get hold of this it's going to be all over the news and papers.'

Wee Hamish stared out into the dark expanse of garden. Or perhaps he was staring at his own reflection in the glass. Difficult to tell. 'To be honest, Logan, I've rather let my attention waver on that side of the business. Once upon a time I knew the operation inside out, but . . . well, I get a lot more tired than I used to.' A shrug, bony shoulders moving beneath the cardigan. 'Reuben's been looking after our pharmaceutical arm. Like he's looking after many things. . .'

Silence.

'Logan, you know I love Reuben like a son – bless his violent little cotton socks – but he's a foot soldier, a lieutenant. He's not a leader.' Another trembling sip. 'If I leave him in charge it'll end in war.'

'I'm not taking over.' Logan put his glass down on the coffee table.

'I know, I know. But if I can't trust Reuben to run things, what can I do? You don't want it, he can't handle it; do I sell up to Malcolm McLennan instead?'

'Malk the Knife's dangerous enough *without* handing him Aberdeen on a plate too. He's already got everything south of Dundee.'

The wheelchair bleeped, then whined back a few feet, before spinning around to face Logan. Wee Hamish wasn't smiling any more, instead a frown made hills and valleys in the pale skin of his forehead. 'I shall endeavour to find out who is responsible for your burning victim. And don't worry, if whoever did it is on my team, they'll be getting a . . . disciplinary hearing. This isn't the kind of legacy I want to leave behind.'

Outside, Logan's fifth-hand Punto was bathed in the glow of a security light. A huge man leaned back against the bonnet, tree-trunk arms folded over a great barrel of a chest. His three-piece suit looked brand new – the waistcoat straining over that vast belly. Shiny black brogues. Face a patchwork of scar tissue and fat, knitted together with a greying beard. A nose that was barely there any more.

Logan nodded. 'Reuben.'

No response.

OK. . . Logan took his keys out. 'Thought you were more of an overalls and steel toecaps kind of guy.'

Reuben just stared at him. Then slowly hauled himself off the bonnet.

The Punto's suspension rose about three inches.

Logan drew his shoulders back, brought up his chin. 'Go on then, out with it.'

But Reuben just turned and lumbered off into the darkness, brogues scrunching on the gravel. Didn't say a word.

Logan stood there until the huge man disappeared, then slid in behind the wheel. The world was full of bloody weirdoes.

The windows of the caravan next door glowed pale yellow in the darkness and Logan climbed out of the Punto, engine ticking and pinging in the silence. On the other side of the River Don, the lights of the big Tesco glittered through the trees.

A noise, behind him. . .

Logan spun around, hands balling into fists.

Nothing.

Grove Cemetery was a mass of silhouettes, reaching up the hill to the railway line and the dual carriageway at the top. The first three rows of headstones were just visible in the orange streetlight. Beyond their reach everything was black and silent. Just the faint rumble of late-night traffic working its way through the Haudagain roundabout.

'Hello?'

Stand very still, don't breathe, *listen*. . .

Nope, he was on his own. Which was just as well – no one about to see him acting like something out of a cheap horror movie.

Twit.

Logan found his house key and— Stopped. Another knot of bones hung from the door handle. More bloody chicken bones, wrapped up in a ribbon that was stained a greeny-grey by the sodium glow.

'Very funny.' He unhooked the bundle and chucked it

into the bushes that separated the tiny caravan park from the riverbank. 'Little bastards.'

Just because the Grampian Country Chickens factory used to be across the road, didn't mean people had to be a dick about it.

Sunday

4

'. . .sometime in the next week. And we'll have more top eighties hits between now and nine, but first here's the weather. . .'

'Unggg. . .' Logan rolled over and peered up at the bedroom ceiling. A slice of golden light jabbed through the gap in the curtains, making motes of dust shine against the scarlet walls. He reached out a hand, but Samantha wasn't there – her side of the bed a rumpled mess of duvet and pillows. Always was a restless sleeper.

The alarm clock blinked '06:15' at him in cheerless green.

'. . .expect the sunshine to continue all the way through till Tuesday morning, when an area of high pressure from the east's going to bring rain with it. . .'

He blinked and yawned, scratched, then flopped back in the bed. 'Come on, you lazy sod: up.'

Maybe in a minute.

Logan dug his knife into the jar. 'Tea and toast, tea and toast, la-la-la-la tea and toast. . .' There was only just enough Marmite in the jar to leave a thin skid mark across the melted butter. Better than nothing. He slouched through to the living room, taking breakfast with him.

A permatanned face on the TV grinned out at the piles of books and cardboard boxes littering the room. '. . .*February next year. I went to see two of the film's stars on the set. . .*'

The little red light on the answering machine blinked at him. Four messages. Probably all from Steel, moaning at him.

Two women appeared on the telly, sitting in director's chairs in front of a poster for *Witchfire*. They smiled and waved at the camera. Pretty, in a superficial, Hollywood, FHM-calendar-girl kind of way. One with natural-looking ginger hair, the other with full-on postbox scarlet like Samantha's. The words 'NICHOLE FYFE' and 'MORGAN MITCHELL' appeared across a banner at the bottom of the screen.

Logan pressed the button on the answering machine and the electronic voice droned into the untidy room, '*MESSAGE ONE:*' It was replaced by DCI Steel's familiar, gravelly tones. '*Laz? You there? Pick up.*' Pause. '*I'm no' kidding, get your arse—*'

Delete.

On the TV, Mr Fake-Tan simpered. '*And you're a redhead now!*'

The one called Nichole laughed. There was a slight trans-Atlantic twang to her accent, but the Aberdonian was still there underneath: '*I know, isn't it great? We both had to do it for the film, but I really like it, it's so liberating. And absolutely no one recognizes me: it's like being a completely different person!*'

Morgan twirled a lock of her screaming red hair, smiling at the camera as if she was about to rip its clothes off and make it do unspeakably kinky things right there on the studio floor. Her accent was pure New York, '*Everyone should try it at least once. Unleash the naughty, people!*'

'*MESSAGE TWO:*' was followed by, '*Laz, I'm serious—*'

Delete.

'*Nichole, what's it like starring in something as big as* Witchfire?'

'*It's immense. My first really meaty dramatic role, and—*'

'*MESSAGE THREE:*' A man's voice, sounding depressed. '*Hello? This is a message for Logan McRae. Logan, it's Preston's the architects, it's been two years since we got the roof on the flat. . .*' Sigh. '*And I wondered if you're any nearer making a decision about going ahead with the build?*'

Should really call him back.

Delete.

'*—was such a shock: I'd actually auditioned for Mrs Shepherd.*' Morgan flapped her hands, grinning. '*And I was up for Rowan, but apparently* someone *was just too fabulous—*'

Logan ripped a bite out of his toast, chasing it down with a slurp of tea.

'*MESSAGE FOUR:*' An ominous pause. '*Logan, it's your mother. You* know *I don't like talking to this thing—*'

Delete.

'*—so much more fun not having to be a goody two-shoes the whole time.*' Morgan placed a hand on her chest. Lucky hand. . . '*Three years on* CSI New Orleans, *and I really wanted to get to grips with a darker character for a change. Get back to my roots.*'

'*YOU HAVE NO MORE MESSAGES.*'

He finished off the toast. Have to buy another jar of Marmite. And maybe some squeezy cheese. Breakfast of champions.

'*Nichole, I have to ask you about coming back to Aberdeen after Hollywood.*'

'*It's so great to be home! People in the north-east are so real and down to earth, it's incredibly refreshing after all that –*' onscreen, Nichole Fyfe made quote bunnies with her fingers – '*"show business" stuff.*'

Quote bunnies. What kind of person did that?

'*And I understand you're running a competition so one lucky viewer can win a walk-on part in—*'

Logan jabbed the remote control's off button and the picture disappeared into darkness.

In the bedroom, Madness were banging on about finally being old enough to buy condoms. He slouched through to join them, drinking his milky tea between hauling on socks and pants and trousers.

'. . .and "House of Fun". Speaking of fun, fancy winning yourself an exclusive VIP tour of the new Witchfire movie being filmed right here in the north-east? Well, stay tuned because you're in for a treat after David Bowie. "Let's Dance"!'

Bloody film was like a virus.

He pulled on a white shirt that deserved a much better iron than the one he'd given it, sooking his fingers clean of butter and Marmite before doing up the buttons.

Tie, or no tie? He picked a couple from the wardrobe, then stood there, staring at the sheet of paper taped to the glass.

A blaring rendition of 'If I Only Had a Brain' came from his mobile. Logan blinked. Checked his watch. Been standing there like a turnip for five minutes.

Shudder.

He sank onto the bed and worked his feet into his shoes with one hand, answering the phone with the other. 'What?'

Rennie sniffed. 'And good morning to you too.'

For God's sake. 'You're not six.'

'Fine. We've got another battered Oriental male – this one's from Laos. They beat the crap out of him, then took a hammer to his knees and ankles.'

'Anything?'

'Won't say a word. According to the ambulance crew, he was off his tits when they brought him in – doped to the eyeballs, reeking of cannabis.'

'What about the jewellery heist?'

'Like juggling mud. Been dragging people out their beds all night – thanks for that, by the way, always nice to be sworn and spat at for a whole shift. Really boosted my morale.'

'So what you're saying is: you didn't get anywhere.'

'That's not fair! Not my fault the gang haven't tried shifting the stuff yet, is it? Maybe they've taken it down south, maybe they're stashing it for a couple of years, or shipping it overseas. How am I supposed to deal with that?' Moan, whinge, complain, grumble, whine. On and on and on.

He stuck his phone on the bedside cabinet, let Rennie enjoy his wee petulant moment while he laced up his shoes.

When he picked up the phone again, Rennie was still going.

'. . .never get any credit. And how come I'm always on nights? It's not—'

'Much though I'd love to sit here and listen to you bitch the day away, I've got work to get to, so—'

A knock on the caravan's door, loud and insistent.

'God's sake. . .' Logan put a hand over the mouthpiece. 'JUST A MINUTE!' Then back to the phone, marching out of the bedroom and across the hall to the front door. 'Get on to the lab – I want those forensics chased. And don't let them give you any crap about "three to six weeks". *Tuesday*, by the latest.'

'Would you like a magic flying unicorn while I'm at it?'

'No, but I'll take an egg buttie – on my desk for quarter past seven. And a tea.' Logan turned the key in the lock. Swung the door open. 'And don't think you're—'

Something exploded in his face, hard, driving pepper and bees through his nose, making the edges of the world scream with yellow fog as he crashed back onto the carpet. Thunk – his head bounced off the plasterboard. One knee caught the edge of the doorframe. 'Nnnghn. . .'

Everything tasted of hot copper wire.

Something wet on his face.

Blink.

'Gagh. . .' Tiny scarlet drops burst out of his mouth, then pattered down onto his cheeks and forehead.

Get up. GET UP NOW.

Ow. . . Fire burned through his head, radiating out from his nose. Screaming at him. Making his ears ring.

A huge bulk blotted out the sunshine streaming in through the door: Reuben. Not in the suit and tie any more. He was wearing a pair of blue overalls, the cuffs frayed and stained dark with oil and dirt, the knees too. A pair of heavy boots on his feet, the leather scuffed away in patches, metal toecaps glistening within.

Oh. Shit.

Logan scrabbled back against the wall.

But Reuben didn't step inside and kick the living hell out of him. Didn't stomp on his head and ribs. Didn't pummel his face to mince. Instead the big man wobbled a bit, clutching the door frame, mouth hanging slightly open, eyes bleary and blinking.

The sharp, smokey stench of stale whisky and sweat came off him in a greasy fug. Chest heaving as he hauled in a breath through his flattened nose. The words came out slurred, riding a little mist of spittle. 'I know . . . I . . . I know what you . . . you're doing.'

He rocked back and forward a couple of times, the knuckles on his right hand sticking out like rivets on a steel sheet. 'You . . . you're not gonnae . . . get. . . Fuckin' kill . . . kill you. . .'

Then Reuben's legs gave up and he slid down the side of the caravan until he was slumped on the top step, shoulders juddering, tears running through the webs of scar tissue, snot glittering through his patchy moustache.

And dangling from the door handle, another knot of little bones.

Bastard. . .

Logan wiped at the drop of scarlet staining the report, leaving a dirty smear through the words. He leaned back in

36

his chair, head tilted to the ceiling, clutching a wodge of paper napkins to his nose.

Detective Sergeant Rennie tutted. 'Took me ages to type that up, and you're getting blood all over it.'

Logan's office was just big enough to fit a couple of filing cabinets, a chipped Formica desk, two whiteboards, a creaky swivel chair, and a visitor's seat that looked as if it belonged in a skip.

Rennie shifted in it, making the vinyl squeak. He'd gelled his hair up into a blond tuft at the front, his cheeks glowing with sunburn, a curl of skin peeling off the end of his shiny nose. '*And* you didn't eat your buttie.' It still sat in the middle of the desk, half unwrapped from its tinfoil shroud. Congealing.

Logan glowered at him. The words came out all bunged up and flat. 'Do you want to be partnered with Biohazard for the next month? Stuck in small confined spaces with him? Because I can arrange that.'

'Had to go down the baker's: canteen's still closed for the refurb.' He sniffed. 'Be cold by now.'

'Just . . . bugger off.'

The door banged open, rattling the memos pinned to the wall. DCI Steel posed in the doorway. Grinning.

Logan gave her a glower as well. 'It's not funny!'

'Is it no'?' Her suit was as unfashionably baggy as her neck; crow's feet and wrinkles turning her face into a jumble of planes and lines. But it was the hair that really stood out. And up. And in every other direction too. As if she'd brushed it with an angry cat. 'Looks funny to me.' She wafted in, bringing a fug of stale-cigarette-stink with her.

Steel gave Rennie a wee slap on the back of the head. 'Shift it, Tintin.'

He grumbled, then hauled himself out of the visitor's seat. He pointed at the tinfoil package on Logan's desk. 'Booby-trapped buttie going spare, if you want it?'

Steel settled into the seat. 'Looks like you might make a decent DS after all.' She reached out and plucked the thing from the desktop. 'Now be a good boy and sod off. You've got tramps to find, and the grown-ups need to talk.'

She unwrapped the foil and took a big bite. Then froze, face creasing up around a soured mouth – red lipstick spidering out into the skin. 'Urgh, this is *cold*!'

Rennie disappeared, giggling, closing the door behind him.

Logan pulled the napkins from his nose and peered at the paper, stained a deep poppy red. He dumped them in the bin and grabbed a fresh handful from the pile. It was as if someone had lodged a burning coal in the middle of his face, filling his head with smoke and fire. 'If you want to give me a hard time about the jewellery heist: don't. We're doing everything we can.'

'Doc Ramsey tells me you're lucky it's only broken. Could've been a lot worse.'

'And yes, there was another racial attack last night, but the victim refuses to talk. Won't even admit to speaking English.'

'Says you're in for a full-on panda set of shiners when the swelling goes down. Like a grumpy raccoon. We should get you a stripy jumper and a big sack with "Swag" written on it.'

He stared up at the ceiling tiles. Big brown stains made continents on the pockmarked grey squares. 'If it's not the jewellery heist, and it's not the racial attacks, what is it?'

'Do you know you can die of a nosebleed? Seriously: fifteen minutes and you're a corpse.' She checked her watch. 'How long's it been?'

'Feel free to sod off at any point.'

She took another bite of buttie, chewing around the words. 'It's no' that bad if you pretend it's just an egg sandwich. You got any salad cream?'

'Top drawer.'

'Any porn?'

'*Just* salad cream.'

A shrug. She dug through the desk, coming out with two blue sachets he'd liberated from the canteen. 'So how come you let Reuben get away?'

'I *didn't*.' Logan dabbed at his nostrils. The napkins came away with scarlet blooming across the white. 'He lumbered off before the patrol car got there. Useless sods couldn't arrest books in a library.'

'We'll get him picked up, do him for assaulting a police officer – or what passes for one these days – and get him off the streets for a year or two. Can't be bad, can it?' She tore open the sachets and squeezed them into the roll. 'Should've let him punch you in the face ages ago.'

'Have you not got flying monkeys to train or something?'

Another bite left her with a smear of white on her cheek. 'Where are we with the necklace guy?'

'No witnesses. The Joyriders' Graveyard isn't exactly *on* the beaten track, which was probably the point. We ran a check on all the burned-out cars. . .' He waved a hand at his in-tray, then tipped his head back again. 'Report's on the top.'

'Very good. Want to give me the quick version?'

Sigh. 'Forgot your glasses, did you?'

'Don't need sodding glasses. Nothing wrong with my eyes, I'm just busy: so summarize.'

'DVLA gave us plates to match the chassis numbers. Got DS Chalmers to check out the registered keepers on the police national computer.'

A yawn. 'God, the suspense is killing me.'

'A couple with form for drunk and disorderly. One guy's done four years for assault. There's nothing more than a handful of parking tickets between the rest of them.'

'ID on the victim?'

'Face is gone, and his hands were chained behind him so the tyre dripped burning rubber all over them. They're scorched; apparently we *might* get a partial off what's left of the right thumb, but no one's holding their breath. We could try matching dental records, but for that—'

'We'd need to know who he was in the first place.' Steel chewed in silence, scowling out of the window. 'Do you have any idea what the CID budget's like right now? Can't buy a bag of crisps without the ACC's say-so. And you know what he's like.' She dropped her voice an octave and put on a posh Morningside accent. 'I can assure you, Roberta, that the press are only too happy to make Grampian Police look like idiots on this. I would appreciate your team not helping them out on that front. We need a swift and decisive result!' She let out a long wet raspberry. 'Like we're sitting about on our bumholes doing sod all about it.'

'What do you mean, *"we"*?'

'Lucky our victim copped it on a Saturday night. Be all over the papers come Monday. Editorializing tosspots. . . Get your victim DNA tested, and if the ACC moans I'll drop my breeks and tell him to pucker up.' Steel stuck her feet up on Logan's desk and polished off the last of the buttie. 'Speaking of tosspots, have you done anything about Agnes sodding Garfield yet?' Steel dug into her pocket and hauled out a wad of 'WHILE YOU WERE OUT' stickies. She chucked them onto his desk. 'All from the mother. Says she's going to the papers if we don't get our finger out and find her wee girl.'

Logan picked them up and dumped them in his bin. 'She's *not* a wee girl, she's eighteen. And she's not missing: she's run away with her boyfriend.'

'Don't care if she's sodded off to join the circus – her mum's going to make a pain in the arse of herself till we find her. Can you no' at least *look* as if you're trying to find her?'

40

Yeah, because he didn't have anything better to do. 'Is that it? Nothing else you want?'

Steel sooked her fingers clean. 'Could murder a cup of coffee.'

Logan groped for the office phone, then punched in DS Chalmers's number.

She picked up on the second ring. *'Guv?'*

'Got a minute?'

'Be right through.'

Steel waved at him. 'Tell whoever it is to bring coffee!'

Logan blinked at the printout a couple of times, then handed it back. The bleeding had stopped, but burning army ants were marching through his sinuses, trying to force his eyes out of their sockets. A scrunched-up tail of white paper stuck out of each nostril, just in case his head started leaking again. 'Nothing at all?'

DS Chalmers stood to attention in front of his desk, her curly hair more or less under control in a lopsided ponytail. She consulted her notebook. 'I chased them up at eight, on the dot; told them to put a rush on the DNA, and got an earful of moaning about the new procedures, and the re-organization, and the software upgrade, and it's Sunday. . .'

Steel settled back in the visitor's chair, eyes clamped on Chalmers's buttocks. 'You don't say. . .'

'Yeah, the SPSA got this big IT company in to rationalize everything, and nothing works anymore. Apparently there's a pensioner in Dumfries that's come back as a positive DNA match for eight murders, thirty-seven housebreakings, six arsons, and five rapes. Not bad for a woman in a wheelchair.'

Logan ran a finger along the side of his nose, gently probing the edge of the plaster that crossed the bridge. Sore. 'Did they get anything off that partial thumb?'

'Gave it a go, but nothing came back. Which *could* mean

the victim's not in the database.' She put the notebook away. 'So, maybe it's not gang-related after all? If he was a dealer we'd have his prints in the system, right?'

'Not if he'd never been caught.'

Steel took one last look at Chalmers's bum then sat up straight. 'Aye, well someone caught him yesterday, didn't they.'

5

Isobel hauled off her purple nitrile gloves and dropped them in the pedal bin, then dumped her green plastic apron in after them. Then stood with her back arched, pregnant bulges sticking out, hands rubbing at the base of her spine. Eyes closed, teeth gritted. 'Ungh. . . You know, when I had Sean I held off going on maternity leave until the last possible moment. Won't be making *that* mistake again.'

Behind her, the Anatomical Pathology Technician was slotting the victim's ribcage back into place, whistling the theme tune to *Doctor Who* as she worked.

Logan dropped his facemask and gloves in the bin. Then unzipped his SOC suit. 'Cause of death?'

'I need a sit down first.' She waddled towards the door. 'And maybe a nice cup of camomile tea.'

Logan followed her through into the pathologists' office – a small room with two desks facing opposite walls. One was covered with stacks of paperwork, the other completely clear, except for a power-lead and an empty in-tray.

Isobel groaned her way into the seat and puffed out her cheeks. Stuck her legs out and rotated the feet at the ankles.

First one way, and then the other. 'Are you sure you don't want an analgesic?'

He shrugged one shoulder. 'The only benefit of a punch on the nose – can't smell the post mortem. And I had some paracetamol before we started.'

'You always were such a martyr.' She opened a desk drawer and pulled out a blister pack of pills. 'Take two. No alcohol for six hours.'

Logan popped a couple of tablets out onto his palm, then knocked them back dry. Like a pro.

Isobel nodded. 'Damage above the fire line was extensive, the dermis and epidermis are virtually gone. But it looks as if whoever killed him shaved him first. No hair on the head, groin, armpits, or chest, and they didn't do a particularly smooth job of it either.'

She dumped the pills back in her desk. 'In addition to the shaving and burning tyre, your victim was stabbed three times, left-hand side. Twice between the fourth and fifth rib, once between the fifth and sixth. The first two punctured the lung; the third went straight into the left ventricle, rupturing the heart.' She levered her right shoe off with the toe of the left. Let it clunk to the threadbare carpet tiles. 'Oh, that's better. . .'

An off-white kettle sat on top of a filing cabinet. Logan stuck it on to boil. 'So the burning didn't kill him?'

'The ribcage was full of blood, so the knife wound was definitely ante-mortem. Mind you, given the state of his liver, he would probably have been dead within eighteen months. Your victim was a *very* heavy drinker: his stomach had nothing but alcohol in it. Something else – the hyoid bone was cracked.'

'Stabbed, burned, *and* strangled?'

'No. Strangulation is a binary state, you're either strangled, or you're alive. Your victim aspirated smoke into his lungs, so he was still breathing when the tyre was set alight.' She

44

levered off her other shoe. 'So it's more like: burned, strangled, *then* stabbed.'

'Hmmm. . .'

The kettle rumbled and rattled, then clicked and went quiet again. Logan popped a camomile teabag in a bone-china mug. It was decorated with a kid's drawing – a skeleton lying on a table, while a stick-figure woman in a green dress stood over it with a big bloody knife. The words 'MUMMY AT WORK' picked out in wobbly lowercase. He poured boiled water into the mug, filling the room with the smell of dead flowers, then handed it over. 'It'd have to be *strangled*, burned, then stabbed. No one's going to be daft enough to strangle someone who's on fire, are they?'

'Unless the hyoid bone was damaged by heat, rather than compression. It's an incredibly delicate structure, we're lucky it survived at all.' Isobel blew steam from the surface of her tea before taking a sip. 'I hear you're having problems identifying the body?'

'Still waiting on DNA. Bloody SPSA reorganization means everything takes three times as long.' He spooned some instant coffee granules into a second mug.

'A forensic anthropologist could work up a facial reconstruction from the remains. That would help, wouldn't it?'

Logan pulled a face. 'Steel's already got a wasp in her pants about the CID budget. We're not to authorize anything without her say-so. And I'm guessing forensic anthropologists don't come cheap.'

'About the same as a decent childminder.' A scowl. 'Or a thieving au pair.'

'What do I look like, made of money?' DCI Steel's voice echoed around the office. 'DNA's still our best bet – you don't get bumped off like that in a mob hit and not be dirty.'

'But a forensic anthropologist—'

'No. N.O. spells: "Shut up and stop bugging me about forensic anthropologists."' She slumped back in her office chair. 'Take the sodding hint.'

'But Isobel—'

'I don't care if the Ice Queen wants raspberry ripple ice cream with brown sauce and gherkins, we're waiting for the DNA.' Steel scrubbed at her face with her hands. 'He'll *be* in the system.'

Ah well, can't say he hadn't tried.

'What about Reuben?'

She narrowed her eyes. 'What about him?'

For God's sake. 'Have they picked him up yet?'

'Do you *really* think I've no' got more important things to worry about than who punched you on the bloody nose? You probably deserved it.' She held up a hand, thumb and forefinger squeezed tightly together. 'Hell, I'm this far away from doing it myself!'

'Thanks. Thanks for the support. Really appreciate it.' Logan marched out of her office and slammed the door behind him. 'Cow.'

'I heard that!'

Of course she did. Ears like a bloody vampire bat. He stuck two fingers up at the wood.

The corridor funnelled the noise from the main CID room, open-plan muttering and barely controlled chaos. Greasy coils of garlic, salami, and cheese tentacled through the air carrying with them the ghosts of pizzas past. His stomach gurgled.

Somewhere, deep within his head, someone was doing a Steve McQueen impersonation from *The Great Escape*, hurling that bloody baseball against the walls of the cooler. Thump-thump. Thump-thump. Thump-thump.

He turned his back on the siren scent and slouched through to his own office instead. A lanky figure with sticky-up blond hair was draped all over the visitor's chair, feet up on Logan's desk. Eyes closed, head back, mouth hanging open, making little grunting noises.

Logan opened one of the filing cabinet drawers, then slammed it shut.

'Gaaah!' DS Rennie jerked upright in his seat, eyes like nervous pingpong balls, jittering feet sending a pile of forms scattering to the carpet. 'I'm awake, I'm awake.'

'What are you still doing here?' The old office chair creaked as Logan settled into it. 'You were snoring.'

Rennie stretched: arms up to the ceiling, legs hovering an inch over the tabletop. 'You've been ages. . .'

'Post mortem.' What the hell happened to his desk? The whole thing was covered in other people's paperwork. Why did every lazy sod in CID think *this* was the perfect place to dump their crap? 'Now get your bloody feet off my desk.'

'Sorry, Guv.' Rennie screwed the palm of one hand into his eye socket, yawned again, shuddered, then sagged in the chair like someone had stolen all of his bones. 'Went through all the witness statements and CCTV footage from the jewellery heist: three males, all in their late teens – early twenties. Local accents. Initial getaway car from the scene was a VW Golf.' He hunched his shoulders and dug his hands into his armpits. 'Cold in here.'

Logan picked the forms up from the floor, added them to the rest, then started separating them out into piles for whoever touched them last. 'Number plate?'

'Fake. Well, not fake-fake – they'd nicked it off a blue Citroën Berlingo in Mannofield.' Another yawn. 'Bet you a fiver they abandoned the Golf and torched it before going on in a second car. So we'll get nothing off it, even if we can find. . .' He blinked at Logan, then frowned. 'What?' Brushed a hand across his cheek. 'Have I got pizza on my face?'

'We found a burned-out VW Golf in the Joyriders'

Graveyard: reported stolen Saturday morning – last seen by the owner, Friday tea-time. It was still warm.'

'Plenty of time to get to the jeweller's, cut the alarm cables, get in, tie up the proprietor and his bit on the side, rob everything, then sod off into the night.'

Logan took a biro from the mess on his desk and tapped it against his chin. 'Interesting.'

'Ooh,' Rennie sat forward in the chair. 'Maybe your victim's one of the team? Someone got greedy, or they thought he was a snitch?'

'Would explain the gangland execution, wouldn't it?'

A knock at the door, then DS Chalmers stuck her head in. 'Guv?' A huge grin split her face, teeth all small, pointy, and glinting. 'We just got DNA back: it's a match.'

Looked as if DCI Steel was right after all. There'd be bacon flapping its way past the window any minute now. 'Get on to the PNC, I want—'

'Criminal record?' She held up a manila folder.

'And—'

'Current address?' She placed a printout in the middle of Logan's desk, then stood back, showing off her happy little teeth. 'And there's a pool car waiting outside for us.'

Cocky, ambitious, and efficient. Maybe not such a bad combination after all.

Chalmers took them out through the city limits, heading north on the Inverness road, sitting in the outside lane of the dual carriageway, doing eighty, with the blue flashers going. '. . .and you'd think he'd be a bit more grateful, wouldn't you? At least now he knows where his precious Range Rover is. But he was a complete arsehole about it.'

Logan watched the fields go by, fluffy white sheep and big rectangular cows polka-dotting the swathes of almost luminous green. 'Uh-huh.'

'OK, so it's a burned-out hulk, but he'll have third-party fire and theft, won't he? Don't know what he's moaning about, really. Just because we haven't got a clue who stole it in the first place. . .'

'Right.' A fortress of pine trees flanked the dual carriageway for a minute, needles shining in the sunlight, the earth below wreathed in brambles and sharp-edged shadow. And then more fields. Aberdeenshire at its bucolic best, sliding by outside the car while DS Chalmers jumped from topic to topic in a perpetual-motion monologue.

'. . .and I know blow's never really *that* difficult to get hold of, but it's everywhere right now. Cannabis as far as the eye can see: Inverness, Aberdeen, Ellon, Keith, Peterhead, it's like a plague. . .'

'Mmm. . .'

Down the hill to Blackburn, through the roundabout, and on. The sky was a blanket of sapphire blue, streaked around the edges with misty white. Warm in the car. Logan blinked. The army ants had all congregated in the bridge of his nose, and now the little sods were having a hoedown. In clogs.

'. . .can't believe the SPSA are *still* fiddling about and reorganizing stuff. Honestly, can you think of a single person who's actually in favour of all this? Nothing but cost-cutting pirate bollocks – not surprising the SOCOs are all grumbling about industrial action. . .'

Sodding Isobel and her 'analgesics'. Might as well have downed a couple of kiddie Aspirin for all the good they were doing. Should've taken some of the *proper* painkillers from the caravan: the ones that made the world go all fluffy, warm, and soft. Like sleeping on a giant kitten.

'. . .just have to look at this guy – we get a hit on his DNA, but nothing on the fingerprints. You know why? Because they can't leave well enough alone, that's why. If it's not broken, poke and fiddle with it till it is. Honestly. . .'

'Hmm.' Might be nice to move further out of town. The caravan was OK, not that much smaller than the flat, and it was all on the ground floor – which was a bonus. And the view wasn't bad out over the fields, and trees, and the River Don. Just had to ignore the sewage treatment plant directly opposite. Other than that it was OK. Be nice to have a bigger place though.

'. . .continual budget cuts. I bet we could catch half the neds in the area if we just stuck a couple of cameras up at the Joyriders' Graveyard. Make our lives a hell of a lot easier. . .'

Bennachie humped on the horizon, the mountain rising up between the trees. Not much to look at from a distance, the Mither Tap looking like an abandoned breast: nipple pointing at the sky.

Silence. Just the sound of the engine, and the tyres growling on the tarmac at eighty miles per hour.

Logan glanced across the car. DS Chalmers was looking back at him, one eyebrow raised – as if she'd just asked a question.

He cleared his throat. 'In what way?'

'Well . . . can't they see that it's interfering with the actual job? Surely that's more important than saving a few quid?'

Ah. He went back to the window. Trees and fields and cows and sheep. 'Austerity measures. We've all got to do our bit. All pulling together, in the same boat, etc. Pick your cliché.' The sun was warm through the glass. Soporific. He closed his eyes for a minute, just to let them rest. Switch off the lights on the ants' hoedown. 'Think yourself lucky – you only have to moan about it. Some of us have to implement this crap.'

A spaniel loped along the pavement, unaccompanied, sniffing each and every lamppost before cocking a leg and leaving its calling card. Logan looked up from the manila folder's contents and peered out at a line-up of identikit houses. 'You sure this is the right street?'

'No.' Chalmers turned the wheel and they drifted onto another road lined with yet more pale-cream buildings with the occasional patch of sandstone cladding thrown in for fun. White PVC windows, lockblock drives, satellite dishes, and a tiny garage where a front room should have been. All topped with fresh brown pantiles. Detached homes built so close together you'd be lucky if you could walk between them without your shoulders brushing either side. 'Place is like a maze. . .'

She did a three-point turn and headed back the way they'd come. A wee boy on a yellow bike with tassels on the handlebars cycled slowly by, excavating the inside of his nose as if it held buried treasure.

'Has to be around here somewhere. . .'

According to the Police National Computer, Guy Ferguson was the lucky recipient of umpteen warnings, and three stints of community service. Everything from shoplifting in John Lewis when he was twelve, to drunk and disorderly when he was fourteen. Then there was a string of vehicle offences – theft from opening lockfast places, unlawful removal, vandalism, driving without insurance. . . One count of breaking into the corner shop and making off with the till. Almost went to prison eighteen months ago when he was caught helping himself to the contents of ladies' hand-bags in the Kintore Arms.

And that was the last thing on his record. Either Guy had cleaned up his act, or he'd finally figured out how not to get caught.

'God's sake. Everything round here's Castleview: Castleview Place, Castleview Avenue, Castleview Crescent. Where's the castle? Can you see one?'

Logan flicked back to the mugshot at the front of the file. 'Developers are like politicians – never believe anything they say.'

In the photo, Guy looked as if he'd just been dragged through an Alsatian, backwards. His left cheek was a patchwork of bruises, his eye swollen almost shut, split lip and swollen jaw. Apparently some bloke objected to Guy stealing things from his wife's handbag. An earlier pic showed a plain young man with doormat eyebrows, acne-flecked cheeks, and a moustache that barely qualified as enthusiastic bumfluff.

Very gangsta.

Chalmers pointed through the window. 'Here we go.' She pulled up in front of yet another barely detached sandstone-clad box, blocking the Audi and Renault parked on the driveway. Then wiped her hands on the steering wheel, leaving a shiny film behind. 'Guv, about the death message. . .'

'Let me guess, you're not keen?' Logan slipped the print-outs back into the file. 'Our victim had form for stealing cars and breaking into places to rob them. Sound familiar?'

'The jewellery job.'

'Car was stolen a couple of streets away from here, used in a robbery, then dumped and burned just past Thainstone Mart. Next to Guy Ferguson's body.'

Chalmers left another layer of palm sweat on the steering wheel. 'They do the job, then his mates turn on him after they've divvied up the loot. Maybe he was holding out on them?'

'Could be.' Logan climbed out into the warm afternoon. 'What about the registered keeper?'

'Straight up, far as I can tell: no record in the PNC. Pretty hacked off to lose the car too, was a present from his dad.' She straightened her wrinkly suit, then marched up to the front door and rang the bell.

A minute later, it was opened by a wee girl in a bright yellow dress with bears on it, head a mess of black curls. She looked up at DS Chalmers with big blue eyes, then stuck her thumb in her mouth.

A voice came from somewhere inside: a man. 'Who is it, Bella?'

The thumb came out with a soft pop. 'My name's Bella and I'm five and I'm getting a pony for my birthday.'

Chalmers hunkered down until she was roughly at eye-level. 'Hello, Bella, my name's Lorna. Can you tell your mummy and daddy the police are here and they need to speak to them?'

A nod sent her curls bobbing, then she turned and shouted back into the house. 'It's the pigs!' Before squealing her way down the corridor, arms waving above her head. 'You'll never take me alive, Copper!'

Chalmers cleared her throat. 'Well that was . . . nice.'

A man poked his head out into the corridor. Pulled a face. Then sauntered towards them: jeans, flannel shirt, the top of his head poking through a crown of greying frizz. He wiped his hands on a tea towel. 'Sorry about that – someone let her watch *Life on Mars* the other day and she's been impossible ever since.' He gave them a smile. 'How can I help?'

Logan stepped forward. 'Mr Ferguson?'

The smile slipped a little. 'Yes?'

'Can we come in please, Mr Ferguson? We need to talk.'

The living room was bright and airy, the sounds of music and laughter coming through from the dining-kitchen. Mr Ferguson sat on the edge of the couch, his wife perched beside him. She fidgeted with the hem of her orange cardigan, working it back and forth between her fingers, pulling little tufts of fluff from the wool.

She looked over her shoulder at the open door. Slipped a fleck of orange fuzz into her mouth and chewed on it.

The wee girl who'd swore they'd *never* take her alive was sitting at the table, shovelling peas into her mouth while an older man cut something up on her plate.

Mrs Ferguson pulled another tuft of orange fluff. She stared off over Logan's shoulder, not making eye contact. 'What's he done now?'

Her husband sighed. 'Why do you always have to do that?'

'I'm not doing anything, I'm being realistic. Of course Guy's done something, why else are *they* here?' She pointed at Logan and Chalmers.

'Sheila, he's—'

'That boy could cause a fight in a cemetery.'

Mr Ferguson laid a hand on her knee. Smiled at Logan again. 'Guy's a good kid, he just . . . he's easily led.'

Logan licked his lips. Cleared his throat. 'I'm afraid we have some bad news. . .'

Mrs Ferguson's mouth fell open, eyes wide. Then she stood, walked over to the door and closed it, shutting out the sounds of laughter. 'I see.'

'Oh God. . .' Her husband rocked back and forward in his seat. 'Oh God, no. . .'

She blinked, wiped the heel of her hand across her eye, then brought her chin up. 'We only saw him this morning. He was supposed to be getting out on Wednesday.'

'Oh God, Guy. . .' Mr Ferguson dropped his chin onto his chest and sobbed, fingers digging into the soft cushions of the couch. 'Oh God. . .'

Logan glanced at Chalmers, then back at Mrs Ferguson. 'You saw him this morning?'

'At the hospital. They said he was going to be all right. Just keeping him in for observation.' She settled onto the arm of the couch and wrapped an arm around her husband's heaving shoulders. 'Was it . . . did he suffer?'

'He was in hospital?' Oh, shite.

'They were fooling around and he got petrol all over his hands. How can someone die from burned hands?' A thick line appeared between her eyebrows, two more slashing down from the corners of her mouth. 'It was that MRSA, wasn't it?'

'Ah.' Logan stood, put his hands in his pockets. Took them out again. Shuffled his feet. 'There may have been a bit of a . . . mistake.'

6

The pool car's sirens carved a path through the afternoon traffic. Chalmers jinked the car around an eighteen-wheeler loaded down with bags of gravel. 'Don't think I've ever been so embarrassed in my *life*.'

Logan pressed the mobile against his chest. 'Slow down! I said I wanted to go up to the hospital, not end up in bloody A&E.' Then back to the phone. 'What do you mean, he's not there?'

A small pause. Then Sergeant Big Gary McCormack's bunged-up Aberdonian accent grumbled down the line. *'What do you think I mean? I mean, he's not there. Sent a car round there three times this morning and there's still no sign of him.'*

'He's six foot tall, five foot wide, and looks like someone took a burning cheese grater to his face, *how* can you not find him?'

'Are you asking for another punch in the face? I've got a whole city to keep safe here, dayshift's got better things to do than run around after your ungrateful arse!' A clunk and the line went dead. The bastard had hung up on him.

Logan rammed the phone back into his pocket. 'Typical.

Ask them to do one simple thing and— Bloody hell!' He grabbed the handle above the passenger door as Chalmers threw the car into the roundabout, tyres screeching all the way.

She ground her hands around the steering wheel. 'They're going to make a complaint, aren't they? I don't want that on my record, how am I supposed to make promotion with that hanging over my—'

'Let them complain. The lab didn't screw up on the fingerprints, they screwed up on the DNA. It's not the victim's: it's the killer's. So as soon as we get to the hospital. . .?'

'We get the killer.' Chalmers brought her little pointy teeth out to shine. 'One week on the job and I've solved a gangland execution.'

Logan stared at her. 'You do know I'm sitting here, don't you?'

At least she had the decency to blush. 'I meant, *we've* solved a gangland execution. Team effort. . . Sorry, Guv.'

'Just drive.'

Footsteps clattered back from the spearmint-green walls. Paintings and arty photographs lined the corridor. People in dressing gowns shuffled to the side, leaning on the handrails, watching them march past.

Up the stairs.

Chalmers hurried on ahead, one of the uniformed officers seconded to Aberdeen Royal Infirmary clomping along behind her in full ninja black.

The other one hung back with Logan, puffing and panting as they climbed. 'Could we . . . wc no' have . . . have taken the . . . bloody lift?'

And let Gungho Gertrude get there first? No thanks.

They burst out onto the next floor.

Chalmers was staring at the ward signs hanging from

the ceiling. She did a slow three-sixty, before shrugging her shoulders and poking the uniform in the shoulder. 'Well?'

'Must be the next floor.'

Sod.

Logan went back through the doors to the stairwell, pulling out his phone on the way and scrolling down to Steel's name. It rang as they charged up the stairs. Bang – out into another bland green corridor that smelled of boiled socks and murdered cauliflower.

Steel finally picked up. *'Oh, it's you is it? Where's my bloody paperwork? I told you I wanted it on my desk by lunchtime, no' next sodding—'*

'We know who killed the necklacing victim.'

Pause. *'You do?'*

One of the uniformed officers checked the ward signs, then marched off to the left. Chalmers hurried after him, Logan and Mr Too-Many-Pies bringing up the rear.

'Guy Ferguson. He was in on the jewellery heist. Victim was probably one of his gang. He's in ARI right now: we're on our way.'

'Buggering hell. . . It's only been a day and a half, and I've already solved the thing. Keep telling everyone I'm a genius.'

'*You've* already solved?' Logan barged through a set of double doors into another stretch of sickly green. 'You're as bad as bloody Chalmers.'

'My intrepid leadership is what did it. I'm no' saying you didn't play your own small part—'

'Do I get any sodding credit at all?'

Up ahead, Chalmers and the other uniform were shouldering their way into a ward.

'Laz, you're big enough and ugly enough to know how this works: credit, like a happy wee party balloon, floats up the way. Blame, like jobbies, falls down.' Rustling came from the other

end of the phone. *'Now, be a good boy and keep an eye on my party balloon while I hurry over there to collect it.'*

Aye, right.

Logan held the phone out at arm's length, then made a harsh hissing noise. '. . .ant hear what . . . signal . . . hello? Hello?'

'Don't you sodding dare, Logan McRae, or I'll ram my boot so far up—'

'Isn't. . . Hello?' He hung up.

Darth Vader's theme tune burst out of the phone's speaker, the word 'STEEL' flashing on the screen. He switched it off and jammed it back in his pocket. Served her right. He nodded to PC Pies. 'OK, we'll—'

The ward door banged open and three young men scrambled out, white trainers squeaking on the cracked terrazzo floor. They weren't wearing identical tracksuits, but it wasn't far off it, the tops pulled on over hoodies and baseball caps. One slammed into the wall, twisted round a couple of times, then sprinted straight towards Logan.

More squeaking as he scrabbled to a halt, eyes wide, staring at the huge constable. 'Shite!' And he was off again – accelerating the other way, following his mates.

Constable Pies lumbered into a run, giving chase.

Logan shoved open the ward door. The other uniform was feeling his way along the wall, one hand clutched tightly over his groin, sweat running down his pale face.

Chalmers appeared behind him, the front of her suit spattered with something brown.

Logan jabbed a finger at the PC. 'You: get back there and secure the prisoner.' Then glared at Chalmers. 'Don't just stand there dripping, get after them!'

The trail of destruction wasn't that hard to follow – overturned carts, little old men shaking their walking sticks and bellowing obscenities, little old ladies shouting far worse.

Off in the distance, a pair of double doors boomed against the walls. More swearing.

DS Chalmers stuck her elbows out and her chin in, sprinting after them.

Logan skipped to a halt, then turned and charged through into the stairwell again, taking the steps two and three at a time before bursting out on the lower level. Where it was nice and quiet.

There were only two ways out of Aberdeen Royal Infirmary from here: double back towards the exit onto the side road opposite the auditorium, or keep going and out past Nuclear Medicine. Unless they just popped out through a fire door. . .

Too late to worry about that now.

He hurtled along the deserted corridor, passing empty beds and wheelchairs. An abandoned lunch pod.

An intern flattened himself against the wall, clutching a huge brown X-ray envelope to his chest, as Logan sprinted past.

Up the stairs at the end, heart pounding in his ears. Through the doors at the top and— PREGNANT LADY, PREGNANT LADY!

Logan's shoes skidded on the patchwork of flooring and duct tape, stopping him just short of a wheelchair full of red-faced, teeth-gritted, soon-to-be motherhood, one leg encased in plaster to the hip. The man pushing the chair turned as Logan battered past, setting the shiny 'CONGRATULATIONS!' balloons spinning and bumping into each other.

'Watch where you're bloody going!'

And then BOOM – the door from the main wards smashed open and one of the tracksuit hoodies flailed into view, arms and legs windmilling as he tried to dodge a porter pushing a trolley heaped with metal bowls and trays. It didn't work.

The hoodie careened straight into him, the pair of them landing in a tangle of limbs as the trolley's contents clanged and clattered across the cracked floor.

Then he was up on his feet again, lunging for the exit.

Only Logan got there first.

He slammed into the hoodie's side, sending them both crashing into the automatic doors before they could open. They hit the rubber matting in a tangle of arms and legs.

'Gerroffus, gerroffus!'

The door hissed open.

'Police!' Logan grabbed a handful of hood and hauled. 'Hold still, you wee shite. . .'

'Aaaagh, gerroffus!'

Something thumped into Logan's side. The hoodie put his head down and threw another punch.

Right in the armpit. Buggering hell, that *stung*.

Logan let go of the hood and snatched at the other arm – fumbling till he got a good hold on the wrist, then bent it over on itself, forcing the palm towards the forearm and keeping it there.

'AAAAAAAAAGH! GERROFFUS!'

Another bang and the door burst open again: another tracksuit hoodie. This one hurdled the porter's overturned trolley, clearing it by at least two feet, going like the hounds of hell were snapping at his heels.

BOOM – DS Chalmers charged through after him. Mouth open, sharp little teeth bared. 'COME BACK HERE!'

Hoodie Number One landed another punch. 'Gerroffus!'

Logan gave the wrist one final twist. . . And something inside went '*pop*'.

A moment's stillness, then he exploded, screaming, legs thrashing.

His mate leapt over them and out through the door into the sunlight. Chalmers wasn't quite so lucky. A flailing leg caught her mid-leap and she went crashing to the ground, face first. Hoodie Number Two didn't look back, didn't slow down, just kept on running.

Chalmers lay where she was, groaning.

'Gerroffus, gerroffus, gerroffus.' The wee sod was losing a bit of energy and volume now. The words punctuated by little sobs.

Logan dragged the cuffs from his pocket and forced one end on over the hoodie's misshapen wrist. Got a squeal for his troubles. Did the same with the other one, fastening both hands behind the guy's back.

Then Logan struggled to his feet, reached down, and helped Chalmers stand. 'Nice swan dive.'

She glowered at him. 'I would've got him, if you hadn't tripped me!' Fresh dots of red welled up on her skinned chin.

He hauled the crying hoodie upright. 'Blame Laughing Boy here.'

She turned her head and spat a frothy blob of red on the rubber matting. 'Bit my tongue. . .'

DS Chalmers limped in, clutching an icepack to her chin. 'How'd you get there before us anyway?'

The ward was broken up into rooms of four beds a piece. Clunky screen things on flexible arms sat above the head-boards, flickering adverts at them promising a glorious world of entertainment for any patient willing to pay for it.

Guy Ferguson had the bed by the window, propped up on a cliff-face of pillows, blinking slowly in the sunlight. His arms disappeared into what looked like shoe boxes covered in gauze bandages. Shiny metallic 'GET WELL SOON' balloons were anchored to the rail at the foot of the bed, glittering in the sunshine, trailing coils of ribbon like poisonous jelly-fish. Grapes, lads' mags, and bottles of Lucozade cluttered the bedside cabinet.

His acne had cleared up since the mugshot, leaving his cheeks and forehead a moonscape of pockmarks. The eyebrows were even thicker, but the bumfluff moustache hadn't improved any.

Logan sat back in his padded seat, and pointed Chalmers at the empty plastic chair on the other side of the bed. 'One of the benefits of spending a *lot* of time in hospital: you get to know all the shortcuts.'

'Oh.' She sank into the chair, winced, then slumped slightly. 'I've put in a lookout request for our missing hoodie; the other two are on their way back to the station.'

A pair of handcuffs fixed Guy's ankle to the bed, by the balloons. As if there was a risk of him floating away. Which, given the amount of morphine he was apparently on, probably wasn't a bad idea.

'So,' Logan helped himself to a grape, 'do you want to come clean and save everyone a load of trouble?'

'Trouble?' He squinted one eye, then did the same with the other, as if Logan was bobbing in and out of focus. Both eyes were red-veined and puffy, the pupils dilated, tears glittering along the bottom lid. A little laugh. 'Trouble. . .'

Stoned out of his tiny mind.

'Your mates, the hoodies: who are they?'

'Trouble. They're trouble . . . that's what mum always says. . .'

'What about the man you killed, was he trouble too? Did he try to screw you out of your share of the jewellery, that it? What was he, the inside man?'

'Doctors came round. . .' Guy held up the boxy things hiding his hands. 'They're going to cut off my fingers. . . All . . . all the ones on the left, and . . . and two on the right. . . My fingers. . .'

Chalmers poked a finger into the bedclothes. 'That's what you get for necklacing someone, isn't it? Serves you right.'

'All burned. . . Can't save them.' A deep breath. Then he screwed his eyes tight shut and bit his bottom lip. 'Going to cut them off today. . .' Tears rolled down his cheeks, glinting. As if that was going to make them feel sorry for the murdering little bastard.

He'd burned his hands so badly they'd have to amputate more than half his fingers: maybe Isobel was right? Maybe Guy Ferguson *was* stupid enough to strangle someone on fire? 'You did it, didn't you?'

'I. . . I can't—'

'You killed him. You chained him to a stake, stuck a tyre over his head and set fire to it.'

'It wasn't—'

'Twenty minutes, that's how long it takes someone to burn to death like that. *Twenty* minutes.'

Guy's mouth fell open, bottom lip sticking out, tears spilling down his cheeks. 'I. . . I don't—'

'Guy Ferguson, I'm arresting you on suspicion of murdering an unknown male yesterday afternoon. You do not have to say anything—'

'I did it. . .' He sniffed, then blinked in slow motion. 'I killed him. . .' Guy wiped his eyes on his forearm, tears darkened the white bandage. 'What else could I do? He was screaming and burning and I couldn't get the tyre off and it's all over my hands and they're on fire and it's horrible and it hurts and I had a . . . I had the knife.' A deep, rattling breath. 'So I stabbed him. And stabbed him, and stabbed him, and my hands are on fire and it hurts so much and . . . I couldn't just leave him like that!'

Ah. . . Logan sat back in his seat. 'He wasn't part of your crew for the heist?'

'His face . . . you should have seen his face . . . screaming.'

'He was burning when you got there?'

A nod. 'We . . . we ditched the car, divvied up the watches

64

and rings and necklaces and stuff, and . . . and there he was.' Guy held up the boxes where his hands should have been. 'They're going to cut off my fingers, because I tried to help someone. . .'

7

A woman's voice blared in the corridor outside the hospital room. 'I don't bloody care – you let me in to see my son right now!' Mrs Ferguson.

DS Chalmers sniffed. 'You think he's telling the truth?'

'Well. . .' Logan leaned against the room's little sink, staring down at the bed.

Guy was curled over, boxed hands against his chest, great heaving sobs rocking him back and forward.

'Guv?'

'Necklacing, it's . . . it's a big-city gangland organized-crime thing. Not something I can see a bunch of teenage wannabes doing. So . . . maybe. Probably.'

'He did it so the victim wouldn't suffer any more.' She puffed out her cheeks, hissing out a breath. 'Did the right thing, and it's going to cost him his fingers.'

'When everyone's calmed down a bit we'll interview his mates. See if they corroborate.'

That voice again. 'I DEMAND TO SEE MY SON!'

Here we go. . .

Logan pointed at Chalmers. 'Tell him to let them in.'

As soon as she stuck her head around the door, Mrs

Ferguson barged her way past the uniform on guard, into the room. 'Guy?'

Mr Ferguson scurried in behind her, crying. 'They told us you were dead.'

Guy's mother wrapped him up in a hug. 'My baby. . .' Then she straightened up and glared at Logan. 'YOU! You told us he was dead. How could. . .' Her eyes went wide, staring down at her son's ankle: at the handcuff. 'HE'S IN A HOSPITAL BED!'

'It's not—'

'HOW DARE YOU!' She clenched her fists, took a step forward. 'You take that off him, and you take it off him *now*.'

The stairwell echoed with footsteps and murmured conversations, overlaying the background hum of the hospital. Then Logan's phone joined in – Darth Vader's theme again. Should have left the damn thing turned off. He pulled it out. 'It's not—'

'*Have you got him? Where are you?*' She sounded like a small child with a new puppy. If the kid had smoked forty a day for its whole life.

Chalmers pushed through the doors onto the ground floor, holding them open for Logan.

'We're heading back to the car, but—'

'*There! I see you!*'

He froze.

DCI Steel was marching along the corridor towards them, mobile held against her ear, a big Cheshire grin pulling her wrinkles into a starburst. '*Who's Aunty Roberta's special wee soldier then?*'

He hung up. Stood there, waiting for her.

Steel gave a hop-skip, then grabbed him by the shoulders and gave him a little squeeze. Then frowned. 'Where is he? How come you're no' taking him in?'

'He's . . . upstairs under guard. They're amputating most of his fingers this afternoon.'

'And you're *sure* he's our boy?'

DS Chalmers held up her notebook. 'Confessed to the killing, and the jewellery heist too.'

'Excellent!' Steel let go of Logan and gave Chalmers a hug. Holding on for long enough that the DS started fidgeting.

Logan took a deep breath. 'There's something I need to—'

'The ACC looks like he's won free boobs for a year; scheduling a press conference for half three.' She released Chalmers. 'You're both invited. Is this no' great?' Steel poked at the screen of her mobile, then held it up to her ear. 'ACC wants a word. . .'

'Actually, Guy Ferguson—'

'Aye.' She stuck a finger in her other ear. 'Dougie? Is his nibs about? Yeah. . .'

'Look, it's not as simple as—'

'Sir? I've got him here. . . Yup, under arrest and under guard as we speak.' The grin got bigger. 'Well, you know us: CID always gets its man.'

'Seriously, we need to—'

'I'll put him on.' Steel held the phone out to Logan. Nodded at him. 'Go on then.'

Sod.

He took the phone. 'Sir?'

'*McRae, well done.*' The Assistant Chief Constable's put-on posh telephone voice wasn't enough to cover up the Teuchter underneath – all elongated vowels, dipping for no reason in the middle of random words. '*Excellent to get a result so quickly.*'

'Sir, it's—'

'*No, no: credit where it's due. Why haven't you applied for that permanent DI's position in Peterhead yet? You're obviously qualified, and a shoo-in after this!*'

68

A frown. 'There's a permanent DI's job?'

Steel cleared her throat, stared up at the ceiling tiles. 'I . . . Must've slipped my mind.' Scheming old bag.

'Didn't Roberta tell you? I could have sworn I asked her to disseminate it to the troops. Anyway, you should definitely get your name down.' He lowered his voice a notch, as if there was a secret on the way. *'Listen, we're having a press conference here at half three, and you know me: I like to ensure my team gets the kudos it deserves. Make sure you've got a decent suit on, don't want them thinking we all fell off the back of a tractor, do we?'*

Deep breath. 'Actually, sir, it's a bit more complicated. . .'

'You don't have a clean suit?'

'No. I mean yes, I've got a clean suit, I mean it's Guy Ferguson. He claims someone necklaced the victim before he got there. He tried to get the tyre off. And when that didn't work Ferguson stabbed him so he wouldn't just . . . burn to death.'

Steel's eyes went wide. 'You . . . *what?*'

Logan turned his back on her. 'Ferguson got molten rubber all over his hands trying to save the victim. They're going to amputate most of his fingers this afternoon.'

Silence on the other end of the phone.

'Sir?'

The posh telephone voice was slipping. *'Are you telling me you arrested a good Samaritan?'*

'He confessed. And he was in on the jewellery heist too. We've got two of his associates in custody and—'

'How the hell am I supposed to spin that? For God's sake, McRae, could you not have arrested someone who wasn't a hero?'

'But the jewellery heist—'

'Please tell me he's not photogenic.'

Acne scars, thick eyebrows, junior moustache. 'No, he's not photogenic.'

A sigh. *'Well that's something at least. . .'* The ACC hung up.

Logan returned Steel's phone. 'Why didn't you tell me about the DI's job?'

'Don't change the subject: you made me look like a right fanny!'

'Tried to tell you, but you wouldn't listen, would you?' He turned and headed back into the hospital.

'Hoy!' Steel's voice boomed down the corridor behind him. 'Where do you think you're going – we're no' finished!'

'Visiting hours. Got someone to see.'

Interview room three was baking hot, the usual pervading odour of cheesy feet and stale digestive biscuits was joined by a thick layer of oniony BO. Its owner shuffled his bum in his seat – the one on the wrong side of the scarred Formica table. The one bolted to the floor.

Sammy McCloist, seventeen and a half, squint nose, sideburns like a pedestal mat, hair down to his hunched shoulders. The fibreglass cast on his right wrist reached all the way from the palm of his hand to just before the elbow. Brand new, and it was already filthy.

He opened his mouth, but the git in the suit sitting next to him put a hand on his arm.

'My client has nothing to say on that matter.' McCloist's lawyer smiled. He was huge, broad and tall enough to tower over everyone, even sitting down. Big hands, big chin, big ears, hair cut short trying to disguise the big bald spot.

'Really.' Logan checked his watch: quarter to three. 'Well, you know what, Sammy? That's fine with me. Right now we're getting a warrant to search you and your mates' houses. Think we'll find anything interesting?'

A sniff. 'You broke my bloody wrist.'

'You were resisting arrest. Remember?'

'My client strenuously denies your interpretation of events. He was visiting a friend when you attacked him.'

'Do you know we've recovered DNA from the jewellery heist? Nice clear sample. Right now they're seeing which one of you it matches.' Which was a lie. The way things were going, they'd be lucky to get any DNA results back before Christmas.

'It cannot possibly match my client, because my client wasn't there. My client—'

'Was visiting his sick granny. You said.'

'Then there's really no reason for us to continue this interview, is there?' The massive lawyer stood. 'We have co-operated fully with your investigation, now it's time for you to release my client.'

Sammy grinned. 'Going to sue your arse off for breaking my wrist. Police brutality, that is. I'm going to own your *house*, man.'

Logan shook his head. 'Sammy, Sammy, Sammy. One: you don't want my house. Even *I* don't want my house. Two. . .' He sat forward, lowered his voice to a whisper. 'We've got a witness. When you broke into the jewellers, someone outside recognized you.' Another lie, but worth a try anyway.

Sammy curled his top lip. 'That's bollocks!' He thumped his cast on the tabletop. 'No one could've recognized us, 'cos we was wearing masks the whole time.' He sat back, folded his arms, nodded. Smiled. Look how *clever* I am.

The lawyer sank into the chair and buried his face in his hands.

The Procurator Fiscal wandered over to the window and stared out at the view. A hint of grey was creeping in at the temples of her dark-brown hair. Blue tweed Jackie Onassis suit, cherry-blossom nail varnish. Distinguished, in a cougary kind of way. 'Could you not have found a less . . . complicated solution?'

Sitting at the boardroom table, Logan shrugged. 'It wasn't really up to me, ma'am.'

From here, most of central Aberdeen was laid out in a patchwork of slate and flat roofs, bristling with satellite dishes and obsolete aerials. Big fat seagulls spiralled in the pale-blue sky, like bleached vultures, hunting for scraps and any dogs or children small enough to carry off.

'There's no way we'll get a conviction for murder, not in the circumstances. . . Manslaughter, at a stretch, but it won't be popular.' She rested her hands on the windowsill. 'We'll have to prosecute him for the jewellery robbery, of course. *That's* going to play well in the press.' A sigh. 'Inspector McRae—'

'I didn't do it on purpose.'

'No, I suppose not. But still. . .' She turned, took off her glasses and polished them on a little yellow cloth. 'Do we have *any* good news about the necklacing case?'

'We're—'

'If you're about to say, "pursuing several lines of enquiry", I'm going to stab you in the eye with a pencil. And don't think I won't get away with it.'

Ah. . . 'The fact he was necklaced out at the Joyriders' Graveyard has to be significant. Up a rutted track on a dead-end road past Thainstone Mart – it's not exactly somewhere you just stumble across on your way to the shops, is it?'

'So whoever it is has local knowledge.'

'They've probably got form for unlawful removal as well, or know someone who does. We're still waiting on a full DNA work-up; you know what it's like these days. Until we've ID'd the victim it's going to be hard to get anywhere.'

She slipped her glasses back on. 'I don't like this, DI McRae. I don't like this at all.'

'We could get a forensic anthropologist in? Do a facial reconstruction?' He cleared his throat. 'You know, if we had the budget. . .?'

Her eyes narrowed. '*Find* the budget. I'm authorizing it.

This case is now Grampian Police's number one priority.'

Steel would love that.

'. . .no, that's *not* what I'm saying at all.' The Assistant Chief Constable waved a finger and twenty flashguns went off, reflecting off his high forehead, catching him in all his chunky glory. He must have shaved right before the briefing, because the lower of his two chins was an angry shade of puce flecked with tiny spots of scarlet. 'What I'm saying is we have to treat these two cases separately. That's how the law works.'

The briefing room was packed with row after row of journalists and TV crews, all sticking their hands up and asking questions at the same time:

'Was the surgery a success?'

'Would you say Guy Ferguson is a hero?'

'Why did your officers tell his parents he was dead?'

'Why is Grampian Police persecuting a man who sacrificed his fingers trying to save someone?'

The ACC thumped his hand on the table. 'We're not persecuting anyone, and it's irresponsible to suggest otherwise. What Mr Ferguson tried to do for the victim was admirable, breaking into a jewellery store and making off with thirty-four thousand pounds' worth of merchandise was *not*.'

Sitting next to him, the Press Liaison Officer put one hand over the microphone, leaned across and whispered in his ear. Probably something along the lines of, 'Stop antagonizing the bastards. . .'

Standing at the back of the room, behind a forest of microphone booms, Logan checked his watch. Fifteen minutes in and they were already struggling.

Steel nudged him in the ribs, her ancient-ashtray breath congealing around his head. 'You're a jammy bugger.' She

73

jabbed him again. 'See if it'd been me? No way I'd let you weasel out of it: you'd be up there getting your wee pink bum paddled with the rest of them.'

'I'm not weaselling out of anything. The ACC said he'd do it on his own – not everyone's out to cover their own arse, *some* senior officers actually look after their team.'

A snort. 'More fool him, then.'

Logan kept his eyes fixed forwards. 'PF wants us to get a forensic anthropologist in.'

'Oh, *I* see: I told you no, so you ran off and clyped to the Fiscal. Judas.'

Up on stage, the ACC ran a hand across his shiny fore-head. 'I'm not at liberty to discuss that for operational reasons.' Which meant he didn't have a clue.

One of the journalists stood: a scraggy man in an ill-fitting suit, all bones and sharp edges, nose hooked like a beak, Dictaphone pointed like a handgun. 'Assistant Chief Constable! Michael Larson, *Edinburgh Evening Post*: how come Grampian Police refuse to mount a proper search for missing teenagers Agnes Garfield and Anthony Chung?'

The ACC's mouth fell open for a moment, then a frown crawled across his face. 'I'm not at liberty to discuss that.'

Steel elbowed Logan in the ribs again. 'Did I no' tell you to get your bloody finger out and do something on that one?'

'I haven't had time, it's—'

'Now look what you've done. And who do you think's going to get it in the neck, because you've no' bothered your arse? Me. That's who. Like our delightful ACC needs another excuse. The sweaty chunky wee sod.'

Larson, from the *Edinburgh Evening Post*, shook his head. 'ACC Irvin, why won't you even *listen* to the parents' concerns? Do you just not care, or what?'

The press officer leaned forward until the microphone was

inches from her face. 'OK, we're drifting off topic here. I need everyone to restrict themselves to questions about the case at hand.'

The journalist turned, looking around at the assembled press. 'Sounds to me like Grampian Police are doing a cover-up, right?'

ACC Irvin thumped his hand on the table again, hard enough to make the microphones wobble. 'We are not covering anything up!'

'Then answer the question: how come you lot care so little about Anthony and Agnes's safety that you can't be bothered looking for them? Eh?'

8

'. . .complete and utter disaster.' The pathologists' office was empty, so Logan shifted Isobel's 'MUMMY AT WORK' mug out of the way, then perched one bum-cheek on her desk. 'The ACC looked as if he was going to have an aneurysm.'

Samantha laughed down the phone at him. '*So you ran away and hid in the mortuary?*'

'I'm not hiding, I'm. . .' He switched his mobile from one ear to the other. 'I beat a tactical retreat till Steel and the ACC calm down. And yes: my nose still hurts, thanks for asking.'

'*Coward.*'

'What am I supposed to do? Everyone's acting like Agnes and Anthony are this pair of lost wee kids, but they're old enough to get married, join the army and get shot at. . . So what if they've run off to be together? Who are they hurting?'

'*You going to be late again tonight?*'

'It's Agnes's bloody parents causing all the trouble. Don't like to think about their wee girl out there shagging Anthony Chung.'

'*Moan, whinge, moan. Don't forget to pick up some milk on your way home. And you're all out of Marmite too.*'

'Like they've not been at it for years already. You know what horny little sods teenagers are, any excuse and. . .'

He sat up straight, setting Isobel's china mug rattling against its saucer: the mortuary's outer door had just slammed shut. Then came the sound of footsteps, echoing down the corridor outside.

'Got to go – someone's coming.'

'Don't be such a wimp; you're a DI now, take your medicine like a man.'

'Acting DI, and no thanks.' He hung up and jumped down from the desk. The footsteps were getting closer. As long as they kept on going, through to the cutting room, he'd be fine. Just have to sneak out once they were in there.

Crap. . . The footsteps stopped right outside the pathologists' office.

Logan spun around on the spot. Had to be *somewhere* to hide in here. Behind the filing cabinet? Not enough space. Under one of the desks? . . . Yeah, and how would he explain *that* when they caught him? Looking for a contact lens?

Might be worth a go.

He pulled out the nearest chair—

The door swung open and he froze, halfway into a crouch. 'Guv?'

Logan looked up, and there was Rennie, frowning down at him.

'You OK, Guv? Only you look like you're about to curl one out on the floor there.'

Heat bloomed in Logan's cheeks. 'I was just—'

'Should probably pull your trousers and pants down first though,' a grin broke across Rennie's face, 'going to be hell of a mess otherwise.'

Logan stood. 'Did you want something, *Sergeant*?'

'See, if I was going to take a dump in someone's office,

77

I'd do it in their desk drawer. Or in the filing cabinet, under "J" for jobbie, that way it's all organized and—'

'Rennie!'

'Oh, right. Yeah.' He stood to one side and swept his arm out in a grandiose gesture, as if he was a magician introducing his glamorous assistant. 'Got a Dr Graham here to see La Monarch De Iceberg.'

A woman stepped past Rennie, into the room. Short, big smile, tiny diamond earrings twinkling between strands of long blonde hair. Big brown boots, blue jeans, and a pink twinset. Petite and girly. She stuck out a thin hand for Logan to shake. It was like an industrial car crusher. 'I hear you need a forensic anthropologist?'

Already?

Logan took his hand back while it still worked. 'You're keen: we only put the call out an hour ago.'

She flashed him a smile that made little crow's feet around her eyes. 'Are you kidding? Jobs like this are hen's teeth: had to get here before any other bugger did. Forensic anthropology's a cut-throat business.'

'Dr Graham—'

'April, please.' She shook her head. 'I blame the telly – they show all these glamorous actors running about the place, solving murders, then everyone and their dog thinks, "Hey, why don't *I* train to be one of them bone people?" Seriously, you can't throw a brick these days without braining two dozen unemployed forensic anthropologists.'

'That's very—'

'You know,' she frowned up at him, 'you should've put some ice on that, it would've brought the swelling down. Might be too late now, but it's probably still worth a go. Trust me: if there's one thing I know, it's being punched in the face.'

Logan's fingers stroked the side of his swollen nose. 'OK. . .'

'Are the remains ready?' She got a step closer. 'I'd really like to get cracking as soon as I can.'

He backed away, until the desktop dug into the back of his legs. Retreat no longer an option. 'They're through the house. . .'

'Good stuff.' She spun around, as if she was mounted on castors. 'Right, lead the way, and we—' Her pillow-sized handbag swung out as she turned, caught Isobel's china mug and sent it flying.

It hit the carpet tiles with a delicate ping, then shattered into a dozen glinting fragments.

April stared down at it, mouth hanging open. She cleared her throat, clutched at the demon handbag, kneaded at the tan leather. 'Oh God. . . It was an accident.' She shuffled sideways, into the filing cabinet. 'It . . . I'll pay for it. I didn't mean to break it.'

Rennie hunkered down and picked a shard up between thumb and forefinger, dropping it into his palm. 'Don't worry, it's just—'

'No, you don't understand, it. . . They're just waiting for me to screw something up, so they can barge in and take over.'

Logan leaned back against the desk. '*They*?'

'The other forensic anthropologists. I told you it was cut-throat, didn't I? I'm good at my job, and it was an accident, and—'

'It's OK. We didn't see anything, did we, Sergeant?'

Rennie dropped another sliver into his palm, then shook his head. 'Mug? What mug? Was missing when we got here, someone probably nicked it. Bunch of thieving bastards round here.'

April smiled at them, eyes shining. 'Thanks.'

Rennie picked up the last of the shards. 'Don't thank us – we didn't do, or see, anything.' He went to tip the remains into the wastepaper basket.

Logan hit him. 'Don't be thick – she's going to look there, isn't she? Wrap it in toilet paper and dump it in the gents' bin. Then go see if anyone's caught Reuben yet.'

A wink. 'Got you.' And he was off, cradling the shattered mug like a baby bird.

Logan ushered April out into the corridor. 'So, what, you just happened to be in the area?'

She followed him through the double doors into the cutting room. 'It was on the news this morning. So I jumped in the car and called your pathologist – met her at the Forensic Society conference at RGU two years ago. In this job, it pays to network.'

The doors whumped closed behind them, letting the air wrap them in its chilly arms. Not quite cold enough to make their breath plume, but close.

Overhead strip-lights glinted back from the stainless-steel work surfaces, cutting tables, and wall of refrigerated drawers. White tiles clicked beneath Logan's shoes as he marched over and read the labels slipped into the little holders on the doors. 'UNKNOWN VICTIM: MURDER ~ 003613' was second from the bottom on the left. He clacked up the handle and hauled the drawer out.

April looked down at the white plastic body-bag. 'Are forensics finished with trace evidence?'

'Yes.'

'Everything's done?'

'Just said that, didn't I?'

'Good. In that case. . .' She snapped on a pair blue nitrile gloves, took hold of the body-bag's zip and pulled it down.

The scent of raw meat and scorched barbecue oozed out into the cold room.

'Hmm. . . I know it sounds daft, but it's *so* nice to get a fresh one. Normally, the smell of them. . .' She peered down at what was left of the head, up on her tiptoes, then down again, then left and right, as if she was expecting it to do something. Not touching anything. 'I need a practising medical professional with five years' experience, and you'll have to sign a release.'

'Isn't my body.' He looked at the mortuary doors. 'If Dalrymple's about, she can do it.'

'There's a fair bit of work to be done. . .' April headed for the nearest cutting table and dumped her demon handbag on it, popped open the clasp and went rummaging inside while Logan went off to find the Anatomical Pathology Technician.

'You see, that's the real trouble. . .' April slipped the blade through the last strands of tendon and eased the head away from the body. She'd changed into an orangey-grey sweater, the turtleneck pulled up over her nose and mouth, like a makeshift facemask. 'Britain's too small – remains get found too quickly. What you want is somewhere like America, or Australia, dump your victim out there and it'll stay hidden for years.'

She placed the head down on a white plastic tray. It rocked a couple of times, then lay there, screaming up at the ceiling with its cracked yellow teeth.

Logan adjusted his mask. 'How long's this going to take?'

On the other side of the room, the duty doctor sat in one of the chairs dragged through from the staff room. Dr Ramsey: a short man in a baggy suit, with a threadbare goatee beard, chubby cheeks, a mini-quiff at the front and a bald patch at the back; Ramsey had his feet up on an empty brain bucket, and his head buried in a copy of the *Aberdeen Examiner*. 'MAN BURNED TO DEATH IN SICK "NECKLACING" MURDER' in big black letters above a photo of the Joyriders' Graveyard out by Thainstone Mart. 'Well, you could always move.'

'Don't get me wrong: I've thought about it a couple of

times, but I'd miss Scotland too much. All that sunshine and warm weather just isn't natural. Mind you, must be nice not to have to fight for every single job.'

'Dr Graham: how long?'

The forensic anthropologist glanced up at him. 'Well, I've got to remove the residual skin, clean the skull, work out the correct tissue depth, add the markers, model the musculature, then the skin, hair. . . Like I said, it's a fair bit of work, but obviously I'll go as fast as I—'

A loud bang came from outside, in the corridor: the mortuary door slamming against the wall. Then a voice: 'WHERE THE BLOODY HELL IS SHE?'

April wrapped her gloved hands around the head. Bared her teeth. 'Dempsey.'

BOOM and the cutting-room doors flew open. A man stood on the threshold, his round face flushed and trembling. Two streaks of grey ran back across his head from the temples, as if he'd been a badger in a former life. It went with the yellowy-tweed suit. He jabbed a sausage finger at April. 'You unprofessional bitch!'

Rennie stumbled in after him. 'If you don't calm down, sir, I'm going to have to—'

He spun around. 'Don't let her fool you: this is *my* job, not hers. She's got no business being here.'

April cradled the head against her chest, pressing the scorched flesh into the off-orange fabric. 'That's not fair, Jack, I got here first.'

'I have an agreement!' He threw his chest out, shoulders back. 'And it's *Dr Dempsey* to you, Graham.' He dug into his jacket and pulled out a sheet of paper. 'See? The local pathologist called in *my* services, not yours. Now put down my remains and go peddle your clumsy excuse for forensic anthropology somewhere else.'

Still holding the head with one arm, she grabbed the

82

clipboard from the cutting table. 'I've got a release, do you have a release? No, you don't.'

'Don't you "I've got a release" me: you only got that under false pretences. This is my job and you bloody well know it!'

Rennie took the sheet of paper from Dempsey's hand and peered at it for a moment. Then looked up at Logan. 'It's from Pukey Pete. Blah, blah, blah, Dr Peter Forsyth cordially invites you to assist with the identification of an unknown male found last night suffering from severe burns to the head, neck, and chest. . .'

'See? I told you: this is *my* job.' He beamed, teeth bared, eyes narrowed to piggy little slits. 'Now sling your hook, Graham.'

April brought her chin up. 'I was asked to come by Dr McAllister.'

'Well I was asked *first.*'

Raised voices echoed down the corridor, the noise amplified by all the cold hard surfaces in the cutting room. Rennie peered through the gap between the doors. 'They're still going at it.'

'Pffff. . .' Logan hissed out a breath, then leaned back against the corridor wall. 'Any news?'

Blank look. Then a blink. 'Oh, right: Reuben. No. They've tried his house, Wee Hamish's place, the garage in Mastrick, all the bookies he runs, the docks. . .' Shrug. 'He's gone all ninja on us.'

Sod. He let his head rest against the gritty wallpaper. At least the ants were fading away. 'Fancy a cup of tea?'

'You sure we should just leave them alone? What if they start smashing things up?'

'Why do you think I locked the remains back in the fridge? Anyway, if they break anything, Isobel will hunt them down and kill them.' Logan pushed the door to the pathologists' office open. 'Get the kettle on, and. . .'

Dr Forsyth was hunched over his desk, cheeks glistening with tears as he packed files and personal effects into a large cardboard box. Out of his rumpled SOC suit, he was still . . . rumpled. A small man with a neatly trimmed beard and a pair of thick glasses in NHS-black frames. He flinched. Stared at Logan for a breath, then went back to clearing out his desk.

Rennie grabbed the kettle from the top of the filing cabinet and gave it a shoogle. It barely sloshed. 'Afternoon, Doc. Fancy a brew?'

'I'm. . . I handed in my resignation.'

'Ah. Right.' Rennie backed out into the corridor again, pointing towards the cutting room. 'I'll fill the kettle, get it on, and we can all . . . have a nice cuppa.'

Logan waited until the door closed behind him. 'Are you OK?'

A sniff. 'No. That's the point.' He wiped a sleeve across his eyes. 'I can't do this any more. All the pain and the suffering and the relatives and the press and the courts and the bloody press. . .'

A smile. 'You said "press" twice.'

'Did you know they doorstepped me for that Rubislaw Den murder? Right outside my house. I was taking Natasha to playgroup. . .' He dumped a box file in on top of some pilfered Post-it notes. 'I've tried so *hard* to keep what I do separate, and they do something like that?' He wiped his hand across his cheeks, then dried it on the leg of his trousers. 'And the *smell*. I wash and I wash and I wash and it never comes off. . .'

Logan nodded. 'I'm sorry.'

A knock came from the office door. Dr Ramsey was blinking at them from the corridor. 'Turns out some shoplifter's fallen down the stairs in the custody block.' He pointed over his shoulder, back towards the bulk of FHQ. 'If Tweedledee and Tweedledum ever stop shouting at each other, let me know.'

'Thanks, Doc.'

'Anthropologists. . .' Ramsey rolled his eyes, then sloped off, shoes scuffing on the floor.

Dr Forsyth hurled another manila folder into the box, following it up with one more for every word: 'Just – can't – take it – any more.' He picked the box up, cradling it in his arms as if it were a severed head. 'And all the time they're telling us to cut costs, as if what we do is. . .' He trembled, flecks of spittle frothing in the corners of his mouth. 'Like we're sitting about drinking coffee from golden mugs and eating bloody *chocolates*.' A shrug. 'Sorry. It's just. . .'

He lowered his head and shuffled from the room. As he opened the door, the raised voices came through again:

'Oh, don't give me that, Graham, you've always been jealous of my success!'

'I'm not arguing with you about this, Dempsey. I was here first.'

Dr Forsyth looked back over his shoulder. 'Please. . .' A frown. 'Tell Isobel I stuck it for as long as I could.'

'It's my bloody job! Now pack up and bugger off!'

'My life coach says I have to—'

'Life coach? What kind of bloody idiot—'

The door clunked shut again.

Rennie backed into the room, carrying the kettle in one hand and a packet of Jaffa Cakes in the other. He waggled the orange-and-blue box at Logan. 'Creepy Dalrymple didn't lock her locker. What's the point of hiding things in your locker if you don't lock it?' He stuck the kettle onto its base and flicked the switch. 'Clue's in the name.'

Logan scrolled through the messages on his phone,

deleting all the rubbish – most of which came from Steel. 'Mmm. . .'

'Exactly.' Rennie clunked a couple of mugs down on the desk. 'It's gone all quiet out there. Think they've kissed and made up? Bet they're at it on one of the cutting tables, getting their forensic anthropology freak on. Jumping each other's bones.'

No wonder Steel never had any time to do her own paperwork, she was too busy sending pointless text messages. Delete. Delete. Delete.

Logan looked up from the little screen. 'The ACC still on a rampage?'

'Nah, gone home. It's Her Nibs you've got to worry about.' The kettle rattled away to itself, grumbling steam out into the room. 'Guv . . . this jewellery heist. . .'

Here we go. Logan put his phone away. 'You were asleep. We got a confession.'

'Yeah, but I put in all the work and it's not—'

'Never is.'

'But it *isn't* fair. And look at this. . .' He pulled out his notebook, flipped it open, and held it up. Someone had written 'FIND THOSE BLOODY TRAMPS, YOU LAZY WEE BAWBAG!!!' above a list of three names and a crude drawing of male genitalia. The handwriting was obviously Steel's. Rennie clacked the thing shut and stuffed it back in his pocket. 'She drew a cock in my notebook. What am I supposed to do if I've got to produce it in court? Think the judge'll be impressed?'

The kettle clicked, then fell silent.

'She keeps lumping these crappy make-work jobs on me. How am I going to make my mark, if she keeps—'

'*Make your mark*?'

A blush spread across his cheeks. 'Well, it's. . . You know what I mean.'

'No wonder she drew a dick in your notebook; lucky she didn't do it on your forehead. Anyway, you should be happy.'

He picked up the kettle and filled the mugs. 'Ha bloody ha.'

'She did the same thing to me. In her twisted little mind, it's her way of singling you out. Testing you.' Logan patted him on the shoulder. 'Don't know how to break it to you, but you're her *favourite*.'

Rennie sagged. 'Oh God. . .'

'Oh yes. Say goodbye to getting home at a reasonable hour, and hello to bizarre calls in the middle of the night.'

More sagging. 'And how come I'm the one stuck hunting down tramps? It's not like Hairy Mary, Scotty Scabs and Fusty Forman did anything serious: two blokes and an auld wifie shoplifting cheese, bacon, and vodka doesn't really count as organized crime, does it?'

'And you can forget about seeing Emma. But get ready for lots and lots of questions about your sex life, even though you're never home in time to actually have one.'

'Probably drunk themselves to death weeks ago. They'll be lying dead in a ditch somewhere, covered in smoked streaky and Cheddar, getting all mouldy and fusty. . .' A shudder. 'Bad enough when they do it in winter, but in this weather?' Rennie's bottom lip poked out. 'Can't we get the GED to look for them?'

Logan smiled. 'Trust me: soon as our beloved colleagues in the General Enquiries Division find out that Steel's lumped you with finding these guys, they'll disappear faster than you can say, "Someone else's problem."' Logan fished his teabag out and dumped it in the wastepaper basket. 'Besides, there's only three of them. Don't be such a wimp.'

Rennie ripped open the Jaffa Cakes, then tipped out a half-dozen brown flying-saucers onto the desk. 'It's not three any more, it's two. Got Hairy Mary in the mortuary – found her under the Wellington Bridge with a bottle of turps in one hand and her knickers round her ankles.'

'Sexual assault?'

A shake of the head. 'Call of nature, from the state of her.' He bit a Jaffa Cake in half, talking with his mouth full. 'Poor cow. Imagine going out like that? Everyone seeing you?' He chewed, then swallowed. 'You want to take a look at her?'

Dirty bugger. Logan pulled in his chin. 'Do you *really* think that's appropriate, because I—'

'No! Not look at her with her knickers down. . . I mean take a look and make sure I'm not screwing anything up?'

'Oh.' That was OK then. 'Don't be such a big Jessie.'

'Come on, Guv. . .' He popped the final Jaffa Cake in his mouth and fluttered his eyelashes. 'Please?'

Sigh. 'This is the *last* time, understand?'

A grin. 'Thanks, Guv!'

Rennie was right – the corridor was quiet, not so much as an angry murmur coming from the cutting room. Logan pushed through the double doors . . . and stopped.

Dr Dempsey was sitting flat on his wide tweed bum in the middle of the room, both hands clasped over his nose, while Dr April Graham skipped back and forward in front of him, knees bent, feet barely moving. Fists up in classic Muhammad Ali pose.

She threw a couple of sharp right jabs into the air, making little puffing noises. 'Told him to stop pushing me.'

9

Logan shifted the hot mug of coffee from one hand to the other, wedging the manila folder under his arm as he struggled with the doorknob. Down the corridor, the main CID office was noisy: the dayshift coasting towards quitting time, the backshift grumbling about all the jobs they'd been lumbered with on a Sunday evening.

Click, and the handle *finally* turned. He pushed through into his own private sanctuary— Crap.

Detective Chief Inspector Steel was sitting in his chair, feet up on his desk, electronic cigarette clamped between her teeth puffing artificial smoke into the room. 'Where the hell have you been?'

He dumped the mug on the desk, then swatted at her feet with the folder. 'Out.'

She didn't move. 'Did I no' tell you about those bloody teenagers?'

'For God's sake, they're shacked up somewhere, banging each other's hormone-addled brains out. It's not—'

'I don't give a badger's hairy arsehole if they're on *Jeremy Kyle* with "My Girlfriend Won't Swallow": I told you to get

89

your finger out and visit the bloody parents and at least *look* as if you're doing something.'

'They—'

'No.' She slammed a hand down on the desk. 'This isn't a debate, it's an order. Finger – out – *now*. You made the ACC look a right prawn.'

'You know what? Sod it.' He pulled out his warrant card, in its little leather holder, and tossed it into her lap. 'I'm with Doc Forsyth: screw this for a game of soldiers. I never asked you to make me up to DI, did I? No, I was quite happy where I was, but you had to have someone to run around after your backside, doing all your bloody paperwork.'

'There we go.' She checked her watch. 'Lasted a whole *two weeks* as acting DI before threatening to flounce off in a strop. That's a record for you. Was starting to worry you'd grown up a bit.'

'I'm serious.'

'Oh, don't be such a big girl's blouse.'

'I've had enough.'

'Moan, moan, whinge, bitch, moan. Now I know where Rennie gets it from.' She flipped open the little leather case and peered at the warrant card within, holding it out at arm's length. 'Jesus, there's a face only a proctologist could love.'

He grabbed his coat from the hook by the door. 'Enjoy your paperwork.'

'Park your arse.' She pointed at the visitor's chair on the other side of the desk. 'Soon as Disaster McPherson's finished screwing things up in Holyrood, you can go back to being a lowly defective sergeant. God, you're such a drama queen.'

'I am *not* a drama—'

'You don't see me whingeing on about running CID till Finnie returns from his wee jolly to Malaga, do you? Even though the sodding ACC's down here every five minutes bitching about the budget and the rotas and the overtime bill? No: because I'm a team player, one of the lads, knuckling under and getting the job done like a pro.' She had a dig at the underside of her left breast, scratching and tugging at the bra-line. 'Course, the extra cash helps.'

Logan stared at her. 'You got a pay rise?'

Scowl. 'Don't change the subject. You, Logan Bum-Face McRae, need to get your act sorted. Being a DI's no' about running all over the place, arresting people and getting punched in the nose: it's about taking a strategic overview, staying in FHQ at the centre of your wee web of influence and *organizing* things, making the best use of the available manpower. And solving bloody cases!'

'Like you ever—'

'Now get your backside in gear and go see those poor missing kids' parents!'

Silence settled into the room, then a hiss and click as Steel's electric cigarette gave another puff of steam.

'What happened to, "being a DI's no' about running all over the place"?'

'Parents need to see a senior officer, no' some junior idiot in uniform wiping their nose on their sleeves. And if you'd done something about it in the first sodding place, you wouldn't be in this mess.' She chucked his warrant card back at him. 'Now sod off before I decide to motivate you some more.'

In the main CID office a lone detective constable was bent over the fax machine, cursing and swearing as she pounded away at the keypad. Other than her, the place was deserted: most of the dayshift would be down at their lockers already, getting changed to go home – or hiding so they wouldn't have to answer the phones and get dragged into anything at five to five on a Sunday evening – while the backshift were off actually doing things, leaving the little corrals of chest-high partitions and scuffed beech desks to sulk unloved beneath stacks of forms and reports, empty sandwich wrappers and dirty mugs.

Logan tried the small walled-off annex at the side of the room – the one with a brass plaque mounted on the door: 'THE WEE HOOSE'. Someone had stuck a Post-it note to the thing, with 'CONDEMNED FOR PUBLIC HEALTH REASONS!' scrawled across it.

Inside, DS Bob Marshall was frowning at a pile of receipts and an expenses form. His desk looked as if a stationery cupboard had thrown up on it. A big orange-and-black biohazard sign was mounted on the wall in front of him. As if anyone actually needed any warning. . .

The other three desks were almost tidy, no sign of their owners, just the shelves laden with box files and manuals, the whiteboards covered with case lists for each DS complete with notes and dates.

Bob scribbled something down on his form. 'If you're here to moan about them not catching Reuben yet: don't. It's sod all to do with me.'

Logan slumped into his old familiar chair, the one with the wobbly castor and the creaky hydraulic thing, and the coffee stain on the seat that always made it look as if he'd had an unfortunate accident. Loved that chair. He ran a hand along the rough plastic armrest. 'You're a jammy sod, Bob.'

'Mmm. . .' He didn't look up. 'Think I can claim for that bottle of whisky I bought for the Levinston stakeout?'

'Being a detective sergeant. OK, so you've got to put up with all the crap from the DCs and Uniform – and run around after the DIs like you're their nanny – but it's not bad, is it?'

'Maybe I can kid on it's for an informant?'

Logan swivelled left and right, then back again. The bearings groaned underneath him. Just like the old days. . . 'You're not allowed to have unregistered informants: anything

Chiz-related would have to go through the Secret Squirrel Squad. Put it down as a teambuilding expense under Finnie's "Forward To Tomorrow" cost-code. By the time he gets back from Malaga no one will remember what it was meant to be used for anyway.'

'Ta.' Bob's biro scribbled something down on the form.

Logan creaked the seat around in a full circle, drawing his knees in at the last minute to avoid the leg of the desk. 'See, that's what I'm talking about: you're out on stakeouts with a bottle of Glenfiddich, and I'm up to my ears in spreadsheets, cost centres, and budget plans. I remember when—'

'Yeah, being dragged about, moaned at, and told to do stuff is just *great*. At least you get a shot at being DI, when's my go?' He grabbed another receipt from the pile and scowled at it. 'You want anything in particular, or are you just slumming it for fun?'

'Going out to the Garfield and Chung houses – fly the flag for community policing.' Hydraulics go up, hydraulics go down, hydraulics go up.

'The missing kids?' Bob stood and picked a beige corduroy jacket off the back of his chair. 'Suppose you want *me* to drive.'

Logan stopped playing with the chair. Narrowed his eyes. 'What did you have for lunch?'

Bob pulled the jacket on. 'Why?'

'Bob. . .?'

'Cauliflower and lentil curry from that wee place on Belmont Street.'

Which explained the Post-it note on the door.

'In that case, you can stay here and finish your expenses. No way I'm sharing a car with you.'

'That's discrimination.'

'Self-bloody-preservation more like.'

The Wee Hoose's door opened and DS Chalmers marched in, carrying a stack of printouts, glasses perched on the tip of her nose. She smiled. 'Keeping it warm for me?' Pause. 'The chair?' Then dumped the paper on the desk behind him.

Right: not his chair any more. Not his desk. He stood. 'It's your lucky day, Chalmers – instead of sitting here being gassed to death by Biohazard Bob, I'm rescuing you. Grab your jacket, we've got parents to visit.'

Agnes Garfield's mother glowered at them from the doorway. 'Well, perhaps if you'd done something when we told you she was missing, she'd be home by now.' Her long brown hair was pulled back in a ponytail, and she fiddled with the ends, teasing them apart with yellow-tipped fingers. A smoker. But instead of stale cigarettes she stank of Ralgex and spearmint.

Posters festooned Agnes Garfield's bedroom walls: brooding vampires with greasy hair, monobrowed werewolves, Harry-Bloody-Potter. . . Then there were a few for books that looked as if they'd been lifted from the local Waterstones: *The Night Circus*, *Golden Compass*, *Witchfire*, *Narnia*. . . One wall was completely given over to bookshelves stuffed full of paperbacks, the occasional hardback sticking out like a tombstone.

The window was open a crack, letting in the scent of freshly mown grass and the smoky promise of a back-garden barbecue from somewhere nearby. Agnes's room was at the back of the house, with a view out over the rooftops towards the sprawling housing estates of Danestone on one side, and rolling countryside on the other. Fields of violent-yellow rapeseed shone like burnished gold in the evening light.

Logan stepped back. The computer desk in the window recess didn't have a single piece of clutter or dust on it. 'And they haven't been in touch at all?'

Agnes's mum stuck her chin out. 'If they had, we'd have said something! Think we kicked up all this fuss trying to get you to *do* something because we thought it would be fun?'

'Girls that age . . . well, they're not girls any more, are they? Eighteen years old: they're adults.'

'Our Agnes would *never* run away from home. She loves us. She's safe here. She *knows* that.' The yellowed fingers pecked at her hair, like jaundiced crows going after roadkill. 'It's that bloody Anthony Chung. He's done this. Abducted her. I said so, last time you were round, but you didn't do anything about it, did you? Bloody police. . .'

DS Chalmers patted her on the shoulder. 'We're going to do everything we can, Mrs Garfield.'

Agnes's mother scowled at her. 'Don't you patronize me. If you'd taken us seriously and *done* something in the first—'

'Why don't you leave us to it for a bit, and we'll come down when we're done?'

The chin went up again. 'You won't find anything. I've been through this room a dozen times, there's nothing here. Agnes has no secrets from me. You need to be out there, hunting down that bloody Chung!'

Chalmers smiled, showing off those pointy little teeth. 'I know, but you want us to be thorough, don't you? We'll be down soon as we're done.'

A sniff. A thinning of the lips. Then she jabbed a finger at Logan. 'If he'd done his job when he came here, instead of drinking tea and eating my biscuits, she'd be home by now.' A nod. Agnes's mum backed out of the room and slammed the door.

'Pfffffff. . .' Logan sank down on the single bed. The wooden frame creaked, the mattress sagging beneath him. 'Before you say anything, it was DI McPherson. Sent me out here, told me to poke about a bit, reassure them, then get

95

back to solving *actual* crimes. Course, then he gets seconded to the Scottish Parliament on the Force Integration Project – as if they didn't have enough bloody numpties screwing things up already – and hey presto, suddenly it's *my* problem.'

He glanced up. . . The roof was covered in pale-yellowy-green and white stars. Had to be hundreds of them up there, filling the ceiling from edge to edge. Oh to be young and daft again.

Chalmers poked her way through the bookshelves. 'Whenever my mother hated any of my boyfriends, it just made them more appealing. Even Hamish Campbell with his big teeth and stickie-out ears. Dad hated him too, and after that I'd have run away with him in a heartbeat. . .'

The bedside cabinet contained a mix of hankies, granny-pants, and a tiny collection of cheap jewellery – each piece individually wrapped in tissue paper. Logan slid the last drawer back into place, then pushed aside the little troupe of fluffy toy animals to peer into the gap between the mattress and the wall. Nothing.

'What you looking for?'

'A diary. Address book. Something like that.'

Thump. A black leather journal landed on the duvet. It was held shut with a black ribbon.

Logan picked it up, weighed it in his hand. 'Where was it?'

Chalmers pointed at the bookcase. 'Top shelf, next to the collected Roald Dahl.'

Left in full view, where anyone could find it? Bizarre.

He undid the ribbon and flicked through the pages to the last entry. It was dated three weeks ago, the day before she disappeared. He held it out. 'Read.'

'OK. . . Er. . .' Chalmers dug out her glasses and slipped them on. '"Today was a good day, I didn't cry once, and Mum made tuna casserole for tea. Jemma and Penny want to go see a band on Saturday night, but I've got a history test to revise for, so I don't think I can go". . .' A sniff. She looked up from the pages. 'Nothing very dramatic. Nothing that says, "I'm running away to set up house with my boyfriend."' Chalmers flipped back a few pages. 'Here she's talking about watching TV. . .' Back another two. 'They went to the shops and bought some new socks and she got a book. . .' Further back. 'She wants to have a couple of friends over for dinner, but her mum won't let her, says they're a bad influence. And Agnes is *actually* OK with that.' Chalmers curled her top lip. 'Kid's got no spine.'

'Does she mention Anthony Chung at all?'

'Not so far. Mind you. . .' Chalmers nodded at the neatly ordered bookcase, then the tidy desk, then the chest of drawers with a single porcelain figurine of a dragon on top of it – perfectly centred in a lace doily. 'Doesn't exactly come off as a wild child, does she? Even her books are alphabetically arranged by author. When I was her age I was getting blootered every weekend with Duncan Peters in his parents' summerhouse, while they were out getting the weekly shop from Asda.'

Logan stood. 'So she was keeping secrets from the diary?'

'With a nosy mum like that?' Chalmers closed the book and tied the ribbon. 'Or maybe Agnes is just really, really boring. . .' Frown. 'You notice there's no photos in here? No birthday parties, or holiday snaps, or hanging out with friends? Just book and movie posters?'

'Parents seem genuinely worried about her. Maybe a bit too much?'

'Think they've killed her and buried her in the basement?'

'Wouldn't be the first time someone did it.'

Chalmers slid the diary back on the shelf. 'Is it just me, or is there something . . . wrong with the room? You know, like. . .'

Silence.

'Like what?'

'Don't know. Like someone doesn't really live here? It's too ordered, too tidy, there isn't any personal stuff.' She picked a stuffed tiger from the group on the bed. 'Look at these: none of them are worn, or tatty, or threadbare. They've never been loved, they're just things.' She gave the tiger a hug. 'Maybe the thing that's missing is the childhood?'

Logan looked down at the tidy little room. 'Or maybe her mum just tidies the hell out of everything any time Agnes goes out? She's the type. And what sort of freak calls their kid "Agnes" for God's sake? Should report them to child protection.' He took the tiger from her and dumped it back on the bed. 'Five more minutes with the parents, then we're out of here.'

'Yes, Guv.' She followed him out of the bedroom.

'Tomorrow you can get on to the bus stations and the airport and the ferry terminal – have someone knock up "Have you seen Agnes?" posters.' He started down the stairs. 'Then go round all her friends. I want to know if she and Anthony Chung talked about going anywhere.'

10

Logan stopped at the foot of the stairs.

The voices coming from the lounge were muffled by the closed door, but it was easy enough to hear Agnes's mum and dad arguing about whose fault it was that she'd run away. An eighteen-year-old girl whose mother poked her nose into everything, who wouldn't let her have friends over, who went through her things every time she was out. No wonder she'd legged it the first chance she got.

There was a cupboard under the stairs, the door a blank slab of white. It'd been fitted with a bolt on the outside, held shut with a brass padlock. The kind that had tumblers instead of a key. He squinted at the architrave, the words 'AGNES'S ROOM' were just visible – scratched into the wood, then rendered almost invisible by layer upon layer of gloss paint.

He gave the padlock a tug. Solid enough. But the trouble with these tumbler locks, especially the cheaper makes, was how easily you could crack the combination by levering the dials apart while you turned them, feeling for the click. . . There. Then the next one. . . Two more to go, and the hasp popped free of the lock.

Chalmers stared at him. 'How did you *do* that?'

'Gets easier when they're used a lot. Loosens everything up.' Logan drew the bolt, and swung the door open.

Inside, the little cupboard had been turned into a little room. A single mattress filled the available floor space, no sheets, just a sleeping bag and two stuffed toys: a teddy bear that looked as if one more go in the washing machine would finish it off, and a once-white rabbit turned Frankenstein's monster with random-coloured patches and big clumsy stitching.

A bookshelf sat at the tall end of the wedge-shaped cupboard, with more paperbacks, and plastic action figures: wizards, witches, and vampires. Half a dozen grey and black roses were long dead in a vase, tied up with a black ribbon. Very cheery.

He beckoned Chalmers over. 'This look more like it?'

She climbed inside, kneeling on the mattress as she poked through the books on the shelf. 'Harry Potter's got a lot to answer for.'

'She's *eighteen*.'

'Yeah. . .' Chalmers pulled a hardback from the collection and frowned at it. 'She's got this same book upstairs.' The front cover was some sort of dragon thing curled around a woman dressed like a gypsy. Chalmers opened it. Raised an eyebrow. Then turned it so the innards were facing Logan. 'Interesting.'

The book had been hollowed out. She pulled out a spiral-bound notebook, flicked through a few pages. 'Oh dear. . .'

'What?'

'"Rowan looked at him lovingly. 'I'm really glad you bit me Edward,' she said enthusiastically, 'this way we can be together forever when we get to magic school!' He smiled at her knowingly, and thought about how much he loved her, because she was perfect. 'I know,' he said romantically, his eyes smouldering like a million suns falling into a million black holes, 'I can't think of anyone I'd rather battle the Dark Lord of the Werewolves with than you! You're so much cleverer than that little swot Hermione.' And she knew he meant it, because she was the only one who could make his cold dead heart beat again. . ."' Chalmers turned the next couple of pages, pursed her lips. 'Oh, look at that. Then they have sex on the carriage floor while Harry watches and plays with his wand. Then he sticks it up Edward's. . .' She shuddered, put the thing back in the book and slammed it shut. 'God, I hate slashfic.'

'Slashfic?'

'Think *really* bad fan fiction, only you have everyone shagging each other. It's kind of. . .' She looked over Logan's shoulder. 'Mrs Garfield, did Agnes spend a lot of time in here?'

Agnes's mum was standing by the open living-room door, arms folded across her chest. 'We keep that cupboard *locked*.'

'So Agnes wasn't allowed—'

'She was obsessed with those bloody wizard books when she was younger. She'd. . . When she was little she'd sneak in there and play. I know we shouldn't have indulged her, but we did. Keep meaning to clear it out, but every time I tried, she'd burst into tears and scream till she was sick.' Mrs Garfield narrowed her eyes, then looked away down the hall. 'What kind of grown woman wants to be a wee wizard boy in a stupid book?'

Logan pulled on a smile. 'Don't suppose there's any chance of a cup of tea, is there? DS Chalmers will lend a hand, won't you, DS Chalmers?'

She looked up at him from the cupboard. 'I—'

'Excellent. Milk and two for me, thanks.' He stood back so she could climb out. 'I just need to make a couple of calls – get the ball rolling – then I'll be right through.'

'You want *tea*?' Mrs Garfield's mouth hung open. 'You've not done anything yet!'

'Like I said, I need to make a few calls. And DS Chalmers needs to ask you some questions about Agnes's friends.'

Chalmers blinked. 'I do? . . . Oh, right, yes, that's right. Questions. Er, shall we?'

As soon as they'd disappeared into the kitchen, Logan shut the lounge door again, then clambered into the cupboard under the stairs. There was just enough space to kneel at the tall end without banging his head on the sloping ceiling.

He frowned up at it. Now there was something you didn't see every day. A pentagram covered the plasterboard, scratched out in red ink. It sat within a couple of circles, with squiggles in various bits, and what looked like Latin around the outside.

Why were teenagers *such* a bunch of freaks?

A pair of wingnuts sat on the inside of the doorframe. Logan peered outside again. The bolt fitted into a metal bracket held in place by the wingnuts. So if you cracked the padlock, opened the door, unscrewed them, put the padlock back on the now unattached bolt mechanism, then climbed inside – you could pull the door shut, do up the wingnuts again, and no one would know you were in there. From the outside it'd look as if the cupboard was still locked.

He shifted the action figures to one side of the shelf and picked his way through the books. Three of them were hollowed out hardbacks, like the one with Harry and Edward getting intimate. One held a notebook, with curly leaves and squiggles inlaid into the red leather cover. It was full of cramped black handwriting, interspersed with sketches of magic circles and other occult thingies. The next held a little woollen dolly, no bigger than the palm of his hand, with button eyes and a lock of brown hair fastened to its chest with a safety pin; a wizened chicken's foot wrapped in tartan ribbon – like a really cheap kilt pin; a hairbrush; and a test-tube of something dark and viscous.

Book number three was a lot more interesting. Logan tipped the contents out on the mattress. One pack of cherry-scented pipe tobacco. One old-fashioned long-necked pipe. One blister-pack sheet of little orange pills. And one clear plastic Ziploc bag with what looked like catnip in it. He opened the bag and took a sniff: the sweet, sweaty smell of marijuana.

What kind of person smoked weed in a pipe, like an auld mannie?

There was a lot of it too – enough to get a coach-load of students off their faces for a week. Enough to count as possession with intent to supply.

Logan sat back on his haunches. Why would someone run away and leave that much pot behind? Maybe Agnes got into difficulties with her supplier, or another dealer, and needed to get out of town in a hurry?

Assuming she actually managed to leave Aberdeen before they caught up with her. . .

Well, while he was here, might as well be thorough.

He unzipped the sleeping bag and turned it inside out: nothing. The mattress was old and saggy, soft enough that he could lift the corners up and over and poke at the floorboards underneath. More nothing. He let the corner fall back and a puff of fusty dust billowed out into the air.

Logan turned and struggled to haul the mattress up from the short end of the cupboard. Bloody thing was like manoeuvring a dead body. . .

There: a plastic folder lay on the floorboards. He grabbed it and the mattress thumped back into place. More dust.

Inside the folder was a stack of press clippings about *Witchfire* being filmed in Aberdeen – the actors burbling about what a great script it was; the author hedging his bets as to whether it would be any good or not; some toad from the local council banging on about job creation and tourism opportunities; a photo op with the actors doling out soup to homeless people; another with a troupe of little kids in school uniform on the movie set, all grinning and holding swords. But the biggest thing was a copy of the script, marked up with green and yellow highlighter pen:

Witchfire

A Golden Slater Production

Based on the book by William Hunter

Script V: 4.0.2

The name 'NICHOLE FYFE' was written in red ink on the top-right corner. . . Nichole Fyfe. . . Nichole Fyfe. . . Wasn't she the blonde woman? The one in that awful Disney romcom about undertakers last year? The one on the telly that morning with the red hair?

Logan pulled an evidence bag out of his pocket and stuck the weed and pills into it, sealed the sticky flap, and wrote down the details on the form printed onto the plastic.

'. . .I mean it isn't right, is it? Boy like that sniffing around our. . .' Mrs Garfield's mouth clicked shut as Logan walked into the room.

The kitchen was warm, the units painted a terracotta colour, French doors lying wide open, as if they were in the middle of the Mediterranean and not a housing estate in Northfield, overlooking the backside of Middlefield Primary School.

Chalmers nodded towards a mug on the counter. Her mouth turned down at the edges. 'Milk and two.'

Probably came with free spit.

Logan dumped the evidence bag next to it. 'I found this in your daughter's room under the stairs.'

Chalmers whistled. 'That's a *lot* of marijuana.'

Agnes's mum squared her shoulders, voice getting louder with every word: 'You planted that, didn't you? You planted it to deflect attention from the fact your lot are doing nothing to find my bloody daughter! You sick—'

A man's voice blared out across the kitchen. 'For God's sake, Doreen!' Agnes's dad shuffled in: black goatee, long greying hair swept back from his high forehead with a black Alice band, wearing a T-shirt and torn jeans. Like a middle-aged skateboard dude. He even had a tattoo snaking down his left arm. 'It's hers, OK? They didn't plant anything.'

Doreen Garfield's mouth hung open. 'You *knew* about this?'

'Why do you think I kept buying all that incense? It covered the smell. The weed kept her . . . level. Meant she didn't need the pills as much.'

Doreen grabbed Logan's mug and sent it hurling across the kitchen, tea spraying out behind it like a banner. 'HOW COULD YOU NOT TELL ME?' It hit the wall by Agnes's dad's head and exploded.

'You wouldn't listen! You're so busy controlling everything, you never stop to talk to her.' He slapped a hand against his chest. 'I did, OK? While you were busy making rules and trying to control everything and everyone, I sat down and listened to what *she* had to say.'

'How could you?'

He brought his chin up. Stared Logan in the eye. 'She was doing so much better: had a boyfriend, got good marks in her exams; she was going to Aberdeen University in September to do accountancy. . .'

Doreen dug her fingers into her hair. 'It's all that . . . *Chung* boy's fault. If he'd left her alone, we'd—'

'Oh, come off it, she dotes on him. You have no idea how depressed she was when you said she couldn't see him any more, have you? No sodding clue at all.'

'He was a bad influence on—'

'You're the bad bloody influence! She didn't slit her wrists for *fun*, did she?'

Silence.

'She tried to kill herself?' Logan closed his eyes. Gritted his teeth. Counted to five. 'Did you not think it would be important to actually *tell* us that when you reported her missing?'

'It was. . . We didn't want it spread all over the papers. What would she think if she saw it? That we betrayed her?' He looked away. 'She's been doing so much better.'

'When did it happen?'

'Just after Christmas. I found her in the back garden with a bottle of tequila and a packet of razor blades. . .' A little shudder twitched at his shoulders.

Doreen took another mug from the dishwasher and put it on the working surface. The porcelain rattled against the terracotta tiles, shaking in time with her hand. But her voice was perfectly level as she plucked a teabag from the box. 'That's why we read her diary every week. We have to be sure she's not . . . having those kinds of thoughts. We have to be ready to help.'

The kettle growled and rumbled back to the boil.

Logan pulled out his notebook. 'Does Agnes have a car?'

Her mother shook her head. 'We don't allow her to drive. Not on her medication – it wouldn't be safe.'

Agnes's dad bent and picked up the bits of broken mug from the floor. 'What if she's hurt herself?'

Logan slipped the evidence bag into his pocket. 'The fact

that Anthony Chung is missing too means they've probably run away together. Let's not get all worked up over nothing.' He turned towards the door. Then stopped. 'Now before we go, is there anything else you're not telling us?'

11

Chalmers pulled away from the kerb as Logan fastened his seatbelt. Her mouth was one thin line, tiny wrinkles standing out at the side of her eye. Face fixed dead front.

Logan turned his phone on. 'I take it there's a reason you're sulking?'

'I'm *not* sulking, *sir.*'

'Come on then, out with it.'

Her jaw twitched a couple of times, as if she was biting down on something bitter. 'With all due respect: you sent me off to make tea while you were searching the cupboard under the stairs. The little woman makes the tea while the big strong man does the actual police work.' She wrenched the steering wheel left, taking them out the end of the road. 'Let me guess: you didn't think my pretty little head was up to it. Making the bloody tea's all we're good for.'

'I see.' He scrolled through his list of contacts until the number for Control appeared. 'Feel better now?'

'It's *sexist.*'

'Seriously?' A smile broke across his face, then bloomed into a grin. 'I've lost count of the number of times I've had to go make tea with the grieving relatives while Steel's off rummaging through their stuff. That's what happens when you're a DS: you're the distraction.' He hit the button, listening to it click, then ring on the other end. 'And when *you* make DI, you can get your own back on whatever poor sod gets lumbered with you. . .'

A woman's voice boomed in his ear. *'Control room.'*

'Yeah, it's DI McRae, have you picked up—'

'Hold on. . .' A pause. Some rustling. Then a muffled conversation. *'Yeah, it's him again. Wants to know if we've got the big ugly bloke that works for Wee Hamish yet.'*

'Hasn't he got nothing better to do?'

'You'd think, wouldn't you?'

'I can hear you, you know!'

And she was back, full volume. *'Just checking now, sir.'*

Click. Then a creaky version of some waltz. He was on hold.

Chalmers took them out onto the main road, heading back past yet another building site. The whole place was a breeding ground for sandstone-clad little boxy homes with tiny gardens and garages too small to get an actual car in.

Logan reached into his jacket and pulled out the red leather notebook from the cupboard. Stuck it on the dashboard. 'Found that, hidden in one of the hollowed-out books.'

She gave a small, one-shouldered shrug. 'What is it?'

'Some sort of witchcrafty journal thing. Got magic circles and things. . . Hello?'

The voice of Control was back. *'Yes.'*

'Yes what?'

'Yes he was picked up an hour ago by Alpha Three Nine. Was in the Burning Buck, absolutely plastered. They're checking him every fifteen minutes to make sure he doesn't choke on his own vomit.'

Chance would be a fine thing.

'Give it a bit, then stick him in interview room three.

We'll be back in. . .' Five minutes to traverse Kintore, half an hour to mollify Anthony Chung's parents, call it another twenty minutes from there back into town. . . 'Make it an hour.'

Pause. *'Yeah, you better take that up with the desk sergeant.'* And she was gone.

Chalmers picked the book off the dashboard, weighing it in her hand as she drove. 'Agnes knows her mum and dad are checking up on her, so maybe she keeps a fake diary in the bedroom where they can find it, and a *real* one in the cupboard under the stairs.'

'Read it. And call the Procurator Fiscal: I want a GSM trace authorized on Agnes and Anthony's mobile phones. Then get on to every hospital in Scotland – tell them to look out for attempted suicides.'

'Can you imagine someone *watching* you all the time like that, never giving you any privacy? I'd have run away years ago.'

The last-known address for Anthony Chung – before he ran away to rescue his girlfriend from her demented overbearing mother – occupied a corner plot in a swanky development on the southern edge of Kintore. Big houses with big gardens and big cars parked outside. The Chung residence even had a set of wrought-iron gates, mounted on sandstone pillars, but there was nothing behind them – the driveway was empty.

Chalmers pulled up at the kerb. Left the motor running. 'Not looking good, is it?'

Logan climbed out into the sunshine.

The whumping blades of a helicopter thrummed from somewhere over Kirkhill Forest; a child's happy squealing came from nearby, punctuated by the high-pitched yip of a small dog; the distant bagpipe drone of a lawnmower.

Tuneless whistling from the man three houses down as he washed his Range Rover Sport.

Logan opened the gate and marched up the drive. A portico jutted out of the building, making a little rectangle of shade from the sun. He pressed the button on the intercom and classical music sounded deep within the house, followed by a dog barking. Something big, with lots of teeth.

A minute later, Ravel's Bolero faded away. Still nothing from the intercom. But the hell-hound sounded like a gun going off, over and over again.

Logan gave the bell another try.

Chalmers wandered up beside him. 'Maybe they're out?'

'Or maybe they're just— Sodding hell, what *now*?'

Steel's ringtone blared out of his pocket. He hauled out his mobile and pointed Chalmers at a sweep of lockblock leading around the side of the house. 'Try round the back.'

She looked up at the house, rubbing her thumb across the tips of her fingers. 'What if the dog—'

'If it could get outside, we'd be running for our lives with no arse in our trousers by now. Go.'

As soon as she was gone, he took the call. 'I'm doing it, OK? I've just been to the Garfields', and now I'm at the Chungs'.'

'What's happening with that sodding necklacing victim? How come you've no' got an ID yet?'

He stared up at the pale-blue sky. A plane roared into view, fresh out of Aberdeen Airport, banking around to head south, or east, going somewhere else. Lucky sods. 'How many things do you think I can actually do at the one time? I'm looking for—'

'What did I tell you about organizing things? You're no' supposed to be running about—'

'You told me to come out here! *You*, not me.'

A harrumph. *'Aye, well. . . Don't change the subject.'*

'We'll get an ID when we get an ID. Now bugger off and let me do my job.' He hung up. Chewed on the inside of his cheek for a moment. Maybe telling Steel to bugger off wasn't the best of ideas. He switched the thing off.

Chalmers appeared through the gate again. Stopped by the side of the house, and scraped the sole of her shoe across the kerbing that bordered the path. 'All locked up round there. The only thing moving in there is an Alsatian the size of a horse. So Mr and Mrs Chung are either hiding under the bed, the dog's eaten them, or they're out.' Then more scraping.

Logan took out a business card and printed a note on the back of it in small careful letters: 'SORRY WE MISSED YOU. CAN YOU GIVE ME A CALL SO I CAN ARRANGE A TIME TO COME OVER AND DISCUSS ANTHONY?' Then stuck it through the letter box.

Chalmers had finished with the kerbing, now she was dragging her shoe across the grass. . . 'Where to?'

Logan marched down the drive towards the gates. 'Nothing else we can do here. Time to call it a night.'

Logan slid the viewing hatch open and peered into the cell. Blinked. Then backed off a couple of paces, wafting his hand in front of his nose. The sharp-edged stench of stale alcohol curdled the air, making his eyes water. 'God, it's like a brewery in there. . .'

The Police Custody and Security Officer wrinkled her nose. 'He was doing tequila shots when they picked him up. I hear he'd downed a whole bottle of Bells on his own first.'

Logan stepped up to the hatch again.

The cell wasn't much bigger than a hotel bathroom. The red-brown terrazzo floor was littered with discarded clothing, bright sunlight streaming through the little square panes of glass that made up the window. They cast glowing cubes of light on Reuben's naked back, making the tuft of hair between his shoulder blades shine.

He was lying on his side, bum to the door, naked except for a pair of dark-blue pants and a single sock. Snoring. Like a pig from a horror film.

The PCSO shuddered. 'Took three of us to get him into the recovery position.'

'He give you any trouble?'

'Nope: all nice and calm. Told Michelle he loved her, then did the same to Mark. But me?' She sighed. 'Always the bridesmaid. . .'

Reuben twitched and a deep rattling grunt echoed out into the corridor.

She clacked the hatch closed again. 'Be still my beating heart.'

Logan looked back, along the corridor. 'Any chance you can stick him in an interview room?'

'Couldn't even wake him for the Duty Doc's examination. That lump of raw sex is dead to the world. Going to have a stinker of a hangover tomorrow morning.'

'Good.'

The nurse looked up from her copy of Immanuel Kant's *Critique of Pure Reason* and smiled. It made little dimples in her plump cheeks. 'Evening, stranger.'

Logan smiled back. 'Evening, Claire, how's Bill's piles?'

She stuck out a hand, palm down, fingers spread, then wiggled it from side to side. 'You know what he's like. Loves a curry, never thinks of the consequences. Men, eh?'

'That's why you ladies love us.' He pointed down the corridor to the private room at the end. Blinds drawn. 'She in?'

'Well, she popped out for a bit of shopping, but she's back now. Why don't you go in and I'll be along in a bit?'

*   *   *

Logan let himself into the room. Dark. He squinted in the gloom. 'What, you're a vampire now?'

He crossed to the other side and hauled the curtains open. Sunlight streamed in, glittering back from the stainless-steel fixtures. Leaning on the windowsill, he looked down at the little chunk of grass pinned to the ground by thin trees, their green leaves shining in the warm evening. A wee grey shape lumped into view, then hunkered down, eating.

'That rabbit's back again. And I think he's got a knife. . .'

'Don't be daft.' Sam sat up in the bed. She must've had her hair done since lunchtime, because it was a shocking shade of bright scarlet. The tattoos on her arms poked out from the short sleeves of her Skeleton Bob T-shirt. She threw the covers back, exposing a pair of red shorts and thigh-high black-and-white stripy stockings. 'You bring me a present?'

He stuck a bottle of Lucozade on the bedside cabinet, then followed it up with a copy of *Skin Deep* – 'Cyanide Girls Gone Wild' and a *Now* – 'Nichole Speaks: Acting Saved Me From A Life Of Crime'. Then collapsed into the visitor's chair, arms and legs hanging loose. 'God, what a *day*.'

'Did you get milk and Marmite?'

'In the car.' He slipped his shoes off and stuck his feet up on the bed. 'Steel's being an absolute . . . pain in the neck. You'd think I'd get some sympathy for getting punched in the nose, wouldn't you?'

Samantha poked his left foot. 'You've got a hole in your sock.'

'But no, all she does is moan and whinge.'

'Honestly, it's like going out with a hobo. Give it a decent burial and buy some new socks. Maybe even, shock horror, in a colour other than black?'

He smiled at her. 'Thought you goths loved black.'

'Not when it comes to underwear.' She bounced a couple of times. Then scooted forward, until she was kneeling on the edge of the bed, looming over him. 'I want a new tattoo. Something spiky and swirly, with a cat.'

'Of course, Steel's only moaning because the ACC's sand-papering her backside over this necklacing thing. Press are going mental after we caught the guy who killed him.'

'Speaking of cats, I think we should get one. Well, a kitten.'

Logan groaned. 'Can't we just—'

'A little fuzzy kitten. We'll call it Cthulhu!'

'Cthulhu? Isn't that a bit—'

'Shh!' Samantha froze. 'They're coming.' Then she jumped back into place and wriggled under the sheets. Winked at him. 'Not a word!'

The door opened and Claire stuck her head in. 'Fancy a cup of tea?' She wheeled the trolley in, stacks of cups clinking against each other. Then filled one from a metal teapot the size of her head. 'How's herself doing today then?'

Logan helped himself to a slosh of milk and a Jammy Dodger. 'Wants another tattoo. And *apparently* we need to get a cat.'

'That's a lovely idea. Be company for you while she's in here. Don't know about the tattoo though. . .' She looked down at him, her eyes softening around the edges. 'Go on, take another biscuit, I won't tell anyone.'

He did – custard cream – dunking it in his tea as she lumbered the trolley out of the room. Then the door clunked shut behind her.

'It's OK, she's gone.'

Samantha sat back up again. 'Don't get me wrong, Claire's OK, but if I have to sit through one more discourse on the philosophical nature of being, or her husband's piles, I'm going to scream.'

'Play nice with the nurses, they can put spiders in your mouth while you sleep, and *then* where will you be?' He ate his biscuit. Drank his lukewarm tea.

Samantha picked up the copy of *Now*, flipping through its glossy pages. 'I'm serious about that cat, by the way.'

'I think Rennie's going to quit.'

'Thought his wife was planning on turning into a baby factory. How's that going to work if he's got no job?'

'Steel drew a knob in his notebook. Keeps riding him about finding those shoplifting tramps.'

'Hmmm?'

'You know what she's like. Pick, nag, poke, sarcastic comment, arse-related threat. . .'

'Yeah. . .'

'It's a bit of cheese, bacon, and vodka. That doesn't need a detective sergeant, that needs a uniform PC who's done something stupid and needs taught a lesson.'

'Oh, for God's sake.'

'What?' Frown. He looked up – she had her face buried in the copy of *Now*. 'Are you even listening?'

She peered at him over the top of her magazine, then turned it around, showing off the centre spread: a big photo of Nichole Fyfe in jeans and an oversized white shirt, laughing, with His Majesty's Theatre in the background: 'COMING HOME TO ABERDEEN ~ MY SECRET SHAME AT TROUBLED TEENAGE YEARS'. Samantha gave the thing a shake. 'If you hire a publicist to tell the whole sodding world about it, it's not a bloody secret!'

'Oh, I'm sorry. I didn't realize I was *boring* you.'

'Anything to get their face in the gossip mags. "Oh look at me, I'm special and clever!" "Listen to some crap I made up to make myself sound interesting this week!" "Talk about me! I don't exist otherwise!"'

He wiggled his toe through the hole in his sock. 'Then why do you keep buying the things?'

'"Secret" my pale tattooed backside. She probably thinks we'll read this rubbish and go, "Gosh, she's such an inspirational figure! If *she* can go from a delinquent with a criminal record to a multimillionaire film star, maybe *I* can too!" When really she's just boasting about how much better she is than the rest of us. I tell you, it's—'

Logan reached out and snatched the magazine.

'Hey!'

'If you hate this stuff so much, you shouldn't be reading it. It's bad for your blood pressure.' He dumped *Now* on the floor beside his seat. 'Call it an intervention.'

Samantha thumped back into the pillows with her arms folded across her chest. 'Spoilsport.'

'That's me.' He dug into his pocket and pulled out a chunky boxed set of CDs. Then waggled it at her. 'I got you the new Stephen King on audio book, but if you're not interested. . .?'

The scowl on her face faded to a smile. 'You're a rotten sod, Logan McRae.'

'Thought so.' He nipped out to the nearest vending machine for a Crunchie, an Irn-Bru, and a packet of prawn cocktail, and when he got back they just sat there, talking about everything and nothing: tattoos, Steel, kittens, neck-laced bodies, holiday plans, being punched in the face. . . Until finally Logan checked his watch and groaned. 'Right, got to go. Early start in the morning.'

Samantha looked up at him, a little dent between her eyebrows. 'See you tomorrow?'

He put his empty tin on the bedside cabinet, next to three unopened bottles of Lucozade and the stack of unread maga-zines. Then stood. Took hold of her cold hand and kissed her on the cheek. 'Wouldn't miss it for the world.'

Monday

12

'. . .unnngh. . .' Logan rolled over and lay on his back, one arm covering his eyes. 'Go away. . .'

The doorbell's ding-dong chime ripped through the caravan.

He sat upright, stared at the clock. Six o'clock – fifteen minutes before the alarm was due to go off. Sodding hell, why did everyone. . .

Wait a minute: last time someone rang his doorbell in the morning he got punched in the face. Maybe this was one of Reuben's 'associates' come round to make sure Logan was in no fit state to press charges? Because he was propping up a concrete patio somewhere in Elgin.

He rolled out from beneath the duvet and onto the gritty carpet, hand searching the space under the bed. Discarded socks. Shoebox. Plastic bucket. His fingers curled around the wooden pickaxe handle.

That'd put a dent in someone's morning.

Unless they had a shotgun. . .

He hauled on a pair of trousers, not bothering with pants or a shirt, and padded his way to the caravan's front door.

Stopped to one side, flattening himself against the stripy wall-paper, ear pressed to the wall. Listening.

Nothing.

Tightened his grip on the pickaxe handle.

OK.

Wasn't hard to imagine someone standing out there, watching the spyhole, waiting for it to dim as Logan stepped in front of it, then BOOM – a shotgun blast, tearing through the wood and then his chest. One more to the head, and that was it. Drive off into the early morning traffic.

Light spilled in around the letterbox. So it was darker in here than it was outside. That meant no shadow on the spyhole.

Logan crept over and peered out.

No one on the top step. And no one standing outside the caravan either. Just the turning circle streaked with shadows as the sun climbed its way up a duck-egg-blue sky. Early morning midges out for a pre-bloodsucking ceilidh, glittering like flecks of gold. A lone magpie pop-hopping across the roof of his geriatric Fiat Punto.

Deep breath.

He turned the key in the lock and wrenched the door open, jumping out, waving the pickaxe handle, teeth bared. . .

No one.

The magpie stopped on the Punto's bonnet, head cocked to one side, staring at him. Then it took off for the nearest tree, cackling. Ha bloody ha.

A small cardboard box sat on the doorstep, mummified in brown packing tape.

He nudged it with the pickaxe handle, but it didn't explode or start ticking, so he picked it up and went back inside. The magpie stayed where it was, laughing at him.

Logan slammed the door on it, dumped the box on the

kitchen working surface and stuck the kettle on. Six in the morning. What kind of scumbag rang people's doorbells and ran away at six in the morning?

No address on the package, no sender's details. He grabbed a knife from the draining board and slit the brown tape. Inside, the little box was full of shredded newspapers – the *Press & Journal* from the look of it – and nestled, right in the middle, another knot of chicken bones. This one was tied to what looked like a bouquet garni, the herbs wilted, greying, and dead.

He tipped the whole lot out and picked through it, but there was no sign of a note. Just a junior starter kit for making soup. He weighed the bones in his hand. Bloody kids. In what way was this funny?

Through in the bedroom the alarm clock went off, blaring some cheesy eighties pop song.

Cup of tea, shower, then off for another jolly day at work. God, how *lucky* was he? The only thing that could make it any better was—

His mobile added its voice to Bananarama's. 'If I Only Had a Brain': Rennie.

Logan grabbed his phone from the bedside cabinet and hit the button. 'What?'

'*Morning, Guv. We picked up your good Samaritan's missing mate last night, the one who did a runner from the hospital? Denies everything about the jewellery heist, but his story's bang on with everyone else about the necklacing victim.*'

The bathroom was in a bit of a state: towels on the floor, the hollow bones of dead toilet rolls building up behind the toilet, a sour smell coming from the shower curtain, soap and toothpaste acne speckling the tiles and mirror above the sink. The patch of mould that looked a bit like a face. Should really give the place a bit of a clean. . .

'Bugger.'

'*Sorry, Guv, but I thought we kinda knew all this anyway?*'

'Wasn't talking to you. . .' Logan leaned over the sink and peered at the battered lump in the mirror. Both eyes were sunk into dark-purple bags. Wonderful.

'*Anyway, thought you'd want to know: Ding-Dong's down to interview Reuben this morning, soon as his solicitor's been round. And you'll never guess who's representing him.*'

Logan poked a finger into the swollen bruised skin. Didn't hurt, just looked bloody awful. 'Not in the mood.'

'*Hissing Sid.*'

Great. He let his forehead clunk against the dirty mirror. 'When?'

'*Dunno. PCSO says Reuben woke up about five and spewed his ring all over the floor; got a hangover like a car crash right now, so I doubt Mr Moir-Farquharson will be strutting his slimy stuff before ten-ish.*'

Welcome to Monday morning.

High above, the sun burns like a furnace, baking all the people below as they trudge their way through their desperate little lives. Unaware that *things* walk amongst them.

A couple laugh on the pedestrian area beneath her viewpoint, wrapped up in each other like ivy around a tree. They ignore everyone marching past – the shining lights, the grey, and the darkness.

There: a woman with a small child in a pushchair. No one knows that she's an angel, because they can't *see* her. They think she's just another fattie in a tracksuit, smoking a fag, wheeling her screaming kid about on the way to the dole office.

And there: the man with the dark-blue suit and the sunglasses, stuffing a green Markies bag into his leather satchel. Pale-blue aura swirling around him as he tries to decide who he's going to eat today.

No one sees it but her.

She walks in the door to the ladies' lingerie department. Plastic people in bras and pants, frozen poses for the masses. Some will come alive at night and hunt for mice and rats, cooking them on the hot radiator pipes before swallowing them whole.

An old woman pushes past, trailing thin lines of black mist that hiss and crackle.

Rowan looks away before she can turn around. Not safe. Not safe at all.

Down the escalator, into the bowels of the shop, where beasts graze the food department, hunched over their trolleys. Like torturers over their victims.

Don't make eye contact. They can smell the fear, but unless they see your eyes they don't know whose it is.

She reaches for a sandwich . . . then pauses. Counts three to the left. Then one down, because it's Monday. Bacon, Lettuce and Tomato. BLT. Blood, Ligature and Tallow. Good enough.

One of the beasts stops behind her, breath heavy on the back of her neck as it reaches past with a thick hairy paw to stroke the sandwiches she's already touched. Feeling for her. Hungry.

She clutches the BLT to her breast and ducks, slipping to the side and away. Glances back at the end of the chiller cabinet to watch it sniffing the sacrificial offerings.

Right, past the little forests in the little pots. Then more plastic statues, these ones wearing dresses and cardigans.

Exit. Exit. EXIT.

A hand on her shoulder makes her squeal.

She spins around, and a puzzled face stares back at her: skin like midnight, hair like dark curly wool.

'Sorry, miss, but I think you forgot to pay for that.'

Rowan looks down at the sandwich. The paper container is crushed against her chest, the shards of dead pig sticking out between the bread, like blades. Then back up at that kind face with the beautiful eyes and the halo of gold. 'Someone's following me.'

The angel in the security guard's uniform looks over his shoulder. 'What does he look like?'

'A man, with jeans and a leather jacket and his hair all over the place. . .' She points back towards the food section. It's a lie, but the truth would only hurt him, the beasts are too powerful. Rowan digs in her pocket and comes out with a crisp five-pound note, presses it into the angel's hand. 'Please, don't let him know I was here.'

The angel nods, then turns towards the tills. 'I'll get your change.'

And as soon as he's two steps away she's out the door, running.

Logan pushed through the double doors into the cutting room. The little speakers mounted to the tiny stereo unit were droning out Jim Morrison's tone-deaf call for an infant to set fire to him. Not exactly appropriate.

Dr Graham was perched on a stool, hunkered over the cutting table at the far end of the room, fiddling with what looked like a box filled with blue rubbery lumps. A skull sat on a white plastic tray beside her, next to a pile of books opened to display thick blocks of graphs, figures, and tables.

Logan turned the music down. 'All on your own?'

Dr Graham looked up at him. 'Miss Dalrymple let me in. Hope that's OK? Wanted to get cracking.'

She took a Stanley knife down one corner of the box and peeled off the cardboard like the skin of an orange, exposing the blue rubbery flesh below. 'Moment of truth. . .' Dr Graham dug her fingers into the blue stuff and pulled – ripping it away to reveal a yellowy-white skull. Then held it up and scrubbed at it with the palm of her hand. 'Perfect.'

126

'This our victim?'

She placed the cleaned skull on a little plinth, slotting it onto a rod set into the base. 'Resin cast. Dr McAllister wouldn't let me use the real one for the facial reconstruction. It's a bit of extra work, but on the *plus* side it no longer counts as human remains, so we can forget all that rubbish about having to be supervised by a "registered medical practitioner with five years' experience". . . As if I'm going to take a can opener to someone's skull, or use it as a football.'

Logan leaned against the cold stainless-steel surface. 'So what's the diagnosis?'

'Well, he's definitely dead.' She grinned. Then cleared her throat. 'Sorry. I've mapped out the tissue depth and cut the markers, so all I need to do is apply them and I can get on with the real work. . .' A little crease appeared between her eyebrows. 'You didn't put ice on that, did you.'

'Didn't have any. And fish fingers didn't work.'

'No, probably not.' She pulled over a small metal tray, laid out with discs of pale rubber, as if she'd cut them off the end of pencils – each one marked with a number in black ink. 'You know, with bones we can tell almost everything about a person: what they ate, where they lived, where they lived before that, height, weight, sex, ethnicity. . .' A dab of glue went on the end of a disc, then she fixed it right in the middle of the skull's forehead.

'What happened to Dr Dempsey?'

'Sulking. Threatening legal action.'

'You hit him first?'

A shrug. Marker number one was joined by two and three. 'He pushed me.'

Logan nodded up at the shiny black globe hanging from the ceiling over the central cutting table, like a store security camera. 'Tell him it's all on film.'

'Your victim was male, Caucasian.' Four, five and six

followed the ridge of the eyebrows. 'To be honest, he's been spoiling for a fight for years, ever since I got sent to Iraq instead of him. Said he should be the one digging bodies out of mass graves, not me. . .' She sat back and tilted her head to one side. 'Blue, brown or green?'

Shrug. 'Blue?'

'Brown's more neutral.' Dr Graham dipped into her massive handbag and pulled out a wooden box, a little bigger than a pencil case. When she opened it, three pairs of glass eyes stared back at Logan. She plucked the brown eyes from the box, then fiddled around with rubber batons and glue until they were staring out from the skull instead. 'There we go, much better.'

Seriously? It looked like something out of a cheap horror film.

'Can't you just do all this on computers?'

'What, like they do on the telly?' Markers seven to ten were longer, sticking out of the upper and lower jaws. 'Facial reconstruction's half science, half art. You have to really *know* bones. How's a computer ever going to do that?'

'Go on then.' Logan went into his jacket pocket, pulled out the junior soup starter kit that had been left on his doorstep, and dumped it on the cutting table. The bones rattled against the stainless steel. 'What can you get from a bunch of chicken bones and some manky herbs?'

She peered at them, then added the next couple of markers to the skull. 'They're not chicken bones, they're phalanges. Finger bones. Human.' A smile. 'Do I pass the test?'

'Finger bones?'

A sigh. 'OK, we'll do it properly. . .' She pulled an A4 lined notepad from beneath one of the books, flipped over to a clean sheet, then stuck her left hand flat down on it and drew around the palm and fingers with a pencil. Then untied the bundle. 'This one –' she held up one of the little

128

bones – 'is a proximal phalanx from the middle finger.' She placed it on her wobbly outline of a hand in the right place. 'This one's an intermediate. . . *Might* be from the index – going by the growth on the distal articular surface – but it's impossible to tell for sure without having all the other bones for comparison.' It went on the drawn hand. 'And lucky number three is a proximal from the thumb.'

'They're *human*?'

'Yup.' She lowered the last bone into place. Then picked it up again. 'I don't know who cleaned them for you, but they seriously need to go on a training course. Boiling bones damages the joints, look,' she wiggled the end at Logan, 'see how it's all pitted and porous?'

It looked like a pale Crunchie bar with all the chocolate sucked off. She shook her head. 'Very amateurish.'

Oh God. *'Boiled?'*

'Yup – there's much more efficient and less damaging ways to clean skeletal remains: boiling breaks down the cortical bone, that's why you can see that cancellous bone underneath. If you haven't got Dermestid beetles to clean the remains, then simmering's the way to go – long and slow, like you're making stock.' She put it down again. 'I don't know who you're using, but they should be ashamed of themselves.' Another marker went on the skull.

'Boiled. . .' Something cold slithered its way down Logan's spine.

She picked up the last marker in the set, then frowned at him. 'Are you all right? You've gone all pale.'

'When? When were they boiled?'

Dr Graham backed off a pace. 'Look, I identified them, didn't I? Can't you just tell your bosses I'm not faking it here? I really *do* know what I'm talking. . .' Her eyes narrowed. 'Did Dempsey put you up to this? Is he the halfwit who ruined them?'

129

'Was someone eating them?'

'Because if he did, you shouldn't touch him with a barge-pole. He's a bitter, twisted old sod and I'm doing a good job here!'

The cutting table was cool beneath his fist. 'Was someone eating the meat off those bloody fingers or not?'

She pulled her chin in. Then picked up the bone again, held it up to her nose and sniffed. 'You smell that? Bleach: that's why it's so chalky and crumbly. Who'd eat something they'd boiled in bleach?'

Oh thank God. . .

Dr Graham picked all the bones up and held them in the palm of her hand. 'It wasn't a test?' They made a dry sand-paper sound as she rolled them back and forward. 'Seriously?'

'Someone's been leaving them outside my house.'

'Phalanges?' She put them back on the paper hand. 'My life coach told me Aberdeen was weird. . .' She cleared her throat, then dug a ruler from her stack of books and measured each of the bones in turn. 'You can estimate height and sex from phalanges, but it's unreliable. And I mean *seriously* unreliable. I wouldn't even put it in writing.'

Logan licked his lips. 'Thought they were chicken bones.'

'You have to promise not to quote me on this, but best guess: these belong to a woman, about five-two, five-four, something like that. There's a touch of arthritis, so she *might* be in her fifties, possibly sixties? They've been boiled, so you can whistle for DNA, but you could try stable isotope signature analysis?'

'Human fingers.'

'There's a professor I know in Dundee who does pro bono work for police cases. I can give him a call if you like?'

'I've been chucking them into the bushes. . .'

Rowan shifts sideways on the wooden bench, making enough room for the woman with the shopping bags to puff down beside her. Pregnant. Taking the weight off her swollen ankles. A tight coil of green and blue spirals out from her tummy, making a question mark in the air that shimmers with anticipation.

St Nicholas Kirk graveyard basks in the warm morning, the ancient granite headstones turning their crumbling lichened faces to the sun. The church building gnaws at the sky with jagged dark-grey teeth, dirty stained-window eyes glowering out at the dead and the living alike.

A comforting place.

The Kirk is my mother and father. It is my rod and my staff. My shield and my sword. What I do in its service lights a fire in God's name.

Rowan forces down another mouthful of Blood, Ligature, and Tallow, sitting on the bench with her ankles crossed beneath her, curling around her sandwich, shoulders hunched. Newly dyed hair hangs over her face, hiding her eyes.

No one recognizes her as a redhead.

The broodmother unbuttons the top of her shirt and flaps the collar, trying to force cool air in over her swollen udders. 'Ungh. . . This heat!' Then she pulls a rumpled newspaper from one of her carrier bags and uses it as a makeshift fan. 'Ahh, that's better.'

She has no idea what's growing inside her. . .

Another mouthful – forcing it down. Should have bought some water.

'You know, Steve says I always moan when it's too cold, but dear *God* I can't wait for it to rain.'

Rowan just nods.

The broodmother dumps the newspaper on the bench between them, then pulls out a plastic bottle of apple juice. Cracks the seal and drinks deep. It smells like sunshine. 'Pfffffff. . . Can't believe it's this hot. We went on honeymoon to Kenya and it wasn't this hot.'

Between them, the headline shouts in big black letters: '"I COULDN'T LET HIM SUFFER" ~ BRAVE GUY TELLS OF NECKLACING VICTIM'S HORROR' and a photograph of an ugly young man in a hospital bed.

The woman sighs. 'Horrible, isn't it? How could anyone do something so . . . *horrible*?'

A shrug, then Rowan rubs at the scars on her left wrist. Like thin shiny worms wriggling beneath her fingertips. 'Maybe he deserved it?'

'No one could ever deserve *that*.' The blue and green swirl trembled. 'Oooh . . . junior's on the move again. Tell you: I feel like that bloke out of *Alien*. Only he was lucky – he didn't have a little monster's foot in his bladder.'

If only she knew.

Broodmother looks out at the sea of deathstones. 'I was here when they had that service for Alison and Jenny McGregor, did you see it? Got Robbie Williams's autograph. . .'

A man walks in through the ornate pillared frontage that screens the graveyard off from Union Street. He's *here*. The man has a mobile phone pressed to his ear, a bag from Primark in his other hand. And an aura like a house fire – black and orange and red tongues of smoke trailing in his wake, caressing the tombs.

'Of course, that was before Steve. And *now* look at me.'

The wide path from the main street to the church is made up of paving slabs and ancient headstones, worn almost smooth by generations of feet. The living trampling on the dead. She can almost hear them groaning as he marches past the bench.

'I tell you, they say giving birth's the greatest thing you can ever do, but it's the bit before that's a pain in the— Oh, are you off?'

Rowan marches after him, staying far enough back to not be touched by his filthy stench: the cracking lines like burning

132

blood. The beasts are too powerful and so was the woman with the aura of black, but a *witch*. . . Now that's something different.

The Kirk is my mother and father. It is my rod and my staff. My shield and my sword. What I do in its service lights a fire in God's name.

13

'It's not my fault, OK?' Logan grabbed his jacket off the hook by the filing cabinet in his office. 'Not like I ordered them off the bloody internet.'

Steel blocked the doorway. 'How could you no' know they were human?'

'Yes, because you're such an expert on anthropology. Who leaves *actual* finger bones on someone's doorstep?' He picked up the phone on his desk, punched in the number for the CID main office. 'Who's this: Guthrie?'

Little sod sounded half asleep. *'Yes, Guv?'*

'I need you to go through the missing persons reports. Looking for someone between forty-five and sixty-five, right-handed, with arthritis. Five-one to five-six.'

'Aye, right.' Steel had a dig at the underside of her left boob, one side of her face all creased up. 'Like that's no' going to throw up a million hits.' Dig, dig, dig. 'Think my boobs are getting bigger?'

'Male or female?'

'Probably female, but check both just in case.' Logan put the phone down on the grumbled complaints.

'I think they're getting bigger. . .' She squidged them

together, making a crevasse of wrinkly cleavage. 'Look.'

'No.'

'What about your mate the scumbag journalist? He got his fingers lopped off, maybe he's sending you the bits as a wee gift?'

'I need a search warrant for Reuben's house. And he's got a workshop, or a lockup or something, out in the countryside – we need to search that too. He's killed someone, maybe a rival dealer, that's where he's getting the bones from.'

'You're no' right in the head. When did you last hear of a little old lady drug dealer?'

Logan hauled open the bottom drawer of the filing cabinet and pulled out a bundle of empty evidence bags, held together with an elastic band. 'There was that one in Torry last year with the cannabis farm in her garage. And the granny selling coke in Northfield. And the bunch of pensioners running that meth lab in Huntly.'

Steel scowled at him. 'They were retired chemistry teachers, it doesn't count.'

The drawer clanged shut again. 'Reuben's the only—'

'God's sake, you're obsessed. Why would Reuben boil the bones clean? Why no' just send you the fingers?'

'Well, who else would it be?'

A face appeared over Steel's shoulder. DS Chalmers, glasses perched on the end of her nose. 'Guv? Sorry to interrupt, but we've got activity on Anthony Chung's bank account. Debit card was used to withdraw two hundred and sixty pounds this morning from the Clydesdale Bank cash machines outside Marks and Spencer on Union Street.'

Steel turned around. 'Believe it or no', Sergeant, we do actually know where Markies is.' She squidged her boobs together again. 'Do these look bigger to you?'

A blush rushed up Chalmers's cheeks. She stared at Logan. 'Guv?'

135

'Pull the security camera footage from the machine. Then go through the CCTV tapes – find out where he came from and where he went.'

She scribbled it all down in her notebook. 'They're still in Aberdeen: only a matter of time before we find them.'

Steel let go, and her breasts sagged and separated again. 'Unless someone's chibbed him and nicked his cards.' She pointed at Logan. 'You, Bone Boy, when did you find the last lot?'

'This morning, in a box on the top step.'

'Then it's no' Reuben, is it? He's been banged up in here since six last night.'

'So he got someone else to deliver it for him. It's a threat. He wants. . .' A frown. What? What on earth would Reuben get out of it? 'OK, I haven't got a clue what he wants, but you don't send someone finger bones for fun.'

'See if you're right, and this is some OAP drug dealer from Manchester, or Birmingham, or Christ knows where, I'm going to sodding kill you. How are we supposed to solve that?'

Logan pocketed his phone and his keys. 'Chalmers – when you're done with the CCTV, go dig up a list of Agnes Garfield and Anthony Chung's friends so we can start interviewing them.'

'Yes, Guv.'

'And get me someone in uniform with their head screwed on the right way round: search trained. I'm going out.'

Even with her police-issue boots on, PC Sim barely made it past Logan's shoulder. Her dark-brown hair was swept back and imprisoned in a tight bun, just under the rim of her bowler. That and the glasses made it look as if she was trying to get her head to go faster. She wrinkled her nose. 'You live *here*?'

Logan hefted a roll of blue-and-white 'POLICE' tape out of the pool car's boot. 'What's wrong with here?'

She turned around on the spot, then pointed at the sewage treatment plant on the opposite side of the river. Then the dirty big supermarket. Then the graveyard. Then up past that to the dual carriageway where the eighteen-wheelers thundered. 'Where do you want me to start?'

'Hmph.' Logan dumped the tape in her arms. 'String this up between the trees. I want a twelve-foot cordon around the caravan.'

'Just saying.' She unravelled the end of the tape and tied it around the trunk of a big beech.

'And you should have seen it when the chicken factory was right behind us.'

A pair of magpies swooped down, landing on the pool car, hopping on the bonnet, heads cocked to one side, watching as Sim picked her way through the trees that ran behind the caravan, twisting the tape around trunks and branches. Then out around a bush, then another tree, then the caravan next door, until she had a wobbly-sided rhomboid. 'Should we not have a whole team or something?'

'Don't want this splashed all over the *Aberdeen Examiner* tomorrow morning. Low-key.'

'Smart thinking.' She smiled at him. 'And the cordon of blue-and-white, with the word "Police" written all over it, isn't going to be a giveaway at *all*.'

The magpie cackled from the bonnet of the pool car.

'Just. . . Shut up and put your suit on.'

'Yes, Guv.'

Logan stood, hands in the small of his back, trying to stretch the knots out. The white Tyvek SOC suit let a little puff of broiling-hot air out of the elasticated hood, sweat trickling down his sides. Should've stripped off before putting the damn thing on.

PC Sim was on her knees in the bushes behind the caravan,

137

picking her way slowly through the twigs and leaves. Singing a medley of show tunes to herself, the words all muffled by her facemask. Then she sat back, mid-song, and stared at something in her hand.

Logan slouched his way over, blue plastic bootees scuffing on the tarmac. 'Find one?'

'This them?' She held up a small knot of bones, but didn't hand it over. It was held together with a blue ribbon: that would be the one he'd chucked away on Saturday evening.

'That's them.'

Sim pulled an evidence bag from the box beside her, dropped the bones inside, then sealed it up and scribbled the details down on the form printed into the plastic. 'So there's this one, the broken bits from the ivy, and the ones from the kitchen bin. That it?'

Logan shrugged. 'Should be another couple around here. . . There were more, but I chucked them out. The scaffies did the rubbish collection last week.'

'That's a shame, I'd have *loved* to go rummaging through a communal wheely-bin full of other people's mouldy poop.'

'Poop?'

'Poop.'

Sim rocked from side to side, as if she was on some sort of dodgy exercise video. Sweat your way thin in a Tyvek SOC suit. 'I give up.'

Logan sank down onto the top step, back resting against the caravan door. Cool sweat made a clammy hand of his shirt, gripping his spine. 'There were at *least* three more sets.'

'And you chucked them all in the bushes?'

'I think so. Maybe. . .'

The magpies were back, perching on the roof of the caravan opposite. Heads bobbing and weaving as they stared down at him. Waiting for him to do something exciting. Well, they were in for a long wait. Cheeky wee buggers.

Sim peeled off her safety goggles; the glasses underneath were all steamed up. She pulled the facemask out and let it dangle on its elastic around her neck. Her whole face glistened. 'I've been through them a dozen times. If they were there, they've gone now.' Then the hood came off. Her bun had disintegrated into a frizzy clump. 'Jeepers, it's *hot* in here.'

Jeepers?

'You're a weirdo, you know that, don't you, Sim?'

'Maybe. . .' She frowned, then unzipped the front of her suit and cleaned her glasses on the black police-issue T-shirt underneath. Popped them back on. 'Anyone round here got a dog?'

'The Dawsons in three have got a border terrier, and the McNeils in seven have a yorkie. Not exactly the place for Alsatians and St Bernards.'

'Well, dogs might have eaten. . .'

A raucous cackle sounded from the caravan roof. Then one of the magpies hopped off the edge and swooped up onto the tree behind her. More laughter.

Sim stared up into the tree. 'Is that a nest?'

Logan peeled off his own hood. 'Little sods sit up there and giggle at each other from about five in the morning. Like Waldorf and Statler.'

She walked over to it, jumped a couple of times for the lower branch, then stomped her foot. The perils of being short. 'Oh . . . poop.' She waved at him. 'Give us a leg-up.'

'Seriously, you think the magpies nicked them?'

'Well, if the ribbons are shiny, why not?' She peeled off the blue plastic bootees. Looked at him.

Why not. He linked his hands together and gave her a boost.

She clambered up him like a drunken chimpanzee, until she was standing on the lowest branch. Then up onto the next one. And the one above that.

Logan stepped back. 'When you fall and break your neck I'm going to tell everyone I told you not to do this.'

'If you like, we can go back to the station, have a threat-assessment meeting, come up with a health-and-safety plan, hire some scaffolding, get someone qualified to erect it, someone else to inspect it, and then—'

'Just don't fall off.'

She reached up and grabbed the branch with the nest on it.

The magpie bounced up and down, hurling abuse as Sim pulled herself up and peered into the nest.

'Anything?'

'Some bottle tops, a set of car keys, bit of tinsel, and an earring.'

'Bones?'

'Sorry, Guv.' She turned and looked down at him. 'Looks as if. . .' Her eyes went wide. 'Jeepers!'

There she went again: *jeepers*, like something out of *Scooby-Doo*. 'What?'

Sim wrapped one arm around the branch, and pointed with the other one at the roof of Logan's caravan. 'You better see this.'

He frowned up at her. 'If you're—'

'Seriously, Guv: you need to see this.'

Fine. Whatever.

Logan fetched the wheely-bin from the side of the caravan and dragged it over to the front door, climbed onto the top step, then clambered up onto the bin until he was kneeling there. The black plastic wobbled beneath him. Fall off a wheely-bin and kill himself, how great would that be? Bloody stupid idea. . .

He grabbed the lip that ran around the caravan roof and pulled himself up to his feet. Then stared down at what was spread out across the gritty roofing felt, mouth hanging open.

Jeepers was right.

14

'What the hell is wrong with you?' DCI Steel threw her hands into the air. '*How* could you no' know?'

The whole caravan park was cordoned off. Old Mrs Foster and her cockatoo stared out of the kitchen window of number four, mouth a wobbly scarlet slash as a line of SEB techs in white oversuits shuffled slowly past searching the ground for any more bits.

'Well. . .' Logan waved a hand at his home. Two techs were wriggling their way underneath it with tweezers and evidence bags. 'It's a residential caravan, it's got a flat roof, you can't see it from the ground.'

'You're supposed to be a detective, for God's sake!'

'It wasn't—'

'How could you live under that and no' know?'

Someone tugged on Logan's sleeve. 'Guv?' PC Sim looked up at him. 'They say they need to know when your roof was fixed last.'

He stared at her. 'If you're suggesting it's the last guy who fixed it, I think I might have noticed him dying up there and rotting away!'

Steel snorted. 'Going on recent evidence, I sodding doubt it.'

'No, Guv, they need to get up there to examine the remains and . . . you know . . . don't want to go through the ceiling.'

'There's nothing wrong with my roof.'

'Aye, except for the poor dead sod on it.'

He closed his eyes. Counted to ten. Only made it as far as six. 'Don't you have something more productive to do?'

Steel shook her head. 'Surprisingly enough, the skeleton lying on top of your sodding caravan roof is pretty high on my to-do list. Why can it never be straightforward with you? Why's it always—'

'I didn't bloody put it there, OK?' He jabbed a finger at the roof. '*That* wasn't me.'

'Guv?' PC Sim again. 'Council's turned up.'

A scuffed flatbed truck was beeping its way backwards off of Mugiemoss Road into the caravan park. One side of the thing was all dented, rusting scratches clawed their way through the city council logo. A small yellow cherry-picker was tied to the back.

Cheaper and quicker than sodding about with scaffolding.

Five minutes later, the cherry-picker was trundling along the tarmac, driven by a pug-faced man in a set of council overalls and a high-vis vest. A massive black moustache covered his upper lip, drooping down on either side in a permanent hairy scowl.

Steel held up her hand. 'All right, Sunshine, that's far enough. We'll take it from here.'

He stopped the cherry-picker, but didn't get out. His voice was a hard-core Teuchter drawl. 'You certified to drive one of these, quine? 'Cos if you're not, you're not driving it. Health and safety.'

'Who're you calling "quine"?' She stuck her chest out. 'I'm a detective chief bloody inspector, and—'

'I dinna care if you're the Queen's proctologist, no one's

driving this thing without a cert from the council.' A nod. 'Health and Safety'd have my arse in a buttie.'

She scowled at him, pulled the fake cigarette from her pocket, clicked it on, stuck it in her mouth, and sooked on it a couple of times. A puff of steam dissipated in the warm summer air. 'Right, someone get Burt Reynolds here an SOC suit. He's our new chauffeur.'

'Aye, aye. . .' Burt Reynolds and his amazing moustache leaned out over the edge of the cherry-picker's railing, gazing down at the roof of Logan's caravan. 'There's a sight you don't see every day.'

The cherry-picker's basket was at least eighteen feet off the ground, high enough to give a good view of the whole roof. It rocked slightly as Steel and Logan moved over to get a better look.

Steel grabbed the handrail. 'This thing safe?'

'Once found a skull when we were digging up a road outside Rhynie. Fat Doug wanted to take it home for an ashtray. He was aye a bit strange.'

The yellow-grey bones were laid out on the flat roof like some sort of art installation: a toothless skull resting above crossed femurs, the bottom jaw on the other side, then the pelvis and sternum, all held within a rough circle made up of ribs and vertebrae. Little piles of soil dotted the roof around it.

Logan pointed. 'Can't have been there for long. There's no moss or anything growing on them.'

'Ah.' Burt Reynolds from the council nodded. 'Maybe it's Keith Richards?'

Steel shrugged. 'If it is, he's lost weight.' Then she hit Logan on the arm. 'Told you it wasn't Reuben.'

'How can you possibly—'

'This is way too frou-frou.' A sniff. 'Besides, the lardy sod would've gone through the roof like Ann Widdecombe in a brothel.'

The downstream monitoring suite had been given a fresh coat of magnolia since last time, so now it was miserable, pokey, and stank of paint fumes. Logan wedged the door open with one of the plastic chairs. 'Better?'

'What do you think.' Steel banged the flat of her hand down on top of the small TV screen mounted above the length of grey working surface. 'Go on, you wee bugger. . .'

The picture fizzed and crackled. Then interview room three appeared on screen, slightly distorted by the angle of the camera.

Reuben was sitting on the other side of the table, facing the camera, massive shoulders slumped, his hair all flat on one side and sticking up on the other. Could almost smell the second-hand booze oozing out of every pore, even from here.

If it bothered the man sitting next to him, it didn't show. Sandy Moir-Farquharson's suit probably cost more than Logan made in a month. Maybe two. The white shirt immaculate and crisp, the tie perfectly centred. He had a little less hair, and it was almost entirely grey now, but he still had exactly the same patronizing air. '*And tell me, Inspector, when was my client supposed to have conducted this alleged assault?*'

Logan poked the screen. '"Alleged" my arse.'

The man sitting with his back to the camera checked his notes. '*Half six, yesterday morning.*' DI Bell was nearly as wide as Reuben, but half a head shorter. He'd taken his jacket off, rolling up his sleeves to reveal a hairy pair of arms that wouldn't have looked out of place on a gorilla.

'Come on, Ding-Dong, ask him about the bones.'

Steel sighed. 'You're bloody obsessed.'

'*Then your complainant is clearly mistaken in his identification.*'

The lawyer pulled a sheet of paper from his briefcase. *'I have here a sworn statement from a Miss Chloe Slessor stating that my client was with her all night in a . . . romantic capacity.'*

'The lying cow!'

Steel whistled. 'Romantic? Reuben? Jesus, can you imagine that humping away at you? Be like a warthog shagging a Fabergé egg.'

'Does your complainant have any witnesses to corroborate his fictitious version of events?'

'Ooh: think you're the one who's shagged now, Laz.'

'As a police officer, DI McRae—'

'I'm sorry, Inspector, are police officers above the law now?' Hissing Sid's smile was sharp and reptilian. *'Don't they have to comply with the same burden of proof as everyone else?'*

'He punched me on the bloody nose!' Logan grabbed the little microphone wired into the wall and pressed the red button. 'He punched me on the bloody nose!'

On screen, DI Bell flinched. Then dug a finger into his ear, wiggling the little wireless earpiece. *'Ow. . .'*

Logan pressed the button again. 'Sorry. Ask him about the bones.'

'Reuben,' DI Bell leaned forward, *'who do the bones belong to?'*

A sniff, then a frown. *'Eh?'*

'The ones you've been sending to DI McRae.'

He looked at his lawyer, then back at the inspector. *'Are you off your hairy wee head?'*

'Who was she? Who did you kill?'

Silence. Reuben sat back and folded his huge arms.

Steel snorted. Then grabbed the microphone from Logan's hand. 'Yeah, good one, Ding-Dong, really smooth. He's *bound* to tell you now.'

'My client hasn't killed anyone, Inspector Bell. My client is a law-abiding citizen and resents the accusation.' Hissing Sid clicked

his briefcase closed again. '*Might I just warn you that Grampian Police are already looking at one count of wrongful arrest: I really wouldn't go throwing about accusations like that without some serious proof.*' He unfolded his long limbs and stood, towering over the table. '*Now as you clearly have nothing relevant to discuss with us, and no evidence, I suggest you release my client immediately. This interview is over.*'

15

CLANG – the wastepaper basket clattered against the wall and rebounded, spewing napkins, eviscerated crisp packets, chocolate-bar wrappers, and empty Pot Noodle cartons all over the stained carpet tiles of the viewing suite.

DS Chalmers flinched, spinning her chair around, eyes wide. She blinked a couple of times, then took off her headphones. 'Frightened the living Jesus out of me. . . Good job I've got excellent bladder control, or it'd be like Niagara Falls in here.'

The viewing suite was even smaller than the downstream monitoring one – jammed into a space barely big enough to qualify as a cupboard with a huge grey security cabinet for police van CCTV hard drives against one wall, and a little wall-mounted work surface on the other. Two sets of AV equipment sat side-by-side on it, grainy footage of Aberdeen flickering away on a pair of tiny flat-screen TVs.

Chalmers sat in front of them, with a stack of ancient-looking VHS cassettes piled up on the work surface beside her.

Logan ran a hand across his eyes. 'Sorry.' Then he squatted down, picked up a dead packet of prawn cocktail and dumped it back in the dented bin. Followed it up with a chicken-and-mushroom Pot Noodle carton. 'Been one of those days.'

'I've been trying to find Agnes Garfield and Anthony Chung on the city-centre CCTV footage from this morning. Which is a complete nightmare. But. . .' She pressed a button on the console, then spun what looked like a volume knob. On the screen, people rushed into rewind, backing rapidly across Union Street as the lights changed. 'I did manage to track down that cash-machine transaction.'

'Bloody European Court of Human Rights. *No*, you can't do things the *sensible* way any more, the way they've been done for years, now you've got to have the scumbag's slimy lawyer mouthpiece in the room when you interview them. As if the job wasn't difficult enough as it is.' He rammed a cheese-and-onion corpse in the bin, then a Mars bar, pickled-onion Monster Munch, beef-and-tomato. 'And people wonder why Scotland has a reputation for the unhealthiest diet in Europe. . .'

'Hold on, I'll get it up.' She ejected one tape and replaced it with another.

No way he was touching the used hankies with his bare hands. Just because the viewing suite was on the ground floor, right across the corridor from the CCTV room – manned twenty-four hours a day – it didn't mean some filthy sod wasn't in here wanking themselves ragged to footage of drunken Friday-night girlies flashing their boobs at the cameras.

He plucked a biro from the desk and used that to hook them into the bin instead.

'Here we go. . .'

Logan looked up to see a queue of three people, distorted by the cash-machine camera's fisheye lens. First up was a wee man with a hoodie, a leather jacket, and a bobble hat – even though it was the middle of May. Behind him was a woman, looking back over her shoulder every three or four seconds, as if someone might be after her. The person behind her was a dick in a suit, making a big show of checking his watch every fifteen seconds: don't you know how *important* I am?

Logan shook his head. 'It's the wrong footage. Where's Anthony Chung?'

Bobble-hat-and-hoodie took his money and walked away out of shot. Little Miss Nervous took his place.

Chalmers pressed pause. 'According to the Clydesdale Bank, this is the transaction from Anthony Chung's debit card. Two hundred and sixty pounds.'

Little Miss Nervous had far too much makeup on, ginger hair exploding out from underneath a baseball cap with '*WITCHFIRE*' embroidered into it. Her heart-shaped face was slightly out of focus, the layers of mascara and black eye-shadow giving her eyes a serious Tim Burton vibe.

Logan frowned at the screen. 'Is that—'

'She's dyed her hair, the glasses have gone, and she's lost a bit of weight, but it's definitely her.'

Agnes Garfield.

'What's she doing with Anthony Chung's debit card?'

Chalmers pressed play. 'Getting some cash out for him? Maybe she's got none of her own, so they're living off his?'

'Two hundred and sixty's a lot of cash to get out at one time. They're going somewhere, or buying something big. . .'

'Not enough for plane tickets, too much for train tickets. And if she was clearing his account out, why not withdraw the full three hundred? Bank says he's still got another three and a half grand.'

Logan dumped the biro in the bin with the suspicious tissues. 'Two sixty would buy you a reasonable quantity of weed. She left hers at home.'

'We followed her through the CCTV from Markies, Union

Street, Schoolhill, then she disappears down some steps beside the theatre. There's nothing else on camera.'

'GSM trace?'

She flashed her teeth in a quick grimace. 'Sorry, Guv, we're getting nothing on Anthony or Agnes's phone. They've either got their mobiles switched off, they're out of battery, or they've ditched them. Control are keeping an eye on it – if there's any activity they'll let us know.'

So much for a quick and easy result. 'Anthony Chung: he's got a car, hasn't he?'

'Nissan Skyline. The insurance must be costing his parents a fortune.'

'Get a lookout request on it.' Logan nudged the wastepaper basket back where it came from. Just have to do this the old-fashioned way. 'Right, someone's got to know where they're staying, so—'

'I've put together a list of Agnes and Anthony's friends.' She flipped open her notebook and held it out. The page was covered with names and addresses. 'And I've booked out a pool car for the rest of the day.'

He smiled. 'Then let's go see who's in the mood for squealing.'

'Yeah, we were like, you know, *completely* best friends.' Dan Fisher leaned against the countertop, stringy tattooed arms poking out from the short sleeves of his crumpled shirt with the pub's name embroidered onto it. 'Ton and me was like . . . Han and Chewie, right?'

'Were?' Logan settled onto the bar stool. 'Past tense?'

'Yeah. . .' A shrug. The lobe of Dan's left ear was stretched around a hollow cylinder, big enough to poke a tube of Smarties through. Three silver hoops above that, one more through his nose, and a stud in his bottom lip like a metal cold sore. Black hair, collar-length on one side and shaved to the scalp on the other. 'We kinda fell out a bit. You know, with Rowan and everything. He was all,' Dan put on a broad American accent, cranking up the volume, '"She's a Goddamned nympho in the sack, you ain't gonna believe what she did last night. . ." Always boasting, and I. . .' He bit his bottom lip. 'I didn't think he should treat her like that.'

Chalmers flipped to the next page in her notebook, pen at the ready. 'Rowan?'

A nod. 'Yeah, she doesn't like being called Agnes. Can't blame her, right? Stupid name.'

'And that's why you fell out with Anthony Chung?'

Dan pulled out a smartphone and poked at it for a moment, then held it out. Grainy camera footage flickered across the screen. A group of young men and women in a pub some-where, everything stained satsuma orange by the indoor lighting. Laughter crackled out of the little speaker, and the picture moved in on a couple snogging in the corner of the booth. His hair was longer than hers, black and shiny, hers was brown, wavy, pulled back in a ponytail. He slipped a hand up the front of her T-shirt. And then the kissing stopped and she jerked away from him.

It was Agnes Garfield, though not as pretty in pixelvision as she was in the 'Have You Seen This Woman?' posters. *'Damnit, you've got to let it heal!'* She slapped him hard enough to make his sunglasses fly off. *'Bastard!'* And then she was off, shoving out of the booth and stomping out of shot.

Silence. Then the guy picked up his glasses and hurried after her. *'Rowan, please, come on, I didn't mean it. . .'* Everyone else laughed.

Dan pressed stop, then put the phone away. 'Only just had it pierced.'

'And that was a regular occurrence.'

'At least twice a week. She's a great girl. Bit screwed up, but she *completely* dotes on him – even though he treats her

152

like crap. Screwing around behind her back, pissed and stoned all the time, telling her it's her fault and she makes him do it. And she just *takes* it, forgives him, lets him get away with it.' Dan fiddled with the big hole in his ear. 'You know what happened on Valentine's Day? He made her get his name tattooed on her thigh. I mean, tattoos are cool and everything, but he was just marking his territory, right? Can you believe that? Wanker.' Dan coiled one hand into a fist. 'But she doesn't see it, you can't talk to her any more. . .'

Logan took a sip of his water. 'So you fought.'

'Yeah. . .' Dan opened his mouth, stuck a finger under his top lip and lifted, showing off a gap where a tooth should have been. 'Got in a couple of decent punches, but Ton's like a bloody ninja, isn't he?'

'And let me guess, Agnes wasn't exactly grateful you'd stood up for her?'

'Came round that night and kneed me in the nads.' He looked off down the bar, where a pair of huge women were bellowing out Sid James laughs, cleavage all a-wobble. 'How could she let him treat her like that, you know? I would've looked after her. . .'

'. . .at it like, I dunno, just arguments and fights and that.' Clive McWilliams took a long drag on his cigarette, then oozed it out in a slow breath. Smoke curled in the thick moustache and ludicrously long goatee beard. He couldn't have been much older than nineteen, but he had the facial hair of a Victorian industrialist. The muscle shirt was smeared with blood, as was the black apron and the white wellington boots. 'She just . . . you know, gets under his skin.'

'And he beats her.'

'Nah, it was never physical, they're just that kind of couple. Like to fight. Like to make up. Course, I wouldn't blame him if he gave her a slap now and then: she won't shut up

153

sometimes. Other times she just sits there staring at him like he's Jesus or something. You know?'

The smell of old fish and spilled diesel wafted across the quay. Off in the middle distance three massive seagulls were fighting over a cod's head, screaming at each other as they swooped and dived.

'And are the fights worse when he drinks?'

'Nah. . . Well, you wouldn't be able to tell, 'cos he never *stops* drinking.'

Chalmers looked up from her notebook. 'What about when he takes drugs?'

'What, weed?' A laugh. Then the last smouldering stub of cigarette pinged out over the edge of the quay and into the rainbow-filmed water. 'Not exactly drugs, is it? Just a bit of mother nature's finest to help a body unwind. God knows where he gets it from, but it's *mint*. . .' Clive's mouth clamped shut, he rolled his shoulders forward, looked off into the middle distance. 'Not that I would know anything about that, Officers.'

'Any idea where they're staying?'

Clive rubbed his hands down his bloody shirt, then dug a hairnet out of his apron and pulled it on. 'No idea. But wherever it is, she's probably winding him up something chronic.'

'. . .and I mean seriously loopy.' Penny Cooper sucked at her teeth for a bit, staring up over Logan's shoulder at the secur-ity monitor mounted above the whiteboard. Then she sighed, broad shoulders moving beneath the black T-shirt. Enough gel in her ash-blonde hair to make her look like an electrocuted Jedward. 'OK, she's pretty enough, if you like that whole brash perky look-at-my-boobs thing, but still. . . Welcome to Freaktown, population: Agnes.'

The bookshop staff room smelled of stale kebab and onions,

154

the microwave buzzzzzzing away to itself on the countertop. Breezeblock walls painted white, and covered with posters for kids' books and serial-killer thrillers.

Penny peered through the microwave door. 'Always takes forever, doesn't it?'

'Do you have any idea where they might have gone?'

'He's been banging Stacey the whole time, and Agnes *still* won't take the hint. Tell you, I lost count of the times Ton's tried to ditch her, but she'd just turn up the next day with a litre of voddy and a six-pack of Stella, and that would be that. This one time, he dumped her right before Valentine's Day and she went out and got his name tattooed right on her thigh. How weird would you have to be?'

Logan glanced over at Chalmers: still scribbling away in her notebook.

'So you're saying he's a heavy drinker?'

'Agnes the nutter drove him to it. Always burbling on about Harry Bloody Potter and *Twilight*, and that stupid *Witchfire* book. Seriously, what is she, *six*?'

Duncan Cocker's cigarette sent a smoke signal into the vivid blue sky. 'Yeah . . . dunno, really.' He leaned back against the grey harled wall and loosened his tie, tucking the pile of house schedules under one arm. 'They're kinda. . .' A shrug rearranged the creases on his cheap grey suit, the fabric thin and shiny, like its owner. 'You know?'

Not even vaguely.

The back garden was big enough for a swing set, a slide, and a Wendy house that looked as if it'd been built by a drunken chimpanzee. Lichen flecked the patio slabs. A gas barbecue and a set of plastic furniture lay abandoned in the middle of the grass.

Off in the middle distance, a tractor rumbled along the edge of a field. Rapeseed flowers glowed violent yellow, as if someone had taken a highlighter pen to the landscape. A pigeon whrrrrooooed in the thick leylandii hedge.

All very bucolic.

Logan shaded his eyes against the sun. 'So he drank, he smoked dope, and he dumped her?'

'Well . . . they were always doing that. Storming out, "I'll never speak to you again, you lying bastard." "Screw you, you mental bitch." And next thing you know they're tying each other's tonsils in knots with their tongues. Even when he's cheating on her.'

Chalmers stopped scribbling in her notebook and stared at him. 'And Agnes is OK with that?'

'Oh, she makes him pay for it, but basically: if Ton's happy with it, she is too. Tell you, he's had *dogs* less loyal than her, and I'm talking Alsatians.' Duncan made a little circular motion with the tip of his cigarette. 'You hear about her tattoo?'

'And you're sure they've not been in contact? No missed calls, or texts?'

'Nah. Ton's like that though: man of mystery. Doesn't like being pinned down.' Duncan checked his watch, took another puff. 'Bastards should be here by now. Got another couple to show round at half two.'

Logan moved across the patio, so the sun was warm against his back and not blazing in his eyes. 'Any idea where they'd go? Ever talk about escaping somewhere else? Down south, maybe?'

A frown creased Duncan's thin face. Then he swept a hand outwards at the fields and trees. 'Why'd you want to escape all this? It's, like the best place in the world.'

'They *never* talked about leaving Aberdeen?'

'Sometimes, when he's stoned, Ton bangs on about how great San Francisco is, but. . .' Duncan leaned forward and dropped his voice to a whisper. 'There were some Chinatown

Triad guys after him: that's why his mum and dad had to pack up and do a runner over here. The way Ton tells it, there's this big gunfight behind some restaurant and he caps two of them, but they get his cousin. Bang, right between the eyes.'

Chalmers moved a step closer. 'He told you he killed two people in San Francisco?'

'Pffff. . . Nah, shot them in the leg and that. *Totally* self-defence.'

'And you believed him?'

'Yeah, well . . . Ton's my main man, you know?' Duncan shifted the schedules from one armpit to the other. 'Don't know what I'm gonna do if he don't come back.'

Logan passed the brown paper bag over, then settled down on the bench. Sunlight beat down against his cheeks, the sharp salty tang of the sea mingling with fresh-cut grass. Three huge offshore supply vessels were lined up a mile from shore, probably waiting their turn to slip into harbour.

The grass dropped off in a steep incline down to a tarmac path, then a railing, then another steep drop – concrete this time, then a wide strip of pale-gold sand. A mother lumbered along it, following a pair of wee girls that giggled their way to the water's edge, then scurried away squealing as the waves tried to eat their bare toes.

Chalmers rummaged about inside the bag and came out with a couple of fries. 'Thanks.'

'Did you notice?'

She chewed, swallowed. 'They're a pair of nutjobs and they deserve each other?'

'Apart from that.' Logan unwrapped his cheeseburger and took a bite. Talking as he chewed. 'No one mentioned Agnes taking drugs. It was all him.'

'Her dad did.'

'Yes, but did he actually see her do it? Or did he just smell the marijuana on her? Maybe the weed was in her house because she was holding it for her boyfriend.'

'Her boyfriend the complete scumbag.' An onion ring disappeared in two goes. 'He gets high all the time, plastered too, he cheats on her, and she's *still* running around after him like a lovesick puppy. . .' More fries. 'Makes you vomit, doesn't it?'

'Takes all sorts.' Another bite of burger. Chewing, staring out at the glittering blue sea. 'We need to chase down this Stacey he was seeing on the side. Might still be at it.'

One of the wee girls turned to run away from the North Sea again, tripped, went sprawling on her face in the sand, and was swallowed by a tiny wave. Cue screaming and bawling.

Logan helped himself to one of Chalmers's onion rings. 'Why are they hanging about Aberdeen, though? If you're going to run away, you run away, you don't stay in the same place where people are going to recognize you. . .' He dipped a couple of chips into a dollop of mayonnaise. 'What about the diary?'

'Next on my to-do list. Spent most of the morning going through CCTV footage.' Chalmers tore the top off a sachet of salt and sprinkled it into her brown paper bag. 'When I was little, Dad would load us all in the car and down we'd come from Inverness for a long weekend during summer holidays. Play on the beach. Go to Duthie Park. Eat ice cream and rowies.'

'Maybe they're not running away at all. Maybe they're hiding?'

'Do they still have that petting zoo out by Hazlehead?'

'What if Anthony Chung isn't just into smoking dope? What if he's been selling it too?'

Chalmers stuffed more fries into her mouth. 'I used to love the llamas. Like mutant sheep on steroids.'

'Run a PNC on the pair of them when we get back to the station.'

'Already did it.' She sooked her fingers clean, then pulled out her notebook and thumbed through the pages. 'Here we are: Anthony Chung, done for drunk and disorderly behaviour twice, no jail time, just fines. One charge of driving without a valid tax disc. Two warnings for possession of a controlled substance, but they didn't find enough weed to do him for intent to supply.'

'Agnes?'

'Choirgirl, compared to him. She *was* given a warning the week before she went missing – local production company filed a complaint about her breaking into their film studio. A Mr Alexander Clark from ClarkRig Training—'

'Wait: Alexander Clark. *Zander* Clark?'

'His name's on the complaint. They had to get security to eject her three times, then she broke in.'

'Why was she breaking into a porn studio?'

16

'Porn?' DCI Steel's mouth twitched at the corners, nostrils flaring, eyes widening. 'Seriously?'

'Got thrown off the set three times. Then she broke in.' Logan hung his jacket on the back of his chair, then settled in behind his desk. Some sod had dumped a big pile of interview transcripts in his in-tray, as if he didn't have anything better to do. . .

Steel clapped her hands together. 'Well, don't just sit there: get us a pool car and we'll go a-visiting!'

Logan stared at her. '"Being a DI's no' about running around"—'

'Oh, don't be such a whinge. You said this Andrea's a suicide risk, right?'

'*Agnes*. Do you ever pay any attention to anything I—'

'Be derelict in our duty if we didn't follow up on an important lead that could save a young woman's life. So get your arse in gear. I'll come along and . . . supervise.'

'I don't need you holding—'

'No, no,' she held up a hand, 'I insist. A good senior officer knows when to step in and lend a hand with the troops.'

'How very team-spirited of you.' He didn't move.

Steel bounced up and down on the spot, like a horny terrier. 'Porn, porn, porn, porn, porn!'

Like working in a kindergarten.

He hauled himself up and pulled his jacket on again. 'If you're going to do that all the way, you're going in the boot.'

'Porn!' She did a little hop-skip, then turned and trundled down the corridor. 'Been ages since we've seen the chunky monkey. Think he'll still remember me?'

Logan closed and locked the office door. 'Wish I didn't.'

'I heard that.' But she didn't stop.

He followed her down the stairs, through the station's rear doors, and out onto the rear podium car park. It was bordered on two sides by the concrete bulk of Force Headquarters, the mortuary on the third, and the back side of King Street, turning it into a sun trap.

A couple of uniforms were lounging against the little dividing wall that ran along the ramp down to road level, faces turned to the sky, sunglasses glinting, their bare arms going an angry shade of Barbie pink.

Steel hauled out her cigarettes and popped one in her mouth. Then patted down her pockets. 'Arsebiscuits. . .' She looked at Logan. 'Well?'

'Thought you'd given up.'

'Quitting is for wimps. Besides, if I'm going to be stuck with your miserable mug all afternoon, I'll need a wee nicotine buzz going. It's this or the whisky.' She cupped her hands around her mouth in a makeshift loudhailer. 'Hoy, Chuckle Brothers, either of you got a light?'

Someone tugged at Logan's sleeve. 'Guv?'

He turned, and there was PC Sim, blinking in the sunlight. She sneezed a couple of times, like a shotgun going off in a bath. Then wiped her nose. 'Sorry.' Another sneeze. A blink. Pause. 'Big Gary says you're not allowed out till you've seen your visitor. Sir.'

'I don't *have* any—'

'Sorry, Guv, it's. . .' She screwed up one side of her face and then the sneezing was back.

Logan left her, doubled over by a battered police van, and hauled out his phone. Punched in the number for Sergeant McCormack. 'What visitor?'

'Aye, and hello to you too. Sim get you?'

She was still at it – sneezing and sneezing and sneezing. 'What visitor, Gary?'

'The visitor who's been waiting in the reception room for the last twenty minutes.'

He stared up at the building, looming in black and grey over the car park. 'You could've bloody said! I've been in my office for the last—'

'Your guest's getting a wee bit tetchy, by the way. Might be an idea to come see them before you sod off with old Wrinklechops.'

'Who? Who's waiting for me, Gary?'

A pause. *'You'll see.'*

By the time Logan had reached reception, Big Gary was standing behind the desk, a huge fat smile on his huge fat face. He grinned through the safety glass, then pointed off to the right. 'In there.'

The reception-room door was shut. Logan keyed his passcode into the pad mounted on the wall beside it, then stepped inside. . .

Sod.

Hissing Sid was sitting at the little grey table, arms folded across his chest. Shirt and suit jacket immaculate beneath the scowl. The lawyer checked his watch. 'I have been waiting here for precisely twenty-two and a half minutes. Do you have any idea how inconvenient this is?' A sniff. 'There isn't even a wireless network for visitors.'

Logan nudged the door shut behind him. 'Reuben's guilty and you know it.'

'If you had any evidence to that effect, you wouldn't have had to let him go, would you?'

'He punched me in the face. I was there. I bloody well saw it!'

Hissing Sid brought his chin up. 'I don't appreciate your tone, Acting DI McRae.'

'Think you'll appreciate my boot up your—'

'I'd love to sit around listening to threats of police brutality, but thanks to you I'm running behind as it is.' He reached down beside him and came out with his briefcase. Clicked it open, then pulled out a small brown envelope and placed it on the tabletop. Then went back in for a standard white DL one. He placed it beside the brown one, then pushed them both across the table towards Logan. 'These are for you.'

Logan backed up a step. 'A brown envelope, seriously?'

'If you're inferring that it contains a bribe, you're mistaken. The contents should be self-explanatory, but if you're feeling challenged by any aspect, you can always contact my office and make an appointment.' He clicked his briefcase shut again. 'Now, if you'll excuse me, our time is up.'

Logan stared down at the pair of envelopes. 'What is it then, blackmail?'

A small smile slithered around Hissing Sid's mouth. 'For blackmail to be effective, the target has to have done something wrong. Otherwise there would be nothing to blackmail them about. Have *you* done something wrong, Acting Detective Inspector?'

He backed off another step. The door handle pressed into the base of his spine. 'Of course not.' At least, nothing that Hissing Sid could have found out about. . . Could he?

'Then you have nothing to worry about, do you?'

'But what—'

'DI McRae, do you have any idea how much my services cost per hour? While my client had cleared me to brief you on the contents of these envelopes, you kept me waiting so long that the allocated time is now gone. And as my client is an old family friend I am unwilling to charge him more to make up for your tardiness.'

'But—'

'Make an appointment with my office.' Then Hissing Sid stood, staring at Logan with expressionless grey eyes. 'Now, if you don't mind. . .?'

Logan stepped to the side and let him out.

Hissing Sid limped across reception and out through the front doors into the sunny afternoon.

Back in the reception room, Logan closed the door. Two envelopes from a 'family friend' of Sandy Moir-Farquharson. Didn't take a genius to tell who that meant: Wee Hamish Mowat.

Maybe it *was* a bribe after all – drop the charges against Reuben, and all this could be yours. . .

Logan picked the envelopes up. Weighed them in his hand. Or maybe—

A bang on the door and he flinched hard enough to jump a foot to the right. Then stood there, pulse throbbing in his ears, making his arms itch.

Steel's voice blared through the wood. 'Come on, get a shift on: there's fresh porn getting all cold!'

Logan stuffed the envelopes into his pocket. Well, it wasn't as if he could just leave them lying about, was it? God knew what was inside. . .

'. . .and we're making substantial progress with the enquiry.' Steel slouched in the passenger seat, one foot up on the dashboard, one arm dangling out of the car window, mobile phone jammed between her ear and her shoulder as she rearranged her bra.

The security guard was a lump of muscle squeezed into a brown polyester shirt. He peered in at Logan, then over at Steel – just in time to catch her digging about in her cleavage with her spare hand.

The guard frowned. 'You sure she's police?'

'Wish I wasn't.' Logan pointed past the barrier at the car park, laid out in front of the two-storey office block. It was crammed with vehicles. 'Anywhere?'

'. . .That's right, sir, several lines of enquiry are opening up, and now we've got that forensic anthropologist on board. . . Yes, thank you, sir, it was a good idea of mine, but I can't take *all* the credit.'

Typical.

The security guard checked his clipboard, then took a couple of steps away from the car and spoke into a two-way radio. Whatever he said, it was too quiet to make anything out. Especially with Steel droning away.

'. . .no, sir, it's too soon to promise an arrest's on its way to the media, but between you and me: we're confident. . . Yes. . . Right. . .'

And then the guard was back, holding a pair of ID cards dangling from fluorescent orange lanyards. He handed them through the window. 'Make sure your pass is visible at all times. Go round the production block, there's overflow parking in front of Soundstage One. Five miles an hour, tops.' He leaned into the car again. 'Not fifteen, not thirty: five.'

'Just make sure someone knows we're coming.'

The parking barrier jerked up and Logan eased the pool car over the threshold into tinsel town. Or what passed for it in the north-east of Scotland.

A pair of big grey warehouses sat behind the office block. Logan followed the road around at a glacial five miles per hour.

'. . .aye, sir, you can count on me.' Steel hung up, then peered out at Soundstage One. It was at least four storeys tall, with a big '1' stencilled up the front in gold paint. 'You and me are in the wrong business, Laz. Looks like the dirty movies is where the money is.'

'We're making substantial progress?'

A tanned young woman in denim shorts and a cut-off T-shirt flip-flopped past pushing a rail of what looked like nuns' costumes.

Steel grinned. 'That's your global recession for you. Every bugger's got to cut back on the frivolous stuff like food and heating, but they'll no' give up their porn.'

Logan pulled up in one of the bays marked out in yellow paint beside the soundstage door, ignoring the 'REVERSE PARK ONLY' notice. 'The ACC's going to know it was all bullshit. We're no nearer finding out who necklaced that poor sod than we were two days ago.'

'The ACC believes what I tell him to believe.' She slapped Logan on the chest. 'Now shut up: you're harshing my pre-porn tingles.'

A thin young man marched over from the office block, a leather satchel slung across one shoulder. Long hair, knee-length shorts, blue plimsoles, 'BOD IS MY CO-PILOT' T-shirt, and thick-rimmed glasses. Half a dozen friendship bracelets dangled tatty braided tails from his left wrist. He reached the car as they climbed out. Grinned at them. Then pulled an iPad in a red leather case from his manbag and fiddled with it. Then nodded. 'Hi, you're . . . Logan and Roberta, right? Can I see your passes?'

Logan handed them both over.

'Right, I actually need you to wear these, OK? And make

166

sure they're visible. We've had a bit of a problem with un-authorized people. . .' He gave the passes back.

As soon as Logan put his on, the young man took a photo of him with the iPad. He did the same with Steel. 'Cool, all in the system. OK, well, my name's Jack,' he jiggled his own pass at them, 'I'm the go-to guy round here, so if there's anything you need: let me know. Right, let's do this.'

Jack turned on his heel and marched off around the side of Soundstage One.

Steel licked her lips, a frown creasing up the terrain of her forehead. 'Why am I getting a bad feeling about this?'

They followed him, past a stack of foam and fibreglass bodies, most of which had bits hacked off.

He looked back over his shoulder. 'I know, creepy right? You should see them when they're all wired up by the FX guys, it's totally amazing. Got to hold onto them till we finish pickups, just in case.'

Steel dropped her voice to a hissing whisper. 'What kind of porno needs a big pile of mangled corpses?'

Logan stuck his hands in his pockets. 'Jack, you been here a while?'

'Since the very start! It's been . . . an amazing experience. Seriously, what an introduction to the business, right?'

'Do you remember an Agnes Garfield?'

'Oh, my, God.' He rolled his eyes, one hand pressed against his chest. 'Could she have *been* any more of a nutbag? It's creepy when people get obsessed like that, isn't it? I mean, it's only a film, right?'

Steel shrugged. 'Wouldn't know.'

'Right, here we are.' Jack swept his arms out, encom-passing the front of another dirty big warehouse, this one with the number '2' painted in silver all up the front and over the massive sliding doors. If anything it was even larger than the first one. 'Oh-oh, we've got a red light, so we're going to have to wait here for a minute or two.'

Logan rested his back against the warm metal wall. 'They had to throw her off the studio lot three times?'

'I *know*, and then she broke in! Can you believe it? There's props missing from the stores and everything.' A sigh. 'That's why we've all got to be like super vigilant about passes. Even the actors have to wear them between scenes.'

Steel puckered her lips. 'What, stark bollock naked with a stiffy and wee ID card dangling about?'

Jack's smile slipped a little. 'A . . . stiffy?'

'Aye, between scenes. When they're no' humping?'

His mouth fell open a half-inch. Then clacked shut again, and the insincere smile was back. 'Well, that's us got a green light now. Shall we?'

17

Steel stood in the doorway and stared. Soundstage Two was massive, broken up into different sets. The biggest was a four-storey block of flats in partial cutaway, the rooms full of battered furniture and grubby wallpaper, with what looked like a water tank at the bottom. Three people in dirty coveralls and facemasks were spray-painting stains onto one of the rooms.

Then there was a shanty town at the foot of a cliff, and the inside of what might have been a fishing boat. They all backed onto vast sweeps of green fabric marked with little yellow crosses. But other than a handful of people doing set-dressing, the locations were deserted. All the real activity was taking place around the set in the far corner – a sort of circular House of Commons, with raked green leather bench seating and carved woodwork, arranged around a central island of red carpet and a massive brass lectern.

Half of the set was green-screen, but they'd built a segment of wall with more benches, a couple of balconies, and a curved ceiling painted blue with gold stars.

Two figures walked towards the middle of the round floor. One was wearing a black robe speckled with gold embroidery, his bald patch surrounded by thick grey hair that cascaded down to the middle of his back. The other was . . . stunning: long ginger curls, elfin face, little upturned nose, and a perfect bow of a mouth. Nichole Fyfe. Much more impressive in the flesh than she was on the TV yesterday morning. A dark scar jagged down through her pale skin, starting at her left temple, across her big blue eye, and all the way down her cheek, separating the freckles. Black jeans, black leather frock coat, red silk shirt, black leather gloves. A long-handled old-fashioned pipe jutted out between her teeth – just like the one he'd found in Agnes Garfield's Harry Potter hideaway – puffing smoke signals out in the studio lights.

A camera dolly followed them along the track – its operator sitting on the round stool mounted to the metal framework, fiddling with knobs and buttons, while someone else pushed the thing back into place.

A voice crackled out through speakers, hidden somewhere on the set. *'OK, that was great, but this time, Nichole, can you break in across Charles's line about the bodies all bearing the devil's mark? You're not interested in his superstitious nonsense.'*

Jack pulled a face, then jerked his head towards a cluster of monitors and cables. 'Oops, better be quick.' He hurried over, beckoning Logan and Steel after him.

Enthroned on a folding director's chair, at the heart of the nest of cables, was a huge man – tall and wide, with a bizarre hairstyle that looked as if he'd attached a lopsided shark's fin to his head then sprayed it scarlet. The goatee beard was an unnatural shade of Just-For-Men black. His thin rectangular glasses glinted in the reflected light of a little TV screen. 'OK, everyone, we're running scene three-sixty-two. . .'

'Excuse me, Zander, sir, you've got visitors.'

The big man didn't look up from the monitor. 'I've told

you, Jack, you don't have to call me "sir". We're all artists here. . . Aaaaaaaaaand: action!'

The whole place went silent.

Then a voice crackled through the speakers. '*Three-sixty-two, take four.*' Followed by a clack.

Nichole Fyfe looked up at the man in the robes. 'She has to be stopped.'

A sigh. 'I understand your concerns, but she's a good finder. One of the best we have.'

'She's a psychopath! A *monster*!' Nichole's blue eyes blazed. 'She's worse than the people we're hunting.'

Steel tugged at Logan's sleeve, then warm stale cigarette breath whispered in his ear. 'Is the shagging going to start soon? Only I'm no' looking forward to the old git getting his knob out. Even if he manages to get it up, it'll be all grey and wrinkly.'

'You have to understand: we have an *obligation* to uphold the peace.'

'You can't do that by murdering people!' Nichole turned and marched towards the camera as it backed off along the dolly track. 'I didn't join the Fingermen for this.'

Steel made a small moaning noise. 'Mind you, if *she* wants to get her kinky on I'm all for it.'

'Will you shut up?'

'Rowan!' The man in the robes limped after her. 'Mrs Shepherd found the Devil's mark on every one of those—'

'Of course she did!' Nichole spun around, hauled the pipe from her mouth and jabbed the man with the end. 'Look hard enough and you'll find one on anyone. Give me a knife, a flame, and fifteen minutes, and I'll find the Devil's mark on any minister you like.' Another poke. 'I'll find one on *you*.'

Steel licked her lips. 'Bet she goes like a jackhammer on a sunny day.'

171

'Shhhh!'

Nichole Fyfe spun around and marched past the camera, off the set.

'Rowan. Rowan! COME BACK HERE!'

Silence.

Zander Clark leaned forward and pressed a button on the microphone mounted beside the monitor. 'Aaaand, cut! That's a print, everyone, well done.'

A round of applause rippled through the crew.

Jack stepped up and tapped the director on the shoulder. 'Sorry, Zander, but the police need to see you?'

A frown crossed the huge face. 'What do the police. . .' He stared straight at Logan. 'Detective Sergeant McRae!' And the frown turned into a smile. Now he looked exactly like the photo on the pass dangling from his neck. 'How *nice* to see you again, it's been too long. And have you brought. . .' More smiling, and a little clap of the hands. 'Detective Inspector Steel, how's your lovely wife?'

Steel sniffed. 'How come no one's got naked yet?'

Blink. Then the smile turned into a grin. 'No, no, Inspector, haven't you heard? Those days are behind me: we're filming a proper Hollywood blockbuster here.'

'Oh. . .' Her shoulders drooped. 'No bonking at all?'

'One nude scene, but it's very artistic and intrinsic to the plot.' He leaned forward and keyed the microphone again. 'Charles, Nichole, you were *superb*. We're going to set up for three-six-three.' Then he let go of the button. 'Now, it's not that I'm not happy to see you both again, but you wouldn't *believe* how much something like this costs every minute, so. . .?'

Logan stepped to one side, letting a woman with a big tray laid out with makeup scuttle by. 'We need to talk to you about Agnes Garfield.'

The smile disappeared from Zander's face. He stared up

172

at the lighting rig above their heads for a moment. Then a sigh deflated his huge frame. 'Give me fifteen minutes, then we can talk while they're dressing the set for three-sixty-four.'

'God, she was a *complete* nightmare.' Zander slouched in his seat, arms draped along the back of the row. The viewing room wasn't huge – just big enough for fifty or sixty cinema seats arranged in half a dozen rows. A ceiling-mounted projector flickered images onto the screen at the front of the room, where a handful of people murmured down the front, spinning back and forward through footage of people in frocks shouting at one another.

Logan settled into a seat a couple down from the director. 'So she tried to break in?'

'Not to begin with, no.' A shudder set his jowls wobbling. 'She was so sweet at the beginning: wanted to study film at Glasgow University, was a huge fan of the books, could we give her a job as a runner so she could get some industry experience?'

'According to her dad, she was going to Aberdeen Uni to do accountancy.'

'She was OK at the start – did what she was told, always showed up on time, and her knowledge of the books was just . . . encyclopaedic. Every time the writer had a problem she'd be right there, polishing his ego and keeping him happy. Even came up with some great local PR exercises: competitions in the papers, cast and crew helping out at a soup kitchen, guided tours of the set for some primary school, dramatizing a real witchcraft trial from the fifteen-hundreds. . .' Zander sighed. 'Then everything changed: she started arguing with the designers and the chippies and the painters about the sets not being *exactly* like the book. Then she had a go at the script team for making changes to the story and the dialogue – as if it'd even be possible to do the book line-for-line on the screen.'

DCI Steel slumped into the row of seats in front of Logan, clutching a wax-paper cup in one hand and a Danish pastry in the other. 'Can't believe there's no shagging. . .'

'Every time she did it I'd sit her down, and we'd have a talk, and she'd apologize and promise she'd do better, and beg for another chance. And like the big softy I am, I'd agree.'

'Have you no' got any archive footage or something we could look at? You know, for old time's sake?'

'But in the end, she was haranguing the actors about how they were interpreting the characters, or speaking their lines, and I had to ask her to leave.'

Steel peeled the plastic lid off her cup and dark bitter tendrils of coffee coiled out into the cinema. 'Doesn't even have to be that hardcore, just a bit of girl-on-girl slippery. . . What?'

Logan glared at her. 'Could you give your libido a rest for five minutes? You can download some porn when you get home, OK?'

'Anyway, after we asked her to leave she started hanging about outside the studio, following people home, making a nuisance of herself. She snuck in a couple of times and had to be evicted. Then she did it in the dead of night and sprayed "thieves and liars" all over the Assembly set, slashed up some of the costumes too.'

Steel's face curdled, arms folded beneath her boobs. 'Was only asking.'

'We're not even doing the Thieves And Liars scene: it's a huge book, we had to get rid of something. So I made a formal complaint.' He brought his chin up, bringing a big swell of neck with it. 'I know it was mean of me, but this is a multi-million pound production, I can't have some hormonal teenager *sabotaging* it.'

'Zander?' A tall gaunt man with hollow eyes and a

tight-fitting polo shirt stood in the aisle a couple of rows down. The projector's light glittered back from his shiny bald head, as if he'd been polishing it. His voice had the deep rumble of grinding icebergs, and as he spoke the saggy skin around his chin and neck rippled. As if he'd once been a lot bigger, but someone had let all the air out. 'Do you have a minute to look at the cut for one-twenty-nine?'

Zander took off his glasses and pinched the bridge of his nose. 'David: I was just telling them about Agnes Garfield.'

The gaunt man grimaced. 'We should've pressed charges. People like that don't deserve. . .' He frowned at the back of Steel's head, then stood and stared at Logan. 'Anyway, one-twenty-nine.'

He turned and walked back to the front of the room, fiddled with a remote control, and the screen filled with black. Then a bleep. Then a dramatic shot of a woman in a Grim Reaper cloak, rich with black embroidery, on over a red leather jumpsuit. She threw the hood back. Bright scarlet hair tumbled about her face, teeth bared. . . It was the other actress – the one who'd been on the TV with Nichole Fyfe, making naughty with the camera.

What was her name, Mary? Maureen? No: *Morgan.*

There was something . . . not right about her slate-green eyes, something dangerous and unhinged.

Zander patted Logan on the arm and pointed at the screen. 'She's magnificent, isn't she? *Terrific* actress.'

The camera pulled out. Morgan was standing over someone kneeling on the ground, hands behind his back, a tyre wedged over his chest, head and one arm forced through the hole in the middle.

'*Thomas Leis, you have been found* guilty *of witchcraft—*'

Logan stood, the seat clacking back upright. 'You're neck-lacing him?'

'*I'm not a witch, it's a mistake!*' Tears and snot glistened on his face, eyes wide, mouth twisted.

'—*condemned to burn at the stake until you be dead.*'

Zander sat forward, squinting at the screen. 'Shh. . .'

'*I didn't do anything!*'

'*Coward.*' She pulled out a book of matches – close up on her hands as she struck one, then twisted the book so they all caught fire – then a low angle, looking up past the terrified man at her standing there.

'*PLEASE!*'

'We found a dead body, Saturday evening,' Logan pointed at the screen, 'just like that! *Exactly* like that.'

'*Burn. Like you'll burn in hell.*' A vicious smile. '*It'll be good practice for you.*' The blazing matchbook tumbled through the air, hit the tyre, and blue and yellow flames leapt up, cracking around the rim of the rubber.

The man on his knees screamed, wrenching himself from side to side, making the chains rattle. Close up on his face, wreathed in black smoke. . .

Zander waved a hand. 'Can you pause it there, David?'

On the screen, the burning man lurched to a complete halt, mouth open in a wide scream.

Standing at the front of the room, cadaverous David pulled out a laser pointer and ran a bright red dot around the man's face. 'Do you see it?'

'Yes, compositing really needs to be tighter. And can we lose the snot? It's just a bit. . .' He wiggled his fingers. 'Too mucusy.'

Logan settled back into his seat. 'It's exactly the same set-up: kneeling, chained to a stake, tyre over his head and under his left arm.'

Zander frowned, pulling his chin in, making ripples across his wobbly throat. 'The necklacing of Thomas Leis is a key scene. We're being *very* faithful to the book here – the fans would have a fit if we changed it.'

'It's in the book?'

176

'*Pivotal* to our understanding of Mrs Shepherd's character.'

Steel squinted down towards the front of the room.

The big gaunt man had produced a small plastic bag of something. He pulled what looked like a child's finger from the bag and popped it into his mouth. Crunching.

Her voice was little more than a whisper. 'David. . .?' Then she stood. 'Holy crap in a handbag, it's no', is it? David *Insch*?' She cupped her hands around her mouth. 'HOY, INSCHY? THAT YOU?'

She was off her head. There was no way that was ex-DI Insch. Insch was the size of a barn: a six-foot-two perpetual-motion eating machine with anger-management issues.

David hauled his shoulders back, chest out, chin up – pulling a dangly fold of skin with it. 'Detective Inspector Steel.'

There was no mistaking that withering, disappointed tone.

'It *is* you! The boy Insch, as I live and fornicate. . .' Her mouth hung open in a lopsided grin. 'What the hell happened? You look like someone's draped a deflated bouncy castle over a stepladder.'

'Age hasn't improved you any, has it? You still have the manners of a two-year-old.'

Zander clapped his hands. 'Excellent. I'd forgotten you all knew each other. David, why don't you sort out DCI Steel and DS McRae, and I'll get back to work?'

'But—'

'Time and principal photography waits for no man.'

Insch closed his eyes, massaged his temples, teeth bared between thin trembling lips. 'Cool wet grass, cool wet grass. . .'

Nothing ever changed.

18

'She broke in through there.' Insch pointed at a window about six foot off the ground. A set of black bars were bolted over the opening, a 'WET PAINT!!!' sign hanging beneath them.

Steel puckered her lips, looking up at the bars. 'Nothing like bolting the stable door, eh?'

Insch turned his back on her and marched off down the corridor, soured mouth working on another carrot stick. Strange seeing him walk like that, all rangy and long-limbed, instead of the lumbering mass he used to be.

Logan followed him. 'So how long have you been with Crocodildo Productions?'

'I'm not: doesn't exist any more. The props department is just down here.'

Steel scuttled up beside them. 'What? No. Come on, that's no' funny!'

'As Zander says: no one appreciates the art any more. What's the point going to all that effort to create something beautifully written and acted and shot, when all anyone ever does is fast-forward to the sex?'

'But that's the *good* bit!'

'The final straw came when someone sent him a link to an illegal porn download site. They'd made a compilation of all the . . . *finale* shots from every one of his movies. All his effort and creativity reduced to *that*. No wonder he gave it up.' Insch stopped in front of a door marked 'DEPARTMENT OF VARIOUS THINGS' and swiped his ID card through the reader fixed on the wall beside it. The little red light went green. He nodded towards a security camera mounted in the corner, with a clear field of view down the corridor. 'We had all this fitted after the break-in. Insurance company insisted.'

Steel scratched at her right boob. 'But he can't give up, he was. . . It's not right.'

Insch hauled open the door. 'Of course, I'd always wanted to work in film, so when I bumped into Zander at the Rotary Club we got talking. He invited me onboard for Crocodildo's last cinerotography project: *The Girl with the Dildo Tattoo*. We won twelve Woodies for that.'

Steel curled her top lip and backed off a couple of paces. 'Eew. . .'

He scowled at her. Then dipped into his bag and produced another carrot stick. 'I wasn't *in* it, I was second unit director.'

'Oh, thank God for that. The thought of you, in the nip, humping away at some poor woman. Flaps of skin flippity-flopping all over the shop. . .' Shudder.

She had a point.

'Have you finished?'

A shrug. 'Tell you, if I could bleach away the mental image, I would.'

Logan stepped through into the Department of Various Things, leaving them nipping at each other in the corridor. The props department was about the size of a school assembly room, laid out with racks and racks of costumes in neatly ordered rows on one side, and modular shelving units on the other, laden with various bits and pieces. Everything from standard

179

lamps to swords, bibles to handguns, all marked with little cardboard tags.

He picked a Glock 9mm from the collection. Hauled back the slide, then clacked it back into place.

A voice at his shoulder: 'Good, aren't they?'

Logan turned. 'You just leave these lying around?'

A little woman with big glasses smiled back at him, small fleshy lumps speckling her dimpled cheeks. She was wearing a T-shirt with 'BECAUSE PROP MISTRESS SAYS SO, *THAT'S* WHY!' on it. 'They're using them this afternoon for three-seventy-one, if they get that far. Need a good clean first, checked for blockages – I'm not having a Brandon Lee on *my* watch, thank you very much. Otherwise they're kept in the safe, with the ammunition and the firing pins.'

She dug into a shoulder bag and produced an iPad in an identical red leather cover to Excitable Jack, the film's go-to guy. 'The tags are all barcoded, they're scanned when the guns are signed out and when they're signed back in again.' She held the pad up and pressed something. A click, then a bleep. She turned the screen to face Logan. It was a spread-sheet with names, dates, times, and scene numbers. 'We're very, *very* strict about it.'

'So you've got a list of everything that's gone missing?'

That produced a small grimace. 'Don't get me started. I know this place looks like a junkshop, but every single thing in here has been *handpicked* for a set or a scene. And anything we couldn't buy we've made, so replacing this stuff isn't just a case of nipping down to Asda with a shopping list. When we started out we were way too trusting: cloaks, hats, props, daggers, medals. . . You name it, someone would nick it.'

She wandered over to another set of shelves, this one full of red leather notebooks. The bottom three shelves looked brand new, but the ones on the fourth were in varying stages of wear and tear. 'These are always the favourites. You

180

wouldn't believe how many Dittay books we've had to make.' She picked one up and handed it to him. 'Started off tooling the designs on the leather by hand, but so many went missing we had to get a die made. Everyone wants a souvenir.'

Logan ran a finger over the intricate pattern of curlicues and swirls set into the cover. It was identical to the one he'd found in Agnes Garfield's bedroom under the stairs. 'Dittay books?'

Insch's deep, dark voice rumbled through the room. 'Sixteenth century. They called the list of charges brought against people accused of witchcraft "dittays". That's what got you tried and burned at the stake.'

The prop mistress took the book from Logan's hand and put it back on the rack. 'All the Fingermen have to have at least one. They're quite important to the plot.'

'How many did Agnes Garfield get away with?'

Another grimace. 'Bad enough she took a couple of blanks, but she nabbed the main Rowan one too. Do you have any idea how much effort goes into making them look real and used? How many hours I spent, hunched over that bloody book, writing in all the dittays and sigils and notes. . .'

Insch folded his arms across his chest. Not as impressive a sight as it used to be, especially with the dangly bingo wings poking out from the sleeves of his polo shirt. 'She's lucky we didn't press charges.'

DCI Steel slouched into the prop room, hands in her pockets, shoulders slumped. She pursed her lips, looked around. Sniffed. 'Right: this is boring the arse off me. If no one's shagging, we're going.'

She swung around and stomped off, back down the corridor.

Insch stared after her. 'You know, you could probably arrange some kind of accident. I'd give you an alibi: you were with me the whole time.'

'Don't tempt me.'

They followed her out of the prop room, Insch's hand dipping into the bag of carrots every three or four steps, conveying another bright-orange stick into his mouth. Crunch. Crunch. Crunch. 'Is Rennie still. . .?'

'A pain in the backside? Yeah. He's on a major whinge at the moment, because Steel keeps—'

A woman's voice echoed down the corridor behind them. 'David?'

Insch froze. Then pulled on a smile. And turned. 'Nichole! I've been reviewing yesterday's rushes – the bath scene was terrific, you were great: such emotional intensity.'

Nichole Fyfe had taken off the leather frock coat, dark patches beneath her arms staining the red silk shirt. A ring of what looked like napkins poked out of her collar, presumably to keep her makeup off the fabric. Unlike Zander's and Insch's ID pass, hers hung around her neck on a bright orange lanyard with 'ACTOR ~ ACTOR ~ ACTOR. . .' picked out in black all along it.

She held up a copy of the script. Post-it notes stuck out of the edges like brightly coloured spines, the visible text covered in scrawled annotations and yellow highlighter pen. 'I wanted to talk to you about three-eighty-two. Don't you think Rowan should be more concerned about the inquisition team? Would she really go into the tower block without taking backup with her? I can't emotionally connect with her decision-making here.'

There was a small pause, then Insch blinked. 'I see where you're coming from. . . But if she takes backup then we don't get that sense of deep primordial threat when she finds Issobell Barroun's body.'

'But—'

'And she doesn't want Mrs Shepherd finding out, does she? If one of the team's compromised, then everything becomes a lot more dangerous.'

A little frown pulled at the fake scar on her face. 'So what you're saying is: at this point, Rowan's the only person Rowan can trust? She's isolating herself and that emphasizes her core vulnerability. . . It's a metaphor for her need to be loved. Yes, I can work with that. . .' Then Nichole looked over and gifted Logan with a smile. 'Sorry, I'm *such* a drama queen when it comes to getting the scene right.' She hauled off a black leather glove and stuck out her hand. A network of shiny scar tissue traced its way across the skin of her wrist. 'Nichole Fyfe.'

Logan took her hand – slightly damp – and shook it. 'DI McRae. I used to work with . . . David.' Still felt strange using his first name.

'Right – Logan McRae. I'm sure David's mentioned you.' The smile got brighter for a second, then she picked at the fabric of her shirt, pulling it away from her armpits. 'Sorry, been under the studio lights all day, I'm a mess. Anyway, it's been great. I'm sure I'll see you later.' And she was gone, scribbling something down in the margins of her script.

As soon as the door closed behind her, Insch sagged, massaging his forehead with the fingers of one hand. 'It'll be worth it, it'll be worth it. . .' Deep breath. 'Whatever happened to just turning up on time and knowing your lines? Now everyone's a method-acting nutjob pain in the arse: "What's my motivation, would my character *really* think that in this situation, what's the emotional *heart* of the scene. . .?" Every bloody day.'

Another carrot stick disappeared. Then he turned and stalked back down the corridor.

Logan followed him. 'Seems nice enough to me.'

'You know we send her a car every morning? With a driver, a punnet of raspberries, and three bottles of Perrier. Has to be Perrier, any other brand and she flies off in a strop. It's fizzy bloody water, not insulin. If she deigns to turn up at all. Four hours we were waiting for her this morning. *Four* hours.'

'So fire her.'

Insch stopped and stared at him. 'Don't be stupid. She's the best thing that ever happened to this film.' He pulled out a carrot stick and pointed it at Logan like a magic wand. 'She was still filming *In Death We Trust* when we cast her as Rowan. And soon as they stopped shooting, she dragged Morgan off to stay with a coven in the Midwest US so they could learn about witchcraft. She even learned to smoke a pipe for the role. We told her she didn't have to – we'd fix it in post-production – but she did it anyway. *That's* how dedicated she is.' The wand disappeared between his teeth. 'Just because Nichole's a nightmare to deal with, it doesn't mean she's not a great actress. Not just good: *great*.'

The fire door clunked shut behind them. Insch squinted in the sunshine as they stepped out onto sticky black tarmac. 'So I finally managed to persuade Zander it was still possible to make an artistic statement, but he'd have to get away from cinerotography to do it. Let's face it: the people watching porn are, by definition, a bunch of wankers. We needed a genre that would appreciate the work we put in.'

The car park was bathed in a golden glow, sparking on chrome bumpers and gleaming paintwork. Logan settled back against a BMW. 'When I searched Agnes's house I found your missing Dittay book: the one with all the squiggles and sigils in it. And a script.'

'So we pooled our resources, remortgaged our houses, optioned the rights to *Witchfire*, and got a stack of investors involved. Meant we could afford proper big-name actors, set designers, cinematographers, costumes. . . We've got the budget to do something really special here.'

'Why didn't you press charges?'

Off in the middle distance, Steel was grumbling into her mobile, kicking a stone about like a sulky teenager.

Insch ran a hand along the wattle of skin under his chin. 'She never changes, does she?'

'There must have been a reason.'

'Go back in time five years and you'd have been mad to put money on her running CID. Me: yes. Her: no chance. You'd have more luck betting she'd be out on her backside for gross misconduct. Or banged up somewhere.' A sigh. 'Now look at us.'

'She's *not* running CID. . . Well, she is, but only till Finnie gets back from Malaga: serial rape, case review.'

'Not that I'm complaining, mind: I *love* making movies. And *Witchfire*'s only the beginning, we're already looking about for the next project.' A smile stretched his cadaverous features. 'This is the start of something big, Logan. Aberdeen's going to be the film capital of Scotland. Goodbye Hollywood, hello Stoneywood.'

'So why *didn't* you press charges?'

Insch settled onto the bonnet next to him, the bag of carrot sticks plonked down between them. 'Because Zander is ruled more by this. . .' He poked himself in the chest. 'Than this. . .' The finger doinked off the side of his forehead a couple of times. 'We called the police, went round, demanded our property back, and her father gave us this big sob story about how she'd tried to kill herself and she's a good kid really and we can't blame her for being mentally ill.'

'And Zander. . .?'

'Hook, line, and stinker. Didn't want to be responsible for her taking another overdose.'

'Yeah, well, I suppose you can't blame him for. . .' Logan dragged out his notebook. 'Hold on, her dad told us she'd slit her wrists.'

'That was at Christmas. She took an overdose in February: Valentine's Day.' A nod. 'Nothing like it for bringing out the suicidal romantics.'

'The bastards lied to us, *again*.'

Insch cleared his throat, looked down at his huge shoes. 'I heard about Samantha, and the fire. I'm sorry.'

Everyone was always sorry.

Logan cricked his neck from side to side. 'What about you? How's Miriam and the kids getting on?'

'Apparently Canada's lovely this time of year. Anna's got a boyfriend. Can you believe that? Only eleven and she's got a boyfriend. Haven't seen her or Brigit for two years. . .' Insch chewed on the inside of his sunken cheek for a bit. 'Miriam's getting married in September. He's called *Jeff*, owns a restaurant in Vancouver.' The word 'Jeff' was pronounced as if it tasted bad.

'Sorry.'

'It is what it is.' Insch crunched his way through another carrot. Then stared off into the middle distance. 'Speaking of arsehole boyfriends: I need you to do me a favour.'

Wonderful. 'Oh aye?'

'Nichole Fyfe. Her ex has been causing trouble: turning up at her hotel, declaring undying love, having a go at the security team, threatening her driver, throwing his weight around. Won't take "You were dumped four years ago" as an answer.'

'So she wants to make a formal complaint?'

'This is the movies, Logan. The leading lady doesn't make complaints about her ex-boyfriend stalking her, she gets someone else to do it for her. And I don't want the papers getting hold of it.'

Logan couldn't keep the laugh in. 'Your film's all over the gossip mags, and the radio, and the TV, and—'

'That's not the point. Nichole doesn't want to look like a

big-headed diva who's too good for Aberdeen. And I don't want her distracted and not focusing on her job.' He shoogled the bag, then held it out. 'Want one?'

'So, what: you want me to go lean on him? Read him the riot act? Get him to fall down the stairs a couple of times?'

'You'd rather wait till he hurts someone?' Insch helped himself to some carrots.

Logan closed his eyes for a moment. All these years and Insch was *still* manipulating him. 'I'm not promising anything, OK?'

'His name's Robbie Whyte, twenty-five, lives in Inverurie with his mum.' Insch hauled himself off the car and checked his watch. 'Time's up. I've got a meeting with Trading Standards in five minutes – haven't even finished principal photography and some scumbag's already flogging counterfeit *Witchfire* merchandise – then it's the council historian we use as a witchcraft consultant. Then some arsehole journalist, then a competition winner. . . And at *some* point, I've got a film to make. Make sure you hand your passes back in at the gate when you leave.'

'Right.'

Insch stalked off a couple of steps, then stopped, with his back still turned. 'If . . . there's anything you need, give me a call and I'll see what I can do.'

'Lying bastards *swore* to me there was nothing else we needed to know about Agnes.' Logan put his foot down as soon as the car's bonnet was level with the forty-miles-per-hour sign, overtaking the bus in the inside lane. 'How are we supposed to—'

'Blah, blah, blah, life's tough, people lie.' Steel cracked open the passenger window, letting in the dual-carriageway roar of Auchmill Road. 'Get over it.' She pulled out a packet of cigarettes and jiggled one out. 'Weird seeing Insch again, isn't it? All thin and bony and floppy like that. . .'

'We're taking a detour. Agnes Garfield's mum and dad have got some explaining to do.'

'Bet if you stuck one of them garage air pumps up his bum you could inflate him like a beach ball.' She sparked the cigarette with a Zippo, then clunked one foot up on the dashboard and had a scratch. 'You know, it's just like old times: you, me, Inschy McFattypants. . . Except now we'd have to call him McSkinnypants.' A grin. 'I know: McFloppypants, he'll like that.'

Five minutes later they were in deepest darkest Northfield. Logan hauled on the handbrake. The sound of shrieking children came from the other side of the high school wall, interspersed with shouted commands and laughter.

Steel sooked on the last nub of her cigarette, slouched so far down her seat she was nearly in the footwell. 'You sure about this?'

'They *lied*.'

'Aye, I know that. But what does spanking them for it get you?'

'What else are they lying about?' He climbed out into the warm afternoon and called Chalmers: 'I need you to run me a quick PNC on Agnes Garfield's parents.'

It sounded as if she was in the middle of eating something. '*Give me just a second. . .*' A slurp. Then the clacking of fingers on keyboard. '*Did you see the results from the lab?*'

'Can we just focus on—'

'*The cannabis was about twenty-one percent THC, which is* phenomenally *high. And the blister pack of pills we found was Risperidone. It's an atypical antipsychotic – might be to counteract the weed?*'

No wonder all of Agnes's friends thought she was a basket case.

Chalmers made a little humming noise. Then: '*Here we go. . . The computer says Agnes's dad, Mark Garfield, has been done for speeding, Council Tax evasion, and once for assault.*'

'So he's violent.'

'*Got into a fight in a pub. I can try digging out the details if you want?*'

'What about the mother?'

'*Doreen Garfield: five warnings for threatening behaviour. Once told Agnes's maths teacher she'd rip his balls off and make him eat them.*'

'OK, that's—'

'*Apparently he said Agnes was thick. Another thing: I got a surname and an address for our mysterious Stacey. Her flatmate says she's not been home since Friday night, didn't turn up for work this morning either. Apparently it's not unusual. She's going to give me a call soon as Stacey shows.*'

There was that efficiency again. 'Good. Keep on it.'

'*And I've been looking through that red leather notebook we found in Agnes's cupboard under the stairs, it's exactly the same as the one the character—*'

'Rowan from *Witchfire*.'

'*Oh. . .*' Silence. '*I haven't read the book for years, but I picked up a copy at lunchtime and guess what: the Fingermen burn witches by—*'

'Necklacing. I know.'

This time the silence stretched on and on and on.

'Chalmers?'

'*Sorry, Guv. I'll. . .*' She cleared her throat. '*Anything else I can do?*' Sounding a little desperate.

Steel tapped him on the shoulder. 'See if I'm no' back in the office by five, you're getting my boot for a butt plug. '

'Find out where they are with the remains from this morning. Then take a look at Rennie's racial hate crimes – see if you can come up with anything.'

'*You can count on me!*' And she was gone.

Steel blew a wet raspberry, the spray of spittle glowing in the sunshine. 'Have you *still* no' solved that one yet?'

He walked up the path and rang the doorbell. 'Investigations are still ongoing.'

'And my arse is peanut butter. I'm no' having racist scumbags running round crippling people, Laz.'

'Well, tell you what, I'll wave my magic wand and. . .' The door opened.

Agnes's dad blinked out at them, a tin of Export in one hand, a remote control in the other. 'Mmm?' The smell of beer came off him in thick waves. Not bad going for half four on a Monday afternoon.

'Mr Garfield.' Logan folded his arms. 'Something *else* you failed to mention: she took an overdose in February.'

Garfield shaded his eyes with the hand holding the remote. As if he was trying to change the channel on Logan. Fat chance. 'I . . . didn't think it was—'

'No, you didn't think, did you? She was taking anti-psychotics; how much cannabis did—'

'She didn't. . .' A sigh. Then he turned around and walked back into the house. 'You'd better come in.'

Logan followed him into the lounge. The TV was paused: some sort of generic cop drama where everyone looked like models and no one ever broke wind, scratched their backside, or swore. An open pizza box filled the coffee table, a couple of slices lurking on the cardboard surrounded by discarded crusts. Empty beer cans were lined up like soldiers on the grease-flecked lid.

Garfield collapsed into a stripy armchair. 'Doreen's round her mother's.'

Outside the living-room window, Steel leaned back against the car, pointing at her watch, then her boot.

Logan turned his back on her. 'What part of, "Is there

190

anything else you haven't told us?" did you not understand?'

A swig of beer. 'Agnes slit her wrists because her *mother* decided she wasn't allowed to see Anthony Chung any more. Doctor said she was lucky she didn't wind up with permanent nerve damage.' Garfield waggled the can from side to side, making the contents slosh and fizz. 'She tried to hang herself when she was twelve. So we sent her to a shrink, and that was it: medication.' He reached for one of the last slices, pepperoni acne glistening on greasy cheese. 'Twelve and she's on antipsychotics. What kind of life is that?'

Silence.

'Why the hell didn't you tell us? I asked you if there was anything else, and you looked me in the eye and lied! Did you *really* think it didn't matter?'

A shrug. 'She was doing better. The overdose was. . . I don't know. She was upset because Anthony wasn't enthusiastic enough about her tattoo. They're like that, always. . .' He curled one hand into a claw, the whole arm trembling. 'You know? But she loves him.'

'Did Agnes take her medication with her when she left? What if she has another episode?'

Garfield's mouth turned down at the edges. Then he took a bite, chewing as if it was bitter cardboard. 'She couldn't take it with her. We don't. . . Doreen doesn't want. . . After the overdose we don't let Agnes manage her condition on her own. Doreen doles out the pills every day and watches to make sure she takes them.'

'Then how come she had a pack of Risperidone in her stash?'

'Risperidone. . .?' He shook his head. Washed the pizza down with the last of his beer. 'No, she can't have that: it's only for when the episodes are really bad. It's too strong for regular use. We manage her condition with Aripiprazole.' The empty tin went to stand guard with its comrades.

'Well, she got hold of some, didn't she.' God's sake. Logan marched off a couple of steps, then back again. 'Does she get violent when she's not taking her medication?'

Garfield stared down at the half-eaten slice in his hand. 'We didn't tell you, because we didn't want it splashed all over the papers. Bad enough she has to live with her problems, without every bugger looking at her like she's got two heads. None of their business.'

'Is she violent? Yes or no.'

'Agnes is a sweet little girl. She's more likely to hurt herself than anyone else.' He closed his eyes. 'That's why you have to find her. . .'

19

'Going to be sodding late. . .' Steel had one last dig at her bra, then slammed the passenger door shut.

The rear podium was packed with patrol and pool cars, the Chief Constable's new Bentley standing on its own like a leper with halitosis. Everyone too scared of scratching the thing to park anywhere near it.

Logan plipped the pool car's locks. 'It's five-to. You've got plenty of time.'

'How am I supposed to have a fag, grab a coffee, shout at Rennie, *and* get to the meeting on time?' She hauled up her trousers. 'Didn't even want to go to the sodding thing in the first place. Bunch of stuffed shirts stuck in a room moaning. How are *we* supposed to stop the forensic monkeys going on strike? We're no' the ones buggering them about.'

'And now you've got four minutes.'

Steel glanced up at the lump of concrete and glass. 'Go and do the meeting for us, eh?'

'No chance. I've got a forensic anthropologist to chase up.'

'Be good for you: character building. You can—'

'What's more important: you sloping out of the meeting, or us catching whoever necklaced that poor bugger?'

'Well. . .' A scowl made the wrinkles gang up on Steel's narrow lips. 'While we're on the subject, I told you to tell your bloody mother to sod off and stop whining on about spending more time with Jasmine. She's *your* mother. Fix her!' Then Steel wheeled around and stomped off through the back doors to FHQ.

Logan waited until they'd clunked shut behind her, before sticking two fingers up.

The steps down to the mortuary entrance were a shadowy graveyard for discarded crisp packets and cigarette butts, blown in off the rear podium. He picked his way down the stairs, rang the bell, waved at the security camera, waited for the bzzzzzz. . . Then stepped through the door and into the land of the dead.

Today, the land of the dead smelled like bleach and rehydrated curry.

He stuck his head into the staff room.

Miss Dalrymple had her feet up on the coffee table, a Pot Noodle in one hand and a fork in the other. A gossip magazine was spread out on her lap, 'NICHOLE FYFE: MY SECRET TEENAGE SUICIDE SHAME'. Which explained the scars on her wrist.

Dalrymple shovelled a dangly forkful of noodles into her mouth. The words came out muffled as she chewed: 'Not here.'

'Who's not?'

'Dr MacAllister. She's interviewing candidates to replace our dearly departed Dr Forsyth. He's not having a leaving do, so there's no whip-round.'

'I'm after Dr Graham.'

'Ah yes, the *bone* lady.' Dalrymple popped the fork into the plastic container, then made spidery gestures with her free hand, as if the fingers were sniffing the air for something. 'She's managed to break three beakers, two mugs, and knock over a brain bucket since this morning. How anyone so congenitally clumsy can survive day-to-day life is beyond me.'

'Is she here or not?'

The fingers formed a knot, then spread out to point towards the cutting room. 'If she ever offers you a lift, I'd *seriously* recommend running in the opposite direction.'

'I'll bear that in mind.' The grey terrazzo floor was damp, as if it had been mopped not long ago and hadn't dried yet. Logan left bleach and detergent footprints all the way down the corridor to the cutting-room doors. Then pushed inside.

The sound of gentle snoring came from the corner. Someone had dragged four chairs through from the staff room, lining them up against the stainless-steel working surface with the backs facing out into the room. Whoever it was lay on their side, cocooned by the two sides, an open newspaper draped across their head and shoulders. Like a tramp on a park bench, but in a mortuary cutting room. The only thing missing was an empty bottle of supermarket vodka.

Dr Graham was almost exactly where Logan had left her – hunched over the necklacing victim's skull. There wasn't a lot of the resin cast still visible, instead bands of dark-red clay speckled with tissue depth markers made it look like something out of *Hellraiser*. Dire Straits burbled out of the mortuary stereo.

Logan switched it off. 'How we getting on?'

She looked up, smiled. Then held a finger to her lips. 'Shh. . .' Her voice was barely a whisper. 'Dr Ramsey just got off to sleep. Rough night.'

'Under supervision again?'

She nodded her head towards the third cutting table, where a partial skeleton was laid out on a blue plastic sheet. 'Not

195

that I'm complaining. It's difficult enough to get *one* job, but to have a second fall right in my lap: how lucky is that?'

She peeled off her gloves and dumped them in the bin, then crept over to the other bones. The skull sat at the head of the table, missing the top set of teeth. The vertebrae were arranged in a line underneath, with gaps marking the ones that hadn't turned up on Logan's roof, but nearly all the rib bones were there, laid out in a disjointed fan down either side. Then the pelvis. And then the two femurs. Dr Graham pointed at the hands: thin cylinders of bone arranged on two sheets of paper, each bit fitting inside the wobbly biro outlines. 'As far as I can tell, the fingers you found came from the same body. We're missing the carpals and a couple of metacarpals. And there's no distal phalanges at all, but fingertips are really small and fiddly so it's possible they just blew off the roof. Or they were so mangled after being boiled in bleach they just fell apart.'

Logan pulled a photograph from his pocket and placed it on the table beside the skeletal hand. 'Is this our necklacing victim?'

'Ah.' She frowned at the picture of Anthony Chung. 'Actually, if everything goes to plan I'll get the epidermis on the reconstruction tomorrow. It would've been quicker, but I had to make the mould, and cast the skull, and examine the new skeleton. . .'

'But it *could* be him, right? Isobel said the victim had liver damage – and this guy was a serious drinker. Bottle of vodka a day serious. Two: his girlfriend's obsessed with a book where witch-finders execute people by necklacing them. And three: she suffers from psychotic episodes, and she's been off her medication for weeks.'

'Well. . .' Her eyebrows and cheeks twitched, as if there was something wriggling around under the skin. 'No. It's not him.'

196

'Are you *sure*?'

Beneath his tabloid blanket, Dr Ramsey snorted and twitched, making the chairs creak.

'Shhh. . .' Dr Graham froze, staring at the duty doctor until he rolled over onto his back and the snoring started again. 'Trust me: this isn't our victim.'

'But—'

'If it was, I'd have expected rounder eye sockets and a flatter front to the skull as well. Plus there should be a rounded palate and the incisors would be shovel-shaped, but our victim's teeth are spatulate. I know the body would have looked a bit – and I'm not meaning to be racially insensitive here – *yellowy* during post mortem, but that's because the blood settles in the areas closest to the ground.' She picked up the photo and handed it back to Logan. 'He wasn't from the Far East. And he wasn't in his late teens, early twenties, either.'

'Oh. . .' So much for that theory. It wasn't Agnes Garfield's boyfriend. She wasn't on a psychotic rampage.

Dr Graham patted the clay-covered skull. 'Our friend here was male, Caucasian, and about forty years old. The remains on your roof, on the other fingertip-less hand, are definitely female, mid sixties, five foot three, and her second and third lumbar vertebrae were surgically fused at some point: that might be worth chasing up?'

Logan glanced back at the pale-grey bones. 'How did she die?'

'My life coach says I should always turn a negative into a positive. So: there are excellent opportunities there for further discovery.'

'You have no idea, do you?'

She scrunched up one side of her face. 'Well, there's no knife marks on the bones, or signs of blunt-force trauma, or bullet holes. . . To be honest, it's impossible to tell, *especially* without the rest of the remains. We've got nothing below the knees and we're missing both arms too – he could have hacked them off and she bled to death. Maybe he drowned her? Suffocated her. There's no hyoid, so she could've been strangled. Or he stabbed her in the stomach. Or made her drink bleach. Or—'

'Enough, OK. I get the picture.'

Dr Graham shrugged. 'If you want, I can send a sample off to that friend of mine in Dundee?'

'Do it.'

She picked the left femur from the plastic sheet and hefted it like a club, tapping the hip joint on the palm of her hand. 'I'll just need you to sign a couple of release forms. . .'

'Yeah, sorry.' Logan sat on the edge of Dr Forsyth's old desk, mobile phone pinned between his shoulder and his ear, hunting through his jacket pockets for a pen. Bloody things must be hiding. He pulled out his notebook, his car keys, his warrant card, laying them on the desk beside him. Then a handful of business cards, two packs of individually sealed blue nitrile gloves. Then that white DL envelope Hissing Sid gave him, and then the brown one. . .

They sat on the Formica desktop like tombstones.

A female voice dribbled into his ear. '. . .there yet?'

Blink. 'Erm . . . I think so.' The pen was lying sideways in the bottom of the pocket. He pulled it out and got her to repeat the authorization number and scrawled it down in his notebook, along with the Fiscal Depute's name and the time and date. Covering his arse, just in case. 'Thanks.'

'And this isn't going to take a chunk out of budget?'

'Pro bono, apparently.' He stared down at the tombstones. Puffed out his cheeks. Then picked up the white envelope and tore it open.

'Really? Is this a regular thing, or a special favour, because the

PF would definitely *use this stable isotope thingy a lot more often if it's free.'*

Inside were two sheets of paper tagged with little yellow Post-its marked 'SIGN HERE' with an arrow pointing to the relevant part of the form. Logan's pulse thumped in his ears, pins and needles sparking along his forearms. 'Holy mother of crap. . .'

'*I beg your pardon?*'

'I. . .' He licked his lips. 'Got to go, something's. . . Bye.' He hung up. Put the phone down with all the other rubbish from his jacket pockets. Cleared his throat. Blinked at the sheet of paper in his hand. The words were still there:

I **HAMISH ALEXANDER SELKIRK MOWAT** *(Mains of Clerkhill, Grandhome, Aberdeen, AB22 8AV), being of sound mind, do hereby nominate and appoint* **LOGAN MCRAE** *(23 Persley Park Caravan Park, Aberdeen, AB21 9NS) as sole executor for my last will and testament, and further grant him CONTINUING and WELFARE POWER of ATTORNEY. . .*

Oh dear Jesus. No. No chance. No chance in hell.

Logan tore the brown envelope open and tipped the contents into his hand. It was a cheque for thirty thousand pounds.

'Little shite. . .'

'. . .cheeky bastard gave me a cheque for thirty thousand pounds! Can you believe it? The sodding nerve of—'

'*Oh boo hoo.*' Samantha yawned at him down the phone. '*Are you seriously moaning because someone gave you thirty grand? I mean, really?*'

Union Street sparkled in the sunshine, mica chips in the granite making it look like someone had sneezed glitter all over the place. Traffic thundered across the junction to Rosemount Place, buses and taxis played chicken in the middle of the box junction.

Probably better waiting for the green man.

'I can't take—'

'*You could finally get the flat finished – move out of the caravan and back into an actual house.*'

'Thought you loved that caravan.'

The pedestrian crossing bleeped and Logan marched across, dodging his way through a gaggle of middle-aged men in suits bragging about how much they were going to drink tonight.

'*I do. But you've made it smell all fusty.*'

'Of course, you know what'll happen if I'm an executor for his will, don't you? I'll be a target for anyone who thinks they deserve a slice of the Wee Hamish empire: drug dealers, thugs, loan sharks, protection racketeers, people traffickers, smugglers, pimps. . .'

'*When was the last time you opened the curtains and let a bit of air in?*'

'Reuben's going to *love* that. He. . .' Logan screwed his face shut for a heartbeat. Bloody hell: that explained the random punch on the nose that morning. Reuben knew about the will. Brilliant. Thirty grand and a death sentence.

Right onto the cobbles of Diamond Street down the side of KFC, past the sandwich bar and the hairdresser's.

'*Logan?*'

'All right, all right, I'll open the windows.'

'*And it wouldn't hurt you to give the place a scrub as well. There's a mouldy patch in the bathroom that's beginning to look a bit like Shakespeare. I don't want Shakespeare watching me in the shower, it's perverse.*'

'He's giving me power of attorney too. What the hell am I supposed to do with that?'

'*Do I need to boo-hoo you again?*'

Left onto Lindsay Street, leaving the cobbles for a Frankenstein's patchwork of tarmac and potholes.

'You're getting as bad as Steel.'

A pause. *'You take that back, Logan McRae, or there'll be no kinky bedtime fun for you ever again!'*

Then right onto Golden Square. Tall granite buildings faced out onto what was the bastard child of a roundabout and a car park. Rows of cars ringed a wrought-iron fence with more of them on the inside, facing out. Then another row behind that, circling the statue in the middle. The handful of trees dotted around the place looked in need of a decent drink.

'Logan, I'm warning you.'

'All right, I take it back.' Sigh. 'And I'll do something about the shower.'

'That's better. Now run along and see your lawyer, it's nearly teatime here, and they've been boiling the cauliflower since last Thursday in my honour. Don't want to miss that.' Then she hung up on him.

The receptionist scowled up at him from behind her mahogany fortifications. The glasses balanced on the end of her nose had little wings on the top corners. They went with her purple cardigan. 'Our office hours are nine to five. If you wish to make an *appointment* to see Mr Moir-Farquharson, I can—'

'Is he in or not?'

The smile looked forced, making tiny wrinkles around her narrowed eyes. She glanced sideways at a door on the far side of the room. 'Mr Moir-Farquharson is with a client and isn't to be. . . Hey: you can't go in there!'

Logan hauled the door open. 'What the hell are you playing at?'

Sunlight gilded the wood-panelled room, glinting off the bald head of a shaven gorilla in an expensive suit with 'HATE' tattooed on one set of knuckles and 'PAIN' on the other. Scars knitted their way over the back of his scalp, like cracks in an eggshell. He didn't look around as Logan barged in, just sat there, silent as a slab of meat.

Sitting behind the wide oak desk, Hissing Sid sighed and closed his eyes – pinching the bridge of his nose with his thumb and forefinger. 'Mrs Jefferies!'

Logan shook a fistful of brown envelope at him. 'Attempted bribery of a police officer is an offence under the Criminal Justice, Scotland—'

'How many times do I have to tell you: it's *not* a bribe.'

'Don't give me that shite!' He hurled the envelope across the desk. It hit the lawyer on the chest and fell to the floor. 'Think I don't know a bribe when I see one?'

The receptionist appeared at his elbow. 'I'm sorry, Mr Moir-Farquharson, I told him you were with a client.'

The hulk of muscle in the suit sniffed, then hooked a thumb over his shoulder. His voice was a nasal Borders growl. 'You want I should, you know, remove him from the premises, like?'

Another sigh. Then Hissing Sid pushed his chair back, bent down and picked the envelope from the ground. 'Will you excuse me for a couple of minutes, Mr Harris? I'm afraid DI McRae requires things to be explained to him slowly and with pictures wherever possible.' He stood. 'Mrs Jefferies, will you fetch Mr Harris a pot of tea? I'll be in the conference room with our uncivilized visitor.'

Sandy Moir-Farquharson settled into a chair at the end of the long table, sitting with his back to the window. Sunshine cast dappled shadows on the cars parked around Golden Square, rippling gently as wind brushed through the leaves of the parched trees.

The lawyer placed the brown envelope on the table in front of him and smoothed it out with careful fingers. 'DI McRae, I don't appreciate you coming in here and making a nuisance of yourself when I'm with a client. Or any other time, come to that. If you wish to see me, you can make an appointment with Mrs Jefferies like everyone else.'

'Thirty *thousand* pounds! And what the hell is *this*?' Logan dug out the power of attorney forms and slapped them down on the table. 'Get it through your pointy little head, I am not for sale. DO YOU UNDERSTAND ME?'

Hissing Sid pulled the cheque from the envelope. Held it up. 'As you will see, the payee section has been left blank. Mr Mowat has no interest in bribing you, he merely wishes you to select a worthy cause you'd like to support.' The lawyer went back into the envelope and pulled out a Post-it note covered in cramped handwriting. 'As you would have known if you'd bothered to read my message. All you have to do is fill in the missing details.'

Logan stared at the note. Bloody thing must've been stuck to the inside of the envelope. . . Still, that wasn't the point, was it? 'So you'll have *my* handwriting on a huge cheque from Wee Hamish Mowat? Do you think I'm *stupid*.'

Hissing Sid puckered his lips and raised an eyebrow. 'I'm certainly coming to that conclusion.' He laid the cheque on the table. 'It's really not that complicated. Name the cause you wish to support and I'll have someone complete the relevant details for you.'

'I'd . . . it's thirty thousand pounds!'

'With keen observational skills like that, it's no wonder you made detective inspector. Now, is there anything else? Or can I get back to my client?'

'It. . . What's with this power of attorney bollocks?'

Hissing Sid did the sighing and nose-pinching thing again. 'We could have discussed all this when I came to see you at the station, but instead you had to play your little power games and keep me waiting in that room without so much as a glass of water.'

Heat spread out across Logan's cheeks. 'I didn't even know you were there.' He sank down into the nearest chair. 'Someone was playing silly buggers.'

'Mr Mowat has recently updated his will, and has named you as sole executor. That means on the sad event of his demise you will be responsible for disposing of his assets and ensuring the distribution of behests according to his wishes. If, on the other hand, he becomes incapacitated due to illness he has granted you continuing and welfare power of attorney. That means you are authorized to look after his property and assets, and if necessary make end-of-life decisions.'

'And by "assets" you mean "criminal empire". What am I supposed to do with it: divvy the drugs operation up between Wee Hamish's lieutenants? Give the prostitutes and people-trafficking to someone else? Devolve power to the loan sharks?'

A sniff. 'I really couldn't comment. And you should be careful about making accusations of legal impropriety about Mr Mowat if you don't want to be on the receiving end of a suit for slander.'

'I can't do it. I'm a *police* officer.'

Hissing Sid slipped the cheque back into the envelope. 'Then there is the matter of his bequest to you: six hundred and sixty-six thousand, six hundred and sixty-six pounds. And sixty-six pence.'

Oh God. . . thirty grand was bad enough.

'I'll admit the amount of the bequest is unusual, but I'm sure Mr Mowat has his reasons for giving you two-thirds of a million pounds.'

Logan's bowels churned. 'He can't *do* that.'

'My dear Mr McRae, Mr Mowat can leave whatever he wants to whomever he wants. And for some unfathomable reason he's seen fit to leave you a rather large sum of money.'

'But. . .'

'Of course, it doesn't have to be deposited straight into a UK bank account, or handed over in cash. In order to avoid questions of impropriety it can be discreetly placed in a trust to await such time as you cease being a police officer. Think of it as a nest egg to support you in your retirement.'

'But if someone finds out—'

'Mr Mowat has left provision in his will for my firm to represent you.' The lawyer stood. 'Now, I really must return to Mr Harris.'

Logan stared up at him. 'How am I supposed to—'

'You can see yourself out.'

20

The sun burns like a glowing cigarette end pressed into pale skin. Rowan closes the bathroom window and leans on the sink, head down, blood-red hair hanging like a curtain in front of her face. Don't be sick. She's stronger than that. She did what had to be done.

'The Kirk. . .' The words stick in her throat. She takes a deep breath and forces them out. 'The Kirk is my mother and father. It is my rod and my staff. My shield and my sword. What I. . .' She closes her eyes. 'What I do in its service lights . . . lights a fire in God's name.'

Don't be sick.

'Lights a fire in God's name, lights a fire in God's name, lights a fire in God's name. . .'

The churning fizz inside her settles, leaving a hollow shell behind. Like a chrysalis after the moth has gone. Empty and brittle.

Her black leather gloves leave scarlet smudges on the porcelain.

Tenet Three: 'Leave nothing of thyself behind: lest thine enemies use it against thee.' Rowan turns the hot tap on and lets it run until it steams, then washes her hands. The water runs pink, soaking through the gloves' stitching, leaving the leather shiny like fresh liver.

'What I do in its service lights a fire in God's name.'

She pulls a towel from the rail by the door and wipes the sink clean.

There. That's better, isn't it?

Did what needed to be done.

She raises her head and looks at the woman in the mirror. Empty and brittle. Tendrils of dark red and black make wings across her shoulders, jagged with barbs and thorns and claws.

She bares her teeth. 'WHAT I DO IN ITS SERVICE LIGHTS A FIRE IN GOD'S NAME!' Spittle flecks the mirror.

And slowly the red fades to pale blue, then gold.

A little smile pulls at the corner of her lips.

All better.

'. . .or not? Guv?'

Logan blinked.

'Guv!' Sitting in the visitor's chair, Rennie crossed his arms and stuck his bottom lip out. 'Least you could do is *pretend* to be interested.'

Logan frowned, then checked his watch. 'What are you doing in here anyway? Not even half-seven yet.'

Rennie screwed his face up. 'Aaaaaargh! I just *told* you. I'm in because bloody DS bloody Chalmers phoned me – while I was in bloody bed, by the way – wanting to know where all the hate crime files were. And—'

'Did you tell her?'

'Yes, but—'

'Then what's the problem?'

'What's the. . .' Rennie screamed at the ceiling again. 'Why did you tell her to check up on me? We used to be a *team*. But now it's all: Chalmers this, and Chalmers that.'

'Oh for God's sake.' Logan moved onto the next budget

requisition form: DI Bell wanting DNA analysis for a series of housebreakings. It went on the 'possibly' pile along with a request to set up a surveillance operation in Blackburn, looking for a cannabis farm, and one for a forensic archaeologist to consult on what might or might not be a body deposition site outside Fraserburgh.

'What, I'm not good enough for you any more? I used to be the Robin to your Batman. The Rodney to your Del Boy. The Branston Pickle to your cheese on toast!'

Silence.

Logan stared at him. 'Seriously?'

'The hate crimes aren't Chalmers's, they're mine!'

'The Robin to my *Batman*?'

He shrugged one shoulder. 'I couldn't get back to sleep. Just lay there thinking about all the ways you were screwing me over with this bloody Chalmers woman.'

'No, but seriously: Robin?'

'It's not *fair*.'

Logan shook his head. 'I hate to disappoint you, Rennie, but we're not a gay couple, OK? And I'm *not* screwing you over with Chalmers.'

The other shoulder came up, making him look like a grumpy teenager. 'Well . . . that's how it feels.'

Logan sat back, drummed his fingers on the desktop. 'Tell you what, find me some bloody suspects and you can be the favourite again. And while we're at it: what's happening with your shoplifting tramps?'

'It's. . .' He wriggled in his seat. 'It's not as easy as you'd—'

The door clunked open and Steel stood there, one hand hauling up her trousers, the other plucking the electronic cigarette from her mouth. She narrowed her eyes, making everything all wrinkly. 'What are you pair of dinks doing here?'

Logan pointed across the desk. 'Poor wee Rennie's feeling

all unloved and unappreciated. So he's come in early to moan about it.'

'Oh aye, and what's your excuse?'

'Doing *your* paperwork.'

She smiled, both arms extended as if she was waiting to be crucified. 'Then all is forgiven. Now grab your coat – we're going out.'

Logan stood. 'Another body?'

Steel frowned. 'No: pub. Why does it always have to be work, work, work with you?' She slapped Rennie on the back of the head. 'Arse in gear, Stinky, you've got tramps to find.'

Rennie grumbled his way out of the chair, then out of Logan's office.

She waited till he'd shut the door behind him. Then collapsed into the vacant chair. 'We're screwed.'

'What's wrong this time? Did. . .' Logan sat down again. 'Hold on, if you thought I wasn't here, why did you barge in?'

She dug a hand down her cleavage and went rummaging. 'You *were* here.'

'Yeah, but you didn't know that.'

Rummage, rummage. 'My underwire's killing us. I keep telling Susan, you've no' to put them in the washing machine, but will she listen?'

'Answer the question.'

'We're getting a visit tomorrow from the National Police Improvement Authority. *Apparently* our necklacing case is going nowhere. Boardroom, half two in the afternoon, attendance is mandatory.'

Just what they needed. 'Who they sending?'

'Who do you think: a bunch of cockshites from Strathclyde up to point out the sodding obvious and tell us how to do our jobs.' She gave her cleavage one last dig, then puckered her lips around the fake cigarette, sending a little puff of steam up into the room. 'Well, I'm no' giving up that easy. Tell everyone I want their arses in the briefing room at quarter to eight sharp. And I mean *everyone*. This case isn't turning into a runner, understand? I want its bloody legs hacked off before our Weegie visitors get here. I want it like Stumpy McStumperton, so we can tell them to turn round and sod off back from whence they sodding came.'

Yeah . . . *that* was going to happen.

Logan looked up at the door. 'So come on then, why *did* you barge in here?'

Steel sniffed. 'Sometimes, when you're all out, I like to rummage through your desks and see what lies you're hiding from me.'

Good job he still had the form about being an executor for Wee Hamish Mowat and the dirty big cheque in his pocket then.

Steel pulled a face. 'God's knickers, the place is *hoaching*.'

O'Donoghues was a barn of a place off Justice Mill Lane, the walls painted a mucal shade of shamrock green. As if all the Guinness and Beamish memorabilia wasn't enough of a giveaway. The crowd was three deep at the bar, the tables around the outside already taken.

An all-girl six-piece band crowded the stage: electric guitar, bass, fiddle, drums, accordion, and a lead singer belting out the Stereophonics's 'Have a Nice Day'. They were good. Good, but *loud*.

Logan frowned around him. 'Could we not go somewhere quieter?'

'Don't be so wet.'

'Remember, I'm only staying for the one. Got to go up the hospital.'

'Wah, wah, wah. Get us a table.' She stuck out her elbows and waded for the bar.

210

'It's packed, how am I supposed to. . .' But she wasn't listening, she was barging through the crowd like a wrinkly icebreaker that stank of cigarette smoke.

Well, maybe someone would be sodding off soon? Then he could nick *their* table. He did a slow three-sixty, staring through the mass of bodies . . . then stopped. Someone at a table crowded with empty glasses was standing up and waving at him.

'Guv?' PC Guthrie had changed out of his all-black-ninja-police officer uniform and into a tweed sports coat and a pair of jeans, as if he was channelling the spirit of Jeremy Clarkson. He smiled, the fair hair and pale eyebrows looking like mould on his happy potato face. 'Over here.' Guthrie shifted his chair over a couple of hops, and pointed at an empty one beside him. 'Great band, eh?'

Logan settled into the seat, the other three people at the table rearranging their chairs to make room for him. PC Hannah had a big droopy smile on her face, eyes heavy and lidded in her wobbly head, dark wiry hair sticking out in a frizzy crash helmet. PC Stringer covered his mouth for a belch, blinked a couple of times, then went back to making little knots out of empty crisp packets. Forehead creased up in concentration.

Contestant number three was Dr Graham, sipping what was either a huge gin-and-tonic or a pint of sparkling water. She leaned forward. 'I should have a face for you by mid-morning tomorrow.'

Stringer patted her on the shoulder. 'Your round, April. Can we . . . can we have more crisps?'

Hannah banged a hand down on the table, making the empties clink and rattle. 'Eating's cheating!'

'Making a night of it then?'

Guthrie shrugged, then drained the last of his latte. 'Supporting the troops.'

Another thump. 'Drink!'

'OK, OK. Drink it is.' Dr Graham stood and gathered up an armful of empties. 'DI McRae?'

'Not for me, thanks. Got one coming.'

She shuffled off, looking as if she was carrying nitro-glycerine rather than a few empty glasses, tongue sticking out of the corner of her mouth.

Up on the wee stage, the song jangled to the end and applause crackled around the room, along with the occasional whoop.

The singer let it die down, then her voice boomed out of the speakers. *'Thanks, guys, here's a number we haven't done in a little while, it's called "The Importance of Being Idle".'* And off they went again.

Logan turned and peered over his shoulder, through the crowd. 'Is that Constable Sim up there?'

Guthrie nodded. 'Every other Monday. Good, aren't they?' He cleared his throat, leaned in close, not quite shouting over the band. 'Have you talked to Rennie recently, only he's on a real moan about this tramp thing.'

'It's all he ever does these days: moan.'

'I know, but he looks up to you and. . .' Guthrie sat upright, cranking up the smile. 'Chalmers, thought you weren't going to make it?'

DS Chalmers stood to attention, nodding at Logan. 'Sir. Can I get anyone a drink?'

'Nah, you're good – April's just gone up for—'

There was a crash of broken glass, then a cheer and some swearing. Dr Graham strikes again.

Chalmers looked left, then right, then marched off and came back a minute later with another chair. Parked it next to Logan. 'Hoped I'd bump into you, sir. I went through DS Rennie's notes for the hate crimes, and I think I've got a connection. All the victims are male, from the Far East, and none of them are prepared to make a statement.'

212

'*That's* your connection?'

'No.' She opened her mouth. Then closed it again. Had another go: 'Well, yes it is, but think about it: if you've been attacked by a bunch of racist morons, why lie to protect them? Why not cooperate with the police? Wouldn't you want them arrested and locked up?'

He shook his head. 'Not that much of a shock, is it? Whoever beat them up threatens to come back and finish the job if they speak to the police. Poor sods are too scared to stick their hands up and ask for help.'

'But what if it's more than that? What if our *victims* are involved in something illegal too?'

'And they can't talk without incriminating themselves.' Possible.

'What if—'

A gravelly voice sounded right behind her. 'Hoy, Curly-top, budge up.' Steel was back.

Chalmers stood. 'Sorry, ma'am. Would you like my seat?'

Steel smiled. 'Blatant sucking up, but I'm cool with that.' She thumped a pint glass down on the table in front of Logan: black with a white head.

He sniffed at it. 'I don't drink Guinness, I drink Stella. You *know* that.'

'Tough nipples. They're no' giving Stella away half-price if you flash your warrant card, are they?' She creaked into the vacated seat, clutching a large white wine and what had to be a triple whisky. 'Anyway, it's good for you.'

'You drink it then.'

Steel shuddered, then took a sip of wine. 'No chance. Bloody stuff tastes like licking a leprechaun's bumhole.'

Chalmers shuffled her feet. 'I like Guinness.'

Logan pushed the pint towards her. 'Knock yourself out.'

*   *   *

'. . .thanks, everyone! We're Burn this City Down, and we'll be back after a short break: Jane needs a pee, and the rest of us need Tequila!' A huge round of applause went up, and the band followed the blushing bass player offstage.

Steel settled back in her seat and had a scratch at her left armpit, lips puckered, staring at PC Hannah. 'Come on then.'

The constable gave her a slow-motion blink – one eye lagging behind the other – then smiled, chin pulled into her neck, giving birth to chins. 'Shoot Jamie. Shag Nigella. Marry Delia?'

Steel threw her head back and roared a laugh at the ceiling.

Chalmers wobbled her way through the crowd to the table with a chipped brown tray laden with drinks. 'Right: one latte, one sparkling water. . .' She doled them out to Guthrie and Dr Graham. 'One Jack and Coke for Sophie, one Stella. . .' That went down in front of Logan. 'One white wine with a Grouse chaser. . .' Steel. 'And two Guinness.'

She tucked the tray under the table for next time. 'Cheers, everyone.'

Steel wrapped herself around a mouthful of wine. Smacked her lips. 'Guthrie, your turn: Tony Blair, Ed Miliband, and Nick Clegg.'

Chalmers shuffled her chair closer to Logan's. 'Before I forget. . .' She dug about in her handbag, coming out with a white carrier-bag with a big 'W' on it. 'Got you something.'

Ah. Logan stared at it. Well, this was awkward. 'You don't have to. . . It's. . . I'm certainly *flattered*, but I'm seeing someone and—'

'Oh God no, no.' She held up her hand and shrank back in her seat, eyes wide. 'I'm not. . . It isn't. . . I just thought it would help with the investigation.' She handed it to him. 'Open it.'

He did. There was a paperback inside, thick as a house

214

brick. *Witchfire* picked out in shiny gold above a 'SIGNED BY THE AUTHOR' sticker, another boasting 'SOON TO BE A MAJOR MOTION PICTURE!' and one more with '2 FOR £10!'. The actual book cover was almost invisible. 'I see. . .'

Chalmers took a mouthful out of her Guinness, leaving herself with a white foam moustache. 'Tenet Two: "Know thine enemy, for knowledge is power and power is victory." If Agnes Garfield is *really* that obsessed with the book, maybe we can use it to figure out where she is, or what she's going to do next?'

Might not be a bad idea at that.

Laughter erupted through the group, Steel pounding on the tabletop, tears rolling down her cheeks. 'You're a sick, sick puppy, Guthrie! A cucumber!'

Guthrie shrugged. 'It's not like I'd *eat* it afterwards.'

Logan slipped the book into his pocket. 'Thanks.'

'No problems, Guv.'

The glass of Stella was cold, beads of condensation rolling down the side. He raised it to his lips, then swore. His phone was having a fit in his pocket, vibrating and blaring out 'If I Only Had a Brain.'

Sodding Rennie. . .

'What do you want?'

Rennie's voice was barely audible in the crowded pub. '—ng, don't ha— . . . —er and . . . it?'

Logan stuck a finger in his other ear. 'What?'

'I sai— . . . entire pl— . . . —overed in blood! It— . . . —ody.'

He stood. 'Calm down and try again.'

Rennie did, but it wasn't any better.

Steel frowned up from her whisky. 'What's munching on your pants?'

'Rennie. Says there's a body, blood everywhere.' Logan grabbed his jacket off the chair and pushed through the crowd to the exit.

Sunlight glinted off the roadworks on the other side of the street, a deep hole in the patchwork tarmac ringed around with orange cones and barrier tape.

Justice Mill Lane bustled with cars, taxis and drunken halfwits. A pair of girlies were bent over their friend, at the kerb, outside the nightclub next door, one holding her hair the other stroking her shoulders as she vomited in the gutter. Her short skirt was tucked into her knickers at the back. Classy.

A pack of greasy-looking young men laughed like hyenas outside the slab-faced communist-styled lump of a building that used to be the local swimming pool, trying to get one of their number to wear a stolen traffic cone as a wizard's hat. Someone in the distance roared out the words to 'Bohemian Rhapsody' as if it was a battle cry.

Eight o'clock on a Monday evening. . .

Logan hunched his shoulders against the noise and pressed the phone hard against his ear. 'What body?'

'*OK, OK. . .*' There was a deep breath. '*Kintore. Neighbours complained about the smell, so the local station sent round a uniform. There's a body in the kitchen and blood . . . everywhere.*'

'Has the—'

'*I can't cock this up! I've never dealt with something like this on my own. What? What do I do?*'

O'Donoghue's door clunked open and Chalmers appeared.

DCI Steel was right behind her, blinking into the sunshine. 'What's this about a body?'

'Will you shut up?'

'*I'm sorry, I'll shut up. Just tell me what to do!*'

'Not you.'

Steel stuck her chin out. 'Don't you tell me to shut up!'

He turned his back on her. 'Get your notebook out. I need you to call Control and tell them you're confirming it's a suspicious death. Tell them you need a crime scene manager,

216

the PF, the pathologist, the IB, and enough bodies to search the place and get door-to-doors started.'

'*I can do this. . . I can do this. . .*'

'And get the scene secured – you know the drill: no one in or out. Now give me the address and I'll be there as soon as I can.'

Steel poked him in the chest with a yellowed finger. The words floated out on a tide of whisky fumes: '*We'll* be there. Head of CID, remember?'

21

Blue-and-white 'POLICE' tape stretched across the driveway, tied to a For Sale sign driven into the lawn on one side and next-door's cheery garden gnome on the other. Not exactly impenetrable, but better than nothing.

Bees hummed in the syrupy summer air, thick with the Turkish-delight smell of honeysuckle and roses. A nice street, in one of the older bits of Kintore, only a handful of eighties bungalows breaking up the solid granite cottages and terraced houses. The clacking diesel growl of a train going past behind the property on the way out to Inverurie.

It wasn't the kind of place normally associated with words like 'bloodbath'.

DCI Steel leaned on the roof of Logan's battered Fiat Punto, elbows just missing a gritty smear of vitrified seagull poop. She took a long drag on her fake cigarette. 'What kind of sick weirdo has gnomes?'

Chalmers struggled her way out of the back seat, notebook at the ready. 'Why aren't the SEB here?'

'I mean, it sounds like a venereal disease, doesn't it? Can't come into work today, I've got a bad case of the gnomes.'

No sign of life, so Logan called Rennie on his mobile. 'Where are you?'

'Where are you?'

'Out front.'

'Don't come in!' Clunk, rattle.

'What, are you naked or something?'

Then the front door opened and Rennie lurched out onto the driveway, dressed in a white SOC suit. 'You have to stay out here.'

Steel snorted, then stepped over the gnome-line. 'Aye, that'll be shining.'

Rennie scurried over, the legs of his suit making rustly vwip-vwop noises. 'No!'

She stopped one foot in, one foot out. 'I'm head of sodding CID, you wee shite. I'll decide—'

'This is a secure scene. No one enters or leaves till the Procurator Fiscal and the IB gets here.' He stuck out his chest. 'First rule of crime-scene management: secure the scene.'

'First rule of DCI Steel – do what you're sodding told, or I'll have your scrotum for a shower cap!'

His eyes flicked to Logan. 'Guv?'

'You stick to your guns, Detective Sergeant.'

Steel scowled at him. 'Don't you bloody start.' She pulled her shoulders back. 'Rennie, I'm warning you: get out of—'

'Have you been drinking?' He sniffed, then his mouth set into a hard little line. 'You're not getting anywhere near my crime scene. The PF would do her nut.'

Logan placed a hand on Steel's shoulder. 'Why don't you and Chalmers wait out here, and I'll let you. . . What?'

Rennie shook his head. 'You've been in the pub with her, haven't you?'

'I had *one* pint. I'm still—'

'DI Leith got here five minutes ago, Control made him Senior Investigating Officer, and you know what he's like.'

219

'You called me! We came wheeching all the way out here for *nothing*?'

Rennie opened his mouth, then closed it again. Fingered the elasticated hood of his oversuit. 'I can't let anyone in till the PF and the IB get here.'

Chalmers curled her top lip. '"IB"? How behind the times are you? It's Scenes Examination Branch.'

'That's what we call them, OK?'

'How can you *possibly* be in charge of a crime scene—'

'Oh, bugger off back up north with the rest of the Tartan Bunnet Brigade, we don't—'

'—can't even tell the difference between—'

'ENOUGH!' Steel curled her hands into fists. 'God, you're like a pair of wee kids.'

Silence.

She jabbed a cigarette-stained finger at Rennie. 'You, Procedure Boy, who's FAO?'

Rennie nodded at a patrol car parked on the other side of the road. 'Constable Duncan.'

Steel hauled up her trousers. 'Thrown off my own sodding crime scene. . .' She gave Rennie one last scowl, then turned on her heel and scuffed across the street to the patrol car. Chalmers waited a couple of beats, then followed her.

Rennie closed his eyes and sagged on the spot. 'I'm sorry, OK? I panicked and I didn't know what to do and it was all happening so fast and there's all this blood. . .'

Logan looked up and down the street. Quiet so far, but that would change. 'You're a right pain in the backside, you know that, don't you?'

He drooped even further. 'Sorry, Guv.'

'Don't worry, you did the right thing. No one in or out.' Then Logan followed Steel and Chalmers over to the patrol car.

The passenger door was open, a police officer sitting

220

sideways in the seat with his feet in the gutter, head between his knees. He'd stripped off his stab-proof vest and dumped it on the driver's seat.

Steel poked him on the shoulder. 'You the First Attending Officer?'

He nodded, then blew out a long shuddering breath.

'No' what you expect, is it? Hacked-up body on a nice Monday evening.'

Constable Duncan's voice came out muffled from way down there. 'It was . . . like a horror film. . .'

A young couple passed on the pavement opposite, giggling and murmuring, heads together, eating chips from rectangular cardboard boxes. The scent of batter and hot vinegar coiled out around them. The girl peered into the patrol car. 'You doing someone?'

Logan nodded at the house with its half-arsed barrier of blue-and-white tape. 'You know who lives there?'

Her boyfriend jammed in another handful of chips. 'For sale, isn't it?'

As if the estate agent's sign in the lawn wasn't enough of a clue.

'*Darren.*' She smacked him on the shoulder, leaving greasy fingerprints on his AFC tracksuit top. 'Been empty for ages. Think they went to Dubai or somewhere, you know, for work and that?'

Steel straightened herself up. 'You pair know it's an offence to withhold evidence or lie to a police officer, right? So you'd better think really carefully before answering. . .' She squinted at the pair of them. Squared her shoulders. 'Where'd you get those chips?'

Steel counted out three grubby tenners into Chalmers's palm. 'Three fish suppers, one with pickled onion, a thing of mushy peas, and some tins of Irn-Bru.' She looked down at the

221

constable, still sitting in the passenger seat with his head between his knees. 'You want some chips, Duncan?' No answer. 'Get him one too.'

Chalmers pocketed the cash. 'Ma'am.'

'And get something for Rennie. Nothing fancy – mock chop or something – don't want him getting ideas above his station.'

She brought her chin up. 'Ma'am.'

'Aye, and no spitting in it either.' Steel made shooing motions. 'Well, go on then.'

Chalmers puckered her lips for a moment, as if she was about to say something, then turned and marched off in the direction of the chip shop, back straight, arms swinging at her sides. Left, right, left, right, left, right. . .

Steel settled her bum down on a garden wall and puffed at her fake fag. 'Right, sunshine, time for you to sing for your supper. What happened?'

PC Duncan took a deep breath, then sat up. His face was pale and shiny, like the belly of a frog, greeny-purple bags under his eyes. 'I've never. . .' He swallowed. 'I mean, they make you go to a post mortem, but. . .'

'Your first real body?'

'The *smell*. . .'

Logan flipped open his notebook. 'When did you get the call?'

'I was out looking for a missing Renault Clio. House has been vacant for about eight months, local estate agent's handling the sale. Neighbours phoned the station complaining about the smell coming from the place.' He shuddered. 'Got there and there's no sign of forced entry, so I go down the estate agent's and get the key, come back and. . .' He puffed out his cheeks. 'He was in the kitchen.'

'Victim?'

'Male, IC-one . . . maybe. Difficult to tell. . . Face all

222

battered, cuts and stab marks over his body.' PC Duncan's head went back between his knees. 'Oh God. . .'

Steel examined the end of her pretend cigarette. 'Tortured?'

'They staked him out on the lino. There's blood every-where: on the floor, on the walls. And the flies. . . God, the place is *black* with them.'

Logan wrote it down. 'What about the neighbours?'

Duncan raised his greasy face. 'Mr and Mrs Morris, they're in their eighties. He's in a wheelchair. Don't think they did it.'

Steel blew a raspberry. 'He means did they see anything, you divot.'

'They keep themselves to themselves.'

'Pfff. . .' She stood, stretched, then leaned on the roof of the patrol car. 'Someone up there sodding hates me. We've no' had anything like this for what, two, three years? And soon as I'm in charge of CID, bang: necklacing, skeletons, and some poor sod tortured to death. Could they no' have waited till Finnie gets back?'

Logan sooked the salt and grease from his fingertips, then stuffed the cardboard box back in the plastic bag it came in. 'Fiscal's here.'

Steel crunched through a bit of batter. 'How can they no' wrap fish and chips in paper any more? Used to love that – the smell of hot fat and sharp vinegar and warm newsprint. That's your golden days of childhood right there.'

The Procurator Fiscal's Mercedes purred to a halt behind a grubby Transit van with 'MANKY MYSTERY MACHINE' finger-painted into the grime.

'At least it's no' in that polystyrene rubbish. Whoever invented *that* needs buggering with a hedgehog.'

The passenger door swung open and the Fiscal climbed out, looked around. Frowned. Then marched across the street

223

to Logan's battered Fiat Punto, heels clicking on the tarmac. 'You're eating *chips*?'

Steel dipped a chunk of fish into the tub of snotter-green peas. 'Would've got you some, but you weren't here.'

The Fiscal's eyes narrowed, mouth pinched. 'Have you any idea what will happen when the press turn up and find you lot mooching around eating chips?'

'Thought it would be classier than a kebab.'

'Have you been *drinking*?' The Fiscal thumped the flat of her hand on the roof of Logan's car. 'For goodness' sake, Roberta, *think* about the impression you're making!'

'I'm no' the one shouting and banging things, am I?'

Rennie emerged from the front door of the house and waved at them. 'Ma'am? DI Leith says he's ready whenever you are.'

'Go *home*, Roberta.'

Steel popped a chip into her mouth and chewed.

'I mean it, Roberta!'

A shrug. 'Sod all going on here anyway.' She closed the lid on her cardboard box and passed it to Logan. 'Laz, fire up the Crapmobile, the pub beckons.'

'And never turn up half-cut to one of my crime scenes again.' The Procurator Fiscal turned and clacked towards the house. 'Briefing: tomorrow morning, nine sharp.'

Steel licked the peas from her fingers, then stuck two of them up at her departing back.

Rennie grimaced at them, then lifted up the line of blue-and-white 'POLICE' tape so the Fiscal could duck under it.

'Course you know what this is, don't you?' Steel picked something out from between her teeth. 'Pent-up sexual frustration. PF sees me and gets all excited in her barbed-wire panties.'

'Am I dropping you back at the pub or not?' Logan got in behind the wheel. 'Should've been at the hospital ages ago.'

'Mind you, bet she goes like a Rampant Rabbit wired up to the mains. I could—'

'Do you *want* me to drive off and leave you here?'

'Touchy.' She cupped her hands around her mouth. 'CHALMERS, ARSE IN GEAR: WE'RE GOING!'

The DS appeared from behind a nearby hedge. 'Sorry, Guv, I was . . . looking for a bin. To put the chip boxes in?'

Steel opened the passenger door, then hauled the seat forward and hooked a thumb at Chalmers. 'In the back.' As soon as she was inside, Steel clunked the seat into place again. 'Pretty convenient you went off a-Wombling the minute the PF turned up, isn't it?'

'I. . . Recycling's important.'

'Didn't want to be labelled as a prick for breathing Guinness fumes all over her, more like.'

In that case, she was a hell of a lot more sensible than Steel.

Logan cranked the engine over and drove them both back to town.

The slates are warm beneath her buttocks, the heat seeping through her jeans and into her bones. Rowan leans back against the roof, legs dangling over the edge as the sun sinks towards the horizon. It's nearly nine, but the burnt-fat scent of barbecuing flesh coils through the air from the massive steading development hidden behind the house, mingling with the sharp emerald stain of freshly mown grass.

A fat pigeon crooooow-crooooows from the overgrown beech hedge. Somewhere in the distance a dog barks.

The world is back in its place.

She sucks on her pipe. . . Nothing. The weed's dead in the bowl, so she sparks her Zippo and puts the flame to it again, drawing the smoke deep inside her and holding it there like the Holy Spirit. Calming the turmoil. Settling the waters.

She has done a good thing today, released a tortured soul into the warmth of God's embrace.

A confession.

Repentance.

Acceptance.

Rapture.

Release.

A grin spreads itself across her face, pulling her cheeks tight. She has lit a fire in God's name today, and it will burn for all eternity.

22

Steel's smile grew another inch. She licked her lips and waggled her eyebrows. 'You *sure* you're no' wanting in for a nightcap?'

Chalmers shook her head, backing away from Logan's manky Fiat Punto. 'Er . . . no. No thanks. I'm good. I'll just . . . walk home from here. Need the exercise.' And she was off, marching down the street, glancing back over her shoulder as if she was afraid they were going to start chasing her.

Logan clunked the car door shut. 'Do you have to do that?'

Steel hauled up her trousers. 'What? I was being hospitable.'

'No: you were being creepy.'

'You say potato. . .' She turned and lumbered up the path towards her house. Chez Steel was a big granite pile on a quiet tree-lined road: bay windows on either side of a dark-red door; a garden full of rose bushes, the air thick with their scent and the hum of bees.

A knot of keys appeared from the depths of her jacket pocket, then she unlocked the door and beckoned Logan over. 'Don't just stand there – neighbours will think I've gone funny, bringing scruffy men home with black eyes.'

Logan scowled at her. 'I'm *not* scruffy.'

'You say tomato. . .'

Cheeky sod, there was nothing wrong with his suit. OK, so he got it in the sales at Slaters for forty quid, but what was wrong with that? Couldn't beat a machine-washable jacket and trousers when your job description included dealing with people likely to vomit all over you.

He tugged at his jacket lapel as he followed her over the threshold into a hallway hung with photographs of the family – Steel, Susan, and little Jasmine. Making sandcastles on a beach somewhere with palm trees, flying a kite in Duthie Park, eating sandwiches on Brimmond Hill, playing on the dodgems down the beach. . . The row of coats hanging on the rack featured a bright-red duffle coat, a pair of tiny yellow wellington boots lined up beneath it.

What sounded like a dog eating a cactus, but was probably meant to be singing, oozed from somewhere down the hall – a TV tuned to some awful talent show.

Steel paused at the living-room door and stuck her head in. 'Sooz? Laz is here. You want a drink?'

Click – the noise from the TV died, and Susan appeared. At least ten years younger than Steel, she was the spitting image of a Cary Grant-era Doris Day, only chunkier and with longer blonde hair, wearing a blue summer dress. She smiled, making little wrinkles at the corners of her eyes. 'Hello, stranger, it's been ages.'

He bent down and kissed her on the cheek. 'You look great.'

'Pfff. . . I wish. Two and a half years and I still can't shift the baby weight. You want to see Jasmine? She's asleep, but you could peek in?'

Steel grabbed a handful of Susan's arse and jiggled it. 'Don't know what you're worrying about. I like a woman with a bit of padding, just means there's more of you to love. Now,' she gave the handful a slap, 'you show Laz upstairs and I'll get the drinks in. . .'

Jasmine lay flat on her back, arms and legs splayed out like a drunken starfish wearing stripy black-and-white pyjamas, little toes and fingers twitching as she snored.

Susan sighed, crept into the room, and pulled the blanket over her. Then came back to the doorway and put a hand on Logan's arm, her voice a whisper. 'It's been so long, we were worried you didn't want to see her.'

Great: guilt. 'It's just been a bit of a sod at work. And with Samantha and everything. . .'

'You know you're always welcome here. You're not just a donor, you're a member of the family. And it's good for Jasmine to see her dad from time to time.'

'I know, I know. I'll try harder. I promise.'

'Good.' Susan gave him a little hug. 'Now let's go get that drink.'

Steel added an obscenely hefty measure to her own glass, then put the bottle of whisky down on the breakfast bar. A couple of plates sat next to it, arranged with olives, cheese, slices of salami and cured ham. She helped herself to a slice of prosciutto, stuffing it into her mouth, then chasing it down with a sip of Isle of Jura while Susan went off to fetch the crisps.

Logan rolled his tumbler from side to side between his hands. 'Erm. . .' He cleared his throat. 'You remember that money you inherited?'

Steel sniffed. 'If you're looking for a sub, you're out of luck. Every penny's going on Jasmine's school fees. Well, when she's old enough.'

'I didn't—'

'You got any idea how much these places charge? Three or four grand, aye, and that's not a year, that's every sodding term!'

He helped himself to a chunk of brie. 'I'm not after a loan, I want to know how you . . . you know, decided to take the cash?'

'Hrmmmph. . .' Steel narrowed her eyes. Then jerked a thumb at him as Susan came back from the pantry with a multipack of Monster Munch. 'Sooz: the boy here wants to know why we took Desperate Doug's cash. How come we didn't tell his lawyers to sod off, then go round and piss on his grave?'

Susan dug into the pack and came out with a bag of pickled onion. 'We do that every year, on the anniversary of his death.' She popped the bag open. 'I was thoroughly ashamed the first time, but now we make a picnic of it, don't we?'

'Which reminds me –' Steel hopped down off her stool and crossed to the corner of the room –'time to empty Mr Rumpole's litter tray.'

Logan had an olive while she grabbed hold of the plastic tray by the patio doors and shoogled it until dark poopy monsters rose from the deep. 'You know what I mean: just because someone leaves you money in their will, it doesn't mean you've got to take it. You hated—'

'Desperate Doug MacDuff was a nasty, murdering, raping, wee shite.' Steel scooped the lumps out with a plastic trowel and tipped them into the bin. 'We took his cash so Jasmine could get a better education. The old bugger was dead, anyway.' She opened the cupboard under the sink and pulled out a brass urn from between the Flash and Cillit BANG. Gave it a shake. Pursed her lips and frowned. 'Think he's beginning to run a bit low.'

Logan tried his whisky. Warm and dark. 'So you don't
. . . *regret* taking the money?'

She unscrewed the lid from the urn, then dug a teaspoon
into the opening. 'He's dead. Fuck him.' Steel sprinkled the
ashes onto the cat litter. Then she paused, and squinted at
him. 'Why the sudden interest?'

A shrug. 'I just. . .' Don't tell her the truth! 'I just
wondered what I'd do if it was me.'

'You can either take the money, or you can be a moaning
big girl's blouse. After what that rancid old bastard did, his
debt to me's never going to be paid off. At least this way we
got *something*.' She dumped the spoon in the dishwasher,
then screwed the lid back on the final resting place of
Desperate Doug MacDuff.

Logan peeled off his jacket and draped it over the end of
the bed, hiding Samantha's charts, then wriggled out of his
tie. 'It's like a furnace in here.'

She pulled the duvet up under her arms and settled back
into the pillows. 'Don't whinge. Did you bring it?'

He leaned forward and dug in the jacket pocket, coming
out with Chalmers's carrier bag. The book went on the
bedside cabinet, next to the bottles of Lucozade and tattoo
magazines. 'Chalmers gave me a copy of *Witchfire* in the pub.
I thought she was coming on to me.'

'Ha!' Samantha's voice fell to a featureless monotone:
'That's because you're *so* damn sexy us women just can't
keep our hands off you. Ooh, you stud you. Etc.'

'You can be a sarcastic sod at times, you know that, don't
you?' He went into the other carrier bag – the one stashed
underneath his seat – and produced a tin of Stella. Still cold
from the off-licence. The ring clicked off. 'You want one?'

'Can't. Medication.'

Fair enough. The beer fizzed and crackled its way down,

cutting through the thin layer of grease left behind after the fish and chips. 'Steel thinks I should take Wee Hamish's money.'

Samantha tilted her head to one side and stared at him. 'Have you put on weight? 'Cos you're looking a bit chunkier than usual.'

'You know, there *are* other women out there. Women who might appreciate a thoughtful boyfriend like me.'

'Why are fat people always so touchy?' Samantha picked up the copy of *Witchfire*. 'So? Are you going to take the cash?'

'I'm *not* fat. Steel says it doesn't really matter where it comes from, what matters is what you do with it.'

'Kinky.' Samantha peeled the stickers off the book's front cover and dotted them onto her face. Now her forehead was 'Soon To Be A Major Motion Picture!' and her left cheek was '2 for £10!' She puffed out her cheeks and dumped the book in her lap. 'I'm bored.'

'How can I take money that's come from running protection rackets, drugs, Post Office jobs, prostitution. . .?'

'Bored, bored, bored, bored, bored.'

Typical. Might as well be talking to himself. Logan took another sip of beer. 'What happened to that Stephen King I bought you?'

Samantha's shoulders slumped. 'CD player's knackered.'

'Then get your arse better and come home.'

She smiled. 'Why didn't I think of that?' She flipped *Witchfire* over in her hands and frowned at the back for a bit. Then cleared her throat.

'"Belief can get you killed.

Forbes St John is one of the most powerful and feared men in England: leader of the Holy Inquisition, fourth in line to the throne. So what's he doing lying on his back in a condemned council estate in central Scotland, with his chest ripped open and his heart torn out?

It's 1999, two and a half centuries since a captured Charles III was beheaded in Edinburgh, bringing an end to the Act of Union. As Scotland's ruling body – the Kirk – prepares to celebrate the 250th anniversary of Headsman's Day, the last thing it needs is a diplomatic war with its militant Catholic neighbour.

Rowan Knox, one of the Kirk's elite Fingermen, will have to catch St John's killer without anyone finding out he's been murdered. But that might be the least of her problems. Talk of dark magic, demons, and witches is rife in the inner cities, children are disappearing, and the police are powerless to help.

The darkness is gathering, and Rowan is the only one standing in its way. And if she doesn't move fast, it'll tear her to shreds."'

Samantha shrugged. 'Sounds OK.' She tossed it into his lap. 'Read to me.'

'Do I look like *Jackanory*?'

'But I'm *bored*.'

'Then *you* read it.'

She crossed her arms, thumped back into the pillows. 'Thought the whole point of getting the book was you finding out what Agnes Garfield was up to?'

Sodding hell. 'Fine.' He picked the thing up. 'Acknowledgements. Writing any book is a labour of love, and—'

'Don't be a prat, no one reads that bit. Start at the beginning.'

He flipped forward a couple of pages.

'And do the voices.'

So this was what it was like to have small children.

He took another sip of Stella. 'Chapter one.

"The old woman's hands left bloody smears across the cloth as she smiled from the kitchen door. The whole place stank of meat and lavender and cats, of rendered fat and fear and rubbing liniment.

She dropped the cloth on the coffee table, amongst the jars and bottles. 'Now, are you sure he doesn't want an anaesthetic, dear? It's—'"'

'You're not doing the voices!'
It was going to be a long night.

Logan eased back into the room with a mug of tea from the nurses' station in one hand and a couple of pilfered custard creams in the other. He settled into his seat. 'Quarter past ten, and it's like *Night of the Living Dead* out there. All oldies shuffling about in their slippers wanting to eat people's brains.' He dunked a custard cream then sooked off the rind of mushy biscuit. 'Where were we?'

'Mrs Shepherd just necklaced Thomas Leis. Crazy psycho bitch that she is.'

He put his tea and biscuits down on the bedside cabinet and picked up the book again. 'It's all a bit . . . *violent*, isn't it?'

'Don't be such a wimp. Read.'

'One more hour, then that's it. Some of us have work tomorrow.'

The nurse with the thick eyebrows and tufty black moustache checked Samantha's chart. 'I think it's sweet that you're reading to her. Wish I could get Benny to read to me. He's like a slug when he gets home, just slithers up onto the couch and that's him for the night. One day I'm going to snap and tip a whole carton of salt over him.'

Logan stretched the knots out of his back. 'Well, she can

have another couple of chapters, then I'm off. Crime doesn't solve itself.'

The nurse smiled, kissed him on the cheek – the fine hairs on her top lip tickled – then left them alone.

Samantha rolled her eyes. 'I know, I know: you're a stud-muffin.'

'Do you want more book or not? It's twenty to twelve, I *can* just go home.'

No reply.

'Thought so.' He picked the book up again, skim-reading to where they'd stopped. 'Right:

"His screams echoed around the tiny bathroom, each wave building on the last – deafening and harsh.

Rowan took a handful of his collar and forced his face down beneath the filthy water again. It sloshed over the edge of the bath onto the cracked floor tiles as he bucked and wriggled beneath the surface. Panicking. Hands tied behind his back, ankles tied to the rusty taps. The only way he'd be able to escape was drown. And she was far too professional for that.

She hauled him up again and he coughed, spluttered, then retched, making the water even dirtier than before.

He sagged there, his shoulders jerking as he sobbed. 'It wasn't me, I didn't know. . .'

'You see, Mr Breull, some people think the trial by water's the easiest of the three. I mean, what's a little water compared to trial by blood, or fire?'

He went under again, and she leaned her full weight between his shoulders, pinning him to the bottom of the bath. Counted to twelve. Then pulled him back up.

More coughing, more retching, filthy liquid streamed from his nose.

'One more time: what did you do with Helen Fraser?'

'Please. . . Please, I didn't have any choice. . .'

Rowan slammed his head into the bathroom wall, hard enough to crack the tiles and leave a smear of blood. 'SHE WAS SIX!'

And back under the water he went."'

Tuesday

23

'Ow. . .' A burning knife sliced its way down his spine, then dug its glowing tip into his hip. Twisting. 'God. . .'

Silence.

Then the alarm on his phone warbled again.

Logan jabbed a finger at the screen till it shut up. Sagged in the visitor's chair, legs still up on the bed.

Cramp chewed at his calves. Gritting his teeth, he levered his feet down from the wrinkled hospital sheets onto the grey terrazzo floor – cool beneath his socks. Scrubbed at his face. His voice came out as a deep gravelly growl. 'Unngh. . . Time is it?'

Blink. Took a few goes to get his phone in focus, but eventually 06:30 wobbled into view. 'Crap.'

Whose bloody clever idea was it to read a dirty big lump of a novel till four in the morning?

Samantha was asleep, lying there with her mouth open. Didn't matter how many times he told her the spiders were going to sneak in and lay eggs in her head, she always slept like a corpse. Lucky for some.

He winced his way out of the chair and limp-shuffled through into the room's tiny bathroom. Hauled off his shirt and had a spot-wash in the sink with the bar of institutional soap that smelled like a dentist's office. Rubbed a finger around his teeth till they were all squeaky. Spat. Stared at the baggy-eyed, tousle-haired wreck in the mirror.

It'd have to do.

Logan hauled his shirt on again, crept back into the room, kissed Sam on the forehead, gathered up his jacket and shoes, and tip-toed out of the door.

The corridor was quiet, just the far off wub-wub-wub of a floor polisher, and the all-pervading hum of the hospital. He found a seat and pulled on his shoes.

Someone tutted. 'Oh dear. . .'

He looked up and there was Claire, her blue nurse's uniform pristine and ironed.

She shook her head. 'Did you sleep in your clothes again? You look like someone sat on you when you were wet.'

He tied his laces. 'You're in early.'

'Bill's piles are killing him, and when Bill can't sleep no one else is allowed to either.' A sigh. 'I keep telling him, your haemorrhoids' existence is conditional on your perception of them, the pain you feel is a result of *a priori* reasoning based on your construct of self. Of course he says they're not conditional and his perception of them is derived from experience which makes it *a posteriori*, not some airy fairy *a priori* notion outwith the scope of empirical knowledge.'

Logan stared at her. 'The evenings must be just packed.'

A shrug. 'For René Descartes it was, "I think, therefore I am." With Bill it's, "My arse hurts, so I've got piles."'

He stood. Smiled. 'Any chance you can keep the metaphysics down to a dull roar today? She was up late last night.'

'We'll do our best. Next time, let me know you're staying over and we'll get you a wee bed set up.' She glanced down the corridor towards Sam's room. Then lowered her voice.

'So are you still getting that cat, because if you are, I have a source. . .?'

'She wants to call it Cthulhu.'

'That's . . . er . . . *distinctive.*' Claire patted him on the arm. 'Now, do you fancy a cuppa before you head off?'

The briefing room was full of cardboard boxes, so they convened in the main CID office instead – the whole of dayshift squeezed in between the desks and partitions, staring at the projection screen behind Steel's head. The necklacing victim, smoke and flames caught in freeze-frame, mouth open in that tortured silent scream.

She hauled up her trousers and scowled at everyone. 'Do you *really* need me to tell you what's going to happen if those Weegie bawbags get here and we haven't solved this sodding necklacing thing?'

A wee DC with trophy-handle ears and a squaddie haircut stuck his hand up. 'Is this still a gangland hit?'

'Depends, doesn't it?'

'Only, you know, it's pretty much identical to what happens in this book, *Witch*—'

'We know. Now—'

'Well, what if it's a publicity stunt? You know, the production company are trying to whip up a bit of interest in the media? Get some buzz out about the film. . .'

Silence.

Logan shifted in his seat. Here we go.

The tips of the constable's ears went pink. 'Well, it's . . . possible, isn't it?'

Steel stared at the floor for a moment. 'Are you *seriously* suggesting they chained some poor sod to a metal stake, jammed a tyre over his head, and set fire to it, so they could get a wee slot on Lorraine Bloody Kelly?'

Constable Idiot put his hand down.

'Right, if there's no one else wants to make an arse of themselves, we've had three dead bodies in as many days. I'm no' having another one, *understand*? This is it: no more!'

She dug into a plastic carrier bag and pulled out a bottle of Highland Park. Held it above her head. 'And if anyone catches the bastard before Strathclyde gets here, this is yours.'

Chalmers shifted in her seat. 'What about the victim from last night? Initial reports say they may have been staked out on the kitchen floor and tortured. Two torture victims in three days: could be related?'

'We're no' ruling it out, but we're no' relying on it either.' Steel clunked the bottle down on the table next to her. 'Right, people, just in case you're thinking of running off on your own to play on the swings: chain of command. As these are all high-profile deaths our beloved Assistant Chief Constable is carrying the bucket of jobbies, and I'm in charge of doling them out to whoever's pissed me off the most that day. For now, DI McRae's running the necklacing case, Leith's doing the torture victim, and Bell's on our skeleton. If they hand you a turd, you thank them kindly and deal with it. 'Cos if I hear you're shirking jobbie duty, I'll hunt you down and make sure you're pooping shoe leather for a week. Understand?'

Silence.

Steel squared her shoulders. 'Ladies, and gentlemen, we are *no'* at home to Mr Fuckup today. Who are we no' at home to?'

The response wasn't much more than an embarrassed murmur. 'Mr Fuckup.'

'I CAN'T HEAR YOU! WHO ARE WE NO' AT HOME TO?'

Better this time: 'Mr Fuckup.'

'ONE MORE TIME!'

They bellowed it out: 'WE ARE NOT AT HOME TO MR FUCKUP!'

242

'Damn right we're no'.' She smiled, nodded. 'Now get out there and catch me those bloody killers!'

Logan made it as far as his office, a mug of coffee clutched in one hand shrouding him in bitter steam and the promise of actually managing to stay awake until lunchtime.

'Guv?'

He closed his eyes. Counted to five.

'Guv?'

When he opened them again, PC Guthrie was still standing there, pale eyebrows making a question mark on his podgy face.

Well, it was worth a try. 'Whatever you want, it can wait till I've had my coffee.'

Guthrie followed him into the office. 'Erm. . . Do you remember DI Insch? Well, he's just been on the phone about some bloke going mental at one of his starlets. Says he wants you to deal.'

'Does he now.' Logan eased himself into his seat, back creaking and pinging all the way down. The coffee was spoon-meltingly strong, making things fizz behind his eyes. 'Send a patrol car.'

The constable shuffled his police-issue boots. 'He was kind of insistent it had to be you, Guv.'

Of course he was. Logan put his coffee down. Sighed. Then stood. 'Get a car.'

PC Guthrie hauled the CID pool car into the car park behind a swanky boutique hotel on Queen's Road. A middle-aged man in black trousers and burgundy waistcoat was sitting on a low wall, a clump of blood-soaked tissue held against his nose. Scarlet stains covered the front of his white shirt. He looked up as Guthrie hauled on the handbrake and climbed out into the morning sun.

Logan levered himself out of his seat, something sharp grinding away at the base of his spine.

The man with the bloody nose didn't say a word, just pointed back towards the rear of the hotel and an open fire exit.

Logan nodded at Guthrie. 'Take his statement.'

Guthrie looked left, then right, then dropped his voice to a whisper. 'Thought we were keeping this low key?'

'Tell me, Constable, do you remember what Steel said would happen if you don't deal with your allotted jobbie when you're told to?'

'Ah. . . Right.' A blush made his chubby cheeks glow. 'Yes, Guv. Statement. . .' He pulled out his notebook and shuffled in front of Mr Bleedy. 'Now, sir, I need you to tell me what happened, in your own words.'

Logan left him to it.

Inside the hotel, the corridor was lined in dark-red flock wallpaper with brass sconces every couple of metres casting pools of golden light. Tasteful in a 'tart's boudoir' kind of way. Plain wooden doors sat every eight foot or so, signed with things like 'PRIVATE' and 'STAFF ONLY'. One three doors down lay open, with someone's leg sticking out into the hallway, their blue sock twitching in time to muffled grunts from inside the room.

Kinky.

He peered in. A lanky man lay face down on the floor, one shoe on, one shoe off, struggling beneath a huge lump of muscle in a bomber jacket, jeans and a red T-shirt.

Mr Muscle had one knee in the base of the guy's spine, one arm twisted up behind his back, and his face mashed into the grey carpet tiles. A translucent coil of wire spiralled out of Mr Muscle's left ear and disappeared into his collar. So he was either a concerned citizen with hearing difficulties, or a professional security thug.

Logan leaned against the doorframe. 'Are we all having fun?'

Mr Muscle looked up and gave him a thin smile. His face was round and smooth, like a large, slightly scary baby. 'Mr Whyte here is having a difficult time adjusting to being single. Aren't you, Mr Whyte?'

The lanky bloke wriggled some more, muffled swearing just about audible through the carpet tile's pile.

'Any chance you can let Mr Whyte go?'

'I don't know if that would be advisable.' Mr Muscle pulled a face. 'The last time we tried releasing Mr Whyte, he assaulted one of the hotel staff.'

Logan stepped into the room. Then paused. Something in there smelled like raw meat and wet dog. . . He pulled out his handcuffs and secured Mr Whyte's other wrist, then hauled it over so he could grab the one Mr Muscle had in a death grip. Click. 'OK, let him up.'

Mr Muscle took his knee out of the guy's spine, grabbed him by the shoulders, and hauled him to his feet.

One side of Robbie Whyte's face was scratched and glowing with carpet burn, other than that, there didn't seem to be a mark on him. What he did have was a rumpled quiff, designer stubble, bright-blue eyes ringed in red veins, and a dimple in his chin big enough to hide a Malteser. That, the hairy arms, and the pot belly, made him look like a boy band member who'd gone to seed. His grey T-shirt had 'GOD'S GIFT' printed on it in big flesh-coloured letters. The 'i' in 'gift' was shaped to look like a willy.

'Get off me!' He kicked out, just missing Logan's knee. 'I'll fucking kill you!' The smell of stale beer, whisky, and kebab oozed out of him.

Logan took a step back and produced his warrant card. 'Threatening a police officer is an *offence*, Mr Whyte. As is assault.'

'I never did nothing! NOTHING!'

Mr Muscle tightened his grip on the guy's shoulders. 'Mr Whyte, I strongly suggest you cooperate with the authorities.'

Logan swapped his warrant card for his notebook. 'Where's Nichole Fyfe?'

The big man nodded back over his shoulder. 'Miss Fyfe is upstairs in her room. She's deeply upset.'

'I didn't do *nothing*.'

Mr Muscle gave him a little shake. 'Mr Whyte here has been hanging around the hotel for at least the last three days. Last night he tried to make contact with Miss Fyfe. She informed him that their relationship was over four years ago, and asked him to leave her alone.'

Whyte's face darkened. 'That's *crap*. You bring her in here, and she'll tell you—'

'This morning, Miss Fyfe opened her hotel-room door and discovered a parcel in the corridor outside, addressed to her.'

'It's bollocks. He's lying—'

'When Miss Fyfe opened it, she discovered the severed head of a Yorkshire terrier, wrapped up in press clippings about her involvement with the filming of *Witchfire*.'

'I told you it wasn't me!'

Logan stared at him. 'Seriously?'

Mr Muscle nodded at a cardboard box sitting in the middle of the room's desk. It was still partially wrapped in gold and silver paper. Logan peeked inside. It wasn't a big terrier, the head no bigger than his fist, the fur around the muzzle and neck spiky with dark-red clots, both eyes open, staring up out of the box at him.

At least that explained the smell.

The head nestled in a bowl of scrunched newspaper and pages torn from magazines, all of it stained with blood. Looked as if there were a couple of decent fingerprints on a photo-spread from *Hello!* 'FABULOUS NICHOLE SPARKLES AT ABERDEEN CHARITY AUCTION', the whorls and deltas picked out in scarlet.

'You killed a dog? What is *wrong* with you?'

'I didn't do it! They're fitting me up! Ask Nichole: ask her, she'll tell you it's all lies. He's trying to make me look bad. He's—'

Mr Muscle gave him another shake. 'I arrived with the studio car to collect Miss Fyfe at six this morning. Mr Whyte was waiting outside, hiding behind the hotel bins. I approached him to ascertain why he wasn't respecting Miss Fyfe's request for privacy and he threw an empty bottle of Bell's Whisky at me.'

'I never! He's lying!'

Logan looked Mr Muscle up and down. 'You give evidence in court a *lot*, don't you?'

'Occupational hazard.' His massive shoulders shrugged beneath the shiny bomber jacket. 'But I believe the incident with the bottle will be captured on the hotel's security cameras. After Mr Whyte's assault on my person, I restrained him and contacted Mr Insch for further instructions.'

Logan stopped writing. 'Let me guess, he asked you not to make it official?'

'Sadly, that was before I learned about the package. As I said, Miss Fyfe is *considerably* distressed.'

Not surprising. Most hotels left newspapers outside the rooms in the morning, not severed Yorkshire terriers' heads.

As soon as the cell door closed the sobbing started.

PC Guthrie peered through the clear plastic evidence bag and into the open box. His shoulders dropped an inch. 'Poor little fella. . .'

Logan patted him on the back. 'Get it up to fingerprints. Then off to the mortuary.'

He sucked his teeth, mouth turning down at the edges. 'The Ice Queen's going to *love* that. Can't we just—'

'And I want a full criminal history of laughing boy on my desk in twenty minutes, tops.'

A sigh. Then Guthrie clutched the evidence bag to his chest, staring down at the dog. 'How could anyone do that to a wee doggie?' He shuffled off.

Logan slid back the hatch in the cell door. Robbie Whyte stood in the middle of the small room, arms hanging by his sides, his baggy jeans barely covering his pants, his trainers like boats. That's what happened when they confiscated your belt and shoelaces.

Whyte's shoulders trembled.

Logan knocked on the cold metal door. 'You sure you don't want to just . . . tell someone why you did it?'

'It's all lies. . .' Whyte ground the heel of one hand into his left eye. 'She still loves me. I *know* she still loves me.'

'Thought the expression was, "Say it with flowers." Not, "Severed dogs' heads."' A pause. 'Was it your dog? Or did you just pick one at random?'

'She always wanted a yorkie. Mad, eh? Smelly, yappy, little dog like that. So I got her one off a mate.' He sniffed. Scrubbed at his eyes again. 'Before that talent scout tosser spotted her, she was. . .' Whyte gave a one-shouldered shrug. 'Then she did that bloody advert for tampons – "Look at me, I'm roller-skating with a penguin!" and that was it. *Suddenly* she was too good for us.'

'So you hacked the head off a Yorkshire terrier? That made sense to you?'

'Didn't even take the dog. Can you believe that? Walked out and left us both behind, like we were nothing to her. What sort of person does that?'

'What sort of person decapitates their own dog?'

Whyte hunched over into himself, his voice dropping to

a harsh whisper. 'Nichole's *mine*. She's not anyone else's. She knows that. . .'

Logan slid the hatch shut again, pulled out his phone and scrolled through his contacts until he got to the one marked, 'Nutjobs-R-Us'.

It rang, and rang, and rang . . . then a broad Liverpudlian accent boomed out of the earpiece. 'Logan, haven't heard from you in ages, is everything OK? Are you persevering with the talking therapy?'

'Yeah, I need you to come in and look at someone. . .'

24

DI Leith cracked a yawn, showing off a mouthful of fillings. He blinked, rubbed a hand across the stubble on his chin: grey to go with the short-back-and-sides clinging precariously onto his scalp. The washboard wrinkles on his forehead deepened. 'I'm just asking you to take a *look* at it, McRae. Half an hour. Forty-five minutes tops.'

Logan shifted the folder to his other arm, balancing the polystyrene cup and grease-windowed paper bag on top as he reached for the door handle. 'Can't. I've got a stalker in the cells on animal cruelty and assault charges who's probably going to need sectioned, and Steel's on the warpath about the necklacing case. You heard her.'

Leith slumped against the wall and let loose another yawn. 'We both know it's not going to happen, OK? We can't just pluck a result out of thin air because she wants to stick it to the review team. The trail for our torture victim is still viable. We need to chase it down before it goes cold.'

'So *you* do it then.' He turned the handle and pushed through into his office. A rumpled-looking Rennie was slouched in the visitor's chair, blond hair sticking out at random angles, as if he'd had a fight with the styling gel and lost. The bags under his eyes were even more impressive than Leith's.

Rennie scrambled out of the chair. 'Guv.'

Leith slumped into the vacated spot. 'Thought I told you to go home.'

'Need to talk to DI McRae, Guv.'

Logan settled behind his desk, cricked the plastic lid off his coffee, then unwrapped the bacon buttie. 'He's right: go home. You look like an extra from a zombie film.' The squeezy bottle of tomato sauce was locked away in the bottom drawer, where the thieving sods on nightshift couldn't get at it. Logan liberated it and slathered the bacon in scarlet.

'Come on, McRae, I *can't* do it myself: I've been up all night, the post mortem's at half nine and there's no way that's going to be done before lunchtime. I need an experienced pair of eyes on the ground *now*, not this afternoon.' Leith thumped a blue folder onto Logan's in-tray. 'I'll owe you one.'

'You already owe me one.'

'Fine, so I'll owe you *two*. Please?'

Logan eased open the folder's front flap. Photograph: a blackened bloated body specked with mould, lying on a stainless-steel cutting table. The skin was lined with tiny dark-purple cuts each one surrounded by darker circular mottling that *might* have been bruises. Difficult to tell with the remains being so decomposed. No hair on the head, groin, armpits, or chest. Same as their necklacing victim. Logan closed the folder again and took a bite of his buttie. Bacon crunched between his teeth, filling his head with its smoky salty tang. 'What about Ding-Dong?'

'Detective Inspector Bell couldn't find his arse with both hands if you duct-taped them to it. Come on.'

He licked a blob of sauce from the side of his mouth. 'OK, but if Steel asks, I'm off doing something about the necklaced guy. Deal?'

Leith stood. 'Deal.' Then made for the door.

As soon as it shut, Rennie crumpled into the seat again, arms hanging at his sides, head thrown back, showing off a stubbly Adam's apple. 'Urrrrrrrgh. . .'

'I told you to go home.'

'Why can't everything be like it used to?'

'You're making the place look untidy.'

'No, seriously.' He raised his arms, then let them flop down again. 'Being detective sergeant's a crap job. All the DIs and Steel treat you like crap, all the DCs and uniform whinge and bitch and give you crap about everything you ask them to do. It's like . . . being the filling in a crap sandwich.'

Logan took Leith's folder from the in-tray and pulled out the photos inside. 'My heart bleeds.'

'We used to be so happy. . .'

'So resign. Tell Steel you don't want to be a DS any more.'

A snort. 'Yeah, good luck explaining *that* to the wife.' He wrapped his arms around his head. 'Why couldn't it have been a simple one-punch murder, or a nice easy domestic?'

Logan spread the photos out across the desk. The close-ups of the face were the worst, there was almost nothing human left, just a battered lopsided mess swollen after four days in a warm room, speckled with orange and green mould. Whoever it was had even shaved off the poor sod's eyebrows. The eyes were two black empty slits – always the first to go when decomposition set in.

Each hand and foot had its own photograph, thick lines of bruising circling the wrists and ankles. Fingertips and toes pulped.

Christ. . . Logan wrapped his bacon buttie up in its napkin and dumped it in the bin. Not hungry any more. Even the coffee tasted sour now.

'—never going anywhere? Guv? Hello?'

He blinked at Rennie. The sergeant was staring at him.

No idea. He put the photos back in the folder. 'You think you've got it tough? Ever since McPherson left it's been nothing but paperwork, and strategy meetings, and balancing budgets, and manpower rotas, and operational targets, and key performance indicators.' The folder went back in his in-tray. 'I *dream* of being a DS again. Don't know you're born, that's your problem.'

A big, theatrical sigh swelled Rennie's body, then deflated it back to floppy-armed despondency. 'You'll be sorry when I'm signed off on the stress.'

'At least then I won't have to listen to you whinge.' He pulled out his notebook. 'Tell me about the scene.'

Rennie shuddered. 'He'd been dead on that kitchen floor for *ages*. Flies everywhere.'

'Forced entry?'

'If they did, they picked the lock. No broken windows, no jimmied doors.'

'So whoever it was, they had a key. . .' Logan wrote, 'ESTATE AGENTS?' in his notebook and underlined it twice.

'Or someone left a window open and the satanic wee shite sneaked in and closed it after they killed him and did a runner?'

'Possible. You talk to the neighbours?'

Rennie pulled a face and rolled his eyes. 'Pair of coffin dodgers. Didn't see anything; didn't *want* to see anything.' His voice jumped into a wobbly parody of old age: 'Oh, Sergeant, it's too *terrible* to think about, *why* did the Abernethys have to move to Dubai, oh the world's such a *terrible* place these days, they should bring back hanging.'

'What about the other side, did. . .' A frown narrowed Logan's eyes. 'Wait a minute: satanic?'

'Big time: drew an eight-foot magic circle on the lino in

253

the kitchen. Bloody thing was like a conga-line for maggots.'
He shifted in his seat, pulled his chin back, frowning. 'Why
are you looking at me like that?'

Logan pointed at the door. 'Go: I want copies of the crime-
scene photos on my desk in five minutes. And make sure
there's some good ones of the magic circle.'

'Urgh. . .' Rennie hauled himself out of the chair and
slouched from the room, leaving the office door lying wide
open behind him.

Logan grabbed his phone and put in a call to ex-DI Insch,
stuffing an extra set of photos into the blue folder with the
post-mortem shots while it rang.

The big man's voice boomed out of the earpiece. *'About
time you called back! I told you to have a word with Robbie Whyte,
not arrest him!'*

Call him back? Logan pulled the mobile from his ear and
poked at the screen. Four voicemails and three text messages.
All from Insch's number. Ah. . .

'Been in meetings all morning, so I—'

*'What part of "keep it low key" did you have difficulty under-
standing?'*

'He gave Nichole Fyfe a gift-wrapped severed dog's head
and assaulted two people. I didn't have any choice.'

*'CHOICE? If you'd got your finger out and spoken to him when
I asked you to, it wouldn't have happened and I wouldn't have my
lead actress bawling her eyes out in her trailer unable to do any
BLOODY WORK!'*

Wonderful. A bollocking from Insch. Just like the good
old days.

'You said to get in touch if I needed anything.'

'You think you deserve a favour?'

'I – didn't – have – any – choice. I'm trying to solve three
murders here, OK? I'm sorry if that's *inconveniencing* you in
any way.'

Silence from the other end of the phone. Then, finally, *'What do you want?'*

'How about the name and number of your witchcraft consultant?'

'Wow.' The man in the leather jacket rubbed a hand across his downturned mouth and neatly trimmed beard. 'And you're sure I'm supposed to be in here?' He'd hauled his long blond hair back into a ponytail. That and the beard, the chiselled features, and broad shoulders made Alex Hay look more like a Viking than Aberdeen City Council's chief historian.

Logan tucked the folder under his arm and pointed to the path of raised metal trays beneath his feet, the little metal legs keeping them a couple of inches above the patio slabs outside the back door. 'Forensics have got everything they're going to get; just stick to the walkway and you'll be fine.'

Alex pulled on a smile that didn't seem all that happy with his face. 'Does it always smell like this?'

Logan patted him on the back – it was like patting a brick wall. Had to be solid muscle underneath the leather. 'Don't worry, it'll be worse inside.'

'Worse. Right. Good. . .'

Logan turned the key in the lock and pushed the door open. The smell of meat, long past its sell-by date oozed out from the kitchen, sunk its claws into the base of his stomach and twisted. He blinked, turned his face away, breathing through his mouth. The air tasted as bad as it smelled. 'OK, maybe masks would be a good idea.'

He put one on, then passed the other over. Waiting until the historian had his in place before stepping off the walkway onto the one-foot-square patch of linoleum just inside the door marked with black-and-yellow tape as safe. Then from there straight back onto the first tray of the path set up in the kitchen.

It was a reasonably modern space, but completely empty. No pots, no pans, no toaster, no kettle and no furniture, just the little drifts of fly carcases piled up by the skirting boards. The walls were a disturbing shade of rippling grey.

A ragged pentagram, about six-foot across, sat in the middle of the blue-and-cream linoleum. It was lumpen, spotted, as if it'd been made by melting black candle wax onto the floor, layered over with a series of concentric circles punctuated by incomprehensible words and squiggles. Like a demonic sheriff's badge. The smears and pools of dried blood just added to the image.

Five holes pierced the linoleum, a couple of inches in from the pentagram's points.

Alex paused on the threshold, rubbing his fingertips down the front of his jacket, as if that would keep them clean. He stared down at the gap in the walkway. 'I thought we weren't supposed to—'

'They can't lay the trays where the door goes, can they?'

'Ah, OK, yes, got you. . .' He cleared his throat, then stepped inside. Clunked the door shut behind him.

The noise must have startled the flies, because the walls went from grey to magnolia as they buzzed into the rank air, bobbing and swirling like angry smoke. Alex froze. 'I. . .'

'Ignore them.' The walkway detoured around the pentagram and headed further off into the house. Logan stopped at the top of the five-pointed star. 'Well, you're the witchcraft expert: is that what I think it is?'

'Ah, OK. . .' A cough. 'Do you have any gloves?'

Logan handed him a pair, and the historian struggled them on over trembling fingers.

He hunkered down on the walkway, head moving from side to side. 'It's a magic circle.'

Pause. 'I'm going to need *slightly* more than that.'

'Ah, yes, of course. . .' He puffed out a breath. 'Right, this

256

is basically a corruption of the circles described in *The Key of Solomon*. Going by strict Qabalistic belief, the pentagram shouldn't be there, it's wrong. It shouldn't cross the outer circles either.'

He pointed at the centre of the pentagram, where four words sat inside the innermost band. '*Septen, merid, orien, occid* – north, south, east and west. They orient the circle. The next layer: those things that look like musical notes? They're the letter Tau, last character in the Hebrew alphabet, they stand for the perfection of God's creation.' He shifted over a couple of paces. 'Next band out is, *Eloah, Tetragrammaton, Eheieh* and *Elion* – *Tetragrammaton* represents the true name of God, the rest are emanations. And all around the outside is: *Miserere mei Deus secundum magnam*. Basically, "Have mercy upon me, oh God, according to your loving kindness."'

Logan opened DI Leith's folder and pulled out the crime-scene photographs. Selected one that showed the whole room, then held it out. 'Victim was staked out in the middle.'

Alex held a hand against the base of his throat, as if he was trying to swallow something stuck there. 'OK, that's just *wrong*.' He made a gulping sound. Then a groan. Then lurched to his feet and stumbled for the door, making the walkway clang. Thump, out into the back garden, ripping his facemask off.

The door swung shut again, silencing the sound of violent retching.

25

Samantha made chewing noises down the phone at him, as if she was eating something. *'Well, you can't just do nothing and hope it'll go away, can you?'*

Logan wandered up the street in the hazy sunshine, plastic bag from the wee shop swinging at his side. 'Well, what am I supposed to do? I can't accept a cheque for—'

'You're not accepting it, are you? All you're doing is nominating a charity.'

'But that makes me—'

'No it doesn't. Thirty grand could make a massive difference to some charities, so grow a pair and pick one.'

He stopped, leaned against a garden wall, and peered down the street at the handful of journalists and TV crews loitering outside the Abernethy house, doing bits to camera with the 'FOR SALE' sign and line of 'POLICE' tape in the background. They looked about as bored as it was possible to be and still remain awake. 'It's not right.'

'You're getting as bad as Rennie.' More chewing. *'Fancy Chinese for tea tonight?'*

'Can't, I've got that NPIA review thing. And what am I supposed to do about being executor for Wee Hamish's will?'

'*That I* can't *help you with. Don't stay out too late.*' And she was gone. Some rotten sods just enjoyed other people's misfortune.

Right. Back to work. He tucked the plastic bag under his jacket, the cold leaching into his ribs as he marched up the road. No making eye contact, face the front, act like any other normal person out for a walk. He passed the BBC outside broadcast van, a Renault with two journalists reading newspapers and smoking cigarettes. Not one of them looked up. So far, so good. Then he took a sharp left, ducking under the line of barrier tape and onto the Abernethys' driveway.

The uniform standing guard nodded at him. 'Guv.'

By the time the assembled members of the press realized he wasn't just a passer-by he was through the gate at the side of the property.

A voice behind him: 'Have you identified the remains yet?'

Then another: 'Do you have any suspects?'

And another: 'Is it true the victim was dismembered?'

He clunked the gate shut.

Alex Hay was where he'd left him, sitting on a wooden bench in the back garden with his head between his knees.

'Feeling any better?'

The historian shrugged. 'Sorry, I didn't think it would. . . The smell was a bit. . .'

'Yeah, I know.' Logan produced the carrier bag, dug out a tin of Diet Coke and handed it over. 'Got you a Cornetto. Might settle your stomach.'

Alex cracked the tin and took a sip of Coke, swishing it between his teeth as if it was mouthwash. 'The whole thing's wrong.'

'Violent death always is.' Logan perched on the edge of the bench and stretched his legs out. Helped himself to a bottle of water and a choc ice. 'They wash the body

259

when they're getting it ready for post mortem. Want to see?'

'He was staked out *inside* the pentagram, right? That's the wrong way round. A magic circle like that's for protection, you create one and then you stand in it when you're dealing with Satanic forces. Summoning the devil, or demons, or spirits, or raising the dead, or questioning witches. They can't cross the circle and their powers can't either.' He put the can down and peeled the wrapper off the Cornetto, licking the ice cream from the underside of the cardboard top. 'It's like a condom that stops evil screwing you.'

Logan took out the pre-post-mortem photos again and placed them on the bench between them. 'Didn't do our victim much good, did it?'

'That's *why* it's wrong. In *Witchfire*, Hunter created this kind of hodgepodge of different belief systems, stealing things from all over the place. I suppose that's the joy of writing an alternative history, go back far enough and you can change things to suit yourself: who's going to complain?'

'That magic circle: it's in the book, isn't it?' A lot of the story was a blur, but there were definitely a few magic circles in it.

'The Fingermen call it the Ring Knot, it's meant to keep them safe during interrogations.' He glanced down at the photographs. 'How could anyone *do* that to another human being?'

Logan licked a dribble of melted choc ice from his wrist. 'You'd be surprised.'

'You see all those little wounds? It's called "pricking", they do it to find the Devil's mark. Theory was that when you enter into the Devil's service, he gives you this mark that shows you're his. It's meant to be impervious to pain, so they'd jab you all over with pins and knives, looking for

260

some spot where it didn't hurt. If they found it, that meant you were a witch. And they *always* found it, even if it wasn't there.' He took a deep breath and checked the photos again. 'In the fifteenth century, the *Malleus Maleficarum* was the witch-finders' bible. It details shaving off all the witches' body hair before interrogation begins, because they could be hiding something underneath – a charm, or power, or something else they can use against the inquisitor.'

'But he should've been outside the circle.'

'The circle's for protection: if you were the Fingerman, why would you want to protect the witch?' He stared into the depths of his Coke can. 'Did he . . . was it the loss of blood? You know . . . that killed him.'

'Won't find out till they've done the post mortem.' Logan pulled out the other set of photographs – the ones from Saturday evening – and placed them on top of the first lot. The unknown necklacing victim stared up at them with cooked eyes. 'The trial by fire. Identical to the book.'

Alex just sat there with his mouth hanging open.

A wasp swooped down onto the Cornetto in his hand, buzzing like a happy serial killer.

'Half strangled, then burned alive.'

'In Scotland they veerit you first. . . Wrap a rope around your neck and twist it while you're tied to the stake, waiting for them the light the fire and. . . Ayabastard!' He dropped the ice-cream cone and flapped his hand around, dancing up from the bench.

Logan took another bite of choc ice. 'Why didn't they necklace the body in there?'

'Bloody thing stung me. . .' He sucked on the back of his hand.

'I mean, they necklaced the other victim, why not this one?'

'Bloody wasps. . .'

Logan's phone rang in his pocket. He pulled it out: unknown number. 'Hello?'

'Hello? DI McRae? It's April. I mean, Dr Graham. The forensic anthropologist?'

'It's OK, I know who you are.'

'Good. Yes, well, I thought you'd want to know: I've almost finished the facial reconstruction. Do you want me to start on the skeletonized remains from the caravan roof next?'

'Give me . . .' Logan checked his watch, 'half an hour.'

'If you can get them to OK the budget for it, a facial reconstruction could—'

'Have you heard anything from your friend the isotope man?'

A pause. *'I only sent the samples off last night, he—'*

'Chase him up, tell him it's a priority.'

The historian settled onto the bench, flexing his hand and scowling at the swollen nodule between his knuckles. 'Ow. . .'

'I'll be in soon as I've sorted something out.' Logan hung up and stuck the phone back in his pocket. Stood. 'I'd better get going.'

Alex looked up at him. 'You think it's someone involved in the film?'

'Something like that.'

A sigh. 'Horrible to think it might be someone I *work* with.'

'We're pursuing several lines of enquiry.' He checked his watch again. 'Look, I hate to hurry you, I really have to get—'

'Yes, of course.' The historian levered himself to his feet, sucked at the lump on his hand again, then followed Logan down the crazy-paving path towards the house. 'Do you believe in witches?'

'Of course I don't.'

'In the book, neither does Rowan. A witch-finder that

262

doesn't believe in witches. She doesn't believe in talismans like that either.'

Logan stopped. Turned.

The historian was pointing at the guttering beside the kitchen door.

'Talismans?' Two steps back and there it was: a knot of three small bones, tied with a black ribbon. Just like the ones at the caravan.

'In *Witchfire*, there's a Vodun bokor who uses them to protect himself from his enemies.' A shrug. 'I said the belief system was a bit of a hodgepodge.'

'You told me you were finished with the scene!' Logan shifted the mobile from one ear to the other, foot flat to the floor. The Fiat's engine whined and complained, the speedometer jiggling its way up to seventy as it hammered down the Tyrebagger hill.

The SEB head tech's voice was thin, as if he was forcing it through gritted teeth. *'We* were *finished. There's nothing—'*

'Then why did I just find three human finger bones hanging outside the back door?'

'That's not—'

'Get your people back out there and do it properly!'

'Don't you—'

'You left human remains at a crime scene, John, how, *exactly*, is that doing your job? Now get. . . John?' Pause. 'John?' Typical, he'd hung up. Bloody prima donna.

Logan overtook an eighteen wheeler and tried Chalmers instead.

'Guv?'

'I want you to get over to Agnes Garfield's house and find us a DNA sample. If the parents give you any trouble, tell them it's standard procedure when someone goes missing.'

'*Don't worry, Guv: I get the feeling they'll be a lot more coop-erative now they know she's OK.*'

'Why would they. . .?' The cash-machine withdrawal – she was caught on camera. Sodding hell. 'Her parents don't know. We didn't tell them she'd been spotted taking money out of Anthony Chung's account.' Bloody *idiot*.

A pause. Then Chalmers was back with a smile in her voice. '*Even better: means I get to break the good news. Be no problem getting a sample after that. We— Oh, hold on. . .*' There was a scrunching noise, as if she'd put a hand over the mouthpiece. Then she was back. '*Constable Guthrie says there's a Dr Goulding here to see you?*'

'Put Goulding in an interview room with Robbie Whyte. I want a full psych evaluation.'

'*Emergency detention?*'

'And tell Goulding to find out if Whyte's capable of murder.' Logan stuck on the brakes, pulling into the slip lane to turn right across the dual carriageway.

'*You think he might be the one who. . .*' There was a pause. '*Who did he kill?*'

Good question.

Logan gunned the engine, nipping across the carriageway in the gap between a bread van and a minibus. 'And soon as you've got some of Agnes's DNA, make sure they test it against the necklacing victim and the body we found last night. And the bones from my roof too.'

Chalmers whistled. '*You think she killed all three of them?*'

'Bloody hope so, otherwise we've got a whole *bunch* of nutters out there murdering people.' Nutters. . . Better safe than sorry. 'Get them to test Robbie Whyte's DNA against them as well.'

There was a pause, then the intercom buzzed and the gate swung open. Logan edged the car off the road and onto the long gravel driveway. Little chunks of granite pinged and clunked in the rusting wheel-arches.

Wee Hamish Mowat's house was a big Victorian mansion in solid grey granite. All bay windows and little twiddly bits at the gables and guttering. Logan parked the Fiat next to a bright-red Land Rover Defender that didn't look as if it'd ever been off road in its life.

His phone rang as he climbed out of the car. He hit the button. 'What?'

'Laz? It's Tim. . . Tim Mair? Need to talk to you about some hooky merchandise that's—'

'It'll have to wait, Dildo, I've got something on.'

'OK. This afternoon? About three? I've got some knock-off custard creams you can cadge.'

Bloody Trading Standards and their counterfeit biscuits. 'Fine. Three.'

'I'll need at least. . .' Dildo was still talking, but Logan wasn't listening any more.

The front door opened and there was Tam 'The Man' Slessor's niece, wearing a blue nurse's uniform, white trainers, and a scowl that could sour milk. She folded her arms across her wide chest. 'He's busy.'

Back to the phone.

'. . .in Mastrick, so it shouldn't be—'

'Bye, Dildo.' He hung up, locked the Fiat and scrunched his way across the gravel to the foot of the stairs. 'Do you know it's an offence to provide a false alibi, Ms Slessor?'

A sharp-edged smile pulled at her lips. 'Reuben was here with me the whole time. At it like rabbits, we was. He's a very sensuous lover.'

Dear God, now *there* was a mental image that'd take a wire brush and Dettol to shift. 'He wasn't, he was outside my bloody caravan.'

'Nah, you must've walked into a door or something. Think

265

you can blame it on poor Reuben, when he's never done nothing to no one. You're a lying bastard.'

Logan took a step towards her.

She unfolded her arms, both fists clenched like bags of rocks. The smile grew wider. 'Come on then.'

He stopped. Took a deep breath. Counted to five. 'I need to see Hamish.'

'Mr Mowat's indisposed.'

'I'm not buggering about here, I *need* to speak—'

'You need to back up your rusty wee hatchback and get the hell off Mr Mowat's property, *that's* what you need to do.'

Logan pulled out his warrant card. 'Understand?'

She tilted her head to one side, making a crescent moon of chin-fat. 'You got a search warrant? 'Cos if you don't, you can— Hey! Come back here!'

No chance.

He marched around the side of the house, the sound of Nurse Slessor's trainers crunching on the gravel behind him. For a wee chunky lass, she was quick.

The path wrapped all the way around the house, and round the back the place opened up in a wide swathe of emerald green lawn, punctuated with trees and bushes, a flower bed in full Technicolor riot.

'Come back here!'

The conservatory doors were open, leading out onto a raised decking area surrounded by roses growing in big wooden tubs. Wee Hamish's wheelchair was parked in the sunshine, a tartan blanket draped over his knees, an oxygen mask on his face. Head down, shoulders slumped.

Logan climbed the steps.

A voice came from the garden, shouting over the drone of a lawnmower. Reuben. 'Chloe? What's wrong?'

'He's back!'

Wee Hamish twitched, left hand trembling on the blanket.

'Mmmpht?' Then he blinked watery red-rimmed eyes at Logan. 'Nnngnn, tmmmwht dn we nnn. . .?'

Nurse Slessor thumped up the stairs onto the decking. Grabbed Logan by the arm. 'I'm sorry, Mr Mowat, I told him you were asleep, but he wouldn't—'

'Get off me.' Logan shook her free. 'Hamish, we need to talk. And we need to talk *now*.'

Wee Hamish reached up and pulled off the oxygen mask. 'Logan. . .' A smile. 'To what do we owe the honour?'

'I told him, but he wouldn't listen.' She grabbed Logan's arm again. 'Reuben!'

A crackle of feet on gravel, puffing and heeching, and then Reuben's voice growled up from the garden. 'Bloody hell you doing here?'

'Hamish, I mean it.'

Thump – a steel-toecapped boot on the bottom step. 'Did you not learn your lesson last time?'

Logan turned, shoulders back, chin out. 'You want to try again, Fat Boy?'

Reuben's scarred face creased around dark slitted eyes. 'You're bloody *dead*.'

'Come on then; won't be the first time I've battered the living crap out of you, will it?'

Wee Hamish gave a dry rattling laugh, that ended in a wheeze. 'Children, children. Behave or you'll not get any ice cream.'

Logan stared straight ahead. 'This fat piece of shite ambushed me on my doorstep Sunday morning. And your nurse gave him a fake alibi.'

'I see. . .' A cough. A sigh. 'Reuben, did you ambush Detective Inspector McRae?'

'Course I didn't.'

'Chloe, was Reuben with you at the time of this alleged assault?'

267

'Yes, Mr Mowat.'

Wee Hamish nodded. 'There we are then, you must've been mistaken, Logan.'

'*Mistaken*? I WAS THERE!'

A cold smile didn't go anywhere near the old man's eyes. 'Reuben has an alibi. He tells me he didn't attack you, and I believe him. That's an end to it.'

'Is it hell!' Logan wrenched his arms free from Nurse Slessor's grip and took a step towards Reuben.

The big man grinned, showing off gaps in his teeth. 'Anytime you're ready, sunshine.'

Another leathery sigh from the wheelchair. 'Chloe, why don't you go make us a nice pot of tea. Reuben, I'm sure you've still got plenty to be getting on with.'

Reuben shrugged one shoulder, licked his lips. 'No skin off my nose.' Then he turned and swaggered off, hands in his pockets, whistling the theme tune to *The Great Escape*.

Nurse Slessor sniffed, wiped her trainers on the decking floor – as if she was a bull about to charge – then nodded and walked inside, head held high.

Wee Hamish dangled the oxygen mask from a hook built into the side of the electric wheelchair. 'There: everyone's friends again.'

Unbelievable. 'Reuben was waiting for me, *on my doorstep*, at six in the morning! How can you take that vicious bastard's—'

'Loyalty goes both ways, Logan. I can't expect my people to be loyal to me if I don't reciprocate.' He fumbled with the joystick for a moment, then the wheelchair whined forward and left, right at the edge of the decking. Off in the middle distance, Reuben was climbing back onboard a ride-on lawn mower.

Wee Hamish pointed with a shaky finger, twisted with arthritis. 'Reuben sees himself as an alpha male. And when I go. . . When I go he expects to take over the pack. You're a challenge to his ascension, so he does the only thing that makes sense to him: he lashes out. You just have to be the bigger man, accept that, and move on.'

Just accept being ambushed and punched in the face?

Logan scowled out as the lawnmower puttered into life. 'What if he's got a gun next time?'

26

A pair of fat magpies strutted up and down on the grass, white breasts like little waistcoats, as if they were barristers debating some obscure point of law in a murder trial.

The china cup shook in Wee Hamish's hand, tea sloshing from one side to the other. 'The real worry comes after I'm gone.'

Logan settled back in the folding wooden chair. 'You're not—'

'Oh, don't worry: they gave me six months three years ago. I'm going nowhere without a fight.'

Reaching into his pocket, Logan pulled out the two envelopes and placed them on the little round table. 'We need to talk about these.'

'I looked into your necklacing victim, by the way. We had a couple of . . . *meetings* about it last night. No one's admitting anything.'

'They wouldn't, would they.'

Wee Hamish smiled. 'Logan, when you do something high-profile like that, it says, "Look at me, look what I do to people who cross me!" You have to take ownership of it, or it's worthless as a warning.'

'It's not drugs-related.' It never was.

'Of course, I should never have abdicated responsibility for that part of my portfolio. Letting Reuben have his head was a weakness on my part. A good captain knows every inch of his ship.'

Logan topped up his tea. 'You need to tell Reuben to back off.'

'One thing I discovered this morning, is that we've got a drugs war going on. Nothing big, just a little one: a *skirmish* between some of our local entrepreneurs and a group of businessmen from the Far East.'

'If he threatens me, or mine, I'm going to come for him.'

'Yes.' Wee Hamish chewed on his bottom lip for a moment, eyes creased up. 'I've been thinking about that too. When he finds out I've made you executor, he may become somewhat . . . vociferous.'

'I mean it.'

'He's a simple soul, Logan, not suited to the role of commanding the ship. He won't chart a course around the icebergs, he'll call for ramming speed and head right for them.' Wee Hamish stared out into the garden. 'The sensible thing would be to cut his lifeboat loose. . . But I'm too soft-hearted, that's my problem.'

Soft-hearted? Aye, right.

Wee Hamish nodded. 'I think your wisest course of action would be to take care of that as soon as you hear the news, before he moves against you.'

'I don't want. . .' A sigh. 'I can't be executor. What am I supposed to do, hand out bits of your empire to the rival factions, sit back and hope they don't kill each other and everyone in their path? I'm a police officer.'

'The alternative is that Aberdeen goes full-steam ahead into the iceberg.'

'I can't do it.'

271

Wee Hamish smiled at him. 'Look at this skirmish between the local lads and our Oriental friends: fighting over cannabis farms. A small thing, but it'll get out of hand without someone sensible at the helm. People will always want drugs, Logan. And as long as people want them, someone will supply them. Supply and demand. Controlling it as a central entity means continuity, cuts down on conflict, keeps everyone safe and in their place.'

'So what am I supposed to do, swap my warrant card for a claw hammer?'

He reached across and laid a twitching hand on top of Logan's. The skin was papery; hot as if something deep inside was burning.

'You should do whatever you think best.'

Like run a bloody mile.

Logan parked the crumbling Fiat next to DCI Steel's MX5, successfully lowering the tone of the whole rear podium. Then leaned forward until his head rested against the steering wheel and stifled a yawn, mobile phone still clamped to his ear. 'He basically told me I had to kill Reuben.'

Samantha made a sooking noise, like she was a car mechanic about to deliver very bad news. *'Maybe he's right?'*

'I can't kill—'

'What if he came after me, would you kill him then? Because if not you're in trouble, buster!'

'Well, yes, but that's—'

'What if he hurt Jasmine? Or your brother? Or your mum? . . . Well, maybe not your mum, but the others?'

'I'm a police officer.'

'You're a wimp, more like. Remember the talk we had about growing a pair?'

Someone knocked on the passenger window, and Logan flinched. He turned his head and looked across the car. DCI

Steel peered in at him, mouthing something and pointing at her watch.

Back to the phone, voice dropped to a whisper. 'I don't want to kill anyone.'

'*Might not have any choice.*' And Samantha was gone.

Logan stuck the phone in his pocket and climbed out. 'What?'

'Where the hell have you been?'

'Dr Graham wants to do a facial reconstruction on the skeleton too.'

'Aye, I'll bet she does. I'm no' made of money.' Steel hauled out a packet of cigarettes and lit one off her battered Zippo. 'The Weegie buggers get here at two. I *need* a suspect, Laz.'

He locked the car and made for the steps down to the mortuary. 'How about Agnes Garfield: your missing teenager.'

Steel clumped along behind him. 'She's only a kid.'

'She's eighteen, obsessed with this *Witchfire* book, psychotic, and off her medication.'

Empty crisp packets, cigarette butts, and plastic fizzy-juice bottles were piled up in little drifts on the stairs. Logan picked his way through them then punched his ID into the keypad. 'The Kintore body was lying in the middle of a magic circle identical to the one witch-finders use in the book. All the cuts – that was Agnes looking for the Devil's mark, that's in the book too. There was a knot of bones outside the back door, like the ones outside my house: *they're* in the book. Of course it's her.'

Inside, the hum and roar of the extractor fans made the ceiling tiles rattle.

Logan stuck his head into the staff room, but it was empty. The pathologists' office too. The red light was on above the cutting-room door: probably still working on the poor sod who'd ended up tried for witchcraft on a kitchen floor in an abandoned house.

Steel slapped him on the shoulder. 'You know what this means, don't you? If you'd no' farted about and actually *done* something about finding her, none of this would've happened! She'd be banged up in the loony bin, and those poor sods would still be alive.'

'Think I don't know that?' He pushed through the door into the viewing area – a small room with two seats and a heavy red velvet curtain down one wall. He pulled at the cord behind it and they creaked open.

Dr Graham was on the other side of the glass, where the bodies were normally displayed, hunched over her clay-covered skull, tongue sticking out the corner of her mouth. She looked up and smiled at them. Then turned the recon-structed head around and held it up.

Steel squinted at it. Took a step forward until her nose was pressed up against the glass. 'Does he look familiar to you?'

'Who the hell are you?' Steel picked up the reconstructed head, turning it back and forth while the kettle boiled.

The staff room was just cold enough to be uncomfortable. Half-size lockers took up most of one wall, each of them decor-ated with stickers and bits cut out of newspapers. The one with the 'SHEILA DALRYMPLE' nameplate was covered in *My Little Pony* stickers and unicorns and teddy bears in tutus. A lime-green Post-it note glared out from the saccharine montage, with 'STOP STEALING MY BLOODY JAFFA CAKES!!!!!' scrawled across it in angry letters. A faint whiff of ruptured bowel and rotting meat oozed in through the gap under the staff-room door that led out onto the 'dirty areas', the parts of the mortuary members of the public weren't allowed to see. The places where the bodies were loaded, stored, and dissected.

Logan dumped teabags into mugs. 'Maybe he's one of Agnes Garfield's teachers? Or a friend of the family?'

Steel held the head out at arm's length. Closed one eye. 'Looks a bit like Burns from accounting. . .' She swapped eyes. 'Who the hell are you? Why do I know you?'

Dr Graham fetched the milk from the little fridge. 'What about the skeleton, would you like me to get cracking on that one too? If I can get a cast of the skull on the go by lunchtime I could start in on the tissue depth markers by five-ish?'

'You've no' proved *this* one's any good yet. . .' More squinting. 'There's something missing.'

'Well, it's not an exact science, there's lots of interpretation involved. You can't just push a button and hey-presto it's perfect, we have to make assumptions. Like, there's no way to tell if the subject has a moustache, or tattoos, or a beard, or warts, or a—'

'Beard!' Steel put the reconstruction down on the coffee table, amongst the copies of *Hello!* and *Heat*. Severed head meets celebrity cellulite. 'Give it a beard. Big bushy one and a ratty 'tache.'

'Erm . . . OK.' She scuttled out of the room.

Steel sniffed. 'Still no' convinced this isn't just a big steaming pile of useless.'

Logan plonked a mug of tea down in front of her. 'We need to up the hunt for Agnes Garfield. I've got, "Have you seen this girl?" posters up all over the place, but they're sod-all use now she's dyed her hair and changed her appearance. Have to get the papers involved, TV too; release that footage from the cash-machine security camera.'

'Still don't see it.'

Clunk, and Dr Graham was back with an armful of cotton wadding. She sank into one of the chairs, knocking a stack of gossip mags off the coffee table and onto the floor. 'Oops.' She picked up the head and fiddled the wadding around the jaw, pressing it into the clay. 'It's the stuff they use to pack

275

the heads after they've removed the brain. . .' Some more fiddling. A bit of a trim with a pair of scissors. Then she nodded and held the head up again. With the red-brown clay skin, and the grey wadding beard, he looked like a sunburned Santa Claus. 'How's that?'

A slow smile unfurled across Steel's face. 'The very dab. . .' She pointed. 'Laz, look who it is.'

Logan stared at it. 'Who?'

'God's sake. Do you no' read *any* of the memos I send out?'

'Of course I—'

'It's Roy Forman.' A pause. 'Fusty Forman? The Hardgate Hobo? Come on, you must've seen him, lurching about with that ratty AFC bobble hat on, shouting "Arseholes!" at the seagulls?' Steel sighed. 'He was in the Gordon Highlanders, till they invalided him out with PTSD.'

Dr Graham lowered the head to the tabletop. 'You knew him.'

'Arrested him . . . God knows how many times. His patrol copped a roadside bomb in Iraq – aye, no' the sequel, the first time round – came home blind in one eye with all his mates dead. Crawled inside a bottle and never left.'

Logan frowned at the head. 'So what was he doing out in Thainstone with a burning tyre around his neck? Think he did something to Agnes? Harassed her, or something?'

Steel sat back and smiled. 'I remember this one time, I did Fusty Forman for peeing in some shop doorway, absolutely goat-buggeringly hammered, he was. And soon as I get him back to the station, there's Finnie shouting the odds about. . .' She cleared her throat. 'Well, let's call it a misunderstanding over whether it was OK to claim three lap-dances and a bottle of tequila on expenses or not. And Finnie's mid-rant, when Fusty leans over and barfs chunks all over him. I mean *all* over him.' The smile turned into a grin. 'Bits in his hair and all down his front and everything. So Finnie lurches off, all stinking of sick, and Fusty gives us this big wink. Says he did it on purpose, 'cos Finnie was being a dick to his favourite copper.'

She sat there in silence, looking at the head, the grin fading from her face. 'Poor old sod.'

'*Nooo. . .*' On the other end of the phone, Rennie sounded as if he was on the verge of tears. '*Do you have* any *idea what time it is?*'

'Quarter past eleven.'

'*I was asleep!*'

'Hey, you're the one who moaned because you weren't told about us solving the jewellery heist.'

'*Jewellery. . .?*' A yawn. '*I don't care. Sleep. Need sleep. . .*'

'OK, well, in that case you go back to bed and I'll get Chalmers to look into it.'

Silence. '*Chalmers?*'

'We've found one of your missing tramps: Roy Forman. He was our necklacing victim.'

A thump, a crash, some swearing, then: '*I'll be right in.*'

Logan hung up. Now they knew who the victim was it was going to be a lot easier to solve. Connect Agnes Garfield to Roy 'Fusty' Forman, and that would be that. How hard could it be? He swivelled back and forth in his chair a couple of times.

Then stopped.

There was a sheet of paper sitting in his in-tray, on top of Steel's half-completed budget analysis. It was a PNC search for Nichole Fyfe's ex-boyfriend Robbie Whyte. Guthrie must have dropped it off while Logan was off visiting the Kintore crime scene.

He picked it up and skimmed through it. Shoplifting, assault, blah, blah, breaking into people's cars and nicking things, joyriding. . .

277

A smile stretched across Logan's face.

'Oh, you little beauty.'

The viewing suite still smelled of old Pot Noodles, but now came with an extra stale-biscuit whiff of cheesy feet.

Dr Goulding huffed a breath onto his little rectangular glasses, polished them on a cloth, then slipped them back onto his long, hooked nose. Ran a hand through the thick black hair on top of his head, cut short like animal pelt, grey flecks spreading their way around his temples. A pair of flaming dice sat in the middle of his bottle-green tie. He reached out and pressed play on the video console. 'This is the interesting bit.'

Logan scooted his chair closer as the crackling screen filled with the interior of interview room two. Robbie Whyte was sitting in the dead seat – the one bolted to the floor – Goulding in the one opposite him, the legs and stomach of PC Guthrie just poking into the side of the frame.

Whyte gave his lopsided shrug again. *'I don't know. I found it.'*

The on-screen Goulding nodded. *'You found a dog's head.'* Not a question, just a statement.

'I know she still loves me. . .'

'Sometimes, Robbie, it's hard for us to accept that the huge feelings we have aren't shared by others.'

'No: she loves me. I know she does.' He sat back in his seat and stared up at the camera. *'There was this summer we got a caravan in Lossiemouth. Was a friend's dad's and we stayed there for a whole fortnight. Just her and me and Wee Robbie. Caught fish and cooked them under the stars and smoked so much weed one night we saw a kelpie. . .'*

'I see. You named the dog, "Wee Robbie". Was that your idea, or Nichole's?'

'Going to get married and have kids. Boy and a girl. Always

278

wanted a son, you know? Someone to be a chip off his old man's block.'

A nutjob who'd cut the head off his own dog. Yeah, that was something to aspire to.

The real-life Goulding pressed pause. 'So when she left, she not only rejected him, she rejected his future child as well. A double blow. Then, when his mother died, that was the final straw. He couldn't cope any more.'

'He gave the dog the same name he was going to give his kid?'

'You asked if Robert Whyte would be capable of murder. . .'

Silence.

Logan poked Goulding in the shoulder. 'Well?'

'In killing the dog – the emotional surrogate for an unborn son and his potential future with the woman he loves – Robert's metaphorically killing himself and everything he's hoped for over the last eight or nine years. He's a dead man. You can't hurt the dead.'

'Could he necklace someone? Or torture them to death?'

'My opinion is that Mr Whyte is a danger to himself and others. I'll organize a Mental Health Officer to take a look at him, and we'll get him sectioned for seventy-two hours for tests. If that goes the way I think it will, we'll be looking at a Compulsory Treatment Order under Section Seven of the Mental Health – Care and Treatment – Scotland Act 2003.'

Logan poked him again. 'I know a private security guy who speaks just like that.'

A sniff. 'Sometimes it's important to be formal. Robert's mental health is '

'Did – he – kill – them?'

Goulding frowned and puffed out his cheeks. 'It's much more likely he'd kill the object of his affections, then he'd kill himself.'

279

'According to the PNC,' Logan held up the sheet of paper Guthrie had dumped on his desk, 'he's got form for joyriding. And possession of a controlled substance, three convictions for assault, two for unlawful removal, and he just hacked the head off a dog he named after the son he wanted to have.'

'That doesn't—'

'Robbie used to dump the cars he stole in the Joyriders' Graveyard, where we found Roy Forman's body. He's obsessed with Nichole Fyfe, the necklacing was his way of getting her attention. And when that didn't work, he killed the dog.' Logan sat back in his seat. Game, set, and match.

Goulding sighed, opened his briefcase and slid his notebook away inside. 'They should never have got involved with each other in the first place. Robbie Whyte's needy, and co-dependent. Nichole Fyfe. . . Well, she's an actress.' He clunked the briefcase shut and ran a finger back and forward across the tumblers on the lock. 'They hold their emotions much closer to the surface, because they have to display and manipulate them when they perform. They feed off the external validation, then wonder why their personal lives don't live up to the hype. Which is why they're prone to high levels of drug and alcohol abuse.' A sigh. 'It was never going to work.'

'He's got *form*.'

'Logan, think about it: the stressor event was his mother dying. She's been in hospital for the last month and a half with pancreatic cancer. She died yesterday afternoon – I called an oncologist I know and checked. Apparently Robert barely left her bedside.'

'But he could have—'

'She died. The grief caused a mental collapse in Robbie. He went out and got drunk. And somewhere on the way to the bottom of a bottle, he decided giving Wee Robbie's head to Nichole Fyfe would be a perfect expression of his undying love. If his mother hadn't died, he'd still be just another creepy stalker ex-boyfriend.'

So much for that.

Logan checked his watch: five minutes till Steel's latest update meeting. Just enough time to grab another coffee before getting shouted at for wasting time with this. He stood. 'I'm still going to check his alibi.'

'Of course you are.' Goulding stayed where he was, smiling up at Logan with those dead-fish eyes. 'Actually, while I've got you, why don't we have a quick chat?'

'I've got . . . a thing . . . meeting. You know update on the necklacing—'

'How are you getting on with the talking therapy?'

Sodding hell. This again. 'I'm doing it, OK?'

'And is it helping? Because if not, you can always—'

'I said I'm *doing* it.'

Goulding nodded. 'Good.' He pulled on his suit jacket and straightened his ugly tie. 'Well, you have my number. . .'

Logan stuck his coffee mug down on the desk. 'I know what I said, but it's a bit more complicated than it looked. . .'

'In the name of Satan's nipples, Laz, you *told* me it was him!'

Steel's office was crowded: DI Bell slumped in the visitor's seat like a partially shaved bear someone had stuffed into a shirt and tie; DI Leith leaning against the filing cabinets, Logan by the whiteboard, Biohazard Bob and DS Chalmers hovering in the background by the door.

Logan shifted his shoulders. 'I said it *might* be him.'

DI Bell scratched at a scab on one hairy forearm. 'Back in the real world: we need to do a victimology profile. Look into Fusty Forman's last-known whereabouts, question his drinking buddies, see if they saw him fighting with anyone.'

Leith sniffed. 'Be realistic, Ding-Dong, the review starts at two, we're never going to get something by then.'

'Well, let's have your *genius* idea then.'

'We don't even know it really is Fusty Forman, do we? Just because some clay-head thing looks a bit—'

'Oh come on, of course it's him. Who the hell else—'

'You're dreaming, Ding-Dong, if it was him, they'd have got a hit off the database when they did the DNA, wouldn't they?'

'Bloody lab couldn't even tell the victim's DNA from the kid that stabbed him. Ever since the re-org—'

'What happened to eliminative detection? Don't be a bell-end, it's not—'

'Hoy!' DI Bell jumped to his feet, towering over Leith, fists curled into great hairy hammers. 'Who are you calling Bell-End, you cock-faced weaselly little—'

Steel stuck two fingers in her mouth and blew. A high-pitched whistle screeched out into the room. 'Enough! Biohazard: get onto the labs and poke them in the arse till they do another DNA match. *Fresh* samples, no' the complete and utter cock-up we got last time.'

Bob nodded. 'Yes, Guv.'

'Next, we get. . .' A sigh. 'Ding-Dong, sit your arse down. Leith: apologize.'

Leith chewed on the inside of his mouth, looked away, sniffed. 'Sorry, didn't mean anything personal. Was just an expression.'

DI Bell didn't move for a moment, then licked his lips and sank back into the visitor's seat.

Steel stared at the pair of them. 'Like being a sodding primary school teacher. . .'

Bell picked at his scab again. 'He started it.'

'*As I was saying*: next, we get teams going round every homeless person, tramp, junkie, alky, and beggar on the

282

streets. Try the drop-in centres, hostels, clinics, and hospital. Flash Fusty's mugshot and see if we can get some witnesses.'

Logan pointed at the 'HAVE YOU SEEN THIS WOMAN?' posters sitting on Steel's desk. 'You need to show them Agnes Garfield's face as well.'

'Fine, if it'll shut you up. See if anyone's seen the mental witch woman. Leith, you and Ding-Dong—'

'Aya, watch it!' Biohazard Bob lurched forward a step as the door thumped into his back. He turned and wrenched it all the way open. 'You looking for a fat lip?'

Rennie stood in the doorway, wearing a green bomber jacket, jeans, and a T-shirt with a rock'n'roll tyrannosaurus printed across the front. 'Sorry.'

Steel took another puff on her fake cigarette. 'Detective Sergeant, how *kind* of you to take time out of your busy social whirlwind to grace us with your presence.'

Rennie shrugged. 'Came soon as I heard. And I'm not supposed to be on till ten tonight, OK? I was asleep.'

'Could at least have run a comb through your hair: you look like a burst cushion.'

Which was a bit rich, given the exploding wasps' nest on top of her own head.

'It was my case, and—'

'Don't care. You were supposed to find the poor sod *before* he wound up dead. I gave you the simple job of tracking down three tramps, and now two of them are in body-bags. You're like the sodding Angel of Death.'

'How's that fair, it's—'

'Think you can do us a favour and find the last one while he's still alive?' She pulled a stack of forms from her pending-tray, then flapped a hand towards the open door. 'Go on, shoo, the lot of you, find me someone who saw what happened to Fusty Forman.'

They shuffled towards the door, Rennie leading the way with shoulders slumped.

Steel's voice cut through the mumbling. 'DI McRae, where do you think you're going? Not finished with you yet.'

27

Steel stared up at him, face expressionless as a dead fish. 'Well?'

Logan collapsed into the vacated visitor's chair. Still warm. 'Well what?'

'You know fine well what.'

Silence.

'OK, so I was wrong. Are you happy?'

'Sodding ecstatic.' She stuck her feet up on the desk.

Logan counted the points off on his fingers: 'Robbie Whyte had form; he was connected to the film through Nichole Fyfe; he was off his head; he used to dump stolen cars at the Joyriders' Graveyard. *And* he killed his own dog. What was I supposed to think?'

'Oh, I don't know . . . how about: did he *actually* kill anyone?'

'I've got the uniforms stationed at the hospital checking with the nurses on the oncology ward, and going over the security-camera footage. Maybe he left his dying mum's bedside for long enough to necklace Roy Forman and torture whoever the Kintore victim is?'

'Aye, and maybe my bumhole squirts rainbows and pixie dust.'

Logan scowled at her. 'You know, you're getting more like Finnie every day. The sarcastic motivational speeches, the fishing for info, the rummaging through people's desks. . .'

Steel's eyes bugged. 'You take that back: I'm *nothing* like that frog-faced, rubbery-lipped goat-molester!'

'Look at Rennie. He's doing his best, and you're . . . what, trying to make him cry? You're supposed to mentor—'

'I'm *way* nicer than—'

'He's talking about resigning. That what you want?'

'Pfff. . .' She had a dig at her underwire, making the wrinkly cleavage wriggle and jiggle. 'I'm doing him a favour. Either he can handle the pressure, or he can't. Better to find out now – while someone else can still fix it for him – instead of later when some poor sod ends up dead 'cos Rennie's no' up to the job.' Another dig, then she gave up on her bra and tilted her head back, looking down her nose at Logan. 'Besides, never did you any harm, did it?'

'Yeah,' keeping his voice flat and level, 'you're *such* a saint.'

'You looking for a clip round the lug?' She took a long draw on her electronic cigarette. Narrowed her eyes. 'And how come you've done nothing about that deid body on your roof yet?'

'Not my case; you gave it to Ding-Dong.'

'That's no excuse! Have some pride in your caravan park, man. Your roof, your skeleton, your responsibility.'

'So approve the facial reconstruction. Worked for Roy Forman, didn't it?'

She squirmed in her seat. 'You got any idea what they're doing to the CID budget, it's—'

'Then don't come moaning to me when we can't make any progress. You want a result? Fund the investigation properly.'

A scowl. 'See: you and the boy Rennie moan and whine at me all the time, but you're no' the ones stuck in here with the ACC breathing down your neck like a creepy uncle. . .' She poked the desk with a yellowed finger. 'And another thing: how come your mother keeps calling about taking Jasmine away to Sodding Euro Sodding Disney? I *told* you to have a word.'

'If you don't give Rennie a break, I'm going to give her your mobile number.'

'You wouldn't dare.'

'And then I'm going to tell her how you've always wanted to join the WRI, and can she put in a good word for you?'

'If you think—'

'And *then*, I'm going to show her how to stalk you on Facebook.'

Steel glowered at him, the little red LED in the tip of her fake cigarette flickering angry Morse code. '*Fine*: I'll be nicer to Rennie.'

He stood. Yawned. 'Anything else?'

'Don't push it, Laz, or you'll no' get your present.'

'Present?'

Why did that sound like a threat?

PC Sim had her hands behind her back, walking up Union Street with careful measured steps, in full-on *Dixon of Dock Green* mode. She glanced up at the ribbon of sky trapped between the granite buildings standing guard on either side of the road. The shining blue had faded to milky white, with clots of pale grey spreading like cancer. She sniffed. 'Hope the rain holds off till I get home. Got a load of towels out.'

They crossed over to the other side at the lights outside Waterstones, making for the line of charity shops and banks that lined this part of the West End. Corporate greed and unwanted paperbacks, cheek and jowl.

Next stop Gilcomston Church.

Sim hummed something to herself, smiling in the sunshine, padding slowly along. 'Think we're going to find a witness?'

'Do *you*?'

'Nope. Might just be a uniform plod, but I'm not daft. Body out in the middle of nowhere, killed like that, whoever did it is organized and tidy. A planner. They didn't screech up in a black van and bundle Mr Forman inside. They did it careful and quiet, somewhere no one would see.'

'Probably.'

A lump-faced woman marched towards them, wheeling a double buggy with two screaming toddlers imprisoned within it. The fag sticking out the corner of her mouth twitching with every muttered swear word.

Logan and Sim broke apart, taking opposite sides of the pavement and letting Mummy Dearest stomp past between them.

When they came back together Sim froze, gazing in through a charity shop window.

Logan stopped beside her.

Someone had put up a display with a mannequin dressed head-to-toe in black leather with a red notebook tucked under its arm. A sheet acted as the backdrop with a Ring Knot picked out in black paint on it, all the squiggles and circles and words identical to the one on the kitchen floor out in Kintore. A stack of hardbacks and paperbacks sat on a little wooden table beside the mannequin, a skull perched on the top. All of them copies of *Witchfire*.

Sim nodded at it. 'My niece, Amanda, did it for her English Standard Grade. Got a B. Made the whole family read it then sit down and discuss,' Sim made quote-bunnies with her fingers, '"*symbolism*" and "*themes*", like some kind of resentful book club.'

'Little sods don't know they're born. We never got a choice at school, it was *Of Mice and Men* and sodding *Macbeth* or a clip round the ear.'

'I suppose *Witchfire*'s OK. I mean, if you like that kind of thing. Kind of a cross between *Fatherland*, *Night Watch* and *Silence of the Lambs*. Still, at least it got her reading; always thought she'd turn out thick as bogies, like her dad.'

Logan stared at the display. 'Started reading it last night. Got to the bit where the Moderator tells Rowan about her father.'

Sim's mouth curdled. 'You're not wanting to discuss symbolism and theme, are you? Only once was bad enough.'

Logan headed up the street again. 'Agnes is recreating bits of the book; thought it wouldn't hurt to know what to look for.'

'Tenet Two: "Know thine enemy, for knowledge is power and power is victory."' She shrugged. 'Don't look at me like that, told you we had to read it.'

Gilcomston Church reared up into the sky, the jagged grey steeple towering over the surrounding buildings. The place was an elaborate gothic lump of dirt-streaked granite, its main entrance raised far enough above street level to need a short flight of stone steps up to the wide wooden door. A pair of posters were mounted on either side in Perspex-fronted display boxes. The eye-melting orange one read, 'JESUS LOVES YOU EACH AND EVERY DAY!' and the nuclear-urine-yellow one, 'NEW: SENIORS' BINGO EVERY WEDNESDAY!!!'

Two men and a woman lounged on the steps, wearing tatty parka jackets and waterproofs, dressed for winter even though the last few days had been like a furnace. A collection of carrier-bags made a plastic halo around them, stuffed with clothes and tins. Probably everything they had to their names.

Logan stopped at the foot of the stairs and smiled up at them. 'Morning.'

One of the men scowled out from beneath a threadbare woollen hat, his eyes thin and yellow, flecked with red veins. He clutched a tin of extra-strong Co-op lager to his chest, shielding it with his other hand. The sour smell of stale piss and alcohol hung around him like a thundercloud. 'I ain't done nothing. You can't prove I done nothing, I know my rights.'

The other man and the woman sidled closer together. He had one leg in plaster from the knee down, and his face was a mess of scabs and scratches. That would be Henry Scott, AKA: Scotty Scabs, the only one of Rennie's shoplifting tramps not currently lying on a refrigerated drawer in the mortuary.

The woman had a wad of stained gauze wadding taped over her left eye, her hair like damp straw, fingernails painted bright scarlet. She slid a half bottle of supermarket vodka into her pocket.

Sim held up a hand. 'It's OK, Trevor, we're not here to hassle you—'

'Whoever says I did it is *lying*!'

Logan pulled the mugshot photo of Roy Forman from his pocket and held it up.

Trevor sniffed, wiped a hand under his nose, leaving a shiny trail on the dirty skin. 'Whatever Fusty did, I didn't have nothing to do with it.'

'When did you last see him?'

'He was mental.'

Sim settled down on the step next to him, blinking. Probably from the fumes, they were bad enough from the pavement, up close they must have been horrible. 'Trevor, we're trying to help Mr Forman, we're not here to hassle you. We just need to know if anyone saw him last week. Maybe Friday, or Saturday?'

The woman ran a pale tongue across chapped lips. Her voice didn't go with the ratty, unwashed hair and missing teeth. Posh, and not local posh either, Inverness posh. 'He's dead, isn't he?'

Sim nodded. 'I'm sorry, Sally. That's why we need to—'

Henry Scott burst into tears. 'He's deid, he's deid, he's deid. . .'

Sally wrapped an arm around his shoulders. 'Shhh, shhh, it's all right, Scotty, it's all right.' She squinted her good eye at Logan. '*Now* look what you've done.'

Logan dropped down onto his haunches, so he was eye to eye with him. 'You were Roy's friend, weren't you, Henry? You and Roy and Sally? When did you last see him?'

'It wasn't me, it wasn't, I didn't do it, I didn't steal stuff. . .'

'It's OK, I'm not here about the shoplifting thing and I'm not going to arrest you, I promise. I just need to know what happened to Roy. Did you see something?'

Sally hauled Henry Scott closer. 'You think we're just tramps, don't you? Just drunks and junkies, but we're people too!'

'I know you are, that's why we're—'

'We die all the time and you never do anything about it, do you? You don't care. You're just like all the other fascists.'

Sim sighed. Furrowed her brow. 'We *do* care, Sally.'

'If you cared, you'd do something about it! They take us in the middle of the night and they do experiments on us. . .'

'Who do?'

Her lonely eye whipped left and right, then her voice dropped to a whisper. 'The *government*.'

'He's deid, she killed him: he's deid, he's deid. . .'

Logan shook his head. 'The police are independent, Sally, the government doesn't own us, they can't make us do things. That's why we want to find out what happened. . .' He stared at Henry Scott. 'Wait a minute: you said, "she killed him". Who killed him, Henry? Who hurt Roy?'

Henry Scott stared off down Union Street, towards the East End. His voice was barely a whisper, the words hidden in a barrage of raw onion breath. 'The dark angel. She swoops down from the sky in the death of night and she takes us.'

291

Sally stared at the sky for a moment, then sighed. 'Don't be stupid, Scotty, it's not angels, it's the government! The government took him, I saw them in their big black cars with their guns and suits. They took him to do *experiments*.'

Well, this was going well. They'd only been there two minutes and already they had new suspects: the angel of death, and the government. Welcome to care in the community.

Sally licked her lips again, her other hand stroking the pocket she'd hidden the vodka in.

'It's OK, I'm not going to do you for drinking in public. We're really not here to cause any trouble. Just trying to find out what happened to Roy Forman.'

'It. . .' She let go of Henry, fished out her bottle, unscrewed the top, chugged down a mouthful, put the top back on, and rammed it back in her pocket all in the space of three seconds. 'Fusty was trying to get better. Seeing someone about his problems. Was going to get a job and a family and a dog called Savlon. Maybe *they* turned him into the government?'

'He's deid, she killed him, he's deid, he's deid. . .'

The arm went around Henry again. 'Shhh, shhh, it's all right. They can't hurt him any more.'

'Guys, it's important: when did you last see Roy Forman?'

Trevor hunched his shoulders inside his stained parka jacket, the fur trim all matted. 'Friday night. Soup kitchen down the Green. That's where I saw him. . . I didn't cause no trouble though! Anyone who says I did is a liar!'

Logan pulled out the photo of Agnes Garfield. 'What about her? Do you recognize her?'

'Whatever she says, she's lying. I never did nothing.'

Logan swapped the plastic carrier-bags from one hand to the other and squeezed out of the baker's, past a pair of tracksuit slobs at the end of the queue and onto Schoolhill. Overhead, the sky was heading from grey to greyer, taking the granite buildings with it. He nipped across the road, skirting around the back end of an illegally parked taxi.

Then froze on the pavement.

A small knot of Strathclyde's finest turned and stared at him: Steel's National Police Improvement Authority review team. Two male officers and one female – all wearing Man at CID suits, with not a smile to be seen. The tallest of them, in a sharp black number, sniffed at Logan. His little evil-magician's goatee was about three shades darker than the hair clinging to either side of a high creased forehead. He narrowed his hooded eyes. 'Detective Sergeant McRae, isn't it?'

'Superintendent Smith. Nice to see you again.'

Now that *did* get a smile. 'I trust we're not going to have a repeat of last time?'

'That wasn't really my fault.'

'DS Kelly still limps when the weather changes, don't you Gerald?'

A lump of muscle with a shaved head and big glasses glowered out from beneath heavy eyebrows. 'He was *supposed* to be unarmed.'

'And *you* were supposed to stay in the car.'

The third member of the trio's mouth twitched, but she kept the smile in check. She'd aged a bit since the last time – filled out a bit too, but on her it looked good. Her long black hair was pulled back in a ponytail, frizzy around the edges, her makeup almost enough to disguise the dark circles beneath her eyes, but doing nothing to hide the crow's feet. She nodded at him. 'DS McRae.'

Logan nodded back. 'DS Watson. And it's DI now: acting.'

'Congratulations.' She still hadn't moved.

Superintendent Smith sniffed again. 'All right, that's enough unbridled sexual tension for one day. I want to get lunch before the witch-hunt starts. We'll be seeing you, *DI McRae*.'

'I can barely wait, sir.' Logan stayed where he was as they wandered off towards the Bon Accord Centre. Oh, today just kept getting better and better. . .

Logan dumped the carrier-bag down on Steel's desk, then sank into the visitor's chair and let out a long sigh.

She stared at him. 'Well?'

'Didn't have any stovies, so I got you macaroni cheese instead.' He dug into the bag and came out with a Styrofoam carton. Handed it over. Then went back in for the other one. Creaked it open to reveal a baked potato with tuna and cheese; savoury smells filled the office. 'So far, last time anyone saw Fusty Forman was half-ten, Friday night, at the soup kitchen on East Green, where it disappears under Market Street.'

Steel opened her carton. A quivering mound of glistening tubes in a gloopy yellow sauce, next to a jumble of deep-fried potato. 'You got us chips too!' A smile deepened the wrinkles about her eyes. 'There's hope for you yet.'

'Going to canvas the soup kitchen tonight, but—'

'No you're no'. Overtime budget's bad enough as it is without you pulling a double shift.' She balanced some macaroni on a chip, then shovelled it in, the words, 'Get Ding-Dong on it,' muffled by the mouthful.

'How am I supposed to run the necklacing bit of the investigation if—'

'There's no "I" in team, Laz, but there will be my boot in your arse.' She jabbed up a couple of chips. 'Besides, if you're up all night, you'll be sod-all use to me tomorrow. Ding-Dong's doing the soup kitchen.'

Well that was just brilliant: he did all the work and if something came of it, DI Bell would be the one who got all the credit.

'Fine, Ding-Dong can do it, but if it leads to an arrest—'

'Yes, yes: you shall have a gold star and a sweetie.' More macaroni disappeared. 'God, you're such a *whinge*.'

'Just remember, it was *my* lead.' Logan ripped the top off a tiny sachet of pepper and sprinkled it over his tattie. Then did the same with one of salt. 'The cast and crew of *Witchfire* have been volunteering at the soup kitchen, and do you want to guess who set the whole thing up?'

Steel squinted at him for a moment, chewing. 'Agnes Garfield?'

'Bingo.' He pulled out the plastic cutlery and sawed a chunk off his baked potato. 'We haven't had any hits on her photo when we've shown it around, but for all we know this redhead thing is just the latest in a long line of changes. Could be altering her appearance every other week.'

Steel let out a cross between a sigh and a growl. 'That's all we need.'

'Told you.'

'Not helping, Laz.' She popped a couple of chips in and gave them a sour-faced chewing. 'Had a call from the hospital: Robbie Whyte's alibi checks out, he was at his dear mum's bedside right up till they called time of death. There's no way he killed Fusty Forman or our torture victim.'

Of course he didn't. That would make life too sodding easy.

Logan took a bite. The potato was hot, the tuna cold, the cheese like napalm. 'They get an ID yet?'

Steel blew a wet farty raspberry. 'Face is that battered we can't do a dental match, fingertips are pulped so we've no' chance of getting any prints off him, and the IB says there's about as much chance of us getting viable DNA from the body as Rennie has of winning *Mastermind*. Four days in a warm room and it's all turned to mush.' She shovelled in some more macaroni. 'Might get some from the tooth-pulp cavities, but that's it.'

'What do you think: do another facial reconstruction?'

Steel scowled at him.

Fine. Change the subject. 'Never guess who I bumped into, coming out of the baker's: the NPIA team.'

'Already? Who'd we get?'

'Superintendent Smith, Wee Hairy DS Kelly and DS Watson.'

A groan. 'And are the two of you on speaking terms this week, or are you going to sit and glower and snipe at each other all through the review? Because that would make it even *more* fun.'

'Hey, I got you chips, remember?'

'Because things aren't bad enough with the bloody ACC nipping my arse every five minutes. "Oh the press are up in arms." "Oh the Chief Constable's no' happy." "Oh if only *Finnie* was here. . ." Aye, like the frog-faced tosser could just turn up, wave his magic fairy wand, and solve everything.' Steel skewered a chip, then frowned at it drooping there on the end of her plastic fork. 'Any tomato sauce in the bag?'

'Another thing: a couple of Forman's associates said he was getting professional therapy. Give you odds on Agnes was too. Might be worth following up on?'

'Why'd you no' get any tomato sauce? How am I supposed to eat chips with no tomato sauce?'

'Macaroni cheese with tomato sauce is disgusting. What about a TV appeal?'

'Yeah, well . . . you eat Marmite. That's like a wee jar full of Satan's turds.'

'She's still in the city: she used Anthony Chung's cards. They're holed up somewhere, so someone's bound to spot them.'

'Know how they make Marmite?'

He scooped up another chunk of cheddar-covered tuna.

'I'll get onto the media department. See if they can set something up.'

'There's this mine in darkest England and at the bottom of the mine there's a big crack in the earth.'

'Not listening.'

'And the Devil sticks his arse up through the crack, and they send this bunch of murderers, bastards, and rapists down there to scrape up the lumps and bung them in jars.'

'No way Roy Forman can afford to see a private therapist, so whoever's treating him: it's on the NHS. Shouldn't be too hard to track down.'

'It's true, there's video of them doing it on the internet.' She drummed her fingers on the desktop. 'Come on, I know you've got some in your desk.'

'I'm not giving you tomato sauce.'

A little smile tugged one side of Steel's face upwards. 'Do you a swap.' She leaned down and clunked open the bottom drawer of her return unit. When she straightened up there was a rectangular box in her hand, about the size of a thermos flask, wrapped in anonymous brown paper. She waggled it at him. 'Told you I got a present for you.'

Logan put his plastic fork down and shrank back in his seat. Frowning. 'What is it?'

'Tomato sauce first, present later.'

'Right. . . Well. . .' Logan stood, gathered up his baked potato. 'I'll just . . . go get that then.'

And escape.

297

28

Rennie gave a huge yawn, showing off his fillings, then slumped into the visitor's chair. 'Gah. . .'

Logan looked up from the stack of overtime, expenses, and budget request forms that had magically appeared in his in-box. 'If you're here for a moan, you can bugger right back out again.'

'Been round every drop-in centre and hostel in town, and no one's caught so much as a whiff of Scotty Scabs.'

He checked his watch: one forty-five, which meant Henry Scott would have a decent head start. 'That's strange – he was sitting on the steps of Gilcomston Church when I spoke to him an hour ago.'

Rennie stared, a smile dawning across his face. 'You found him? Cool, is he in the cells, because—'

'I said I *spoke* to him, didn't say I'd arrested him.'

The smile disappeared. 'But I've been looking for him for ages! How am I—'

'I needed information on Roy Forman; gave my word I wouldn't do him for the shoplifting.'

'But—'

'If you get off your backside and hurry over there, you might still catch him. Otherwise. . .' Shrug.

Rennie scrambled out of his seat, reaching the door just in time for it to swing open. He jerked to a halt, staring at Chalmers. 'Oh. It's you.'

She stuck her chin out. 'DS Rennie.'

He folded his arms. 'DS Chalmers.'

God help us. Logan grabbed a biro from his desk and chucked it at Rennie's back. It bounced right between the silly sod's shoulder blades. 'Thought you were in a hurry.'

'Yes. Right. Fine.' Rennie pulled his shoulders back and marched from the room, not even looking at Chalmers.

She pursed her lips, raised an eyebrow, then closed the door behind him.

Logan went back to his forms. 'Steel about?'

'She's sloped off to get a quick cigarette in before the review.'

Small mercies.

He moved on to the next form in the pile. 'How did you get on?'

Chalmers dragged out her notebook. 'Far as we can tell, there's no record of Roy Forman being referred for counselling in the last two years. He saw a therapist for about eighteen months after he got back from Kuwait, but that was it.'

So much for that. 'Never mind, what about—'

'*But. . .*' Theatrical pause. 'I did manage to track down the head of psychiatric care at Aberdeen Royal Infirmary, and he says that there's a handful of therapists offering free treatment to the long-term homeless and victims of violent crime.'

'Did you. . .?'

She peeled a Post-it note from her book and placed it on Logan's desk. 'Thought you might ask.'

Four names, one of them instantly recognizable: Dr David Goulding. Giving free therapy sessions to the homeless. Poor sods. Each of the doctors on the list had a telephone number picked out in careful numerals beneath it.

Chalmers flipped over the page in her notebook. 'According to Agnes Garfield's parents she was undergoing treatment as part of an experimental trial programme at Aberdeen University. Something about a comparative benefit analysis of cognitive behaviour therapy and medication.' Another Post-it note joined the first, this one with a single name in the middle: Prof. Richard Marks. 'I tried talking to him, but he's squealing patient-doctor privilege. We could get a warrant?'

'We could do that,' Logan chucked the form back on top of his in-tray and stood, 'or we could try the old two birds, one stone, routine.'

'. . .and when I read the script, I fell in love with it. Of course I'd adored the books as a wee girl, I mean, who didn't, right? I always knew it'd make a great film, but I never thought I'd be lucky enough to be in it!'

Logan's manky Fiat Punto bounced and thrummed over the cobbles on College Bounds, past the dirty beige-and-grey stonework of King's College – the big vaulted crown on top of the bell tower swathed in scaffolding and gauzy material like some massive spider's web.

Chalmers scowled out from behind the steering wheel. 'It's all double yellows. . .'

'Wow. I know.' The DJ's voice had more cheese in it than Steel's macaroni. 'Right, you're listening to Jimmy's Late Lunch, and I'm here with Nichole Fyfe. Yeah, that's right, local girl made good, and full-on Hollywood superstar: Nichole Fyfe! How cool is that?'

A silky laugh. 'I'm definitely not a superstar, Jimmy. Dame Judi Dench is a superstar, Robbie Coltrane is a superstar, Morgan Mitchell is a superstar. I'm just a wee girl from Kincorth hoping

300

no one's going to start wondering what on earth I'm doing hanging about with all these great people.'

Logan pointed through the windscreen. 'Keep going. Might be a couple of spaces further up.'

'So, are you going to pick another track for us, Nichole?'

'You bet, Jimmy. This is a song that meant a lot to me when I was growing up: it's Eminem with "The Real Slim Shady".'

Chalmers grimaced, then clicked the radio off. 'Can't stand rap.'

A group of students, dressed as ninja chickens, leapt and twirled across the road, pausing in the middle to throw some sloppy kung fu moves about, before sprinting off across a small chunk of emerald grass. White feathers tumbled in their wake.

Logan's phone rang, 'The Imperial March' muffled in his jacket pocket. Steel.

Chalmers rumbled the rusty car up the High Street, ivy-covered university buildings on one side, bland granite tenements on the other. 'Aren't you going to answer that?'

He shifted in his seat. 'Sooner not.'

Eventually the music stopped. Then two beats later it started up again.

'You sure, Guv?'

'Positive.' He pulled his mobile out and set it on silent. Put it away again. If Steel wanted to shout at him for dodging the National Police Improvement Authority review, she'd just have to wait.

Chalmers frowned out at the street. Every parking space was jammed with a shiny new hatchback or a Smart car. 'Look at them. When I went to uni, you know what I had? A bike. And some thieving sod nicked it halfway through first term.'

More students, dressed in long black jackets and little black sunglasses, backpacks over one shoulder, nodding along to a collective beat. Was *The Matrix* old enough now to be considered ironic? Or were they just goths, out for a bit of a mope?

Logan smiled. One of them had a Frisbee.

The phone vibrated in his pocket. Steel just couldn't take a hint, could she? Like Agnes Garfield.

He looked down at the latest poster the media department had put together. Three different versions of Agnes's face: the photo her parents handed over, the one from the cash-machine's security camera, and a third one knocked up on the identikit software. They'd given her blonde hair, just in case. A pretty young woman with freckles and a warm smile. Brunette, redhead, blonde – surely *someone* would recognize her?

Logan popped the poster on the dusty dashboard. 'What happened with the diary?'

Silence.

For God's sake. He stared at Chalmers. She stared straight ahead.

'Sergeant, I told you to read it two days ago. Why haven't—'

Her voice was sharp and brittle: 'I was up till *three* this morning going through it. I wrote you a report and everything!'

'You did?'

'Put it on your in-tray first thing this morning.'

'Ah. . .' Where it was probably buried under four tons of paperwork.

'You didn't even look at it, did you?' Mouth a thin hard line.

'Didn't even know it was there: Steel uses my in-tray as a dumping ground for all the stuff she can't be arsed doing.' He pointed at a shiny, tiny, red Alfa Romeo as it pulled away from the kerb. 'Parking space.'

Chalmers slipped the scabby Punto into the still-warm

302

spot. Then looked out of the window, face turned away from him. 'I would've done it sooner, but there was everything else going.'

Logan undid his seatbelt. 'I know the feeling. But next time, do me a favour and hand whatever it is to me in person. Put it right in my hand.'

A nod, still not looking at him. 'Yes, Guv.'

'In Grampian CID you only ever stick something in some-one's in-tray if you're avoiding them, or you're dumping some-thing unpleasant on them and don't want caught holding it. Think "Pass the Parcel", only the prize is an exploding jobbie.'

He climbed out into the afternoon, phone buzzing away silently in his pocket, vibrating against his ribs like an angry wasp. 'Come on: you can give me the short version on the way.'

The dove-grey sky matched the granite buildings, the breeze tumbleweeding an empty crisp packet and a carrier-bag across the grass. Definitely getting colder. Logan followed the path behind the Old Brewery, taking a shortcut under the concrete Tetris block of the Taylor Building.

Chalmers dug her hands into her pockets. 'First half of the book isn't a diary. It's more like some sort of slavish recreation of—'

'The Fingermen's dittay books. It's a prop from the film, she stole it.'

'Oh. . . You knew.' A little sag, then Chalmers brought her chin up again. 'The second half isn't her handwriting – doesn't match the slash-fiction we found. It's still her, but it's like she's trying to make her writing look like whoever did the first part.'

Across a car park wedged in between the buildings, the yellow hatching of a box junction flaking away and scarred with potholes.

'There's loads of angst-ridden poetry, a bit of moaning about how no one understands her, how she hates the way the medication makes her feel, quite a lot about how she loves Anthony Chung more than oxygen. . . Blah, blah, blah. Standard teenager stuff.'

'She's eighteen.'

'There's nothing in the book about her planning to run away, or where she'd go if she did.'

They marched past Coopers Court, warm for a moment in a beam of sunlight, the concrete lump of a building acting as a windbreak.

'What about the mysterious Stacey. . .?'

'Gourdon, Guv. Stacey Gourdon. Still no sign.'

Not good news: if Agnes was prepared to necklace some random tramp, she wasn't exactly going to bake cookies for the woman screwing her boyfriend. And it wouldn't be Anthony's fault, would it? No, it'd all be Stacey Gourdon's.

Be lucky if they found her in one piece, never mind alive.

'Get on to the hospitals. See if Ms Gourdon is lying in A&E somewhere.' Logan stepped to one side, allowing a young woman on a skateboard to trundle past, blonde hair down to the small of her back, ragged saggy jeans low enough to show off a pair of red pants and a 'DADDY'S LITTLE GIRL' tramp stamp. 'If you were eighteen, running away from home, what would *you* take with you?'

Chalmers's brow wrinkled. 'Toilet bag, makeup, hairdryer, Mr Trousermonkey, favourite clothes. . .'

'What about your diary?'

'No way I'd leave that behind. My mum was like the Spanish Inquisition on a bad day, nothing was safe.'

'*Exactly*. And we know Agnes's mother's. . . Hold on, "Mr Trousermonkey"?'

'Mum made him from a pair of dad's old trousers, when I was wee. He's tartan.'

Up ahead, the ninja chickens were poncing about outside the psychology building, doing their martial arts poses for anyone daft enough to pay any attention.

Logan ignored them, making for the glass doors instead. 'OK, so forgetting your dad's appalling dress sense for a minute, you wouldn't leave your diary. How about a big bag of weed?'

'Never smoked it, Guv. I don't put drugs into my body.'

'Does Guinness not count then?' He held the door open for her. The glass was almost obscured by posters for university am-dram productions of Gilbert and Sullivan and worthy plays, 'DRUMMER WANTED' ads, and coming attractions for the film club's slash-horror season.

'Maybe Agnes didn't know she was going to run away? Spur of the moment?'

Possible. . . 'Then why didn't she sneak back in and take the important stuff?'

Up the stairs to the first floor.

'Maybe she can't? Maybe Anthony Chung won't let her?'

Maybe. . .

The receptionist put the phone down, then peered at them with watery eyes, a twitchy smile uncomfortable on her face. 'Dr Goulding will see you now.'

Logan led the way into an office crammed with books on three walls, four large scrawl-covered whiteboards filling the other. The furniture was a collection of minimalist chrome, glass and black leather. A coffee table sat in the middle of the room, littered with publications: *Psychology Review*, *Behavioural and Cognitive Psychotherapy*, *European Journal of Behavior Analysis*, and the *International Journal of Neuropsychopharmacology*.

The room's owner lay on what looked like a lumpy black recliner, supported by twin chrome rails, a copy of *Magic*

Magazine draped across his face. No shoes, just a pair of black-and-red socks with pictures of flaming dice on them. The faint drone of snoring, little pot belly going up and down.

Logan waited until Chalmers was inside, then slammed the office door shut, hard enough to make the framed diplomas rattle. 'Dave!'

Dr Goulding sat bolt upright, the magazine falling into his lap. 'I'm awake, I'm awake. . .' He blinked a couple of times, then reached for the pair of glasses on the coffee table and slipped them on. 'Logan, why didn't you. . .' A frown. 'Did she keep you waiting?'

'Ten minutes. Told us you were on a conference call to Johannesburg.'

'Woman's a nightmare. Just because I told her she couldn't have the day off to go play golf.' He stood, brushed biscuit crumbs from the front of his stripy shirt. 'Sorry, manners.' Dr Goulding picked up a pair of two-tone loafers and slipped them on. 'Take a seat, please.'

Logan settled into a black leather chair that was all rectangles, then nodded at Chalmers. 'Dave, this is Detective Sergeant Chalmers.'

The psychologist stuck his hand out. 'ChalmersDave-Goulding.' Pronouncing it in a rush, as if it was all one word. 'Please, sit, sit. Do you want tea, or coffee? We had some garibaldis, but. . .' He glanced at the crumbs on the chaise longue. 'Someone ate them.'

Logan pulled out Chalmers's Post-it note, then stuck it in the middle of the glass desk.

Dave sniffed. Then picked it up. 'A list of therapists? You've been seeing someone else?' A frown. 'I have to admit that I'm a little bit hurt by that, Logan. I thought the talking therapy was working, and that's why I hadn't heard from you. You could've said something when I was helping out this morning—'

'The four of you have been treating homeless men and women. For free.'

Bloody Chalmers was staring at him, one eyebrow raised as if she'd just heard he had a vestigial tail.

A frown. 'Well . . . yes. Only trying to do our bit for society. These people are vulnerable and conventional—'

'Do you know if any of you treated a Roy Forman?'

Dave tilted his head to one side. 'You could've just given us a phone: didn't have to come all the way out here. Not that I'm not happy to see you again, but. . .?'

'I need a favour as well.'

'Ah. I see.' He steepled his fingers. 'And *have* you been seeing someone else?'

'Dave, it's important—'

'Understand, my help isn't conditional on your response, I'm just interested.'

Brilliant. Discuss whether or not he'd been seeing another therapist, with DS Chalmers standing there, staring at him. No way *that* would be all over the station by close of play. 'No.'

'Hmmm. . . In that case, what can I do for you?'

'Professor Richard Marks. He was treating a young woman called Agnes Garfield as part of some kind of trial programme?'

Chalmers flipped open her notebook. 'Comparative benefit analysis of cognitive behaviour therapy and medication in the treatment of wide spectrum psychological disorders.'

A little smile curled at the corner of Dave's mouth. 'Is he a suspect in something? *Please* tell me the baldy sausage-faced old moron's a suspect. Is it molesting sheep? I'll bet it is, he looks like the type, doesn't he?'

'We think Agnes Garfield might have killed Roy Forman. Professor Marks is quoting doctor-patient confidentiality.'

Dave blinked. Then his eyes pinched nearly shut and he sank down into his big leather chair. 'Roy's *dead*?'

'We ID'd his body a couple of hours ago from a facial reconstruction. He was the necklacing victim.'

'I can't believe Roy's dead. We'd made so much progress. . .'

'Dave, we have to find her before she hurts anyone else. I need you to go talk to Professor Marks. It's a murder investigation, I can get a warrant if I have to, but if he cooperates it'll make everyone's lives a lot easier.'

A deep breath. A nod. Then he stood, straightened the cuffs on his stripy shirt, and marched for the door. 'Make yourselves comfortable. I'll get Little Miss Stroppy to get you a pot of tea.'

Clunk. And they were alone in the room.

Chalmers sat on the chaise longue thing, then lay back on it, putting her feet up. 'So . . . therapy, eh?'

'I've been stabbed, shot at, blown up, made to eat human flesh,' Logan held up his left hand and showed her the two thin scars in the palm, 'someone nailed my hand to the floor with a nail-gun, then tried to do the same with my head. Someone else set fire to my flat with me in it. My girlfriend's still in the hospital after that one. . .' He wandered over to the window, looking down on a patch of green dotted with trees. The goths from the High Street had heaped up their long black coats in a big pile so they could chase back and forth after the Frisbee, laughing and squealing like children. 'So yes: they sent me for therapy. It was that or be invalided out.'

'Oh. . .' She cleared her throat. 'Sorry, Guv. I didn't. . . Sorry.'

Silence.

Yeah, everyone was always sorry.

'Get on to Control: I want someone watching Agnes Garfield's house. Round the clock. If she wants her personal stuff she'll have to go back for it. Chase up the lookout call on Anthony Chung's car too. And talk to the PF's office: I

308

want a warrant for searching Dr Marks's files faxed over to this office within the hour.'

'I thought you said we could kill two birds with one stone?'

'Just in case. You know what these academics are like, stroppy bunch of sods can't—'

A crash sounded from somewhere down the corridor. Then the sound of raised voices filtered through.

'*Unprofessional bastard!*' Liverpool accent, so that would be Dave Goulding.

'*Get off me! Help! Someone call the police!*' And that wasn't.

'Oh crap. . .' Chalmers scrambled out of the chaise longue and ran for the door.

Logan followed her, charging out into the reception area.

The receptionist was standing by the door to the corridor, one hand to her mouth, eyes gleaming as she shifted from foot to foot. She was muttering to herself, voice barely audible over the shouting and scuffling coming from outside. 'Go on, hit him again, right in the balls. . .'

'*Agh! No biting!*'

Logan stuck his head out of the office door. Dr Dave Goulding had a short bald man in a headlock and was dragging him – kicking and swearing – down the corridor towards them.

29

'I want him *arrested*!' Professor Marks sat on the edge of a
black leather armchair, a wad of damp paper towels pressed
against his bottom jaw. His hair was little more than a
memory, clinging in grey wisps around a shiny bald head.
Big gold-framed glasses covered in fingerprints. No chin. His
face just sagged its way down into his neck. Goulding was
right: the man looked like a sausage. 'You're finished at this
institution, do you hear me? Finished!'

Goulding stood with his back to the window, arms crossed,
eyes narrowed. His right cheek was swollen, the skin shiny,
already beginning to darken into a bruise. 'Shut up, and tell
them what you told me.'

'Coming into my office, shouting the odds—'

'You knew she was dangerous!'

Logan massaged his temples. 'Is this really—'

'He attacked me!'

Goulding took a step towards Professor Marks. 'I'll knock
your bloody head off, you unprofessional git; she killed Roy
Forman!'

'You can't know that it's—'

'Do you have any idea how much time and effort I put

into fixing Roy? And you just set your pet psycho loose to kill him!'

Prof. Marks opened his mouth and ran a pale-yellow tongue across his premolars. 'You chipped my tooth. I should sue you.'

'I'll do more than—'

Logan slammed his hand down on the desk. 'All right, enough!'

Silence.

Goulding settled back against the windowsill again. 'Tell him what you told me, Marks, or I swear to God. . .'

The professor cleared his throat, shuffled in his seat, looked away. 'Doctor-patient confidentiality prohibits me from—'

'He's been in touch with her, since she went missing. He's talked to her.'

Professor Marks stared at him. 'I told you that in *strictest* confidence! You can't breach—'

'Oh grow up. I'm not bound by doctor–patient confidentiality; she's not my patient. If she *was*, she wouldn't be out there necklacing poor bastards who fought for their country!'

Logan glanced over at Chalmers. She sat on the chaise longue, scribbling away in her notebook. Good. 'We've got a warrant on the way. Soon as that gets here, you're either going to talk to us, or we're going to arrest you for obstruction, drag you down to the station, and throw you in a cell.'

'You can't do that. I'm the victim here, it's this violent Scouse—'

'And tomorrow morning, you'll go up in front of the Sheriff and he'll send you off to Craiginches till you decide to cooperate.'

Marks licked his lips. 'You. . . I'm a doctor, I can't just—'

'And meanwhile, Agnes Garfield is out there,' Logan stabbed a finger at the window, 'killing people! Do you *really* want to be responsible for another death?'

'I'm not responsible for anyone's death. Whatever happened to Roy Forman wasn't a result of my actions. If Agnes—'

'She beat the crap out of him, chained him to a stake, throttled him, stuck a tyre around his throat and set fire to it.' Logan reached into his pocket. 'Do you want to see the pictures? Want to see what that looks like?'

Professor Marks's knees twitched, then drew together, as if Logan had just offered to kick him in the balls. 'I'm bound by my Hippocratic oath to—'

Goulding lunged for him and Marks squealed, scrambled back into the armchair.

Chalmers was on her feet, blocking the way, one hand in the middle of Goulding's chest. 'All right, let's everyone just calm down. OK?'

He stared over her shoulder. *Tell* them, Marks.'

The professor closed his eyes, curled into himself. 'I took an oath.'

Goulding stared out of the office window, shoulders slumped, one hand on his forehead. 'Are you really going to arrest him?'

Logan looked up from his phone. 'Soon as they fax the warrant over.'

'Good.'

Thin grey light seeped in through the glass, the room darkening with the afternoon. It was a lot quieter without Professor Marks moaning on about his rights and his chipped tooth. Of course, Chalmers wouldn't be happy – having to babysit Marks in his own office, making sure he didn't do a runner for darkest Fife, or the hedonistic fleshpots of Inverurie – but tough. It was character building.

Or at least that's what Steel always told him when she was handing out the crappy assignments.

Logan went back to his phone. According to the screen,

there were nine voicemail messages waiting and half a dozen texts too. Half of which were from Steel:

```
You rancid wee shite! I'm going to rip
your nutsack off and make you wear it
as a hat!
```

```
You knew I wanted help with this meeting!
```

```
Get your arse back here NOW!!!!!!
```

Again with the scrotum threats. Still, say what you like about Steel, at least she didn't resort to text-speak.
Delete.
He deleted the other ones too, not bothering to read past the first line, all of which contained at least one swear word.
Goulding cleared his throat. 'I know dragging Marks down the corridor by the scruff of his neck must have seemed a little . . . unprofessional, but—'
'You had him in a headlock.'
'Roy Forman was making so much progress, coming on so well. To just throw it all away like that. . .' A sniff. 'Why didn't you tell me he was the necklacing victim? This morning, when I was interviewing Robert Whyte?'
'Didn't know you knew him. If I did, you couldn't have talked to Whyte: conflict of interest.'
The next text message was from Rennie, moaning on about how Henry Scott wasn't there by the time he got to Gilcomston Church, and why was Chalmers always the favourite, and it wasn't fair. Wah, wah, wah.
Delete.
Next one was from Tim Mair at Trading Standards:

```
Where the hell are you, McRae? We said
3 pm! I brought biscuits & everything!!!!!
```

Arse. Three. Ah well, never mind.
Logan poked out a reply with his thumbs:

```
Don't be such a girl. Got caught up on
murder enquiry.
Better leave it till later. Make it
17:15-ish?
```

'Did you know Roy was in Operation Desert Storm? Right behind enemy lines, fighting the Republican Guard. His squad was pinned down by sniper fire, then the mortar rounds started falling. They lost their commanding officer and half of the team. Roy caught a bit of shrapnel in the eye. Half-blind, bleeding heavily, he carried one of his mates three miles back to base camp, under fire the whole way.'

Logan looked up from his phone. 'He told DCI Steel he was caught in a roadside bomb.'

'Look, the point is, he was a hero. He was damaged fighting for his country, and he was out on the streets. And he was getting *better*.' A glower. 'Until Professor Skid Marks got involved.'

The last text was from Dr Graham:

```
Gt the SIA rslts bk frm Dundee
Vktm ws lcl
Gv me a phn & ill tlk U thru thm
```

What the hell did 'SIA' mean? The woman was a night-mare.

Goulding left the window and settled behind the desk. 'How's Samantha getting on?'

Logan thumbed out an answer:

```
I'll give you a call when I'm back in
the station.
How's the facial reconstruction coming?
```

He hit send. 'Just great. We went clubbing in Brechin last night. Going to the Maldives in July – do a bit of scuba diving.'

'I see. . .' He steepled his fingers. 'I've arranged for a Mental Health Officer to see Robert Whyte at four this afternoon. I'd be very surprised if he isn't in a secure ward by the end of the day.'

A nutjob, but not the *right* nutjob.

Logan stuck his phone back in his pocket. 'I think we're getting a cat.'

'That's good. From a therapeutic point of view it's probably a bit more effective than discussing all your problems with an imaginary person.'

For God's sake. He slumped in his seat, both hands covering his eyes. 'Here we go again. . .'

'I'm just saying it's not entirely healthy. And you *know* talking therapy works. Look at all the progress we've made over the last two years: we cured your vegetarianism, didn't we? You're drinking less, you've lost weight, *and* you're a lot less irritable.'

'Leave it, OK?' Jesus, nag, nag, nag.

'Logan, I'm serious: it's really not healthy to keep—'

'Take the bloody hint.' He dropped his hands from his face and jabbed a finger in Goulding's direction. 'I can still do you for assaulting Professor Marks.'

Silence.

Goulding sighed, then wandered over to his wall full of whiteboards. 'I'd like to work up a profile on Agnes Garfield. We know who she is, but it might help tell us *where* she is and what she's going to do next. And much though I hate to impugn the professional reputation of my esteemed colleague: Professor Richard Marks is a dribbling idiot.'

'I don't have any say on the budget for this one.'

'I'll do it for free, on the condition that you catch her. Roy didn't deserve to die like that.'

'Free?' Logan raised an eyebrow. 'In that case, knock yourself out. I'll get the case files sent over. And if it helps, I think she might have tortured someone to death in Kintore too.'

The office door swung partially open, and there was Chalmers. She froze on the threshold, then knocked. As if they didn't already know she was there. 'Sorry, Guv. That's the warrant in now.'

Logan stood. Put his phone away. 'He still refusing to cooperate?'

'Won't say a word.'

'Cuff him, then call Control and tell them to send a patrol car: give Marks the full blues-and-twos treatment. March the little sod out the front door in handcuffs so everyone can see.'

She nodded. 'Guv, about Agnes Garfield. . .?'

'You stay with him till the patrol car gets here. Make sure he's processed properly – fingerprints, DNA, the lot.'

'See, I was thinking: Roy Forman was in the Gordon Highlanders, right? A trained soldier, unarmed combat and all that? Would an eighteen-year-old girl *really* be able to subdue him, tie him up, and burn him like that? Wouldn't he fight back?'

Ah. . . Chalmers had a point. 'Maybe she had help?'

Goulding picked up a dry eraser. 'Roy was an alcoholic. Give him a bottle of meths and a straw and he'd do anything you want.' The eraser cut a swathe through a scribbled mind-map, leaving the ghost of words behind. He picked up a red pen and wrote 'AGNES GARFIELD' in the middle of the board and trapped it in a lopsided box. 'When you stick that

316

idiot Marks in his cell, do me a favour? Make sure there's someone noisy and smelly next door. It'll drive him mad.'

Logan took the grumbling Punto for another tour of the surrounding streets. Still no sodding parking space. In the end he had to dump the car on the Beach Boulevard and walk.

A cold wind stirred sand and grit in the gutter, made the trees shiver.

On the other end of the phone, Samantha sighed. *'Well . . . maybe Wee Hamish is right? Maybe you'll have to sort Reuben out sooner rather than later.'*

'I'm *not* killing Reuben.'

'Who said anything about killing him? I said sort him out. Make a deal with him.'

Logan grimaced. 'Yeah, because Reuben's the negotiating type.'

The little red man went green. A hatchback lurched to a halt, the bmtch-bmtch-bmtch of driving bass thumping out through the closed windows.

'So get him banged up for something. Don't just sit about and wait for the scar-faced fat scumbag to turn up on the doorstep with a machete and a power drill.'

Logan wandered across the road, taking his time, getting the evil eye from the hatchback's acne-ridden boy-racer driver. 'I'm not killing him, and I'm not fitting him up either.'

A scrunching noise – probably Samantha putting her hand over the mouthpiece – then a muffled conversation.

He nipped across the other side of the road, weaving his way between cars and trucks waiting at the roundabout. 'Look, I'm going to have to go. I'll give you a call later, OK? It's—'

And she was back. *'Listen, these bones of yours – the ones outside the caravan – your historian said they were for protection, right? What if they're not there to protect you? What if they're there to protect whoever made them?'*

'And that helps because. . .?'

'Remember, in the book, the Vodun bokor sticks one in Rowan's pack, so she won't track him down?'

Onto Justice Street, where a pair of bulky tower blocks loomed over the surrounding granite buildings, dark windows glinting in a stray beam of struggling sunshine.

'Sorry, but I don't—'

'God, how slow can you be? Think about it: when did you get the first knot of bones? Before Roy Forman was burned, right? Maybe even before she tortured the other guy?'

He stopped. 'She'd planned it all out. She knew I was looking for her, because I'd been to her house. So. . .' A frown. 'She tracked me down, followed me home. . .' Something cold caressed the back of his neck.

Logan spun around, his free hand clenched into a fist.

No one there.

A thin drizzle drifted down from the clay-coloured sky, misting the windscreens of parked cars, painting an anaemic rainbow in that one slice of sunlight.

'Don't be such a big girl. The bone knots are to protect her from you. She's scared of you. You're like a witch-finder finder.'

'Ah, right. . .' Jumping at his own shadow, like an idiot.

'You're welcome. Now, if you'll excuse me, I have to get tarted up for my new physical therapist. He's a bit hunky.' And Samantha was gone.

She was right: Agnes Garfield wasn't a criminal mastermind, or the next Hannibal Lecter, she was just an eighteen-year-old girl with mental health problems who wasn't taking her medication any more.

The poor girl was more scared of him than he was of her.

A warm breath escapes her lips, curling white in the light of the open chest freezer. Shiny packages wrapped in tinfoil, so many precious things. . .

318

Rowan leans forward until her cheeks rest against the cold plastic tray. Soothing. Calming. Damping down the fire in her head.

Everything will be OK.

The fifth tenet: 'Do not fear the darkness, make it fear you.'

She closes the freezer lid and the room goes black, just the gurgle and buzz as the compressor kicks in, taking it back down below zero again.

Shapes fade out of the gloom: the boxy outline of the big chest freezer, the scythe leaning against the wall, the lonely pegboard stained by the ghosts of implements past. The old wooden table. The sickly sweet stench of death.

'Light a fire in God's name. . .'

She takes a deep breath and straightens her back. It's time.

The door opens with a creak onto the next room. A barn, with dusty bales of hay stacked in the corner, heady with the smell of mildew. Mouse droppings make Morse code patterns on the dirt floor.

That won't do.

She picks up the broom and clears a patch in the middle, eight foot by eight foot. Then stands and stares down at the uneven grey surface, lights the black candle and traces the circles out across it. *Septen*, *merid*, *orien*, *occid* – north, south, east, and west. Then the names of God, the symbols, and finally the pentagram.

Rowan smiles. No gaps, no mistakes, a perfect Ring Knot.

The hammer is heavy in her black-gloved hand, and so is the metal stake. It rings like a bell as she batters it into the hard-packed dirt at the head of the pentagram, each blow jarring up her arm into her shoulder, sending up a little puff of dust.

Four more stakes go in and finally it's done.

The man in the corner says something behind his gag,

eyes wide and trembling. He's lying on his side, both hands tied behind his back. His wrists are red and chafed around the rope where he's been struggling, the ankles are the same – bare feet filthy and scratched. Tendrils of orange and red crackle around him, thorns of light scratching at the granite walls. Looking for weapons. Looking for a way out.

When what he should be looking for is redemption.

He's lucky, he gets to be *inside* the knot, protected from the darkness of witchcraft and unclean souls. From people like her. . .

She lays out the tools of her trade – the blade, the pin, the bottle of lemon juice, the can of shaving cream and the razor.

His soul might be protected, but his body is another matter.

Rowan stands, brushes the dust off her gloves. Faces her enemy. Keeps her voice level. 'The Kirk is my mother and father. It is my rod and my staff. My shield and my sword. What I do in its service lights a fire in God's name.'

Tears roll down his pale face.

Make the darkness fear you.

Rowan walks over to him, takes a deep breath, the scent of sweat and oranges and burning fill her head. Then she grabs a handful of his hair and drags him over to the Ring Knot. He kicks and screams the whole way until she taps him on the side of the head with the hammer – just hard enough to make him sag and groan.

Then she unties him and fixes him to the stakes. Spread out like a frog in a science lab, waiting for the lesson to begin.

She closes her eyes. Hangs her head. '*Miserere mei Deus secundum magnam.*'

Have mercy upon me, oh God, according to your loving kindness.

30

The rancid stench of a partial-decomp post mortem oozed out of the cutting room like an unplugged fridge full of raw meat left in the sun. Tuneless whistling joined the smell as Miss Dalrymple – in wellies and a thick rubber apron – hosed the tiled floor, chasing smears of blood down the drain.

Logan tried the viewing room.

Dr Graham was hunched over another resin skull, measuring it with callipers, then consulting a long table of figures. She looked up as he closed the door. Her smile was full of teeth. 'Just working out the tissue depth markers.'

'What does "SIA" mean?'

'Ah, right.' She hopped down off her stool and rummaged through a stack of paper. 'Stable Isotope Analysis. Got the results back from Dundee on that segment of thighbone we sent them. The one from your rooftop skeleton?' She handed him a wodge of paper streaked grey down one side where the mortuary printer's innards were eating themselves.

The report started out with social niceties – how nice it was to hear from Dr Graham again, and maybe they could go out for a drink next time she was in town – then descended into an almost indecipherable wodge of technical speak and wiggly-lined graphs.

Logan frowned at it for a bit. . .

Nope. Not a clue.

He passed it back. 'Any chance of the short version?'

'Well, the fourteen-C isotope analysis bomb-curve dating puts time of death between thirty and thirty-five years ago. Your victim wasn't recent.'

Thirty-five years ago? Agnes Garfield wasn't even born then.

'The thirteen-C and one-eighty stable isotopic composition in conjunction with the eighty-seven-S-R slash eighty-six-S-R isotope ratio and strontium—'

'The *short* version, Doctor.'

Pink bloomed on her cheeks. 'Sorry. To get strontium and one-eighty levels like this your victim had to live north of a line drawn between Montrose and Helensburgh. The thirteen-C data points to a Central European diet, so she wasn't from the States.'

Dr Graham took a sip from a bottle of water, sitting next to her collection of glass eyeballs. 'The analysis says your victim probably came from the north-east of Scotland – basically, draw a lumpy circle containing Kintore, Torphins, Coldstone, Craik, Ardlair, Insch and Inverurie. She spent most of her life in there. Apparently the only other place that'd match the strontium and one-eighty is the backwoods of Sutherland and Ross and Cromartyshire.'

Dr Graham flipped over to the last page. 'One more thing – there's a disjoint between the thirteen-C and the fifteen-N isotopes. Elevated fifteen-N means she was suffering from a long-term illness. Which explains the pitting on the skull. . .' Dr Graham picked up the cast and ran a finger around the eye socket. 'See the marks?'

'And you're positive she died thirty-five years ago?'

322

'Stable Isotope Analysis doesn't lie.'

'Sod.'

She hugged the skull. 'But doesn't that—'

'If it's less than fifty years we've got to treat it as a suspicious death. If it'd been *more* than fifty years we could have written it off as archaeological, because whoever killed her would probably be dead by now anyway. She'd be someone else's problem and I wouldn't have another sodding murder on my hands.'

Logan drummed his fingers on the viewing-room table.

Where the hell would Agnes Garfield get her hands on a murder victim from thirty-five years ago?

Dr Graham cleared her throat. 'Look, I don't want to seem greedy, but Miss Dalrymple tells me you've got a badly decomposed body that needs identifying?'

'Hmm?' He glanced back towards the cutting room. 'Steel won't let me authorize another facial reconstruction, I already asked.'

'Well. . . We could maybe try for the basics. Do you know if they did any X-rays? I'm here anyway.'

Worth a shot. Especially as it looked as if everything else was a washout.

He was back two minutes later with a bulky brown cardboard folder. 'You're in luck, they did the head and chest before they cut him open.'

Dr Graham dipped into the folder and came out with an X-ray of the skull from straight ahead, and one taken side on. She held them both up against the viewing-room window. The light from the room beyond was just bright enough to make the bones shine. 'Can you hold these for me?'

Logan did and she leaned in close, peering, squinting, poking at the film with a finger. The upper and lower jaw were a mess of cracks and shattered teeth – just a couple of molars hanging on at the back, one cheekbone broken into three separate bits.

Then she nodded and stepped back. 'You see how the nasal aperture is quite narrow? And the zygomatic bones are wide and prominent?'

No idea.

She had another squint at the X-ray, scratching at the image where the battered nose met the bone. 'Shame we can't get a good look at the nasal sill. . . But if you add in the interocular distance, short nasal spine, and the rounded palate, it means you're *probably* looking at an Oriental male. And given the openness of the sutures and the fact he's got three wisdom teeth at full occlusion, we can guesstimate an age of somewhere between seventeen and twenty-five. Probably. Give or take.'

Dr Graham shrugged. 'If you can talk them into letting me deflesh the skull, it'd help. Or if you can find me the missing teeth. . .?'

An Oriental male, early twenties, lying tortured in the middle of a Ring Knot from *Witchfire*. Someone who knew Agnes Garfield well enough to go there with her. Someone probably too stoned to put up much of a fight. Maybe someone who'd been screwing around behind her back?

Someone like Anthony Chung.

PC Sim curled her top lip. 'Grave robbing? Seriously?'

Logan handed her the stable isotope analysis. 'She had to get the remains from somewhere. Either she's stumbled on a shallow grave, or she's gone mining for bodies in the local cemetery.'

'Urgh. . . Grave robbing.'

'Look for females from the north-east, between sixty and seventy years old, died up to forty years ago. And they had syphilis.'

Sim scanned the report. 'You know what, Guv? I'm guessing there's *not* going to be enough bodies missing to muddy the issue.'

He pointed down the corridor towards the main CID office. 'Less sarcasm, more looking for dead old ladies.'

She rolled her eyes, then turned and ambled away and through the double doors, arms swinging at her sides like a grumpy wind-up toy.

No bloody respect, that was the problem with officers today.

Still, at least they were getting somewhere for a change. Almost. . .

He unlocked the door to his office, opened it, then froze.

Crap.

Steel was sitting behind his desk, with her feet up, fake cigarette glowing between her bared teeth. 'Make it good.'

Slam the door. Slam the door right now and RUN!

Logan licked his lips. 'How's the review meeting going?'

'HOW THE GOAT-BUGGERING HELL DO YOU THINK?' Spittle flew in the grey light. 'I *told* you—'

'I was out trying to catch her, OK? I wasn't sitting about the boardroom table poncing about with whiteboards and Post-it notes.' He hung his jacket on the hook by the door. 'So if you want to rant and rave for a bit, go ahead. But don't expect me to care.'

Steel narrowed her eyes. 'Bunch of soap-dodging tossbags, telling me how to run a murder enquiry. . .'

'I know something that'll cheer you up: I think we've got an ID on our Kintore victim.'

Steel stared at him. 'Well?'

'According to Dr Graham, he was an Oriental male in his mid-twenties. Can you think of anyone like that Agnes Garfield might want to hurt?'

There was a pause, then a smile spread through the

wrinkles. 'Anthony Chung. He was shagging some tart behind her back, wasn't he?'

'And according to their friends, they were always fighting. Breaking up, getting back together again, having blazing rows. . .'

Steel took a long drag on her cigarette. 'He shafts her over one time too many, she's no' taking her anti-nutbag pills any more, so she goes all witch-trial on his lying cheating, drug-dealing, girlfriend-beating arse. I'm no' saying he deserved it, but still.'

'Told you it'd cheer you up.'

'And I told *you* to find her.' Steel settled back in Logan's office chair and folded her arms, hoiking up her bosom. 'Don't think you deserve your present after all.'

There was a shame.

Steel nodded at a red folder, sitting on the desk by her feet. 'Preliminary post-mortem report. Read.'

'Already? That was quick. . .' He flipped the folder open and skimmed through the contents.

According to the report, Anthony had three-hundred and sixty-five stab marks all over his body, but they were only half a centimetre deep – the blade nowhere near long enough to penetrate an internal organ. And not one of them nicked a vein or artery. Slow, careful, and methodical. . . The probable cause of death was listed as ligature strangulation. So Agnes had veerited him, just like she'd veerited Roy Forman. Only this time she'd finished the job.

A colour photo was printed onto the sheet: a close-up of the wounds on Anthony Chung's chest. Four narrow dark-purple gashes, each one sitting in the middle of a perfectly round bruise, about the size of a two-pound coin. A wobbly hand-drawn sketch showed a knife with a tiny V-shaped blade and a circular guard. Should be fairly distinctive.

Steel gave a wet flobbery sigh, then pulled out the top

drawer of Logan's desk and rummaged through the contents. She emerged with his copy of *Witchfire*, curled her lip and squinted at the blurb on the back of the book. 'Our *friends* from Strathclyde find it "surprising and disappointing" that we've no' interviewed the author yet.'

'They think *he* killed Anthony Chung?'

'No' him, you idiot, crazed fans.'

'Like Agnes Garfield.'

'Like Agnes Garfield, only different.' Steel flipped the book open, held it out at arm's length, and peered down her nose at the pages. 'Any shagging in this?'

'Do you not have a review to be getting back to?'

'Comfort break. Any longer and I was going to throttle your bloody ex. "Oh, I'm such an expert on gang-related violence. Look at me with my big perky boobs. I'm so perfect because I got out of Grampian, and Strathclyde Police are so much more special and clever and—"'

'How's DI Bell getting on with the Chung murder?'

'Ding-Dong couldn't find a hand grenade in a bowl of suppositories.' Another angry puff. Then she dumped the book down on the desk. 'Since you're such a big fan, you can go talk to what's-his-face the writer boy. And while we're at it: we need someone to go tell Anthony Chung's parents he's dead.'

Logan blinked at her. 'But that's Ding-Dong's case, and—'

'Remember what I said about handing out jobbies to people who've pissed me off? Well right now, you're at the top of the list. And since you did such a *spectacular* job of catching Agnes before she killed him,' she shook a pair of jazz-hands at him, 'this turd's for you.'

Great.

'Fine, I'll tell his parents. Get one of them to come in and identify the body.'

Steel's shoulders fell an inch. 'Do you no' think they've

suffered enough? Four days mouldering away on a kitchen floor in May; he's in no fit state to be seen by anyone. Even then, a visual ID's going to be worthless. Just have to poke the labs till we get a DNA match from the teeth.'

Logan nodded, pulled his jacket back on again. 'Goulding's going to do us a profile. Gratis.'

'As long as it's free, he can skip bollock-naked up and down Holburn Street for all I care. Now get your backside over there and explain to Anthony Chung's mum and dad why their wee boy's no' coming home for dinner. And speak to that sodding author!'

'OK. . . Thanks.' Logan hung up and stuck the mobile back in his pocket.

PC Sim eased the pool car around the Haudagain round-about, driving as if the car was full of eggs, or sweating dynamite, windscreen wipers squeaking their way back and forth clearing away the misty drizzle. 'How's the case review going?'

Logan wound up his window. 'Like getting a prostate exam from a grizzly bear.'

Sim licked her lips. 'Are we *really* going to meet the guy who wrote *Witchfire*?'

'Thought you didn't like the book.'

'It's just, if I'd known, I could've taken a copy along for signing.' She stared straight again, picking at the steering wheel cover. 'Not for me, for my niece.'

Yeah, right.

'According to Insch, the guy's going to be there all day, doing script rewrites.'

Sim nodded. Smiled. Picked at the steering wheel some more. 'And you're sure we shouldn't go speak to Anthony Chung's parents first?'

A sigh stole the air from Logan's lungs. 'Their son's dead.

Soon as we tell them, that's it: their lives are blighted forever. Half an hour isn't going to change that.'

'Yeah, I'm not looking forward to it either.'

A battered Daihatsu 4Trak growled past in the outside lane, blue-grey smoke sputtering from the four-by-four's exhaust pipe.

Sim pointed at a manila folder on the dashboard. 'I searched through everything reported in the UK for the last two years – only one dead body still missing: a middle-aged man, killed in a motorbike crash in Shropshire fifteen years ago. They dug up one corner of the graveyard to move a gas main and can't remember where they put him.' She changed smoothly into fourth. 'So I got in touch with every council in Scotland and asked them to check their graveyards, just in case there's an open grave they don't know about, and the occupant's gone walkabout.'

'And?'

'The words "don't hold your breath" spring to mind. You know what councils are like: it'll take months.'

Ah well, too much to hope for an easy solution.

The 4Trak switched lanes right in front of them. PC Sim slammed on the brakes, missing it by inches, her face constricting around two flared nostrils. 'Dirty . . . bleeding . . . poop-head!'

'How can *no one* be missing a seventy-year-old dead woman?'

Sim leaned on the horn, the harsh '*Breeeeeeeeeeeeeeeeeeep!*' cutting through the drizzly afternoon. 'PICK A LANE!'

'Will you calm down?'

'It's flipping idiots like that who cause accidents. . .' Her eyes bugged. 'Did he just give me the finger?'

The 4Trak driver's arm was silhouetted between the front seats. Fist clenched, middle finger extended.

A cold, jagged smile spread across Sim's face. Then she

reached forward and flipped the switch – blue-and-white lights flickered behind the pool car's radiator grille, the siren giving its two-tone wail.

'Can you not just let it go?'

'Sorry, Guv, but we've got a *duty* to uphold.'

In the 4Trak, the middle finger was joined by the rest of its friends. But the silly sod slowed, then pulled into the bus stop up ahead.

Sim pulled in behind, lights flickering back at them from the four-by-four's muddy paintwork. 'Right, you little stinker. . .' She grabbed her hat off the dashboard and climbed out into the drizzle.

Might as well let her get it out of her system.

Logan pulled out his phone and settled back in his seat. Dialled Chalmers's number. 'Professor Marks: has he cracked yet?'

'Guv, was just about to call you. We've got another Oriental gentleman in A&E – says he "fell down some stairs". Managed to shatter both his kneecaps. According to the orthopaedic surgeon he must've fallen on a bag of hammers on the way down.'

Now there was a blast from the past. 'Claw hammers?'

'Can't tell. Gentleman in question is a Hong Gil-dong. Mr Hong entered the country legally on a student visa from South Korea twelve years ago. Never went home.'

Obviously.

Logan drummed his fingers on the dashboard for a minute. 'What was he studying?'

'I. . .' A pause. *'Sorry, Guv, I'll find out.'*

'Want to bet it was horticulture?'

31

A deep bass rumble filled Soundstage Two, low and loud enough to make Logan's lungs vibrate in his chest. All around him, people stood in silence, staring at the four-storey block-of-flats set as Nichole Fyfe scrambled across the roof, chased by three men dressed entirely in black. The action flickered across a massive widescreen TV down on the studio floor.

Half a dozen sprinkler heads were going full pelt, drenching the roof in fake rain, making everything glisten. Then a flash of light turned the world monochrome, followed by another bellow of thunder.

Nichole skidded to a halt at the edge of the roof, arms pinwheeling as a camera swooped up the building on a massive crane.

The three men behind her fanned out, knives and swords sparking in the lights as—

Someone tugged at Logan's sleeve.

He turned, and there was Nichole Fyfe, looking up at him. Eh?

Logan glanced back at the roof. No . . . she was still up there. Back to the one on the ground.

The likeness was uncanny.

She smiled. Then stood on her tiptoes to whisper in his ear, her breath warm and sweet against the side of his face. 'Body double. They won't let me do my own stunts.' A shrug. 'Insurance.' She backed off an inch or two and blinked at him. Then closed in again. 'I wanted to say thank you for . . . well, you know, this morning.'

He moved around, his lips brushing her hair on the way to return the favour. It smelled of mandarins. And something sweet and slightly sweaty. 'I'm just glad you're OK.'

Why was it suddenly getting uncomfortably warm?

Another flash, and a BOOM of thunder.

She wrapped her arms around his chest and kissed him on the cheek. Mouthed, 'Thank you' at him. Her eyes were huge and dark.

Logan cleared his throat.

And then the word *'CUT!'* boomed out of the speakers, followed by Zander's voice. *'Sorry people, we're getting terrible lens-flare off Inquisitor Three's sword. Can we get it sprayed?'*

As soon as the instruction was given an army of people swarmed out onto the roof, and everyone on the studio floor started talking at once.

Nichole stepped back. 'Is Robbie going to be all right?' Then a frown. 'I mean, the real Robbie, not . . . you know.'

'He's going to be detained under the Mental Health Act so they can run some tests. Then he's probably going to be treated in a secure facility for a while.'

'That's good, isn't it? That he's getting help?' She wrapped her arms around herself. 'I can't believe he'd *do* that to Wee Robbie.'

'Sometimes people do strange things.'

She stepped in close and kissed Logan on the cheek again. 'Thank you for looking after him. And me.'

'Yes, well. . .'

332

A dark rumbling voice cut through the background noise. 'Nichole?' Insch. 'They're ready for you in makeup, if you're sure you're up to it?'

She nodded, patted Logan on the chest. 'Thanks again.' Then turned and marched away, arms swinging at her sides, as if she was on parade.

Insch scowled, dug into his pocket, and came out with a little bag of apple slices. Popped one in his mouth. 'You should've spoken to him yesterday. And I *don't* appreciate you chatting up my lead actress.'

'I wasn't chatting. . .' Every bloody time. 'Is the writer here?'

'Mr Hunter is in conference room two. *Try* not to piss him off, or he'll spend the rest of the day hitting the gin and we'll get nothing decent out of him till tomorrow afternoon.'

'Can't promise anything. . .' He craned his neck, scanning the soundstage. 'Now, have you seen PC Sim?'

Conference room two was thick with the dark scent of freshly brewed coffee – a percolator gurgling away to itself in one corner of the large rectangular room. A load of desks had been pushed together to make one huge surface, the top nearly invisible beneath piles of different-coloured paper covered in scribbles and highlighter pen. The blinds were down, leaving the room to slump in the unsympathetic glare of fluorescent lighting. One wall was completely plastered in yellow, green, and orange Post-It notes, the opposite one hiding behind what looked like A4 frames from a storyboard.

The room's only occupant sat in the middle, frowning at the screen of a laptop, a 'WORLD'S WORST DAD' mug sitting by his mouse. Mid-forties; curly hair surrounding a high, domed forehead that shone in the overhead lights; goatee beard; glasses obviously bought to look 'hip' and 'with it', but failing.

Sim grabbed Logan's sleeve. 'Eek! That's him!'

Logan produced his warrant card. 'Mr Hunter?'

The man didn't look up from his screen, just waved a hand at the far corner of the desk. 'Just put them over there, and tell David I've solved his continuity problem with four-fifteen.'

'Police, Mr Hunter. I'm Detective Inspector McRae, this is PC Sim. We need to ask you a few questions.'

He peered at them over the top of his glasses. 'You haven't brought the sandwiches?'

Logan pulled out a chair and sat. 'Sim, why don't you get us all a cup of coffee. I'm sure Mr Hunter would like a refill.'

'Mmmpnnnn. . .?' She fidgeted for a moment, blushed, then scurried off to fiddle with the percolator.

Hunter shifted a stack of scripts to one side, and picked up a copy of the *Scottish Sun*. 'Let me guess, you're here about this?' The headline, 'SICKO SATANIC KILLER COPIES FILM MURDER SCENE' sat above a photo of the house in Kintore, and an artist's impression of the Ring Knot from *Witchfire*.

Logan took out his notebook. 'Do you have a lot of fans, Mr Hunter?'

'Why do the police always have to use people's last names? Is it meant to intimidate us?'

'It's meant to be polite.'

'Then you can call me William. I hate Will, Willy, Billy, and Bill, so don't bother.' He dumped the paper on the table. 'And yes, I have a lot of fans. Got so many emails I've had to employ a young woman to pretend to be me. Which is ironic, it's normally the other way round on the internet. But all that, "Where do you get your ideas from?" "Who would you cast in a film?" "When's the next book out?" was driving me mad.'

'What about . . . the more obsessive ones?'

334

His mouth stretched out and down. 'Nutters, you mean? Every writer gets them. People who think the characters are real, people who think they've got the right to tell you how to do your job, people who want to be Fingermen, people who want me to write their life story. You name it, I've had it.'

Sim plonked a coffee down in front of Logan, her hand shaking hard enough to slop some out over the side and onto the blue pages from a revised script. Then she scurried around to the other side and picked up Hunter's 'WORLD'S WORST DAD' mug and took it round to the percolator.

'And it's got worse since they started making the film?'

'Pfff. . .' He scratched at the curls fringing his big shiny forehead. 'Like mushrooms in a damp basement. Still, I suppose it's a small price to pay. I was fed up of being screwed around by the big Hollywood studios promising the earth, then delivering sod all. Eight times this thing was going to be made, before fizzling out. *Eight* times.' He swept his hands out, gesturing at the table and its piles of paper. 'But this time I get a percentage and a say in the production, so I let them have the rights cheap. Of course, I'm stuck in here, rewriting scenes, but at least the thing's *actually* getting made.' He let his hands fall back to the tabletop. 'Mind you, soon as they found out, the nutters came out in force.'

'Did any strike you as particularly odd, or threatening? Anyone speak about necklacing witches, or torturing them?'

'I don't even read most of them. If I did I'd have no time to get any writing done.'

Sim put the mug back on the table, by the laptop, blushing so hard she couldn't have been far off spontaneously combusting.

Hunter nodded at her. 'Thanks.'

The blush grew even darker and Sim just stood there, staring at him, not saying anything.

He patted her on the arm. 'It's all right, I don't bite. Would you like a signed book? I'm sure there's a copy or three knocking about here somewhere.'

'Eeek. . .'

Logan took out his Grampian Police business card and passed it across the tabletop. 'Your woman who answers the fan mail, can she forward everything suspicious on to us?'

'Don't know if she keeps it, but we can find out. . .' He moved the mouse about and clicked on things for a moment, then his fingers rattled across the laptop's keyboard like machine-gun fire. 'Done. She's in Iowa, so it might take a while. I can never remember how many hours they are behind UK time.'

'But you've not noticed anyone hanging around, behaving suspiciously?'

Hunter raised an eyebrow. 'The place is full of actors and film people, Inspector. All they do is behave suspiciously.'

It looked as if Anthony Chung's parents were actually home this time. An ugly Alfa Romeo four-by-four and a silver Porsche sat on the driveway behind the gates, both of them looking brand new, with custom number plates. Hard to believe that only three people lived in a house that big; a football team would have rattled around in it.

PC Sim pulled up at the kerb and peered out through the rain-flecked windscreen. 'Not short of a bob or two, then. Probably explains why their kid turned out the way he did. Rich and spoiled.'

'And dead.' Logan set his phone on silent, climbed out of the car, and hurried up the path to the front door – huddling under the porch as Sim ambled after him, glancing back over her shoulder every couple of steps at the signed limited edition hardback copy of *Witchfire* on the dashboard.

She straightened her stab-proof vest. Then reached for

the doorbell. Ravel's Bolero kicked in, followed by the bellowing of the massive Alsatian.

There was a buzz, then a woman's voice crackled from the intercom, mounted beneath a security camera. *'Who is it?'* The accent was posh and English. One of those BBC-announcer voices, before they went all regional.

Sim took a step back, looking up into the lens. 'Mrs Chung? It's the police.'

Inside, the dog was going mental. Barking and barking and barking.

'Can I see some identification please?'

As if the ninja black outfit with stab-proof vest, airwave handset, utility belt, and bowler hat with a chequered band around it wasn't enough. Sim held her warrant card up to the camera. 'We need to talk to you about Anthony.'

A pause. Then, *'Yes. Yes, of course. . .'* Click. The intercom went silent.

Sim puffed out her cheeks. 'How do you want to play this, Guv?'

'Rock-paper-scissors?'

Logan sat on the sofa in an opulent lounge. White walls, oil paintings, life-sized marble statue of a tiger with bronze stripes, deep-red leather furniture, and a cream carpet. The kind of room that probably got dirty if you looked at it.

Mrs Chung stood by the oversized marble fireplace, fidgeting with the heavy gold bracelet on her wrist. She was immaculately dressed in a red silk jacket and blue jeans, long glossy black hair framing a delicately featured face. An Alsatian sitting at her feet like a statue of Anubis. She cleared her throat. 'Is this. . . Should I get you a cup of tea or something?'

Sim took off her bowler and held it against her chest. 'Maybe you should have a seat.'

'Oh no. . .'

Even though he'd won, Logan stood. 'Mrs Chung, did Anthony have any distinguishing marks? Any tattoos, or something like that?'

'Oh no, no, no, no. . . Please. . .' She clutched a hand over her chest, scrunching the scarlet fabric into a fist.

'I'm sorry, Mrs Chung, but we believe we found Anthony's body last night.'

She stared down at the coffee table. Rocking back and forward. 'No.'

He took a step towards her. 'PC Sim's right, you should. . .' Logan froze. The Alsatian was on its feet, teeth bared – a deep, bowel-loosening growl directed right at him.

He backed away, slow and careful. No sudden moves. 'I'm very sorry for your loss.'

Sim's right hand slid down to the small canister of pepper-spray clipped to her belt, never taking her eyes off the dog. 'Do you want us to call someone for you? Your husband? Relatives? Maybe a friend?'

She just stared at them. 'Anthony can't be dead. He *can't*.'

A rattling clunk came from the hall outside the lounge – someone coming in through the front door – followed by an American accent, 'Honey? Thought we'd go out tonight. You know, bit of a celebration?'

Mrs Chung sank down onto the arm of a scarlet sofa, the dog still growling at Logan.

'What's eating Enfield?' The living-room door opened. 'Sounds like. . .' A small man in a pastel-green polo shirt froze on the threshold, a sports bag in one hand, greying short-back-and-sides slowly retreating up a high forehead. He blinked at PC Sim, standing there in her police uniform and the smile died on his lips. He took a deep breath, then took off his glasses and hung his head. 'I see.'

'Ray,' Mrs Chung placed a hand against her chest, one

hand fanning her face, 'tell them Anthony can't be dead! *Tell* them.'

Raymond Chung stood at the study window, overlooking a perfectly manicured garden, the borders and bushes aglow with flowers and shining leaves. 'I. . . I must apologize for my wife, Kim gets. . . She dotes on Anthony.' His hands trembled at his sides. '*Doted*.'

Logan settled back against the large teak desk. 'Please: there's nothing to apologize for. It must have been a horrible shock.'

The room was nearly bigger than Logan's entire caravan, lined with crowded wooden bookshelves. A couple of green leather sofas sat on the polished wooden floorboards, a small stack of gardening magazines lined up on a glass coffee table.

'We. . .' A breath. 'We left San Francisco, because Anthony was getting into trouble. Falling in with the wrong crowd. They weren't good for him, so we thought, hey – let's go somewhere nice and quiet and calm. Somewhere he can grow up safe. . . If anything, it got worse.' Raymond Chung sniffed. 'How did it happen?'

No point dragging it out – it'd be all over the papers soon enough. 'He was murdered. Tortured, then strangled. About four days ago.'

'Tortured. Oh God. . .' Ray Chung wiped his hands down the sides of his jeans. 'God, I. . . His girlfriend, Agnes, is she. . .?'

'We're still looking for her.'

'I should've asked first, her parents must be. . .' He blew out a shallow breath, then eased himself down onto one of the sofas. 'Tortured. . .'

'How well do you know Agnes Garfield?'

'She. . . I don't know, it was. . .' He took off his glasses and wiped his eyes with the heel of his hand. 'Sorry. If I'm honest, you know, *one hundred* percent honest, she was always too good for him. Anthony had her wrapped around his ego like creeping ivy. He said jump and she wouldn't even ask, "How high?" she'd just do it. But he doted on her. . .'

'Did Anthony ever talk about running away somewhere? Or moving out?'

'He always gets. . . He always got what he wanted.'

'Maybe he talked about a friend's house? Or a family member?'

'We don't have any family over here. Anthony. . .' A deep breath. 'We left San Francisco after Anthony's cousin got shot. He was dealing drugs on the wrong street corner. My brother and his wife said it was all Anthony's fault: that *he* got Grant involved in it. We haven't spoken in eight years.'

Raymond Chung turned his head, staring at the gardening magazines on the coffee table. Not looking at Logan. 'I. . . I guess I always knew Anthony would end up . . . that he'd. . .' He wiped his eyes again. 'Oh, boy. . .'

Logan stepped over to the large window, giving him a bit of space to nurture his grief. A fat ginger cat picked its way along the fence at the bottom of the garden, tail making snake curves through the drizzly air. 'I'm sorry, I know this must be incredibly distressing. A Family Liaison Officer is going to get in touch with you soon. They'll keep you up to date on the investigation, answer any questions you've got.'

'Will. . . Can we see him?'

Rotting away on a slab in the mortuary, with his teeth ripped out, covered in bruises and burns and cuts? 'I don't know if that's such a good idea. He was very badly beaten, and after four days in the heat, he's—'

'I want to see my son!'

*   *   *

PC Sim humped the mattress back into place, then tucked the sheet in again.

Logan leaned back against the wardrobe. 'Anything?'

Anthony Chung's room was almost as big as his father's study. A king-sized bed, shelves of DVDs and CDs, a dining-table-sized flatscreen TV, games consoles, sofa, desk, big shiny silver laptop, nautilus weight machine, collection of empty beer bottles stacked up into a pyramid.

She fluffed the duvet back where it'd come from. 'Not a sausage. But if his mum's up here making the bed and doing the hoovering. . .?'

He was never going to leave anything incriminating where she'd find it. Not unless he was trying to provoke a reaction. 'So: nothing under the bed, nothing in the desk drawers, or under the socks and pants.' Logan did a slow three-hundred-and-sixty-degree turn, with his eyes half-squinted shut.

Where would a rich, spoiled, manipulative little sod keep things he didn't want anyone to find?

Sim sank down on the edge of the bed. 'What makes you think he's hiding something?'

'Teenagers always are.' Logan nodded towards the window. 'Take a look.'

She picked herself up and wandered over, standing on her tiptoes to peer out at the garden. 'What?'

He joined her, pointing at the black plastic guttering a couple of feet down. Little white twists of paper lay amongst the shrivelled leaves, small cylinders of grey cigarette filters poking out. 'See that?'

A crease appeared between her narrowed eyes. 'So he smokes roll-ups. That's not—'

'Every single one of his friends said he was stoned off his face the whole time. And if he's up here smoking weed, then he's got a stash.'

'Are you sure, Guv?' She did a bit more peering. 'Why

would he put filters in his joints? What kind of person *does* that? I mean, I know he was American, but still. . .'

'So, where did he hide it?'

'Hmm. . .' Sim stepped back from the window. Then crossed to the shelves, fingers walking along the spines of the DVD cases, head tilted to one side – presumably so she could read the titles. And she thought Americans were weird.

Logan pulled out his phone, ignored the list of waiting text messages and called Control instead. 'Did DI Leith get an FLO organized for Anthony Chung's parents?'

The voice on the other end was nasal and gluey. *'Hold on. . .'* She paused for a moment, then a massive sneeze boomed out of the earpiece, followed by some bunged-up sniffing. *'Sodding hay fever. Sorry, erm. . . Here we go: PC Munro, she's down to visit soon as she's finished with a fatal RTI. You want me to put you through?'*

'Just wanted to make sure it was—'

'What?' A scrunching noise, then some muffled voices. *'Sorry about that. The Super wants to know if you've spoken to your visitor yet, only he's lowering the tone of the place.'*

'I don't have any visitors: I'm out at Anthony Chung's house.'

'You've got a visitor in reception.'

'Well . . . why didn't someone say something? I'm not bloody psychic!'

'We tried calling you about a dozen times.'

Brilliant. 'I've been delivering the death message to Anthony Chung's parents.' Oh God. . . What if it was Wee Hamish's lawyer, back for another round of *How Screwed Are You*? Logan licked his lips. 'Who is it?'

More scrunching and muffling. Then, *'Seriously? That's his name? OK. . .'* And she was back full-volume. *'Someone called "Dildo"? From Trading Standards?'*

Logan let his breath out in a long slow sigh. Whatever Dildo wanted, it could wait.

'*DI McRae?*'

'Tell him I'll give him a call when I get back.'

'*But what about—*'

He hung up.

PC Sim was grinning at him.

'What?'

She hooked a thumb over her shoulder at the shelves of DVD cases. 'He's got PlayStation games, and he's got Wii games, but he doesn't have. . .?'

'Is this going somewhere?'

'He doesn't have any Xbox games, but look,' she waved a hand at the stack of electronic equipment in the unit below the flatscreen TV, 'he's got an Xbox. Not a new one either, one of the old suitcase jobs.'

Sim hunkered down in front of the unit and pulled the black plastic games console from the shelf. It was about the size of two shoeboxes, with a big plastic 'X' on the top. 'Isn't even plugged into anything.' She dumped it on the computer desk and pulled on a pair of blue nitrile gloves. 'Should be easy enough to. . . There we go.' A click and the whole top came off.

Inside were two clear plastic bags of weed, half a dozen packs of Rizla papers, a few small metal tins, a little rolling machine, and a box of filters. No wires, no electronics.

Sim lifted one of the bags out and gave it a shoogle. The marijuana inside rustled. 'Wow, that's a *poop*-load of weed. Maybe he was dealing?'

'Anything else in there? Diary? Address book? Anything like that?'

Sim went back to the hollowed out Xbox and rummaged about. 'Nope. Couple of tins of resin, some pills, but nothing old-fashioned like a diary. Kids these days are all electronic.'

Too much to hope for. 'Right, confiscate the drugs, the laptop, and any phones you can find.'

She clicked the top back on the Xbox. 'Who knows, maybe we'll get lucky?'

There was always a first time.

32

The mortuary was quiet: no shrieking bone-saw, no music playing in the cutting room, no roar of the extractor fans whisking away the stench of death. Just the sound of Mrs Chung breathing – jagged, gasping, as if she was about to pass out – clutching onto her husband's arm like a life raft. Adrift in a sea of fear and pain.

Logan cleared his throat. 'Are you sure you want to do this?'

She nodded, setting a couple of tears free to sparkle against her cheeks in the dimmed lighting.

'Because you don't have to. Remember the photos I showed you: he's been very badly—'

'No.' The words came out strangled and choked: 'I need to see my baby. . .'

'OK.' Deep breath.

He gave the nod and Rennie pressed the button. The curtains slid open, revealing Anthony Chung's remains.

They'd done the best they could – covered up everything below his chin with white ruffled fabric – but there was nothing they could do about his face.

Anthony's mother paled. Her whole body shuddered. Then her eyes bugged and she slapped both hands over her mouth, turned and scrambled out of the room. Rennie hurried after her.

'He's. . .' Raymond Chung swallowed, staring down at the ruined features. 'What did they do to his eyes?'

'It's just the decomposition. Remember, we went over this in the family room? It's natural: they're one of the first things to go.'

'Right. . . Decomposition. . .' He blinked a couple of times, sweat glistening on his forehead.

'Mr Chung?'

He licked his lips, then his Adam's apple bobbed, as if he was forcing something down. 'There's something sticking out. On his neck.' Raymond Chung's finger traced a circle on the glass. 'There. The tattoo?'

It was barely visible through the blackened discolouration of the skin, but three jagged spikes poked out from the edge of the sheet drawn up under the body's chin.

Raymond Chung bit his lip. 'Can you. . . Can you ask them to lower the sheet?'

Logan pressed the button on the intercom. 'Can we get the sheet lowered a bit on the left?'

On the other side of the viewing window, Miss Dalrymple stepped from the shadows, dressed in a clean set of surgical scrubs, and gently pulled the fabric down exposing the ghost of a tribal tattoo, broken up by tiny cuts.

Raymond Chung closed his eyes and rested his forehead against the glass. 'It's him. It's Anthony.'

'Are you sure, because there's no tattoo on the photos we've—'

'I know my own son!' His shoulders quivered. 'He got the tattoo the day before he went missing. He said it would impress Agnes. . .' Raymond Chung wrapped his arms around himself. 'Please, just. . .' A shuddering breath. 'I can't do this any more.'

*   *   *

346

Rennie backed into the room, balancing two coffees on the lid from a box of copier paper with one hand, and holding a blue folder in the other, a glossy magazine trapped in his armpit. He placed the makeshift tray on the corner of Logan's desk and sank into the visitor's chair. 'Poor woman nearly turned herself inside out.' He dipped into his jacket and produced a couple of chunky Kit Kats.

'Can't really blame her.'

Rennie unwrapped one of the biscuits, bit into it, took a slurp of his coffee, then slumped back with his magazine: *Heat*, with yet another photo of Nichole Fyfe and Morgan Mitchell on the cover. The pair of them posing in their leather Fingermen getup with shiny swords and handguns. 'CLOSER THAN SISTERS ~ NICHOLE AND MORGAN SPILL THE BEANS ON GUYS, GUNS, AND GETTING THE *PERFECT* MOVIE-STAR BODY!'

Logan creaked the top off his coffee. 'Comfortable?'

'Not bad, thanks.' He flipped through the pages, little bits of Kit Kat sticking to his chin as he chewed. Then stopped, mouth hanging open. 'Ooh, *Matron*!' Rennie held up the centre spread – Nichole and Morgan in bikinis, posing on Balmedie Beach. 'See if I wasn't married. . .'

'She'd still have nothing to do with you.' Logan fired up his email. No sign of any threatening or weird fan mail from William Hunter's web person yet.

'Nah, I'd be a good influence on her.' He turned the magazine the right way round again and smiled down at the photo. 'Keep her on the straight and narrow.'

There were half a dozen or so memos from Steel, a reminder from the ACC about not talking to the press, and four warnings from Internal Services about what would happen if they caught whoever it was who kept jamming up the third-floor toilets with packing peanuts.

Delete.

Rennie took another bite of Kit Kat. 'Guthrie bet me

twenty quid she'd knifed someone when she was thirteen. Silly sod.'

Logan looked up from his email. 'She *knifed* someone?'

'Course she didn't. Her boyfriend battered the crap out of someone with a cricket bat when he was fifteen, but worst she ever did was a spot of unlawful removal and some shoplifting from WHSmiths. Nicking cars and Bounty Bars. Not exactly Moriarty, is it?'

Hmph. He went back to deleting things. 'You're not supposed to do PNC searches on people to settle bets. Lucky I don't report you.'

'Ah. . . Well, it wasn't *really* a—' Rennie's phone rang somewhere deep in his pocket. 'Saved by the bell.' He dragged it out, pressed a button, then stuck it to his ear. 'Yeah. . . Uh-huh. . . Right. . . OK, I'll tell him.' Then he hung up and polished off the last of his Kit Kat.

'Tell me what?'

Rennie grinned, smears of chocolate sticking to his teeth. 'They've found a hole. . .'

Logan peered over the edge of the hole at the dark, damp earth down below. 'And they didn't see anyone?'

Rennie settled his backside against a lichen-covered tombstone and yawned. 'Groundskeeper says it could've happened anytime in the last four weeks. Since the cutbacks, he only comes in once a month.'

The graveyard mouldered away behind a six-foot-high stone wall, circling a crumbling granite church – its walls streaked green with moss beneath the rusting gutters. Brambles ran rampant around the outskirts, tumbling barbed-wire tendrils reaching out to engulf the nearest graves. Silver-haired dandelions nodded their heads, going bald in the breeze. A butterfly bobbing above the long damp grass.

One and a half walls were all that was left of the church,

a corner of thick granite blocks, the mortar crumbling away. Give it another hundred years and there'd be nothing left but a pile of rubble overgrown with weeds.

The hole was about three feet long, and four deep, surrounded by docken spears and violent-fuchsia rosebay willowherb. Soil made a sprawling heap along one side.

'And there was definitely a body in here?'

'Difficult to tell, apparently. When the church burned down in fifty-two it took most of the local records with it. Half the headstones in this section are knackered or missing.'

Logan crouched down; a cascade of dirt spiralled down into the earth. The smell of mouldy bread greeted him. 'Looks like we've got spade-marks on the hole. Should be able to match them if we can find the shovel.'

Another yawn. 'You think it's really her? Agnes Garfield?'

'Mentally unstable woman stops taking her medication, kills abusive boyfriend.'

'Yeah, but digs up bodies in a cemetery?' Rennie ran a hand through his spiky blond hair. 'I mean, I've had some mental girlfriends in my time, but not *grave robbing* mental.'

'Might not even be her.' Logan stood, brushed the dirt from his hands. 'Get the SEB down here: I want to know when this was dug. Is this the skeleton we've already got, or something new?'

'If it is, she's a total nutcase.' Rennie wrapped his arms around himself, yawning and shuddering. 'Anyone capable of doing *that* to poor old Fusty Forman needs locking up. And I'm talking: straitjacket, padded wallpaper, and throw away the key. Not like *he* was cheating on her, was it?'

Just a random act of violence? Not likely. 'He must've done something.'

'Anyway,' Rennie nodded at the hole, 'who's to say she was digging someone up? Maybe she was burying something and someone disturbed her?'

349

Idiot.

Logan pulled out his phone and scrolled through his contacts till he came to the number for the council historian.

'No, think about it, witches are always burying things in graveyards by the light of the full moon, aren't they?'

'She's not a witch, she's a teenager.' He hit the button. Dialling.

'Yeah, but maybe she *thinks* she's a witch? That's why she did that big magic circle on the kitchen floor when she killed Anthony Chung: witchcraft.'

'She drew it because it was in the book. She necklaced Roy Forman because it was in the book.' Logan headed back towards the car, damp grass tugging at his legs. 'That's what she does.'

Rennie slouched along after him, kicking through the weeds. 'Anyway, it can't be the skeleton from your caravan roof, can it? Don't think there's a single headstone in here more recent than eighteen ninety. Your body only died, what: thirty years ago?'

Sodding hell. The idiot was right.

'In that case it's—'

The line clicked. '*Hello?*'

'Mr Hay? It's DI McRae.'

'*Ah. . .*' A breath. '*It's not another dead body, is it? Only after last time—*'

'Someone's been digging up graves.'

'*. . .OK. That's not really my area of—*'

'From about the eighteen hundreds. I need you to find out who was buried where in. . .' He stuck a hand over the mouthpiece. 'Where are we?'

'Sign out front says Kingleath Parish Church.'

'Kingleath Parish Church, about five miles east of Inverurie. Place is a ruin.'

'*Hold on. . .*' There was the sound of fingers hammering

350

away at a keyboard. *'We've had students from RGU in comput-erizing a load of the parish records. . . Ah, you're in luck – they've done Kingleath. Right, where was your grave?'*

Logan peered back towards the hole. 'About fifteen feet from the west wall of the cemetery and a dozen from the north.'

'OK. . . Any nearby graves you can give me names from?'

'Hold on.' Logan slapped his hand over the mouthpiece and told Rennie to go look.

Two minutes later he was back, shaking one hand, clenching it into a fist then out again, blowing on the angry pink rash dotted with little pale spots. 'Sodding nettles.'

'Graves?'

'Nearest one I could read is a Mrs Katie Cook, snuffed it in 1892. About two plots to the left.'

Logan passed the info on and there were more clattering keystrokes.

'Well, in that case we can narrow it down to one of two people: Miss Polly McGrath, spinster of the parish, born 1862, died 1885; or a Mr Nicholas Alexander Balfour, born 1835, died 1890. . .' Pause. *'Nicholas Balfour. Nicholas Balfour. Why does that. . .? Give me a second.'*

More typing. Then a little swearing. Then some rustling. And finally Hay came back on the line. *'I knew it sounded familiar: Nicholas Alexander Balfour was a Victorian spiritualist and medium. He performed séances all over the UK, even did one for Victor Hugo on Jersey in 1853. Balfour was strangled in Inverurie by a widower called Sandy Hugh. Hugh thought his dead wife was going to appear to Balfour and reveal that he'd poisoned her.'*

And then, over a hundred and twenty years later, Agnes Garfield came along and dug up Balfour's bones. Which made sense – after all, she'd arranged nearly all of her last skeleton on Logan's roof, she'd need to get another one from somewhere.

'Thanks.' Logan hung up, and *almost* got his phone back

in his pocket before it started ringing again. 'Oh . . . bugger off.' He answered it anyway. 'Hello?'

A wet gravelly voice, half Aberdonian, half public school. Wee Hamish Mowat. *'Ah, Logan, I have a favour to ask.'*

Crap. . .

He held the phone against his chest. 'Rennie: call Control and see if they've got anything out of Dr Marks yet.'

'Yes, Guv.' Rennie wandered off towards the car, poking away at his mobile phone, spiky blond hair glowing in a sliver of sunlight.

Logan waited until he was out of earshot. 'Hamish.'

'You see, it's a rather delicate matter involving a group of foreign businessmen and a team of local entrepreneurs.'

'The cannabis farms?'

'Have you ever read Darwin's On the Origin of Species?'

He rested back against one of the church's remaining walls. 'We found another Oriental victim this morning. Someone took a hammer to his knees.'

'The theory of evolution is an extremely elegant thing, don't you think? I'm all for survival of the fittest, but sometimes competition for resources can get out of hand and that's not good for the ecosystem. Everything gets out of balance.'

'It's the McLeod brothers, isn't it? They're the ones crippling all these Oriental men. What are they, moving in on their territory?'

'I don't like to take sides in these things, Logan. It's of no matter to me which species outcompetes the other as long as the ecosystem remains intact. And the longer this drags on for, the more damage is done.' A pause. *'Perhaps you wouldn't mind giving evolution a helping hand?'*

The sliver of sunlight that had made Rennie's hair glow like a novelty light bulb gave one last flash, then the clouds swallowed it. A single drop of rain burst on Logan's arm. Then another.

A favour for Wee Hamish Mowat. It wasn't as if he'd be doing anything wrong, would it? The McLeods and the farmers were breaking the law. Both sets needed taking off the streets. Just because it was in Wee Hamish's best interests to see it all come to a sudden halt, it didn't mean it wasn't the right thing to do.

And besides, it would hardly be the first time.

'Logan? Are you still there?'

'I can't do anything without evidence. I need photographs, locations of these cannabis farms, someone willing to testify in court. Proof.'

'Of course you do. I wouldn't have it any other way.'

Logan put the phone back in his pocket.

Off in the distance came a soft crack, followed by the muted bellow of thunder. Getting colder. The skies lowered and the rain hammered down.

33

'I told you: I am not prepared to breach doctor—'

'Patient confidentiality. Can you no' change the record, Doc? This one's like listening to paint dry.' If DCI Steel slouched any further down in her chair, she'd disappear under the table.

On the other side, sitting in the full glare of the camera mounted on the interview-room wall, Dr Marks stuck his nose in the air. The bruise on his cheek was colouring in nicely, heading to a deep violet, giving a bit of life to his jumbo sausage features. 'If you don't *like* hearing it, stop asking.'

Logan opened DI Leith's folder of photographs and laid a glossy eight-by-ten of Roy Forman's fire-ravaged skull on the table. Then another one. Then one where the tyre was still burning. 'Agnes Garfield did this.'

The psychologist shrank back in his chair. Looking anywhere but at the photos. 'I don't see what this is supposed to achieve. Did you *really* think I'd be prepared to abandon my professional ethics just because you show me these? Do you honestly believe I got where I am without recognizing blatant manipulation when I see it?'

A sniff, then Steel jabbed a finger at him. 'You'll sodding

well know the toe of my boot when you see it. Aye, and it'll be coming out of your gob after I ram it up your arse-hole.'

Dr Marks took off his big gold-framed glasses and pinched the bridge of his nose. 'Genuinely: if you're going to resort to threats, try to do it in a way that actually connects to the person you're threatening. So far all you've done is reveal an anal fixation that borders on the manic.'

'I'm no'—'

'"Arse" this, and "arse" that. And you say *I'm* the one who needs to change the record. Then there's all the "scrotum" threats: you'll use it as a handbag; you'll fill it with angry bees and sew it over my bumhole; you'll make soup in it; you'll make me wear it as a gimp mask. . .'

'Laz, show the good doctor your photos of Anthony Chung.'

Logan opened the other folder.

Dr Marks sat forward, one hand curled around his barely existent chin. 'You never really got on with your father, did you, Chief Inspector? You always felt that nothing you did was good enough for him. Did he have a problem accepting your sexuality? He did, didn't he? Always hoped it'd just be a phase you were going through.'

The first picture of Anthony Chung was of him lying on the kitchen floor, surrounded by Agnes Garfield's Ring Knot, his skin coloured with mould and decay, his eyes rotted away to dark slits. Logan laid the photo on the table. 'He would've bled to death, but she veerlted him first. Wrapped a rope around his throat and twisted.'

'It must be hard, keeping it up: the posturing, the swearing, the constant scratching. . . You're like someone's stereotyped idea of a man. More manly than the men you have to work with. I imagine you consider yourself a bit of a womanizer too, don't you? Always trying to compete. . .'

355

She scowled at the psychologist. 'Up your hole with a loo-brush, you saggy-chinned wee cockshite.'

Well, that was helping.

Logan placed the next picture of Anthony Chung next to the first. 'Dr Marks, Agnes Garfield is probably a danger to herself, she's certainly a danger to other people.'

The psychologist popped his glasses back on. 'Your father always wanted a son, and you thought that was the only way to get his approval. So you've built this whole vile persona around the selfish wishes of a dead man. Did he ever—'

Steel slammed her hand down on the tabletop. 'YOU LEAVE MY DAD OUT OF IT AND ANSWER THE BLOODY QUESTION!'

A sigh. 'I can't breach doctor-patient confidentiality. Even *with* a warrant. Even if they try to compel me in court. The people who come to me for therapy have to be able to trust me with their darkest thoughts, desires, and secrets. If they can't, I can't help them.'

Logan put down the next photo – a close-up of Anthony Chung on the cutting table, his chest opened up and hollowed out. 'Where's Agnes Garfield?'

Dr Marks sat back again, looking at Steel over the top of his glasses, his voice soft and low. Soothing. 'It must have been very painful for you, having to live up to so many expectations. But it's not too late to be the real *you*, instead of this . . . projection you've become. I'd love to help, I genuinely would.' A smile tugged at one side of his sausagey face. 'I'd give you one of my cards, but they confiscated them when they took my belt and my shoelaces. But I want you to know that you *can* get better.'

Steel stared at him. 'And you can get bent.'

The Police Custody and Security Officer printed 'DR RICHARD MARKS' on the board beside the door of cell number eight.

Then frowned. Then smiled. She pointed. 'Look: his name's Dick Marks. What kind of parent calls their kid Dickmarks? No wonder he turned out a total knob. . .'

'Just make sure he gets noisy neighbours tonight, OK? Someone who likes to sing on one side, and someone with Tourette's on the other.'

'Do my best.'

Steel was standing just outside the back door, smoking her cheeks hollow and glowering at the rain. It bounced back from the roof of grimy patrol cars, sparkling in the rear podium's security lights. 'He fall down the stairs yet?'

'There's going to be another victim.'

'Little prick. Where does he get off with all that psycho-babble, eh? Sod all wrong with me. . .' She took another vicious puff, the cigarette trembling between her lips. '*He's* the one with bloody issues!'

'Stacey Gourdon. Anthony Chung was sleeping with her behind Agnes's back. No one's seen her since Friday night.'

'That's all we sodding need. Media department are already getting phone calls about Chung and his magic circle. Some greasy bugger's tipped off the papers.'

Brilliant. As if this wasn't hard enough. 'Do they know it's him?'

'Will do soon enough: ACC's doing a press conference at eight. Wheeling out Anthony's mum and dad, so they can tell the world how they're worried about Agnes and want her to be safe.'

'It's not her I'm worried about.'

A couple of uniforms slogged their way up the rear ramp, water dripping from the brims of their peaked caps. No point in hurrying, they probably couldn't get any wetter.

One last puff, then Steel pinged her cigarette butt out into the downpour. It bounced off the Chief Constable's Bentley, sparking against the paintwork. 'And for the record: I don't give a flying monkey's willy-warmer what my father thought.'

A knock at the office door, then Chalmers slipped inside. 'Guv?'

Logan signed the last form in the stack and stuck it in his out-tray. Halle-bloody-luiah. 'Where have you been?'

'Chasing down some leads on the Garfield case.' She shrugged, gave him a half smile. 'Nothing but dead-ends, sorry. But I wanted to ask if—'

'If it's not toe-curling urgent: go home.' He stood, paused, then cricked his head to one side, then back the other way – something in his neck popped and creaked like a fistful of gristle.

'I want to volunteer for the soup-kitchen job.'

'Nothing to do with me: it's DI Bell's shout.' Logan sat back down again. 'Where are we with the GSM trace?'

'Still nothing. I got in touch with their phone companies: neither of them's used their mobiles for a week and a bit. No outgoing calls or text messages.'

He swivelled his chair from side to side, staring up at the ceiling. 'So they've not used their phones for a week, but Agnes Garfield still manages to get in touch with her therapist. . .'

'Probably just picked up a new pay-as-you-go SIM card. Bet Dr Marks has got the number though.' A shrug. 'If we could get him to talk.'

Whatever happened to the good old days, when you could batter a suspect around the legs and back with a length of rubber hose till they confessed? Still, with any luck Goulding was right and a night in the cells surrounded by drunken idiots would break Dr Marks like a stale biscuit. 'Go home. Get some rest.'

'But, Guv, the soup kitchen is—'

'They don't start serving till nine. Gives you nearly an hour and a half. Tell DI Bell I said you're to help him out till midnight, no later. I want you in bang on time tomorrow. And look. . .' He picked Agnes Garfield's stolen dittay book off his desk, then followed it with Chalmers's report on its contents. 'I'm taking both home to read tonight. Just make sure that next time, you *hand* them to me.'

'Yes, Guv.' She smiled, showing off those sharp little teeth of hers. 'Thanks, Guv.'

'Oh, and this soup-kitchen job: don't think you're getting any overtime for it, OK?'

Standing in the corridor, Logan locked the office door. Closed his eyes. Rested his head against the cool wooden surface. Home. . . Quarter to eight: forty-five minutes to get back to the caravan and get the lasagne in the oven.

His phone buzzed in his pocket: text message.

Do U want me 2 pick up some wine or something?

Logan thumbed in a quick reply, then froze.

A voice behind him: 'Guv?'

He slipped the phone back into his pocket. 'Rennie, unless your head's on fire, I'm not interested.'

'Got something for you?'

Probably another moan. He took the keys out of the lock and dumped them in his pocket. 'Thought you were back on days now?'

'No, you're going to love this one. . .'

Logan turned, slumped back against the door. 'I swear to God, if this isn't good, I'm going to knee your testicles into orbit. Deal?'

Rennie grinned. 'You know you've got Chalmers looking

359

for Stacey Gourdon? Well, guess who *I* found?' He contorted his face into a Popeye wink. 'Go on, I bet you can't. . .?'

The cell block reverberated with the sounds of what could almost be called singing. As long as you didn't care too much about lyrics, melody, or adhering to any one key.

Kathy the PCSO led the way to the block of cells where they kept the female prisoners. 'Still haven't found anyone with Tourette's, but the night's young.'

She stopped outside the cell at the end of the corridor. Then slid the hatch open. 'Stacey Gourdon: breach of the peace. Otherwise known as staggering blootered down Belmont Street at three in the afternoon with her dress hoiked up around her armpits and no pants on, shouting at random strangers to, and I quote, "Taste the rainbow of fruit flavours." Uniform turned up and she tried to stab them with her high heels.'

Classy.

Rennie hooked his thumb at the cell door. 'See? What did I tell you?'

Logan stepped up and peered inside.

A young woman sat on the edge of the blue plastic mattress, holding onto the bed, staring at the other side of the room, mouth hanging open, blinking in slow motion. Her short black dress was rucked up on one side, her knees scraped red and speckled with scabs. Bruises made a violet tattoo on her bare shoulder. Short black hair sticking out in all directions, like a punk pixie.

Not dead then.

Logan knocked on the metal door. 'Stacey? You up to answering a couple of questions?'

Her voice sounded as if it belonged at the bottom of a well. 'I didn't do it.'

'Didn't do what?'

'Whatever it is you're trying to pin on me. *That's* the "what" I didn't do.'

'Anthony Chung.'

She turned to look at the hatch. Her mascara and lipstick was all smeared to the right, as if her head was suffering from motion blur. 'Now *that* I did do.'

Stacey Gourdon sat on the chair with her knees up against her chest, picking away at her scabby knees. 'This whole interrogation gestalt is so passé, isn't it? What happened to the good old-fashioned smoky room, with the single light bulb? Sometimes there's comfort in cliché, don't you think?'

Building Maintenance had given interview room two a fresh coat of paint. It was a bit like putting an Elastoplast on a tumour.

Logan sighed. 'For the last time: you *can't* have a cigarette.'

'But I *can* have a lawyer.'

'If you want one. But I'm not interested in you, I want to know about Anthony Chung and Agnes Garfield.'

'Gagh. . .' Stacey's mouth opened wide and down, as if she'd just swallowed something bitter. 'They are *so* high maintenance. A sweet couple, but just . . . completely. . .' Stacey stopped picking and twirled a forefinger at the side of her head instead.

'You know they're missing?'

'You're not asking the right question.'

OK. . . 'What's the right question?'

'Do I know where they are now?'

Logan sat back in his seat. 'And do you?'

'Nope.' She went back to picking. 'Next question.'

'You haven't heard from them at all?'

A chunk of brown scab came loose, the skin beneath it pink and shiny. A dot of red oozed to the surface. 'Of course, Anthony treated poor Agnes appallingly. She was obsessed with him and he wrapped her around his little finger. And you know what? She was just as bad.' Stacey popped the liberated chunk of scab in her mouth and chewed. 'Now, your next question is, "Did she know I was shagging dear Anthony at the same time?" And the answer is: of course she did. He told her.'

'He told her?'

'Oh, he did more than that: Anthony arranged a three-way. Me, him, and fiery little Agnes.' Stacey smiled at Logan, long and slow. 'You might not think it to see me now, but I do scrub up *very* nicely.'

'And Agnes was OK with that?'

'Well, she wasn't really into the whole girl-on-girl part of proceedings, but she did her best. For him. And she did have a *lovely* little body. . .' Stacey sighed, then popped another scab into her mouth. 'We met up every couple of weeks after that, until Anthony got bored. Always fluttering from one thing to another is our Anthony, like a little American butterfly with Attention Deficit Disorder.'

Logan frowned. OK, right now Stacey looked as if she'd slept in a skip and smelled like the floor of a pub after a rowdy night, but under the stale alcohol haze, the smeared makeup, messy hair, and scabby knees she probably *was* a very attractive young woman.

'Agnes did it to please Anthony Chung, but what was in it for you?'

A grin lit up her face. 'Darling, he has the most wonderful weed you've ever smoked in your life. And it pissed Daddy off no end that I was shagging a Chinaman.'

Maybe not so attractive.

'Well, your dad can rest easy: Anthony Chung's dead.'

'Ah. . .' The grin faded from Stacey's face. 'In that case, I think I *will* take that lawyer after all.'

* * *

362

DI Bell stopped in the middle of the corridor. He tightened his grip on the folder under his arm and narrowed his eyes. 'What are *you* doing here?'

'And hello to you too.' Logan locked his office door. *Again.* Second time lucky.

'I don't need you checking up on me, I'm perfectly capable of organizing a simple op at a soup kitchen. I was a DI long before—'

'I'm going home, OK? Had to process someone who was sleeping with Anthony Chung. And Agnes Garfield.'

Ding-Dong sidled closer, big hairy paw fidgeting with the knot on his tie. 'Why?'

'Because soon as she heard Anthony was dead, she clammed up and demanded a lawyer. Sound suspicious to you?'

'And you think this woman and Agnes are in it together? They both killed Anthony Chung and Roy Forman?'

Logan stuck the keys in his pocket. 'Or she's just messing with us, because that's the kind of thing she enjoys. Either way, I'm going home.'

Ding-Dong took a step back, looking away down the corridor in the vague direction of the cell block. 'You think I should have a pop at interviewing her?'

'You can if you want, but it's. . .' A frown. Wait a minute. . . DI Bell's suit looked immaculate, as if it'd just been pressed, the shirt freshly ironed. His shoes shone like new buttons too. And what was that smell? Logan sniffed: aftershave. Ding-Dong never wore aftershave. 'What are you up to?'

'Nothing wrong with being a team player.'

'Yeah, but you're being all possessive about this soup-kitchen thing – a lead *I* turned up, by the way – you want to interview Stacey Gourdon, you're dressed up like you're off for a job interview, and you smell like a tart's underwear drawer. . . What have you heard?'

363

A blush coloured his freshly shaven cheeks. 'I don't see what's wrong with—'

'Making a good impression? It's Steel, isn't it? You're angling for the DCI's job.'

'Now you're just being—'

'What's the ACC told you? . . . They're looking to get shot of her, aren't they? They think she's not up to the job and *you* want to take her place.'

Ding-Dong raised his chin, letting a tuft of black fur poke out over his shirt collar. 'I'm not going to dignify that with a response.'

Logan stared at him for a couple of beats. 'OK, fine. Whatever. Nothing to do with me: I've got an appointment anyway.'

'Good.' He turned and lumbered down the corridor, broad shoulders rolling beneath the straining shirt.

'Watch your back, Ding-Dong. She's bloody vicious if you cross her.'

DI Bell stopped with one hand on the door handle. 'I'll bear that in mind.' And then he was gone.

Logan's phone vibrated in his pocket. Another text message:

Where R U? Thot we sed 8:30?

Speaking of which. . .

He picked out a reply on the mobile's little keyboard:

On my way now. See you soon.

After all, it wouldn't do to keep a lady waiting. Especially not one that could kick his arse from Grampian to Strathclyde.

34

The words of an old song echoed out from the bathroom, mingling with the roar of the shower: a Pink Floyd number rendered with more enthusiasm than talent or musical ability. Couldn't carry a tune if it was bound, gagged, and locked in the boot of a car.

Logan stretched out, flat on his back, the duvet rumpled down about his chest. Warmth oozed through his limbs, pulling him down into the fresh sheets. Mmmm. . .

'Stop grinning.' Samantha settled on the edge of the bed. 'Makes you look like a smug hamster.' The oversized black T-shirt rode up around her thighs, Marilyn Manson glaring out from her boobs with his lopsided contact lenses. One of her knee-length red-and-black striped socks had a hole in it, a little toe poking out – nail painted shiny black. 'See you got rid of Shakespeare.'

A big sigh inflated Logan's chest, then let it go again. Warm and fuzzy. . . 'Couldn't have him ogling you in the nip. That's my job. Union won't stand for it.'

She laid a hand on his chest. Looked away towards the bathroom, then back down at him. 'Do you love her?'

'I love *you*.'

'Don't avoid the question, Captain Stabmarks: do you love her?'

'I . . . No. I used to, but it was a long time ago.'

'Good.' Samantha nodded, a smile curling one side of her mouth. 'Just remember: you're mine, Sunshine.'

A clunk, then the bedroom door opened and DS Jackie Watson stepped into the room, head on one side, drying her long dark hair on a grey towel, a big blue one wrapped around her middle, hiding all the naughty parts. A small furrow appeared between her eyebrows. 'Thought I heard voices?'

Logan turned, but Samantha was gone. 'Just . . . talking to myself.'

'Got to watch that.' Jackie sank down onto the bed, in the exact same spot that Samantha had just vacated. 'Bad enough you work with a bunch of nutjobs without turning into one.' Water droplets shone on her pale shoulders, sitting in the hollows carved into her skin by bra straps.

She reached out and picked Agnes Garfield's dittay book from the bedside cabinet. 'A red leather journal? Maybe it's too late after all. . .' She flipped through it, one eyebrow climbing further and further up her forehead with every page. 'Oh God, you write *poetry* now?'

'It's not mine. It's from the necklacing case.'

Jackie took a deep breath, creating a swell of cleavage at the border of the towel. 'Listen to this:

"I give my love a token,
of all the hearts he's broken,
The lungs that are exploding,
the harsh words that were spoken,
He'll fear what he's awoken,
And back to earth he goes.
In darkness walks the liar,

366

We'll cleanse his house with fire,
Come build the funeral pyre. . ."'

She clumped the book shut again. 'Bet Pam Ayres is shaking in her boots.'

'You know what teenaged girls are like.'

'Think you're going to find her?'

Logan crossed his arms behind his head and frowned at the ceiling. 'Depends how things go tonight.'

Jackie stood, letting the towel fall away as she squatted on the floor and dug about in an overnight bag, coming out with a hairdryer. Plugged it in. 'I need to phone Bill later. See how he got on at the Home Office.' The hairdryer whooshed and howled.

'Chances are she's not going back to the soup kitchen again, not if the place is swarming with CID. . . But maybe we'll turn up someone who's seen her? Someone who knows where she is?'

Jackie raised her voice, over the noise. 'They're interviewing him for a new position: liaising on terrorism suspects.'

'I mean, it's not like she's just going to waltz into a police station and hand herself in, is it?'

'He wants us to move to London. . . Only just got Rory settled in primary, how's he going to feel getting uprooted from all his friends and dumped in some school full of Cockneys and Essex boys? Bloody stupid idea, but then that's Bill all over.'

'And the whole thing's a mess too – Steel's running about like an angry crocodile, Ding-Dong and Leith are at each other's throats, and you lot are up here telling us we can't do our sodding jobs.'

The hairdryer fell silent. Jackie stared at him. 'You've not been listening to a word I've said, have you?'

'Bill's getting a new job; you don't want to move to London. See?'

'And we're not saying you can't do your jobs, we're saying there are *other* avenues of investigation you could be following. No one's even looked into local Wicca groups. And what about the metal stake she used to necklace Roy Forman? She had to get that from somewhere. Then there's the soup-kitchen angle—'

'I know – I came up with it. Assuming Rennie and Ding-Dong don't screw everything up. . .'

The hairdryer started up again. 'Thought you'd be over this obsessing about work thing by now.'

'Agnes Garfield is a card-carrying danger to herself and others. The longer she's out there, the more people she hurts playing Witch-Finder General. It matters.'

A sigh. 'Fine, go. Leave me here in your fusty caravan. But I'm warning you right now: I'm drinking the rest of the wine. And I have to be up at half six tomorrow, so if you think you're in for seconds you'd better get your arse back here before midnight. Understand?'

Logan picked his way through the drizzle, down the long stairs from Union Street to the Green. At the bottom of the first flight a man was huddled in the boarded-up doorway of the sports shop hunched over a sticker-covered guitar, knocking out a reasonable rendition of some country and western tune. The damp woolly hat open in front of him held a couple of coppers and a few fifty-pence pieces. Logan dropped in a couple of pounds and kept on going. Down. And down. And down.

The Green was a lopsided rectangle, buried away in the foundations of the city, lined with tall granite buildings, their grey faces darkened by moisture, lights making glowing orbs in the misty drizzle. Some sort of birthday party was underway in the open-air eating area outside Café 52, everyone huddled under a big green patio umbrella as they belted out 'Happy Birthday to You', a cake topped with dozens of candles blazing away.

Logan kept going, across the slippery cobblestones, towards the back end of Aberdeen Market – a semicircular lump of seventies concrete, its windows dark, everyone shut up for the night. Down one side, Correction Wynd cut straight under Union Street, a handful of restaurants glowing in the shadow of St Nicholas Kirk. But right ahead, the road disappeared into the gloom.

Seagulls screamed abuse from the slate rooftops far above as he followed East Green into the bowels of the city and out of the rain.

A row of neon squiggles glowed around the entrance to Blofeld's Secret Underground Lair, casting multicoloured light on a big bald bloke in a white shirt and bow tie, standing all on his own. Looking for someone to bounce as dance music thunked out of the door behind him.

At the end of the road, where it hooked around before climbing back up onto Nether Kirkgate, a mobile catering unit was parked up on the narrow kerb. The thing was a rectangular white trailer with a fold-down flap on the front beneath a sign: 'LOLA & RUDY'S TASTY TREATS'. Steam curled from the open hatch, and a handful of figures formed an orderly queue in front of it. About a dozen others were gathered in small groups, eating and talking over the growl of a diesel generator. At least three of them were nightshift CID, blending in like lumps of coal in a bowl of porridge.

They weren't the only ones: a brick outhouse with a crew cut, dressed in black jeans and a red T-shirt, stood guard a hundred yards from the catering unit: Mr Muscle from the hotel. The one who spoke like he was giving evidence. Another heavy stood at the far end, hands folded in front of his groin, narrow eyes constantly moving back and forth.

No way Agnes Garfield would come anywhere near the place with that kind of security hanging around.

Logan took two steps towards them, then stopped.

Someone was moving in the shadows, halfway between the nightclub and the soup kitchen, lurking in one of the barrel arches that lined the road. Too dim to make out who. . . Logan wandered across the road, nice and casual, hands in his pockets, keeping the figure in the corner of his eye. Then turned and walked slowly and quietly up behind them.

Whoever it was, they were layered up in a padded parka jacket with a hoodie on underneath, tracksuit bottoms. A woolly hat pulled down over their ears. Then they shuffled to the side and the lights spilling out from the nightclub caught the once-white case of a plaster cast – left leg, from the knee all the way down. His foot was encased in a shapeless black leather boot to keep the cast out of the dirt and damp.

So it wasn't Agnes in disguise, it was Henry Scott, AKA: Scotty Scabs, from the Gilcomston Church steps. The only tramp Rennie needed to complete his set.

Logan stopped creeping. 'You avoiding someone, Henry?'

The wee man flinched, spun around, then backed away until he was hard up against the brick wall. 'He's deid. . .'

'Did you see her again: Agnes Garfield? The woman who took Roy Forman?'

Henry blinked at him, eyes gleaming in the darkness. 'She killed him. He's deid.'

OK. So much for that. 'Are you hungry? Why don't you go get yourself a nice bowl of soup or something?'

'What if the witch gets me? I don't want to be deid. . .'

'She's not really a witch, Henry, she's just lost and sick and can't tell what's real any more.'

370

The rubber tips of Henry's crutches squeaked on the cobblestones. A little sob caught in his throat. 'She killed him. . .'

'You want me to go get you something to eat? Would you like that, Henry?'

'If she catches me, she'll kill me too. . .'

Logan came within an inch of patting him on the shoulder, but Henry flinched away again. 'OK, it's OK. . . You stay here and keep an eye out, and I'll go get you some soup.'

Poor sod needed more than soup. Like somewhere safe to sleep, medication, therapy, and a bath.

Logan made for the mobile catering unit, joining the queue. Only five people to go and it'd be his turn.

Someone tapped him on the shoulder. 'Guv?' Rennie, wearing his leather jacket and a scarlet T-shirt, a paper soup bowl in one hand and a plastic spork in the other. 'Thought you were going home?'

A shrug. 'Any luck?'

'Yeah: the chicken and chorizo casserole is bloody lovely. I'm having thirds.'

'Any luck with *Agnes Garfield*, you idiot.'

Rennie scooped up a sporkful of butter beans and chunks of sausage. 'Nope.' Then stuffed it in and chewed. 'Spoken to all of the regulars, and the organizers, and the volunteers, and you'll *never* guess what. . .' He leaned in close, enveloping Logan in a waft of herbs and spices. 'See that tall thin bloke over there,' he pointed to a figure doling out hot drinks from a catering-sized thermos, 'the one who looks like he's two sizes too small for his skin? That's DI Insch! Can you believe it?'

'If you're looking for a pat on the head, you're too late: I know.' Logan had another peer around. 'Where's Chalmers?'

'Pffffff. . .' The last of the stew disappeared, then Rennie licked his piece of plastic cutlery clean. 'Sloped off, didn't she. Want to bet she puts in for a whole night's overtime anyway? Can't trust people like—'

'If you spoke to all the regulars, you'll know where Henry Scott is, won't you?'

Rennie's mouth popped open for a moment, then he closed it again with a clack. 'Scotty Scabs? He's *here*?'

'If you spent more time doing your job and less time stuffing your face, you'd know.'

'Why didn't you arrest him?'

Seriously? 'Because I'm trying to catch a *murderer*: I couldn't give a toss about shoplifted bacon and cheese. You want him? Go get him.'

'Ah, right. . .' Rennie dumped his paper bowl in the bin fixed to the side of the catering unit, then scurried off, doing a tour of the little groups of people.

Idiot.

Three more minutes and Logan was at the head of the line.

A dark face smiled back at him from the hatch, perfect teeth and a white goatee. 'What can we do for you, my man?'

Logan pulled a copy of the 'HAVE YOU SEEN THIS WOMAN' poster from his pocket and held it out. 'Have you seen—'

A deep, rumbling voice sounded at his shoulder. 'You're too late: DI Bell's already been around with the photographs. Do you not trust him, or are you just trying to muscle in on his operation?' Insch hefted his thermos up onto the counter. 'We're out of coffee, Rudy.'

'No problem, boss.'

Logan shifted his shoulders. 'I'm not muscling in on anything, I'm just—'

'Everyone knows to keep an eye out for Agnes Garfield. We're not idiots.' Insch took the poster from Logan, folded it up, and handed it back. 'Rudy and Lola do the cast and

372

crew catering. That's why everyone's getting free-range chicken and chorizo casserole, penne arrabiata, Cullen skink, and tiramisu, instead of watery vegetable soup and a stale roll. Costing us a bloody fortune, but Zander insists. We're giving something back to the local community, once a week.'

'And it's always a Tuesday?'

'Everyone on the film knows to look out for the Garfield woman. I'm not having her anywhere near my people.'

Which explained the secret-service-style muscle.

A pale woman appeared in the hatch, wearing far too much eye makeup, her spiky ash-blonde hair sticking up in all directions. 'What can we get you, my darling?'

'I don't know. . . Chicken?'

'Coming right up.'

Insch scowled at him. 'I forgot what a bunch of freeloading bastards CID—'

'It's not *for* me, it's for someone too terrified to come over, in case he gets grabbed and killed like Roy Forman.' Logan pointed at the pair of heavies with the earpieces. 'Or maybe it's your rent-a-thugs scaring him away?'

The scowl didn't shift. 'Your bloody colleagues act like they've never seen food before. I swear some of them are having seconds. And it's supposed to be for the homeless!'

Rudy reappeared with the huge thermos and a stack of polystyrene cups in a plastic sleeve. 'There you go, boss: hazelnut latte.'

'Thanks.' Insch took them both, cradling the sleeve against his chest. 'McRae: walk with me.'

The spiky-haired woman placed a paper bowl heaped with glistening beans, chunks of amber sausage, and slivers of chicken, on the counter. A spork stuck out of the top, like an antenna. 'Watch, it's hot.'

Heat leached into his hands as he followed DI Insch away down the tunnel, back towards the nightclub. 'Well?'

'I need you to do something about this counterfeit *Witchfire* merchandise. I don't care if it *is* high quality: I'm not having some thieving git making fake stuff and flogging it. They're doing replica props from the film, and we haven't even finished shooting it yet!'

'Seriously?'

'Why aren't you doing anything about it? I told Mair to liaise with you, because you're the only one in CID who isn't going to sod it up. The rest of these idiots couldn't investigate their own feet for toes.'

35

Insch stopped at a knot of three men, all stick-thin and trembling, long sleeves pulled down to their fingertips, hiding the needletracks. He gave each one a polystyrene cup, then filled it with frothy pale coffee. 'Here you go. . .'

Logan stared at him. 'You do know I'm trying to catch someone who's killed at least two people, don't you? Never mind the grave robbing.'

They moved on to the next group, Insch doling out more hazelnut latte. 'Do you have any idea how much money I've sunk into this thing? Every bloody penny. I don't need people stealing from me as well! And counterfeiting *is* theft.'

Insch kept walking, on towards a couple of women in shapeless grey jogging bottoms and hooded tops, his voice dropped to a rumbling whisper. 'Now try not to act like a lovesick teenager this time.'

'Why would I—'

'Ladies: I come bearing hazelnut lattes!'

Both women turned, one holding a black plastic bin-bag in her gloved hands, the other holding a long-handled grabber. She used it to pluck an empty crisp packet from the pavement and dropped it into the open bin-bag. Nichole Fyfe. 'Ah, David, you're an absolute *lifesaver*!'

The other one dumped the bag at her feet and pulled off her gloves. 'Lovely.' She peeled back her hood, exposing a curly mass of scarlet curls, every bit as post-box red as Samantha's. That would be Morgan Thingummy – the one on the TV Sunday morning making come-to-bed-for-kinky-fun eyes at the camera.

Insch handed them each a polystyrene cup, grinning away like a proud parent. 'Slumming it, I'm afraid: we left the bone china back at the studio.' He pressed the plunger on the thermos and the sticky sweet scent of roasted coffee and hazelnut syrup coiled around them. 'Logan, this is Morgan Mitchell, she's our *incredibly* scary Mrs Shepherd. Morgan, this is DI McRae.'

She curled her hands around the polystyrene cup, peering at him over the edge. Her accent was pure New York, a lot stronger than the one she'd used on the TV and *completely* unlike the voice she'd used on film, necklacing the man whose face wasn't composited properly. 'Well, well, well. . .' A slow, naughty smile. 'Nichole, you said he was cute, but you didn't tell me he was a hunk too.'

It got very hot between Logan's neck and his collar. 'Well, it. . . I. . .'

'That's some pair of black eyes you got there. Makes me think of *Fight Club*, God I loved that film. *Very* sexy.' She stuck out her hand for shaking. 'McRae. . . You're the guy who used to be David's protégé, right?'

'Well, I don't know if I'd—'

Insch thumped Logan on the back. 'Of course you were.' The grin changed into a frown as he hunched forward in front of his stars. 'Now, are you both OK? Need anything?'

Nichole smiled at him. 'We're fine, honestly.' Then she slipped her arm through Logan's. Looking up at him with those pale-blue eyes, the pupils large, dark, and shiny as buttons. 'So, DI McRae, have you come here to sample Rudy and Lola's chicken casserole, or. . .?'

It was definitely getting warmer out here. 'We need to find anyone who's seen Agnes Garfield, or knows where she is.'

'God, Agnes. . .' Morgan made choking noises. 'Don't get me wrong, lovely girl, but jeesh, she could be *intense*.'

Nichole gave his arm a squeeze. 'It was such a shame, she was so desperate to get into film. It was her life's ambition.'

Insch cleared his throat. 'Yes, well. . .'

'Zander was going to give her a trial as my body double. She was *so* excited. And then she just. . .' Nichole shrugged. The movement rubbed Logan's arm up, then down the side of her breast.

'She flipped. Wigged out.' Morgan bugged her eyes. 'Went *totally* pill-popping crazy. I came back from makeup one time, and she was in my trailer trying on my *underwear*. True story. Then she has a complete fit because she says I'm not doing Mrs Shepherd's lines right and the character has to be more creepy, and I'm like, *you're* the creepy one: get out of my bra!'

Nichole took a sip of coffee. 'Well, to be fair, she did a lot of good too. We wouldn't be doing this right now if it wasn't for her. Giving something back to the community's really important and she set it all up.'

Morgan rolled her eyes. 'Ack, you're so *nice* I could stab you.'

Logan pulled out his poster again. 'Have you seen her recently? She might have changed her appearance, dyed her hair?'

Morgan squinted at it. 'Wow. Is it just me, or does she look like she's trying to turn herself into Rowan? All she needs is the scar. . .'

Nichole looked away, back down the tunnel towards the soup kitchen. 'She was here last Friday night. Morgan and I like to help out down here when we can – the usual food's nowhere near as good as tonight's, but the people making it really care about the homeless. I was on bread-and-butter duty and I. . .' A frown painted little creases between her eyebrows. 'I thought I saw someone watching from the shadows. As if they were afraid to come out into the light.' She shrugged. 'So I went over to say hello, see if they needed help. It was Agnes, she. . . She said some pretty hurtful things, then she ran away. I went after her, tried to make her see it was OK, but she lost me in the St Nicholas Kirk graveyard.'

Wonderful. 'Why didn't you come forward?'

'What good would it have done? I didn't know where she was, I didn't know where she was going, how could that help?'

Morgan took a step closer, gazing up into his eyes. Boxing him in. Her pupils were massive too. . . That familiar sweet, slightly sweaty, smell of smoke coming off her. 'I know this is kinda out of left field, but if I asked very nicely, would you arrest me? I could smash something, or, you know, hit someone, but I just want to spend a night in the cells. See what it's like?'

'Agnes isn't well, Inspector McRae, she needs someone to stand up for her, not betray her.'

'See, I gotta film after this one, where I'm this lap-dancer who gets kidnapped by a serial killer, and I figure she must've done time, right? She's hard-as-nails on the outside, but there's this core of vulnerability to her, and I think the experience of getting arrested would really help me *connect* with her?' Morgan placed a hand on Logan's chest. 'On an emotional level?'

He closed his eyes, massaged his throbbing temples. 'I'm *not* arresting you.'

'I played a veterinarian once, and spent a month working in an animal pound. Informed my whole interpretation of the character. It was a *very* powerful performance, I—'

'If you see Agnes, if she tries to get in touch, I want you to call me: day or night, don't care.' He pulled out a couple of Grampian Police business cards and printed his mobile number on the back of each. Then handed them out. 'We can't help Agnes if we can't find her.'

He'd taken half a dozen steps away towards where he'd left Henry Scott, when Morgan's voice echoed out behind him. 'OK, so if getting arrested's out, how about a good spanking instead? I'll let you tie me up and everything.' Followed by raucous, filthy laughter.

For God's sake. . . Logan kept going.

Insch huffed up beside him, the grin replaced by a loose-jowled scowl. 'What did I tell you about chatting up my actresses?'

'In what way was that *my* fault?' Logan stopped opposite the barrelled archway where Henry Scott had been cowering. It was empty now, just a lingering sour odour of unwashed clothes and BO to show that he'd been there at all. The little sod could've waited – Logan had fetched his bloody dinner for him. 'Thanks, Henry.'

'I'm serious.' Insch glanced back over his shoulder. Nichole and Morgan waved at him. He waved back, then lowered his voice. 'Do you have any idea how difficult it is to keep everyone happy and motivated?'

'That why they're stoned all the time?'

Insch stared at him. 'I have no idea what you're—'

'Oh come off it, the pair of them have pupils the size of doorknobs. I'm not an idiot.'

Silence. 'You know as well as I do: criminalizing cannabis usage is a waste of police time and doesn't—'

'Trust me, I've got bigger things to worry about than what your stars are smoking.'

Insch closed his eyes and massaged his temples, breath hissing in and out through his nose. 'Look, I *know* you're busy, I know you've got other things on, but I really need you to stop this counterfeiting ring. It's important.'

Logan pulled the spork out of the mound of chicken and chorizo casserole and helped himself to a bite. Well, Henry Scott wasn't going to miss it, was he? It tasted as good as it smelled, even if it was getting cold.

'Logan—'

'I'll see what I can do.'

Voices echoed through Grampian Police Force Headquarters as nightshift clocked on and shuffled out onto the rain-misted streets, fluorescent yellow waistcoats on over their black uniforms. Moaning.

Logan ran a hand through his hair and flicked the water off against the painted breezeblock wall of the cell block.

One of the nightshift PCSOs scowled at him from the other end of the corridor, carrying a tray with half a dozen steaming mugs on it. His pornstar moustache bristled. 'You're dripping on my floor!'

'I'm not stopping, Andy. Just checking up on a couple of prisoners.'

'Bad enough I've got drunks puking and peeing on it, without you CID scumbags dripping all over the place.'

Logan helped himself to one of the mugs. 'Thanks.'

'Hey!' He snatched it back. 'Those are for the guests. You want a cuppa? Get it yourself.'

'Who stuck an angry badger up your bum?' Logan slid back the hatch on the nearest cell, the one with 'STACEY

GOURDON ~ BOTP' written on the board by the door, and peered inside. 'She give you any trouble?'

Stacey sat on the blue plastic mattress with her back against the wall, blood-flecked knees drawn up against her chest. No scabs left, she must've eaten them all. She looked up, smiled, then made the universal gesture for 'wanker'.

Lovely girl.

Stacey stood and padded across the cell floor on bare feet. 'You here to interrogate me too? Think you can beat a confession out of me? Well, I'll tell you exactly the same thing I told your hairy little friend: I don't have to tell you where I was when Anthony went missing, or where I was when he died. And there's nothing you can do about it.'

Why did it sound as if she was auditioning for the part of 'Suspect number one'? Making herself look more dodgy than she needed to. Playing him. . .

Logan paused, then sighed. Of course she was. 'Yes, well done. Very melodramatic.'

Her eyes narrowed. 'Don't you patronize me.'

'You *really* think this is the best way to get your daddy's attention? Get tied up in a murder enquiry? Maybe sell your sordid little story to the papers? Scandalize the neighbourhood?'

Stacey stuck out her chest, her smile wide, voice silky. 'I had a threesome with the victim and the girl who killed him. I think I'm entitled to some compensation for my grief and distress, don't you? It's not my problem if you—'

Logan slammed the hatch shut on her. 'Andy, feel free to spit in her tea, OK?'

Downstairs, in the lower set of cell blocks, the sound of a pissed-up rendition of 'American Pie' warbled and roared out from the cell next door to Dr Marks's. Whoever was on the other side screamed a non-stop barrage of abuse and threats at someone called Baz for sleeping with his girlfriend.

It wasn't quite Tourette's, but it was the next best thing. Which meant Logan probably owed Kathy a couple of pints at least.

Dr Marks sat on the floor, backed into a corner, rocking gently away, chewing on the side of his thumb. 'I know what you're doing and it's not going to work. Doctor-patient confidentiality is *imperative* in my line of work.'

Logan settled down on the end of the mattress. 'It doesn't have to be like this.'

'You can't. . . I *won't* betray my principles.' Blood dripped from the end of his chewed thumb. He stuck it in his mouth and sucked. 'I won't.'

'If you think a couple of hours in the cells is bad, just wait till the Sheriff gives you a week in Craiginches for contempt.'

'I can't. . .'

'She's out there killing people, and *you* can help us stop her. Think about it.'

He sniffed, blinked. Chewed on his bleeding thumb. 'I can't. . .'

In the cell next door, 'American Pie' was replaced by Billy Joel's 'Piano Man', roared out like a football chant.

Logan stood and smiled down at Dr Marks. 'I'll pop past in the morning: say goodbye before they drag you off.' A wink. 'Have a nice night.'

Police. They spill out of the ugly striped building like woodlice from beneath a rotting log. Marching about, dragging coils of fizzing blue and red behind them like angry tentacles. Reaching along the granite streets, searching, probing.

They should be on the same side, but they're not. They

don't see. Don't see the Beasts and the Angels, the Witches and the Kelpie, the Wraith and the Ogres and the Ghosts. Don't see the Hand of Death as they prowl the street.

They think everyone is Sheep.

They think *she* is Sheep.

But she's so much more than that.

Rowan takes a deep breath and crosses the road – walks out into the middle of them.

The Kirk is my sword and my shield.

A pair of them laugh at a shared joke, shoulders hunched against the rain. They don't even see her.

Then there he is.

In the tunnels beneath the earth he looked so normal, but here. . . His aura is different from the others. It's blue and red, but ribbons of gold and black undulate around his head. A halo of light and darkness. Is he an Angel, or a Hand of Death? Does he even know himself?

And if she told him, would it make any difference?

He turns up his collar and runs across the road to his weary battered Fiat, fumbles with his keys, swearing in the rain, then gets in behind the wheel. Reverses out of the parking space in a cloud of greasy exhaust, his aura lighting up the inside of the car like an angry disco.

Rowan steps out onto the road, watching him disappear into the rain. Then reaches into her pocket and feels the knot of bones, safe in its nest of tissue paper.

Soon. . .

She turns her face to the heavy orange clouds and closes her eyes. The rain is cool and soothing on her skin, tiny cold kisses from the heavens. Making everything—

The hard blare of a car horn makes her flinch. She spins around and there's a patrol car less than three feet away. Its headlights flash at her, and she holds up a hand, then steps back onto the pavement.

The patrol car drives by. Its occupants don't even look in her direction. They think she's just another Sheep.

Rowan steps back out into the road. His Fiat is nothing but a memory written on tarmac with raindrops. But that's all right. She has plenty of time to wander back to where her own car's parked.

After all, there's no need to rush: she knows where he's going.

Wednesday

36

The kettle's grumbling rattle came through from the kitchen, fighting against the sound of breakfast news in the living room where, apparently, everyone was getting great weather except for the north-east of Scotland. As bloody usual.

Logan lay back on the bed, arms folded behind his head. Have to get up in a minute. Any minute now. . .

A clunk and the kettle lost its battle with the weatherman.

Jackie padded through wearing nothing but a Strathclyde Police Judo Team T-shirt, with a mug of tea in each hand and a slice of toast sticking out of her mouth. 'Mnnnphnnn gnnph?'

He sat up and accepted the proffered mug. 'Still raining?'

She pulled the toast out and chewed. 'Give me two reasons why I should stay with Bill.'

Oh great: this again. 'He's Rory's father?'

'That's one. And it's not even that good a reason. He's still a selfish prick.' She tore a bite out of the toast. 'I am *not* moving to London, I don't care if this is the job opportunity of a lifetime.'

The sigh escaped before he could stop it. Logan swung his legs out of the bed. 'If you don't like him, why do you stay with him?'

'That's what I just asked *you*.'

Logan picked yesterday's socks and pants off the floor and dumped them in the laundry basket, before shuffling and yawning through to the bathroom for a pee and a shower.

By the time he got back, Jackie was levering herself into the feat of mechanical engineering that was a concrete-coloured Doreen Triumph bra. Making it look as if she was wearing two halved zeppelins from the 1930s. The shiny crescent-shaped scar above her industrial grey pants disappeared as she hauled on her suit trousers.

At least she only had the one scar.

A linen shirt went over the bra that time forgot. 'What are we doing?'

Good question. Logan sat on the bed and pulled on a fresh pair of socks. 'Same as usual, I suppose.' Next: a pair of lucky bright-red pants, then suit trousers. 'Reaching out because we're lonely. Looking for a little comfort. A little human warmth. . . What?'

She was staring at him with her mouth hanging open. 'I meant what are we doing *tonight*? Not what,' she pointed at them both, 'whatever this is.'

'Oh. Right.' Heat raced up his neck into his cheeks and ears. 'OK. Well, if you're not going back to Glasgow, we could—'

'Are you feeling guilty? Is that it? Guilty because she's in the hospital?'

Logan picked the nearest shirt in the wardrobe. 'Yes.'

'In the name of the wee man. . .' She grabbed her jacket. 'Where did I leave my shoes?' Then stomped out of the bedroom, making the caravan floor shake.

Yes, because it was all *his* fault. He followed her into the living room, hauling the shirt on. 'So you don't feel guilty for cheating on Bill?'

'She's been up there for two years, Logan, you really think

that's what she wants? You feeling guilty for having *sex* three or four times a year?'

A wrinkled satchel of a face frowned out at them from the TV. '. . .*important to remember that these are the people who support police investigations. They help catch killers. How can they do their job if the SPSA keeps changing everything?*'

'You didn't answer the question.'

'I. . .' Her face pinched, eyes narrowed, then she turned and grabbed a pair of low-heeled boots from under the coffee table. 'Going to be late.'

Mr Satchelface was replaced by a woman in an ugly blouse. '*Aberdeen now, and Grampian Police have issued a fresh appeal for information regarding the whereabouts of Agnes Garfield. . .*'

'Jackie, it's—'

'Of course I feel bloody guilty! OK? And I shouldn't, he doesn't *deserve* my guilt – he's a selfish, thoughtless bastard who never even *sees* me any more. Even when he does come home, it's like I'm not there.'

'. . .*any information to call the hotline number, or contact your local police station. . .*'

Jackie thumped down on the couch and hauled on her boots. 'But would I leave him? Nooooo, I had to make it work for Rory's sake, didn't I? Why be happy in life when you can be bloody miserable?'

'So leave him.'

'What about Rory?'

'*In other news, police checkpoints are in place on the A96 between Kintore and Blackburn. . .*'

Logan sat down on the couch beside her. 'What's going to be better for him growing up: you happy, or you miserable?'

'. . .*witnesses following the discovery of what appears to be a satanic murder inspired by the bestselling novel* Witchfire *on Monday evening. . .*'

She stared at the screen. 'It's not that simple.'

'Never is.'

'We spoke to two the film's stars, Nichole Fyfe and Morgan Mitchell.' Onscreen, Mrs Uglyblouse was replaced by the familiar PR setup of Nichole and Morgan sitting in front of *Witchfire* posters.

'What am I going to do, Logan? Leave Bill and come back and shack up with you? You me and Rory crammed in your girlfriend's caravan?'

Oh dear God. . . Don't say anything. Don't even breathe!

Jackie stood. 'That's what I thought.'

Nichole leaned forward. *'First I have to say on behalf of everyone working on the film, that our hearts go out to those poor families.'*

Morgan nodded. *'They really do. It's awful that these guys went through what they did—'*

'I can't. There isn't. . .'

'You're just going to sit here, like a bug stuck in fucking amber till she comes back.'

'. . .so important to stop this happening to anyone else. Which is why we're going to do everything we can to help.'

'I am *not* stuck in amber.'

'LOOK AT YOURSELF! It's been two years and you're still here. Why haven't you finished fixing up the flat? I'll tell you why: because you can't move on. You were always the bloody same!' She turned and banged out of the room.

'Jackie!'

Out into the corridor.

'Jackie, wait.'

She was in the bedroom, grabbing her rucksack from the floor. 'You want a sign, Logan? Here's your sign.' She ripped down the sheet of paper Sellotaped to the wardrobe mirror and hurled it at him. *'That's* what's wrong with you.'

She shoved past, wrenched open the front door, then slammed it hard enough to make the mugs in the kitchen clatter.

Silence.

'—*ask if anyone's seen, or knows anything about these terrible deaths, to come forward.*'

'*That's right, people, you* have *to call the police before anyone else gets hurt.*'

Bit late for that.

Logan bent down and retrieved the sheet of paper. Smoothed it out against the wall. 'LIKE IT OR NOT, YOU'RE STILL ALIVE' printed in big black letters.

'*And now here's Russell with the weather.*'

'*Thanks, Steve. Well, it's going to be an unsettled couple of days—*'

The doorbell rang out its long mournful chime.

He reached for the handle, paused. The pickaxe handle waited patiently, propped up in the corner. He took it and peered through the spyhole.

Jackie scowled back at him, her features distorted by the lens.

He opened the door. 'You already had the last word.'

Her eyes went from his face to the pickaxe handle. 'Didn't think you were so sensitive.' Then she hoiked a thumb over her shoulder at a green-haired lanky young man leaning back against Logan's Fiat. One of Wee Hamish Mowat's boys, with a courier's satchel slung over one shoulder. 'You got a visitor.'

The young man grinned at him as Jackie roared off in her Audi. 'Bit on the side, eh? McRae, you old *hound* you.' Acne scars pocked his cheeks, disappearing into a set of wiry sideburns. Eyes hidden behind a pair of sunglasses. Shoulder-length lime green hair swept back from his forehead. 'Though, how you manage to pull the chicks drivin' this manky piece of crap. . .?' He rapped his knuckles on the Punto's bonnet.

The bloody magpies had been at the car again, spattering

it with grey-and-white droppings, wedging twigs into the windscreen wipers. Logan hefted the pickaxe handle onto his shoulder. 'What do you want, Jamie?'

'No' to be up at this soddin' hour. Brutal, man.' He nodded at the caravan. 'You gonnae invite me in?'

'How's your friend Reuben?'

'Yeah. . ..' Jamie stuck the tip of his pale-yellow tongue out between his teeth. 'I heard you and him had a thing. What can I say? The Rubester's a passionate man.' He pulled his sunglasses down to the end of his nose and winked a bloodshot eye. 'But just so you know: if there's a change of management and that, I'd have no problems workin' with the new administration. Just between us.'

'What – do – you – want?'

Jamie dipped into the satchel and came out with a large brown envelope. 'Been lookin' into your battered Chinkies for Mr Mowat. Sod-all clue who the other side are, but the ones doing the hammerin' are definitively the McLeod brothers.'

No surprise there.

Jamie dropped his voice to a whisper. 'I'm just sayin', you know, if the time comes, you can rely on us. The Reubinator's great and all that, but it's like doing *Strictly Come Dancin'* through a minefield some days.'

'I'm *not* taking over, and I'm *not* killing Reuben.'

'Ahhh. . . Right. Just a wee coma or a bit of brain damage. Gotcha. Anyway, Mr Mowat says he's keen on this batterin' cannabis thing being over soon as. Word is Creepy and Simon McLeod are going after anyone they think's in on it – and they're all about the "cripple first, ask questions later".'

'No coma. No brain damage.'

Jamie shrugged. 'We'll talk later. Meantime,' he waggled the envelope at Logan, 'got a couple addresses for the McLeod's cannabis farms: Blackburn and Westhill. Might wanna get your boys to take a squint?'

Logan didn't move. 'Seriously? Handing over a brown envelope, in a public place? You got someone lurking in the bushes taking pictures?'

He sighed, pushed his glasses back into place again. 'Man, you are *cynical.*' He slipped the envelope under one of the Fiat's windscreen wipers, sending a little avalanche of twigs and grass tumbling onto the bonnet. 'No skin off my nose, man. But if you're no' going to sort it out. . .' Jamie bared his teeth and sooked air through them. 'Gonnae get messy.'

'Always does.'

'Later, OK?' He backed away, grinning. 'And I meant what I said about Reuben.'

'. . .talk of industrial action across the whole Scottish Police Services Authority. We spoke to Grampian Police Assistant Chief Constable Denis Irvin. . .'

Logan turned the radio down a bit, shifted his phone from one ear to the other, and changed down into third as Mounthooly roundabout loomed into view. A vast hump of grass and trees, easily big enough for a full-sized football pitch, like an island in the stream of traffic. 'Look, how difficult can it be? Just get a copy of Anthony Chung's criminal record from San Francisco.'

On the other end of the phone, PC Guthrie groaned. *'You know what getting anything out of the Yanks is like.'*

'. . .inconceivable they'd do anything as counterproductive and ill-judged as strike. . .'

'Someone's got to have a liaison officer with the US Justice Department: try the Serious and Organized Crime Agency.'

'They're even worse than the bloody Americans.'

True.

'. . .assure the people of the north-east that Grampian Police won't let this impact on public safety or pursuing criminals to justice. . .'

A taxi's brake lights flared at the entrance to the round-about, it juddered to a halt, just missing getting obliterated by an eighteen-wheeler loaded down with offshore drilling pipes. Idiot should've been watching where he was going. Logan drifted over into the outside lane. 'If they give you any lip, tell them there's a suggestion he's connected to a terrorist organization.'

'*He is?*'

'No, but it'll get their finger out of their bumholes.'

'*. . .other news, to celebrate national sandwich week, one group of Ellon school pupils aim to create the world's longest chip buttie. . .*'

The junction was coming up. Logan put his foot on the brake. 'Just make sure you say it's "unconfirmed sources". . .' The car wasn't slowing down.

He did it again. Still nothing.

One more time, jamming his foot to the floor.

The rattling Fiat Punto just kept on going.

'*. . .weather's going to remain overcast, but we could see some heavy rain later in the day. . .*'

Handbrake! Logan yanked it on and the rear wheels locked, screeching across the road surface, heading right out onto the roundabout in a stinking cloud of hot rubber. Teeth gritted, eyes screwed to narrowed slits, arms straight out in front, hands wrapped tightly enough around the steering wheel to turn his knuckles bone-white. Right into the path of a dozen vehicles.

'STOP YOU RUSTY PIECE OF CRAP!'

A people carrier slammed on its brakes as he slid to a halt right in front of it. Its horn blared an angry tattoo into the early morning air, the driver's face dark pink as she screamed obscenities behind the windscreen.

'*. . .just to rub it in: here's the Eurythmics with "Here Comes the Rain Again".*'

Logan closed his eyes, rested his forehead against the

steering wheel. Everything inside him sagged, as if someone had pulled the plug out. Not crushed to death in a mangled ball of rusty metal after all.

More horns joined the people carrier's angry song.

He sat up straight, blinked, then wound down his window. Exhaust fumes and burning rubber never smelled so sweet.

The people-carrier's driver was still swearing at him through the glass, veins standing out in her neck like angry snakes.

He held up a hand and turned the engine over again, stuck the Punto in reverse and slowly dragged it backwards onto Causeway End. Pumping his foot on the brake pedal did sod all, so he used the handbrake again.

Christ, that was close. . .

'Tada. . .' Dr Graham whipped the cloth away, exposing a clay head: large nose, high cheekbones, jowls, a small mouth set between two deep crevices. She placed it on Steel's desk. 'Of course, I had to use a bit of artistic licence on the wrinkles, but all in all I'm pretty happy with it.'

Steel screwed up her eyes, leaned forward in her chair and peered at it. 'No' a sodding clue. You?'

Logan shrugged. 'Just a random old lady.'

'Nah: one thing I know about nutjobs, Laz, is they don't do things for no reason. She's no' random, she's somebody special. We just don't know why yet.'

Dr Graham shuffled her feet. 'Don't suppose you've turned up another body needing facial reconstruction, have you? Maybe more skeletonized remains?'

Steel leaned back in her chair and puffed on her fake cigarette. 'Laz, get the auld wifie's head up to Media: I want her on the telly news by lunchtime, all the papers, blah, blah, blah.' She stared at him. 'Sometime before we all die of old age would be good. And try to crack a smile, eh? Won't kill you.'

'Thanks. Very funny. I nearly died, OK?'

'Serves you right for being a tightwad and buying crappy old rustbuckets then, doesn't it?'

'Just. . .' The muscles in his jaw clenched. 'Fine.' Logan grabbed the head – surprisingly heavy, almost as bad as the real thing – and stomped out, slamming the door shut behind him.

Steel's voice oozed through the wood. 'Touchy. . . Now, Doc, about your invoice. . .'

The Wee Hoose echoed with laughter that died as soon as Logan walked in. Biohazard Bob and three PCs cleared their throats, Biohazard sticking something in his pocket as the uniforms shuffled out of the room, faces flushed, not making eye contact.

Logan pushed the door shut with his heel. 'Do I want to know?'

'Probably not.' Bob sank into his chair. 'Nice severed head, by the way: suits you.'

The other desks were covered in piles of forms and file boxes, only one was clean and tidy: DS Chalmers's. 'Where's the new girl?'

'Buggered if I know. . .' He frowned. 'Rennie's right, you're playing favourites, aren't you?'

Logan stared at him. If Biohazard wanted favourites, he could bloody well have them. 'You know what: maybe I *am* putting too much on DS Chalmers's shoulders. So. . .' He plonked the head down on Biohazard's desk. '"Who is this woman?" TV, papers, posters. You know the drill.'

'Noooo.' Bob covered his face with his hands. 'Can't someone else—'

'You're the one feeling neglected.' He pointed at the head.

396

'Steel wants that done ASAP. If it's not on the lunchtime news, you know what'll happen to you.'

Bob groaned. Stood. Then picked up the head. 'Come on, Sexy.' He paused at the door. 'One thing. Chalmers might be the new girl, but there's something you've got to remember. . .' He squeezed one eye shut, leaned to the left, then hurried out, thumping the door shut.

The smell he'd left behind wasn't far off being weaponized.

37

Kelly the PCSO pulled her chin in, eyebrows furrowed. 'What happened to you?'

'Biohazard.'

The cell block was quiet, the singing and swearing of last night reduced to a sort of anxious murmur as people got ready for their turn in front of the Sheriff to find out if they'd be released on bail, or banged up in Craiginches.

'Oh Lord, I got trapped in the lift with him once. *Always* take the stairs, and never light a match.' She led the way to cell number eight and rapped on the door. 'Best to let them know we're out here, in case he's pleasuring himself. Happens more often than you'd think.' She slid open the hatch. 'He's had his breakfast, so don't let the puppy-dog eyes con you into giving him any treats.'

Logan stepped up and peered into the cell. Dr Marks had graduated from the floor to the mattress, curled up in the foetal position, arms wrapped around his head. 'Go away. . .'

'That was one night, Dr Marks. What do you think a *week* in prison's going to be like?'

'They wouldn't even switch off the light.'

'That's in case you decide to do yourself harm in the dark.

Don't want to find your cold dead body in the morning, do we? Probably a good idea to keep you on suicide watch up in Craiginches too. Sensitive lad like you— Sod.' His phone was ringing. 'Have a think and I'll be back in a minute.' He pulled it out. 'McRae?'

'*LoganDaveGoulding, how you doing?*'

He moved down to the end of the corridor and pushed through into the stairwell. 'I'm kind of in the middle of something, Dave.'

'*Excellent, excellent. Look, I've got you a profile for Agnes Garfield.*'

'That was quick.'

'*Had a head start. Do you want the highlights? Agnes's psychological condition means it's unlikely she's operating alone, or in a dominant role. She's a subservient fantasist, looking for someone to make her dreams come true. That coupled with the obsession with books like* Witchfire *means she's trying to live a life that never existed in the first place. She'll probably resort to self-harm when things don't live up to her expectations.*'

'Subservient? Didn't you see what she did to Anthony Chung? Far as we can tell, he's the only dominant—'

'*No. She'd never do anything to hurt or disappoint him. It isn't—*'

'She staked him out on the linoleum and tortured him to death, Dave. Doesn't get more final than that.'

Silence came from the other end of the line.

'Dave?'

'*Then that idiot Marks is even more useless than I thought. His files clearly show she's elevated Anthony Chung to the position of personal deity. There's* literally *nothing he can do that she isn't going to forgive or see as a test of her faith. Infidelity, violence, abnormal sexual behaviour. . .*'

'Well, he must've done something, because he's lying in the morgue with. . .' Logan frowned at the stained concrete beneath his feet. 'Wait a minute: Marks's files?'

'*Have you read* Witchfire? *In it there are three primary forms of punishment doled out by the Fingermen: trial by fire, trial by blood, and trial by water. We've had the first two. She's going to have a go at chucking someone in a river next, and if they don't drown she'll drag them back on shore and burn them.*'

'How did you get your hands on Dr Marks's files?'

'*Agnes started off pretending to be in Rowan's world. It was a harmless fantasy, daydreaming she was someone special with a destiny and power, but she did it so often that it became habitual. The fantasy became real. She's not play-acting any more, she genuinely thinks they're witches and they're evil and they need to be purged to save their souls.*' A deep breath. '*And that's where the problem starts: there's a dichotomy at the heart of Agnes's psyche and it's eating her sense of self. In the book, Rowan's a witch-finder that doesn't believe in witches, but has to punish them. But Agnes doesn't just believe in witches, she thinks she is one. She's trapped between two diametric delusions.*'

'Dave!'

'*I broke into his office, it's not important. What matters is that she's following a pattern: it's not malevolent, it's not because she enjoys it, it's because this is what she believes she has to do.*'

'You broke. . .?' Logan glanced up and down the corridor. No one there. But he lowered his voice to a whisper anyway. 'Are you *insane*? Anything you get from those files is inadmissible. Put them back!'

'*I don't see how: you've got a warrant, haven't you? And who's going to know?*'

'Put – them – back.'

'*She won't be moving about, she'll have a single base of operations, somewhere she feels safe. Somewhere she can paint protective circles.*'

Like the ones on her bedroom roof and in her cupboard under the stairs.

'*She has a romanticized notion of decay, it appeals to the entropy she feels inside, so she'll want to stay somewhere that's been empty for a while. Run-down, abandoned, maybe derelict. Assuming the dominant personality lets her have any say in it.'*

And that explained the half-dozen dead roses.

'Anything else?'

'Yes: tread carefully. Agnes Garfield is a deeply damaged individual, and the world is a terrifying place for her right now. She's the only one standing between us and the powers of evil. In her mind she's a hero. Don't break her.'

Not a monster, just doing monstrous things.

'Thanks, Dave.' Logan hung up and headed back to the cell block. Stopped outside number eight and peered through the hatch again.

Dr Marks hadn't moved.

'Last chance, Doctor. You stood up to us, we got a warrant, you got arrested. You did everything you could, no one can say you didn't.'

Marks just stared at the far wall.

'OK, well, you think about it.' Logan marched over to cell seven and banged on the door, then did the same to number six. The swearing and shouting kicked off again. 'Enjoy.'

Rennie slouched in and collapsed into Logan's visitor's chair. 'Urrgh. . .'

Logan glanced up from his door-to-door forms. 'Well?'

Rennie's suit looked as if he'd slept in it, then taken it off and battered it to death with a cricket bat. 'I quit. Sod this for a game of soldiers.'

'What did Ding-Dong say?'

He wrapped his arms around his head and let it fall backwards, knees clenched together. 'How come Chalmers got the morning off, eh? She wasn't even there all night. *I* was there all night, but do I get the morning off? Of course not, because every bicycle-seat-sniffing tosspot—'

'My heart bleeds for you.'

'Not as if we turned up anything, is it? No one's seen Agnes the Nutbag; someone "thinks" they saw Roy Forman leaving the Green with an unidentified woman, but they reeked of meths and wee, so I wouldn't trust them to ID their own reflection; and by the time I got back to the front of the queue they were all out of tiramisu.'

'*Focus.*'

Rennie blinked at him. 'Right: Ding-Dong. I sneaked into his briefing and he says he interviewed some Stacey woman last night? Apparently she's being very cagey about her whereabouts and the death of Anthony Chung. So she's become a person of interest.'

'He say what's happening to her?'

'Up in front of the Sheriff at ten for the assault and indecent exposure. You want me to check it out?'

Logan swivelled back and forth in his chair for a bit. Then shook his head. 'No: she's a time-waster, looking for something she can shock Daddy with. Forget about her. And yesterday wasn't a complete washout, was it? You found your missing tramp.'

Rennie sank even further into the chair. 'Ah. . . Funny story. . .'

'Oh, you are *kidding* me.'

His eyebrows pinched. 'I had to go running after this guy who rocked up pished and picked a fight with Insch's bouncers.'

'Henry Scott was right there!'

'It wasn't my fault!'

Logan buried his head in his hands. 'I swear to God. . .'

His computer made a pinging noise. Then another one. And another – new emails coming in thick and fast. He glanced up at the screen. Three hundred and sixty-two new messages.

What *now*?

He clicked on the last one to come in:

> From: spellchaser@thecovenoflightandhope.org

> To: fanbox@williamhunterwrites.com

> Subject: You Sick Basterd!!!!

>

> WTF is wrong with U man? Ur book is shit and U can't write 4 shit and Ur a looser!!!

> Wiches is a powr for good in the wurld, an U can DIE!@

There was more of it, but the spelling and grammar didn't get any better. OK. . . He tried the first one to come in instead. It was from William Hunter's webmistress in Iowa, apologizing for the huge number of nutter emails she was about to forward to him. Apparently these were all the dodgy messages that had been left through the website.

Rennie slumped further in the seat and flopped an arm across his face. 'Maybe I could go into private security or something?'

'You're useless at public security, who'd hire you?' Logan's mouse swept across the screen. No way he was going to sift through three hundred and sixty-two emails from random internet crazy people. He used a wizard to set up a rule and forwarded them all on to Dr Goulding instead, along with a short note to check them all for someone capable of neck-lacing Roy Forman and torturing Anthony Chung.

Look at it as penance for breaking into Dr Marks's office.

'Or I could be a PI, like in the films? Simon Rennie: Private Investigator. . .'

'Simon Rennie: idiot, more like.' The phone on Logan's desk trilled. He jabbed the speakerphone button. 'What?'

'*Don't you "what" me, McRae.*' Big Gary on reception. '*Just 'cos you're a DI now, doesn't mean I won't take you over my knee and spank your arse for you.*'

Logan scowled at a grinning Rennie. 'Say something, I *dare* you.'

'*You've got a visitor: one Timothy Mair Esquire from Trading Standards.*'

'What the hell does Dildo want?'

'*I don't know, and I don't care.*' A clunk and the line went dead.

Rennie yawned, arms stretched way above his head. 'Don't take it personally: Big Gary's been biting everyone's head off since he found out someone got his little girl up the stick.' He sagged back into place. 'And before you ask: no, it wasn't me.'

Tim 'Dildo' Mair pulled the scabrous council Transit van out onto Broad Street, the gearbox sounding like someone trying to run a set of maracas through the spin cycle. His eyes were narrowed behind a pair of John Lennon glasses, his black goatee beard bristling around a thin-lipped mouth.

Logan hauled on his seatbelt. 'Seriously? You're going to sulk at me the whole way?'

Dildo didn't look at him, kept his eyes on the road. 'Constable Sim, would you please tell DI McRae that I'm not sulking, I'm trying not to give him another black eye to match the one he's already got.'

Sitting on the second row of seats, PC Sim pulled a face, then wiped her hand on the van's wall. 'It's all sticky back here. . .'

'Look, I'm sorry I missed our appointment yesterday, but I'm having a pretty shitty day, so you can—'

'*Appointments.* As in plural.'

The Transit rocked like someone was kicking it as it accelerated past Marischal College.

'Didn't think you were this delicate.'

'Constable Sim, you can tell DI McRae I'm only doing this because *his* friend Insch promised to give my niece a tour of the set and a part as an extra if I caught who was counterfeiting the *Witchfire* stuff.'

She sniffed at her hand, then wiped it on the back of Logan's seat. 'What do you guys *do* in here to get it this sticky?'

'I'm in the middle of a murder enquiry, OK? I'm sorry that's so bloody inconvenient for everyone, but I've got a killer to—'

'Oh, bite me.'

They rumbled on in silence all the way up past the ugly concrete lump of Aberdeen College, then down the hill towards the massive Mounthooly roundabout.

Little muscles twitched along Dildo's jaw, making the skin ripple.

Fine. Someone had to be the grown-up. 'I'm sorry I blew you off yesterday. Can we just—'

'Let's get something straight: you're just here to provide a police presence, because Insch said I had to use you. I'm in charge, get it?'

'You don't have to be such—'

'*I* did all the legwork. *I* found out who was selling the stuff. *I* found out who was making it. And *I'm* in charge.'

'Fine, you're in charge. You're the big man. All hail, King Dildo the Great, Lord of the Shop Cops.'

Sim scooted forward in her seat, feet making scritchy noises on the sticky floor. 'Why do they call you Dildo?'

He glanced in the rear-view mirror, a smile tugging at the corner of his mouth. 'That's *King* Dildo, to you.'

The council Transit van stuttered to a halt in the corner of a car park, facing a row of shops. A bakery, a newsagent's, a dry cleaner's, a tropical fish shop, an estate agent's with a 'FOR SALE OR LET' sign in the window, and a bookie's: J STEWART & SON – BOOKMAKERS EST. 1974. Heavy metal grilles covered the windows, empty crisp packets and bits of old newspaper were trapped in the gaps.

Up above, the sky was like dark-grey ink dripped onto wet paper, slivers of blue shining between the towering clouds.

Logan undid his seatbelt. 'Ma Stewart. *Again*? Does the woman never learn?'

Dildo reached back behind the driver's seat and hauled out a large sports bag. 'Oh, she's done herself proud this time. . .' He unzipped it, then paused.

Logan's phone was singing Rennie's theme tune.

They couldn't leave him alone for five minutes, could they?

'What?'

'*Guv? You better get back here: Ding-Dong and Leith just had a stand-up in the CID office. Proper toe-to-toe yelling match.*'

'So? Get Steel to—'

'*She's going ballistic – and I mean intercontinental. Ding-Dong lamped Leith one, right on the nose.*'

So much for DI Bell's pretentions to the throne. 'Why?'

'*Leith made that bell-end crack again. They're both standing there, yelling about how the other's screwing up the case, then bang – swinging punches, blood, DCs shouting, "Fight! Fight! Fight!". . . You should've been here, it was great.*'

Dildo pulled a sword as long as his arm from the sports bag. The blade shone and glittered.

Logan frowned through the windscreen at the row of shops. The estate agent's looked as if it had died a death a while ago. All the property notices abandoned in the barred window were stained yellow, their colours faded. Dead flies and wasps made a little line of bodies along the inside of the sills. Bars on the windows. A graffiti-covered shutter over the door. No way in or out. . .

'Guv? You still there?'

How did Agnes and Anthony get into the house?

'Put him on.'

'What, Ding-Dong? Can't – Steel's got him in with Professional Standards for a reaming, he'll—'

'No: Leith.'

'Hold on, I'll see if he's done with the Duty Doc. . .' Rustling and crunching noises came from the earpiece.

Dildo pulled a dittay book from the bag and handed it to Sim, then went back in for what looked like a gold torque – the twisted metal band finished with ivory skulls in the end pieces. Then some T-shirts, a couple of baseball caps with the same *'WITCHFIRE'* logo as the one Agnes Garfield wore to take out Anthony Chung's money, a roll of posters, and what looked like a leather warrant card case. 'Good, aren't they?'

Sim's eyes went wide. 'Ooh, a finder's badge. . .' She flipped open the leather case, and smiled at the shiny badge inside. 'It's *just* like the book.' Then caught Logan staring at her and cleared her throat. 'You know, if I was interested in that kind of thing. . . Which I'm not. Obviously.'

'Thought you didn't like *Witchfire*.'

'Well . . . I never said that, *exactly*. . .'

Dildo went back into the sports bag and came out with a dagger. He slipped the knife out of its black sheath. The blade was as long as his hand, sharpened on both sides, and carved with squiggles and lines, topped off with a dull metal T-shaped guard, a handle wrapped in red leather, and a hexagonal pommel. The whole thing looked hard, functional.

Sim put the Finder's badge on the seat beside her and held out her hand, mouth hanging open. 'Jeepers. . .'

Dildo passed it across. 'According to Insch, they're all

perfect replicas of the film's props, right down to the tiniest detail. Look at the end of the handle bit.'

She turned the dagger around and peered at the hexagonal pommel. 'A real-life pricking knife. . . It's got the witchfinders' crest on it, all mirror image so it's the right way round when you use it to make a wax seal for death warrants.' A grin plumped her cheeks. 'This is so *cool*!'

More rustling from the earpiece, then Rennie was back, his voice little more than a whisper. *'Found him. But do me a favour – he's in a crappy mood already, don't set him off, OK?'*

'Just put him on.'

A crackle, then Leith was on the line, voice all nasal and jagged. *'This better be important.'*

'If it's any consolation, at least you saw it coming. I just opened my front door one morning, and *bang*.' The brotherhood of getting punched in the face. 'Your deposition site in Kintore, how did Agnes and Anthony get in?'

'Did you call up just to take the piss, because if you did, you can—'

'It's not my fault Ding-Dong lamped you one. The first attending officer said the place was locked, he had to get keys from the estate agent's. Agnes and Anthony didn't break in, so they had to have a key.'

'Rennie – give me the list.' Pause. *'I got the boy to chase up everyone who's seen the property since it went on the market fifteen months ago. Plus details of the owners' relatives, and friends. We're working our way through them now. That all right with you?'*

'I wasn't trying to tell you how to do your job, I was just—'

'That's exactly *what you're trying to do. Now why don't you sod off and let me do it?'*

'Come on, Leith, it's—'

'I was a DI long before you, McRae, and I'll be one long after you've gone back to the Wee Hoose with the rest of the detective sergeants. Remember that.' And then he hung up.

Logan held the phone in front of his face. 'Not surprised Ding-Dong punched you on the nose, you miserable *git*.'

Sim swished the dagger through the air, pommel forward, the blade resting back along her arm. Knife-fighter style. 'The balance is great. Does it have the thing?'

Dildo shrugged. 'No idea.'

She took hold of the pommel and unscrewed it. Underneath was a tiny V-shaped blade, half as long as her pinkie was wide. Her grin got even wider. 'It does!' She held it up for Logan. 'They use this end to find the Devil's mark. Any deeper and you risk puncturing something. . . What?'

A small V-shaped blade, no more than half a centimetre long, set on a round metal guard. Exactly like the illustration on Anthony Chung's post-mortem report.

At least now they knew what Agnes had used to torture her ex-boyfriend.

Dildo took the dagger back, slid it into its sheath, screwed the pommel into place again, then dumped the whole thing in the sports bag, followed by everything else. 'Right. Remember, I'm in charge. You pair just stand there and look menacing while I confiscate stuff.'

38

One wall was a solid bank of TV screens. Most of them were dark, just a handful playing various matches and races from the other side of the globe, so a pair of auld mannies could perch on red-vinyl stools and stare at them through milk-bottle-bottom glasses. Swigging from tins of Special Brew at twenty to nine on a Wednesday morning.

Ma Stewart sat behind the counter, one plump cheek propped up on her hand, pulling her face out of shape as she leafed through something glossy with telephoto snaps of celebrities in their bikinis. Big red circles drawn around their thighs and tummies so the reader could indulge in a bit of cellulite schadenfreude. Not that Ma had anything to gloat about, she was like an overstuffed sofa in a violent orange-and-gold silk blouse, unbuttoned to expose a vast crevasse of pale quivering cleavage bedecked with gold chains and little sparkly things. She'd swept her wiry grey hair up into a bun that wobbled on top of her head every time she sighed and turned a page.

Dildo marched over, the sports bag slung over one shoulder, and knocked on the countertop. 'Shop.'

Ma looked up from 'Cellulite Bikini Bodies Shocker!' and a huge smile spread across her huge face. 'Mr Mair, how nice to see you again. Would you. . .' Her eyes drifted across to Logan, then her scarlet lips parted in a wet O, like a bullet hole. 'Sergeant McRae, we haven't seen you in ages! Oh, what happened to your poor face?' She closed her magazine, then reached across the counter and pinched his cheek. 'You're skin and bone! That'll never do.'

The cover had a photo of Nichole Fyfe on it, posing in her witch-finder's costume. 'NICHOLE'S TROUBLED PAST: "ACTING SAVED ME FROM A LIFE OF CRIME"' in lurid Helvetica.

Dildo hefted the sports bag up onto the counter. 'We need to talk.'

But Ma wasn't looking at him. She turned towards the back of the shop and took a deep breath. 'Janice! Janice, put the kettle on: the police are here. And see if we've got any rowies left, poor Sergeant McRae's wasting away.'

The replica sword glittered in the overhead strip-lights. 'You recognize this?' Dildo clunked it next to the sports bag, then went back in and came out with a dittay book. 'How about this?'

A little old man shuffled out of the door behind the counter, hands dug deep into the pockets of a shapeless cardigan. He'd wedged a *Witchfire* baseball cap onto his head, far enough down to make the tops of his ears stick out at right angles. He blew his nose on a tatty grey hanky. 'Dougie says we're running out of blanks.'

Ma patted him on one sloping shoulder. 'I'll chase the suppliers up. Everything else all right?'

'We're doing Peggy's birthday cake in a minute – her daughter's picking her up at quarter past for a day's shopping in Dundee. Takes all sorts.' He folded up the hanky and stuck it back in his pocket. 'You want to come sing?'

A big smile. 'Wouldn't miss it for the world. Just let me see to these nice *police officers*, and I'll be right through.' Then she mouthed, 'Police!' at him.

He just stared at her.

Dildo plonked the pricking dagger, witch-finder's badge, T-shirts and caps down in front of Ma. 'Care to explain these?'

Her thick fingers drummed on the counter, gold and diamond rings shining. 'These. . .? Sorry, I really have no idea what you're talking about. Now, how about a nice cup of tea?'

'How many times do we have to have the talk, Ma? You can't counterfeit other people's merchandise.'

'How about a slice of birthday cake? It's a Victoria sponge, Janice makes the best—'

'I've got a warrant.'

Her face sagged around a scarlet pout. 'But I've not done anything *wrong*. . .'

The last wobbling strains of 'Happy Birthday to You' faded away, then Peggy leaned forward and huffed out the candles in three wheezing breaths. A cheer went up from the assembled dozen-or-so OAPs and she sat back beaming her dentures at them, rubbing knobble-knuckled hands as Ma Stewart cut the cake.

Radio 2 burbled out into the large room. The ceiling was a patchwork of stained grey tiles, the breezeblock walls painted white and covered with posters of kittens and 'YOU DON'T HAVE TO BE MAD TO WORK HERE', the floor with beige carpet tiles patched with duct tape. . .

Metal modular shelving ran around the outside of the room, between the posters, spider plants trailing their pale-green tendrils down from between cardboard boxes of dittay books and baseball caps. Benches and tables filled the middle of the room, some with sewing machines, others with glue and glitter, another handful with assorted tools, bales of fabric, sheets of leather, cutting tools. . . A proper little cottage counterfeiting industry.

The wee man in the baggy cardigan handed out china plates with slices of birthday cake on them. A blue-rinsed woman – hunched over like a quaver – followed him with cups of tea.

Logan took one of each and settled back against a work-bench festooned with blank notebooks. A pile of red leather covers lay next to them – each one tooled with the dittay book's swirls and patterns. He took a bite, and a sip of tea. Good cake. Nice and moist.

Ma swept her hands up, until she stood there like an over-inflated letter T. 'See, how can this *possibly* be wrong?'

Dildo picked up a witch-finder badge, the enamel only half done. 'Because it's illegal.'

'I'm providing a service to the community. These poor dears need something to keep them busy, don't you, Dougie?'

A man in a tank-top, shirt, and tie nodded, making his comb-over bang up and down like a trapdoor. 'Better than listening to some wee tosspot singing ye olde wartime songs at us. I'm seventy-five, not ninety – I saw the Rolling Stones live about a dozen times. *And* the Sex Pistols. "Knees up Mother Brown" my sharny arse.'

Peggy put an arthritis-twisted hand to her chest and rolled her eyes. 'Oh, Mr Galloway, such language!'

He grinned. 'Ah, you love it when I talk dirty.'

Ma's chest swelled up, as if she was about to explode. 'You see? They get out and about, we have nice lunches, tea and biscuits, they get to make new friends, gossip, maybe a little romance. . .?'

A blush spread across Peggy's lined cheeks. 'One knee-trembler after the pub shuts and they never let you forget it.'

'And you *know* what the state pension's worth these days, don't you? Nowhere near enough to keep body and soul together. I provide my ladies and gentlemen with a nice little income and a lovely place to work.'

Dildo sighed. 'That's not the point. It's still—'

'And who's it hurting? The film people aren't making anything themselves, are they? So it can't be illegal. Stands to reason. You can't counterfeit something that doesn't exist yet.'

'Ma, you have to *stop* doing this.'

'They like getting together and making things. And they do such a good job too, have you seen the quality?'

'It – doesn't – matter!'

Logan plucked a pricking knife from a box. They'd fixed the guard in place, but the pommel was missing and the hilt wasn't wrapped in leather yet, the words 'MADE IN ABERDEENSHIRE' stamped into the metal. Eight-inch blade at one end, tiny half-centimetre blade at the other. 'How many of these have you made?'

She smiled. 'Lovely, aren't they? There's a wee engineering works I know that produces the most wonderful metalwork. Between you and me: the manager picks his nose, but you have to overlook that kind of thing in an artiste.'

'How many?'

'Oh, we've got about three hundred in the store, don't we, Charles?'

The man in the saggy cardigan shrugged. 'Can't make any more till we get those blanks in.'

Three hundred. So much for tracking down the murder weapon.

Dildo held up his warrant. 'Right, I'm confiscating this lot. You know the drill: stop what you're doing. And if anyone wants to lend a hand loading it all into the van. . .?'

'It's so unfair. . .' Ma Stewart leaned against the betting shop counter, fanning herself with her gossip mag as Dildo staggered out to the van under the weight of half a dozen cardboard boxes. 'We're only trying to give the old folks something productive to do.'

Logan unscrewed the pommel from a counterfeit pricking knife and ran his thumb across the minute triangular blade. Sharp. 'Where did you get the designs from?'

'You don't want them just mouldering away in a retirement home, do you? They need something to focus on.'

'Knives, costumes, swords, badges, books. . . They're all identical to the film props, so *someone* must be slipping you the plans on how to make them.'

Ma puckered her scarlet lips. 'I have my sources.'

'Someone in the props department?'

'Surely we could come to some sort of arrangement? If I can't sell the merchandise, I can't pay my people. That's not what you want, is it? Them going home empty-handed after putting in so much work?'

'Who – did – you – get – the – designs – from?'

A big sigh swelled her cleavage again. 'All right, all right. Since it's you: I had a contact on the inside. A lovely girl who wanted to help my pensioners. Pretty little thing, and so polite! Shame about her boyfriend. . .'

'It was Agnes Garfield, wasn't it? You're the reason she was stealing stuff from the set.'

'She did not "steal". She *borrowed*.' Ma raised her chin, dragging ripples with it. 'Agnes adores those books, she just wants to make sure people can hold a bit of it in their hands. It was her idea to use my ladies and gentlemen, so they'd have something to do, and a bit of spending money to brighten up their old age.' A tear sparkled in the corner of Ma's eye. 'She didn't even want a cut of the profits. But I insisted: I said to her, I said, "It's only fair you get your share. We couldn't do it without you." We've still got her money sitting here. *Personally*, I wouldn't be surprised if she gives it all to charity.'

Dildo marched back in through the shop's front door, and out through the rear again.

'Why can't more people be like that, Sergeant McRae? Selfless and giving?'

And psychotic, and delusional, and dangerous. . .

'How do you get in touch?'

A smile. 'We phone her, silly. Everyone has a mobile these days. My Norman calls me on mine all the time, ever since he split up from Marcus. So sad. They made a lovely couple, but it's Bobbit and Rascal I feel sorry for. . .'

Mobile. Worth a go. 'What's her number?'

'No one ever thinks of the terriers, do they?' Ma slipped on a pair of half-moon spectacles and peered into a thick address book, lips moving as she scanned her finger across the page. 'Here we are. . .'

Logan copied it down into his notebook. It wasn't the one Agnes's parents had given them, so it looked as if Chalmers was right: she'd ditched the old phone and bought herself a brand-new pay-as-you-go. 'Call her.'

A frown. 'And say what? That the police are here and they want to speak to her? I don't think she'll like that.'

'Just. . . Call her and tell her you've got something from the film company waiting for her. Tell her someone dropped it off, specially for her.'

'Who?'

'I don't know: someone who wants to remain anonymous?'

'Tsk. . .' Ma shook her head, making everything wobble. 'For a man, you're a terrible liar.'

She took out her phone and punched in the number, then let it ring. And ring. And ring. . . 'Hello? Rowan, it's Ma Stewart, how are you? . . . Oh, you know, the usual. Can't complain. . . Yes. . .' She put her hand over the mouthpiece and winked at Logan. 'It's her.' Then back to the phone: 'I don't think so, dear, but I'll check. . . Yes. . . Listen, I've still got your first share of the proceeds sitting here, and Peggy's knitted a lovely cardigan for you. You know, like the one Rowan wears in the tower-block scene? . . . Yes, that's right. It looks smashing. And did you know it's her birthday today? . . . I know!' A long pause, with lots of nodding. 'Yes, no, twenty minutes will be lovely. I'll save you some cake.'

Then Ma hung up and smiled at him. 'There we go. All sorted.'

Twenty minutes. 'Thanks.' Logan hurried out through the door to the car park, already dialling Steel. 'We need an Armed Response Unit: Agnes Garfield's coming in.'

'Laz, I'm no' in the mood for jokes. Bad enough I've got Bell and Leith taking swings at each other like drunken—'

'She's going to be at Ma Stewart's place in about twenty minutes.'

'For real?'

'Positive.'

A pause. *'Now that's more sodding like it! We nab her, we tell those Weegie bastards to stuff their case review up their fundament, then we go down the pub and booze it up till we can't stand. Ha! Hold on, I need to go tell the ACC. He'll cream his frilly pink undies.'*

Five minutes later Steel was back on the phone. *'We're screwed.'*

'Already? How did—'

'Can't get a firearms team to you in twenty minutes. It'll take at least half an hour – silly sods are doing a training exercise in Fraserburgh and took the armoury keys with them.'

Logan checked his watch. 'Fifteen minutes now.'

'Can you no' get her to come back later?'

'Yeah, why don't I do that. And maybe I can ask her to bring some biscuits for when we arrest her?' He took a couple of paces towards the van, then back again. Time to improvise. 'OK, forget the firearms team. Far as we know she's probably got a knife, but that's it. Sim's got her stab-proof vest and a thing of pepper-spray. We'll be fine.'

'We're scrambling every patrol car we can find. She'll—'

'A bunch of cars hammering through the streets with blues-and-twos going? That's not going to scare her off, is it? Plainclothes only: stick to the speed limit, nothing flashy.'

A grumble came from the other end of the phone. *'Fine. But when you get back, you and me are going to have a wee chat about the chain of command. In the meantime, you're no' to do anything stupid. Like let her get away.'*

'I know.'

'I'm serious, Laz! Mr Fuckup is not *coming to visit, understand?'*

'OK,' Logan downed the last of his tea and put the cup and saucer on the nearest workbench, 'so I hide under the counter out front. We wait till she comes through to the back of the shop, then Dildo blocks the back door, I block the front, and Sim tackles Agnes. Any questions?'

The counterfeiting room was virtually empty – all the merchandise loaded into the back of Dildo's council van. The OAP workforce was squeezed into Ma's office, complaining about not being able to sit down, and what did that poor Garfield girl ever do to deserve getting pounced on?

Logan closed the door on them. Now it was just him, Dildo, and Constable Sim.

Sim sniffed. 'You sure we shouldn't get them out of the building?'

'Agnes would see them milling about and know something was up. You got your pepper-spray?'

A lopsided smile. 'She's an eighteen-year-old girl, Guv, not Genghis Khan.'

Logan's phone rang: the Beatles and 'Octopus's Garden'. He pulled it out. 'Dave, I'm kind of busy, so—'

The psychologist's voice was clipped. '*Do you not think you could've asked before clogging up my inbox with three hundred and sixty-two emails?*'

Ah. . . 'Look, I just need you to work your magic and tell me which of them are deluded and which are genuinely dangerous.'

'*Now I've got IT on my back moaning about server space. And if you'd bothered to check: the profile I gave you clearly shows that Agnes Garfield is—*'

Something bleeped at the front of the betting shop. The door.

Sodding hell.

Logan checked the security-camera monitor mounted above the entrance through to the front of the shop. A figure in a hoodie and baseball cap stood in the middle of the screen in fuzzy black-and-white-ovision.

'Sorry, Dave, I've got to go.'

'*Logan, I'm not—*'

He hung up.

Sim peered up at the picture, her voice lowered to a whisper. 'That Agnes?'

'Difficult to tell. . .' The general size and shape was right, but the baggy hoodie and cap did a pretty decent job of hiding any distinguishing characteristics. 'Might be?'

If it was, she was five minutes early and Steel was right: they were screwed. There was no way he'd be able to sneak out front now and hide under the counter. Plan B, plan B, plan B. . .

Logan pointed into the room. 'Move!'

Dildo scurried over to the back door and hid behind a stack of cardboard boxes. Sim ducked under a workbench in the middle of the room. Logan flattened himself against the wall beside the door, on the opposite side to the handle. So when it opened it'd hide him from view.

A voice floated through from the betting shop, high, wobbly at the edges. Definitely female. *'Hello? Ma?'*

'Hello, Rowan love. Oh, I love *the new hair – that colour is just so you!'*

Stop sodding about, you old trout. Send her through the back. . .

'You go on through, there's cake and tea.'

'Em, OK. . .'

Logan licked his lips.

The door handle turned.

Here we go. Nice and easy. No one gets hurt.

The door swung open.

39

Rowan steps into the room. Normally the place is alive with pale yellow and blue: the fuzzy-edged auras of old men and women. Short twists of beige for forgotten dreams. Wisps of grey for lost loved ones.

But today it's empty.

Someone's cleared the benches, emptied the shelves.

The only noise is the radio: a DJ burbling away about how great the weekend weather's going to be in London.

The hydraulic return unit swings the door closed behind her.

Clunk.

Where are all the people?

Breath catches in her throat. Something's wrong. Ma said there'd be tea and cake. . . It was a *lie*.

And then the noise – right behind her – a tiny speaker blaring out a tinny rendition of that song from the *Wizard of Oz*, the one about the scarecrow being thick. It's a ringtone.

A man's voice comes so close she can almost feel his breath on her neck: 'Buggering hell. . .'

The song dies a sudden death.

She doesn't turn around, doesn't have to. 'Detective Inspector McRae.'

The man who doesn't know if he's an Angel or a Hand of Death.

Black tendrils coil around her legs and chest.

The Kirk is my shield and my sword. The Kirk is my shield and my sword.

Blood thumps in her throat, each breath crackling deep inside her.

RUN.

She takes a step forward and a police officer uncurls herself from beneath one of the benches. Blue and red fizzing trails probe the area around her.

Rowan stops.

The Angel of Death clears his throat. 'It's OK, Agnes. You're safe now.' And he manages to sound as if he actually believes that.

Safe? How can she *possibly* be safe?

The door at the back of the room leads out into the alleyway behind the row of shops. All she needs to do is get there.

What I do in its service lights a fire in God's name.

Another step.

Hands wrap themselves around her shoulders. A gentle touch that burns like a fistful of ice.

'You'll be OK, it'll all be—'

She pistons her right elbow back, hard into his stomach, and warm breath explodes in her ear. Everything goes into slow motion. He lets go and falls back, crumpling around himself, hissing in pain.

Tenet Two: 'Know thine enemy, for knowledge is power and power is victory.'

She's watched him through his bedroom window, a towel wrapped around his waist, twenty-six little shining scars

422

making constellations on his stomach. Old knife wounds never really fade.

Rowan's already moving forward as he hits the ground. Up onto the nearest bench, running, dragging the pricking knife from the pocket of her hoodie, pulling the eight-inch blade free from its sheath.

The police officer turns, hair sailing out like a black wave behind her. A little canister of something glints in her hand. Rowan's boot flashes out, connecting with the knuckles and it spirals away. End over end. So slow and delicate.

She keeps going.

A man lumbers out from behind a pile of boxes by the back door. His little round glasses are hollow and empty, his goatee beard stretched wide by his open mouth. 'No!'

Something grabs her ankle. Her knee buckles and the workbench rushes up to meet her. Duck, roll, kick out. . .

There's a grunt and the police officer is going the other way, arms flailing, a ribbon of blood fluttering from her mouth.

And Rowan is on her feet again.

The man has a goatee beard, but he's a sheep. He grabs a chair and hauls it up in front of himself, like he's a lion tamer. But she's not a lion, she's a Fingerman.

She hammers straight into it, slamming him back against the door.

His fist crawls through the syrupy air towards her face. She bats it away with her left, then punches him in the ribs with her right. Something goes crack and his eyes bug.

Rowan pulls back her hand. The pricking knife's long blade drips scarlet.

And bang – everything is proper speed again.

He opens and closes his mouth a few times, making a high-pitched mewling noise that builds into a proper scream.

She steps back and the chair clatters to the floor.

Red blooms across his chest. 'No, no, no, oh Jesus. . .' He

leaves a smear across the wall as he slumps sideways to the floor.

What I do in its service lights a fire in God's name.

She opens the back door, steps out into the alley, then closes it behind her.

Time to run.

Logan rolled over onto his back, hissing a breath out between gritted teeth. Burning coals seared through his stomach, melting all the way through to his spine, filling his lungs with scalding embers and choking ash.

Holy *Christ*, that hurt.

The back door slammed.

He worked his way up to his hands and knees, forehead resting on the scratchy beige carpet tiles.

Up. Get up. Get after her. DON'T LET HER GET AWAY.

The ground wobbled beneath his feet as he dragged himself upright sending fresh needles jabbing into his belly.

Ma's counterfeiting shop was a mess: tables overturned, chairs; a smear of blood on the back wall. . . Dildo was lying on the floor by the door, knees curled up against his chest, a pool of scarlet seeping out onto the floor. 'No, no, no, no, no: I don't want to die, I don't want to die!'

PC Sim untangled herself from a swivel chair and lurched to her feet. Scarlet smears covered her mouth, twin trails glistened their way down the front of her stab-proof vest. 'Gagh. . .' She spat – frothy and red. 'Bit my tongue.' Then stared at Dildo. 'Jeepers. Is he going to be—'

'Don't just stand there: GET AFTER HER!'

Sim blinked a couple of times, nodded, then charged over, wrenched open the back door and disappeared.

Logan limped across and sank down next to Dildo. 'Tim, you're going to be OK. We're going to sort you out. It's OK, it's OK.'

Blood bubbles popped at the side of his mouth. 'I don't want to die. . .'

Logan dragged out his traitorous phone. 'I need an ambulance and back-up to J. Stewart and Son bookmakers, Mastrick.'

'One moment, I'll just—'

'Don't you sodding dare put me on hold! I've got a Trading Standards Officer with stab wounds to the chest, Agnes Garfield is fleeing the scene, PC Sim is chasing her on foot.'

'I don't want to die. . .'

'You're not going to die, Tim, just calm down OK? Ambulance is on its way.'

'All cars, this is Control, be on the lookout for an armed suspect, I-C-One female: Agnes Garfield—'

Dildo stared up at him, face the colour of skimmed milk, lips thin and purple. 'Oh God, you called me "Tim", I *am* dying.'

'Don't be a dick, you're *not* dying.' Back to the phone. 'Where's that bloody ambulance?'

Logan peeled off his shirt and dumped it in the bathroom sink. Scarlet coils leeched out of the fabric into the cold water. He stuffed the whole thing under the surface, then dumped his socks and trousers in after them. Squelched it all together until the water was nearly scarlet, then drained it off and turned the tap on again. Left them to soak while he climbed into the shower.

Hot water pounded against his back, washing Dildo's blood down the drain. Soothing the burning in Logan's stomach.

By the time he was towelling himself dry, his mobile was singing Rennie's theme tune. He snatched it up and pressed the button. 'Any word?'

'Still in surgery, Guv. Doctors say he's lucky to get off with a punctured lung – any higher and it would've nicked his heart.'

That was something at least. He pulled on a clean shirt, the fabric sticking to his damp back. 'They find Agnes Garfield?'

Silence. Then Rennie cleared his throat. *'You've got an appointment with Professional Standards at noon. And Strathclyde are going to do the independent review. You know, as they're up here anyway.'*

'And Steel couldn't be bothered to tell me herself.'

'She's . . . kinda pissed-off at the moment. Last time I went past her office, sounded like she was battering the crap out of everything with a sledgehammer.'

Wonderful. Because today wasn't bad enough already.

'Not like it was your fault though, was it? You had to do what you could in the time that you had. Only other option was to let her get away. . . Erm. . . Sort of. We've got a lookout request on for Agnes Garfield.'

Logan picked his notebook off the bedside table and thumbed through it until he got to the last entry from Ma Stewart's shop and read out the number for Agnes Garfield's new mobile. 'Get a GSM trace on that, pronto. She's probably ditched it, but it's worth a go.'

'Will do.' Pause. *'Dildo's going to be OK. It wasn't your fault.'*

'Just get your arse over here and give me a lift back to the station.' Logan hung up. Returned the phone and the notebook to the table. Sank down on the edge of the bed and stared at the crumpled sheet of paper taped to the wardrobe mirror.

'LIKE IT OR NOT, YOU'RE STILL ALIVE'

His phone trilled and buzzed at him.

Couldn't even leave him alone for five minutes. . .

'What?'

'Mr McRae? Yes, hi, it's Kwik Fit, you left a car outside the garage this morning?'

Nursing it slowly around the massive bulk of Mounthooly roundabout with a firm grip on the handbrake.

He stared at the ceiling. 'How much is it going to cost?'

'*Well, you need two new brake lines, and all your brake fluid needs replaced. The disc and the drums on the rear wheels are corroded, the suspension arm on the passenger-side front is almost rusted through, back tyres are worn almost to the canvas, the exhaust is—*'

'The brakes. How much to fix the brakes?'

'Right, sorry.' Some rustling. 'You know, you're lucky they didn't give out on the motorway, or a junction or something. Really nasty thing to do to someone. . . Right, OK, just to fix the brakes is going to be—'

'Hold on: "nasty thing to do to someone"?'

'Well, yes. Cut their brake lines. It's really irresponsible. And indiscriminate too, you don't just hurt the person in the car, anyone they hit—'

'Someone cut my *brake lines*?'

40

'How can she *still* not be in?' Logan scowled out of the passenger window at the bulky three-storey tenements of Sandilands as they drifted slowly by. The ones nearest the road had been given a fresh coat of paint, but it wasn't helping.

Rennie tootled the pool car along behind a number seventeen bus. ''Cos she's special and clever and doesn't have to actually work like the rest of us?'

'Oh, is she. . .' He pulled out his phone, found her number in the contact list, and thumbed the button. Then listened to it ring.

'When this is all over, think I'm going to take Emma to Paris for a long weekend.'

Logan frowned. 'PC Sim?'

'No, not that Emma, *my* Emma. Why would I take Sim on holiday?'

'Because you're a—'

A click and Chalmers's voice came on the line. '*You've reached Lorna Chalmers. I can't come to the phone right now, but you can leave a message after the beep.*'

'This is DI McRae. When we discussed you joining the soup-kitchen team, I don't remember saying anything about you having the morning off afterwards! Get your arse into the station *now*, Sergeant.' He hung up.

Rennie whistled. 'Oooh, someone's in trouble.'

'Don't be a dick.'

That just got him a grin.

The number seventeen hissed to a halt, indicator blinking as a couple of middle-aged ladies dressed like oversexed teenagers clambered onboard.

A nasal Doric accent crackled out of the pool car's radio. *'Charlie Six, from Control, over?'*

Rennie flipped the switch. 'Morning, Jimmy.'

'Aye-aye, loon, you got DI McRae with you?'

He looked across the car and mouthed the words, 'Are you here?'

Idiot.

Logan stuck his phone back in his pocket. 'What do you want, Jimmy?'

'We've had a wee call from someone says they know who your clay-head thingy is.'

He grabbed his notebook. 'You got an address?'

Rennie sniffed, wrinkled his nose, then did a slow three-sixty. 'Smells like someone's burning old nappies.'

The house was on the end of a row of three terraced cottages, all huddled together at the edge of a patch of woodland on the Kemnay Road. Bennachie was just visible through jagged pine-tree branches, the shadows beneath them dark and deep. Throw in a gingerbread house and Hansel and Gretel would have flashbacks.

Cottages one and two bore satellite dishes and mainten-ance-free swathes of gravel where front gardens should have been, but number three was a riot of colour – flowers and shrubs and herbs laid out in intricate patterns around a winding bark path.

Logan opened the heavy wooden gate and stepped onto scrunchy chips of brown, surrounded by tall spiky leaves. Should've brought some breadcrumbs to scatter behind him. . .

Rennie stuck his hands in his pockets and meandered after him, stopping to sniff the flowers along the way.

The doorbell sounded deep inside the house, a faint diiiiiing-donnnnnng just audible through the wooden front door.

A bee bumbled from one purple foxglove to the next. A pigeon cooed. Rennie rocked on his heels.

Logan tried the bell again. 'You sure they know we're coming?'

'Yup.'

Two minutes later, the door creaked open and a pale lined face peered up at them, eyes squinted almost shut. She couldn't have been an inch over four foot five, grey hair up in a lopsided bun, neck like a deformed sock puppet. She smiled, showing off perfect rectangular white teeth. You could've stood on her Teuchter accent, it was that thick: 'Can I help you?'

Logan checked his notes. 'Miss Mary Gray?'

The squint got even more pronounced. 'Are you the man from the council?'

'Police. You called about a facial reconstruction?'

'Oh, the head! Yes, yes, of course, you'll have to come in, I'm a little deaf when I don't have my glasses on.'

Sweat prickled across the back of Logan's neck. A three-bar fire glowed malevolently in the fireplace, turning the small room into a furnace. Sunlight streamed through the lounge window, two massive spotty cats curled up on the sill, ears fixed in his direction.

Three more cats slumbered in front of the electric fire; a pair of Siamese on the sofa; one on top of a bookcase full of ancient leather-bound volumes, their titles picked out in crumbling gold leaf. A bronze urn gleamed on the mantelpiece, between black-and-white photographs of unsmiling women in heavy black frames.

The sound of tea things clattered through the open door.

Another little old lady snored away in a chair by the fire, mouth hanging open like a damp pink cave, a tartan blanket draped over her knees. A stripy ginger cat sat on her lap, glowering at Logan with emerald eyes when it took a pause from washing its bum.

Mary Gray shuffled back into the room. Rennie was right behind her, carrying a silver tray covered in cups and saucers and a plate of cakes and a big china teapot. He stopped in the middle of the room and looked around him. 'Erm, where. . .?'

Mary waved a hand at a black-and-brown tortoiseshell curled up on the coffee table. 'Shipman! Come on, you naughty monkey, move for the nice man.' She shooed him away and Rennie lowered the tray in the cat's place.

'Miss Gray, you said—'

'Please, sit, sit.' A wide grin. 'Don't mind Sutcliffe and Chikatilo, their bark's worse than their bite.'

Logan nudged one of the Siamese out of the way and sat. It stuck its tail in the air then hopped down to lurk under the coffee table. Rennie perched on the other end of the sofa, right at the edge so as not to disturb the other cat.

'You said you can identify our reconstruction.'

'Oh yes.' She gave the sleeping woman a poke in the shoulder. 'Effie? Effie, do you want some tea and a slice of Battenberg?'

The snoring stopped. 'Eh? Who's that?' Her voice was wet and shapeless, slurred by a lack of teeth.

'Do you want tea and cake, Effie?'

431

'Oh. . . Is it Thursday?'

Logan pulled out the media department's poster and held it out. 'We haven't even got these up yet.'

Mary poured five cups of tea with the delicate precision of a neurosurgeon. 'Now, you help yourself to milk and sugar.' Then she turned, took a deep breath, and bellowed out a cry that would have shattered concrete. 'INA! INA, THE TEA'S MADE!' Mary picked up the plate and squinted at it. Then handed it to Logan, swapping it for the poster.

Battenberg and scones and shortbread. Always a sucker for homemade shortbread.

Crumbs tumbled down his front as he bit into it. 'You know her?'

The squinting got so fierce it looked as if her whole face was going to implode. 'Can't see a thing without my glasses.' Another deep breath. 'INA!'

A large grey cat with dark markings hopped up onto Logan's lap, stared at him, then plonked itself down. A throaty burring noise, and the whole thing started vibrating.

Mary beamed. 'My, my: Lopez doesn't usually like men, you're honoured.'

'Yeah. . .' The large furry body leached heat into his trousers, like a hairy hot-water bottle.

'Just don't touch his tummy, or he'll have your hand in shreds.' One more huge breath. 'INA! FOR GOODNESS' SAKE!'

Another little old lady shambled into the room, tugging a pastel-blue cardigan around her shoulders. She had to be at least ten years older than her sister, liver-spotted scalp clearly visible through her thinning hair. A milk-bottle-bottomed pair of glasses perched on the end of her nose, the legs attached to a gold chain around her neck. 'All right, all right, I'm not deaf.'

'Do you want some tea?'

432

She peered at Logan through her glasses; they made her eyes huge. 'You don't look like the police.'

He hauled out his warrant card and she took it with a trembling clawed hand, the fingers arthritic and twisted.

'Ah. You'll be here about that clay-head thing.'

Finally. 'You know who it is?'

'Oh aye.' She took off the glasses and handed them to Mary. 'See?'

Mary slipped them on and blinked at the poster she was holding. 'Oh, that's much better, I can hear everything now.' Then she passed the glasses and the picture of Dr Graham's facial reconstruction to the old lady in the corner. 'Look, Effie, isn't that something?'

'I had another vision.' In the magnifying lenses Effie's left eye was a sea of red, the iris pale and watery.

'Put your teeth in, Effie. No one can understand a word you're saying.'

Ina hobbled over to the bookcase and pulled out a photo album. She opened it, smiled, then ran a hand across the pages. 'I need the glasses.'

They were passed back along the line. 'Right. . .' She flipped forward a couple of pages, then placed the album on the coffee table, next to the tea things. 'There you go.'

A woman stared out of the album, with seventies hair and sixties glasses, the colours faded to pale yellows, orange and brown. She was the spitting image of the clay head. Dr Graham was *good*.

Under the stern, lined face, were the words, 'A HAPPY HOLIDAY IN LOSSIEMOUTH, JUNE 1978'.

And now the family resemblance was clear: Ina, Effie, and Mary were sisters.

'She's your mother.'

'Oh aye, Agnes Gray: scourge of the parish. She was a firebrand, that one.'

433

Agnes. Same name as their missing teenager.

Effie rattled her cup in her saucer. 'Does anyone want to hear my vision or not?'

Ina settled onto the couch next to Logan. 'Effie's visions are remarkably accurate.'

'How did you know it was her? The picture's not even been on the news yet.'

'Oh, Mary heard about it on the radio and I looked it up on the internet. We do most of our business online these days.'

Effie cleared her throat. 'I walked across a field of gold, towards a huge dog with knives for teeth. Five leaves I counted in the glaring light and five doors too. I fought with a ghost for the price of my soul, but they beat me. Bound me. And drowned me in the pale white deep.'

Silence settled into the baking hot room.

What a load of old bollocks.

Logan finished his shortbread. 'Can you tell me where your mother was buried?'

Ina patted him on the knee. 'She was a very influential witch, you know. Agnes Gray was a *power* in this land.'

Mary nodded. 'People came from as far away as Rhynie and Oldmeldrum seeking her help.'

'Of course, things are different now.' Ina peeled the marzipan from a slice of Battenberg. 'The internet's a wonderful thing – we do spells for people in Australia and California and Moscow.'

Logan put his tea down. 'Spells. . .'

Mary held up her hand as her sister, Effie, drifted off to sleep again. 'Don't worry, we always use our powers for good. And we only ever curse people who deserve it, don't we, Ina?'

'Oh yes, we're very responsible that way. Saddam Hussein, was one of Effie's.'

Nuttier than a bag of squirrels.

'Do you remember where your mother was buried?'

The strip of marzipan was rolled up into a ball, then popped in whole. 'She dug Mother up, didn't she: the Garfield girl?'

'You know her?'

Ina laughed, setting the loose skin under her chin wobbling. 'Oh, our wee Agnes is something, isn't she?'

Mary sighed. 'So much talent for someone so young. She'd read all about Mother in the library. Well, ever since that dreadful *Witchfire* book came out, everyone wants to know about our family. . . Agnes was convinced she and Mother were spiritually linked, because they had the same first name. So we took her under our wings.'

'Taught her the importance of herbs, the secrets of consecrated ground, and the power of bones.'

'You see, that's why you haven't found her. When a witch digs up bones from a graveyard they contain power. And if a normal person's bones have power, *imagine* how much the bones of a witch contain.'

'And Mother was a *very* powerful witch.'

Make that two bags of squirrels.

But it did explain why Agnes Garfield had dug up Nicholas Balfour. If you couldn't find a dead witch to exhume, a Victorian spiritualist was probably better than nothing.

'Do you know where Agnes is now?'

Ina disassembled her slice of cake into its four coloured squares. 'And she was such a quick study. The bones, the earth, the herbs, she understood. And she was always so good about doing little chores about the house, and fetching . . . medicine for Effie's glaucoma.'

For God's sake. . . Logan dumped his plate back on the table. 'You know what? That's great, but she stabbed a friend of mine today, so if you don't mind: answer the sodding question. Where is she?'

435

Ina put her hand on Logan's leg again. Gave it a squeeze. 'We're sorry for your loss. But we've not seen Agnes Garfield for months. Not since we fell out over that horrible young man of hers.'

Mary brought her chin up. 'We tried to warn her. Effie had a vision where he hurt her and made her do terrible things, and she's a *good* girl. But Agnes wouldn't listen.'

A sigh, then Ina's eyes drifted to the urn on the mantelpiece. 'The heart wants what it wants. And when we tried to point out how bad he was for her, she left us.'

'And now we have to make do with the bones of our babies.' Mary picked a grey tabby from the carpet and hugged it to her chest. 'Isn't that right, Lopez?' She glanced up at Rennie. 'Oh don't worry, it's all natural causes. We'd never hurt our little fuzzkins, would we, Lopez? No, we wouldn't.'

Ina stood and shuffled over to the urn on the fireplace. Stroked it with a twisted finger. 'How are we supposed to get more consecrated soil, now? Taxi drivers always look at you so strangely when you get in with a shovel and say, "Take me to the nearest graveyard. . ."'

OK, time to come back from Happy La-La Land. 'Where was your mother buried?'

Mary took the photo album back and shut it. 'The family plot, out by Kemnay. The church is deserted now, probably all overgrown. We don't get out as often as we should.'

Ina licked her lips, tongue snaking in and out of her mouth as if it was scenting the air. 'And you *will* give us Mother's bones back, won't you? So she can be with us where she belongs?'

Yeah. . . Where she'd probably end up ground to a powder and sold to gullible idiots on the internet.

'Found the hole!' Rennie stood up to his waist in nettles, elbows out at ninety degrees to his shoulders, hands curled into paws. 'There's a coffin at the bottom and everything. Looks like something out of *Buffy the Vampire Slayer*.'

The graveyard was completely overrun with weeds: the headstones swallowed by jagged coils of brambles and sheaths of bracken, mixed in with nettles and spires of rosebay willowherb. Little parachutes of gossamer fluff drifted through the heavy air to shine against the thunderhead sky.

Logan shuffled through the undergrowth, brushing cat hair from his trousers as he went, following Rennie's flattened path. 'Any signs of recent disturbance?'

'Nah. The grass is starting to grow back on the stuff she's excavated. If she's still digging up magic mojo compost, she's doing it somewhere else.' He hauled a rust-coloured spine of docken from the jungle of weeds and poked at the hole. 'If she's such a nice girl, how come she's off killing people?'

'Nice?'

'You know, keeping the old dears in graveyard soil, bones, and cannabis. . . Most kids these days wouldn't bother their backsides.'

Cannabis? How did. . .

Of course: the glaucoma 'medicine'. So Agnes *was* dealing after all. And given the state of Nichole Fyfe and Morgan Mitchell, she was probably helping them out as well.

Very public spirited. No wonder Zander kept giving her second chances.

Logan turned and looked back at the crumbling remains of the church. Three walls, no roof, a handful of black bin-bags, an old fridge, and a soggy mattress. Nowhere to sleep. And even if she'd pitched a tent somewhere in the grounds, there would be trails leading through the waist-high weeds.

She wasn't here.

So much for that idea.

All that talk of consecrated earth and the power of bones. . .

Never listen to daft auld wifies, no matter how good their shortbread is.

Logan headed back towards the patrol car, leaving Rennie to struggle with the weeds. 'Get on the phone to the council. I want that grave filled in again before some idiot falls down it and breaks their neck.'

There was a brief shout, a rustle and a crunch.

Logan spun around, but there was no sign of Rennie. 'Oh, for God's sake! Tell me you didn't.'

'Ow. . . Help! It's got me! Aaaaaaaargh! Run: save yourself!' Then Rennie popped up in the middle of a stand of willowherb with a grin plastered across his stupid face and tufts of white all over his suit. 'Got you.'

No wonder Steel picked on him.

Rennie pulled the patrol car in to the side of the road, ignoring the zigzag lines for the pedestrian crossing. Causeway End was a lot busier than it had been just before seven that morning, the stream of traffic wheeching itself around Mounthooly roundabout's bulk moving like a twisting snake of steel and glass.

Logan popped off his seatbelt. 'Tell Chalmers I want her in my office soon as I get back to the ranch.'

Rennie picked another clump of willowherb from the front of his jacket and dropped it in the footwell. Where it promptly stuck to his trousers. 'Bloody stuff's like Velcro.'

'And after that, you can check up on how Guthrie's doing getting hold of Anthony Chung's arrest record from San Francisco.'

Another bit of fluff joined the others. 'Does it really matter? He's kinda dead, so—'

'Because I say so, that's why.' He climbed out, then stuck his head back through the open door. 'I want the names of everyone he was associated with, and if any of them have come into the country in the last six months.'

Rennie's frown turned into a smile. 'Ah: you think Agnes didn't kill him after all. It was one of his old gang mates come to settle a score.'

'Don't be an idiot: of course Agnes killed him. I want to know who put her up to it. If Goulding's profile is right, she needs a dominant personality to tell her what to do.'

'Ah . . . And it's not like any of her friends had the stones to go up against Anthony Chung. Even Dan Fisher, with his unrequited crush, wouldn't dare. And last time he tried, she scrambled his eggs with her knee.' Rennie huffed a breath onto his fingernails then polished them on his fuzzy lapel. 'Oh yeah: I do read the case notes, you know. It's—'

A horn blared out behind them: a dirty big articulated lorry hissed to a halt six foot from the back of the patrol car, its driver giving them the one-fingered salute.

Logan slammed the door and stepped back onto the pavement.

Rennie pulled away and the lorry grumbled after him.

Chasing down Anthony Chung's old associates was probably a waste of time, but at least they'd be doing something.

Logan hurried down to the pedestrian crossing, then worked his way across both dual carriageways to the Kwik Fit garage on the corner overlooking Mounthooly.

He popped over the low wall, squeezed between two parked cars in the MOT section. . . Then froze.

A mud-streaked Transit van sat on the forecourt, right outside the entrance. Rusty dents and scrapes marred the once-white paintwork. Reuben's van.

Time to turn around and—

A low growling voice, right behind him: 'Get in the van.'

Shite. . .

'No. Don't think so.'

A big hairy hand appeared from his left-hand side, it was

439

holding a mobile phone, the screen showing a small photo of Wee Hamish Mowat's sunken face, below the word 'CONNECTED'.

OK. . . He took the phone. 'Hamish?'

'Ah, Logan, I'm so glad to hear that you're all right after your close shave this morning. Do you have a minute to talk?'

Not really. He took a step forward, then turned to face the mountain of muscle and scar tissue – standing there in his grubby blue boilersuit with a face like cracked stone. '*Someone* cut my brake lines.'

A pause. *'I see. That* is *an unfortunate development, isn't it. Very unfortunate indeed. But I need you to put that behind you for a moment and go with Reuben.'*

'Not a chance in hell.'

'Logan, remember I told you about the cannabis farms and the violence and the uncertainty and concern that breeds? Well, I'm afraid this little business rivalry has come to a bit of a head. And I'd appreciate it if you would help Reuben sort things out.'

'You have got to be—'

'I give you my word that Reuben is there to facilitate your role as an officer of the law, nothing more. We all want to see an end to the senseless violence, don't we?'

'Facilitate.'

Reuben grinned at him, the scar tissue on his cheeks pulling it all out of shape.

'Do I have a choice?'

'Of course you do, Logan. Everyone always has a choice.'

Reuben stepped forward, closing the gap until the swollen barrel of his stomach was pressed against him. 'What do you think?'

Logan got in the van.

41

The Transit van growled away from the garage, the gear changes a symphony of grinding metal. A smell of stale fat and old garlic filled the cab, overlaid on something sharp and metallic and the sickly pear-drop scent of fresh plastic.

Logan shifted on the sticky seat. 'How did you know where I'd be?'

'None of your business.' Reuben flexed his shoulders beneath the blue boilersuit. 'And just for the record: I don't cut brake lines. When I come for you, McRae, I'll not be sneaking about under your car with a pair of pliers.'

Probably because the fat sod wouldn't fit.

'"*When*" you come for me?'

'You'll bloody well know about it. You'll get to see it coming.'

Oh joy.

'That's the way it's going to be, is it?'

'You, me, and a chainsaw.'

'You know what, Reuben? You can. . .' Logan frowned. There was a noise coming from the back of the van. A sort of muffled moaning to go with the creak and rattle of the old Transit.

He turned in his seat and peered into the cavernous interior.

Plastic sheeting covered the floor and walls – held in place with thick strips of grey duct tape. A figure was scrunched up in the far corner, sitting with his back to the van doors, knees up against his chest, cable-ties around his ankles, arms behind his back, an off-white pillowcase over his head. It was stained dark brown around the front.

'There's someone in the back of the van. . .'

No reply.

'Reuben: why have you got someone trussed up in the back of your van?'

A shrug. 'Everyone's got to have a hobby.'

Logan dropped his voice to a hissing whisper. 'I'm a police officer, you bloody idiot – do you really think—'

'Mr Fisher here's been a very naughty boy.'

'I don't care if he's mooned the Queen and shagged her corgis, you can't just—'

'See, Mr Mowat says I'm not allowed to kill you, or mutilate you, or hack your balls off and make you eat them. Didn't say anything about you falling down a few times and breaking something though.' Reuben turned his scarred smile in Logan's direction, eyes dark and hooded. 'Now, you gonnae shut the fuck up, or do I pull this van over?'

'You know what, I'm sick and tired of your—' Logan's phone burst into Steel's sinister ringtone. He dragged it out. 'For God's sake, what now?'

'*Where the goat-buggering hell are you? Supposed to be in with Professional Standards getting your bum spanked, no' gallivanting off—*'

As if there weren't bigger things to worry about. If in doubt: lie. 'No I'm not.'

'*Aye, you are – I told Rennie* specifically *to tell you, and he—*'

'Nope, must've slipped his mind. Believe it or not, we've been a bit busy trying to catch a killer today, so—'

'*Oh no you don't: you're the one let her escape in the first place! Now get your arse back here so Professional Standards can spank it.*'

'Can't. I'm in the middle of something.'

'*Laz, I'm warning you—*'

'Got to go.' He hung up on her and switched his phone off. Steel could shout at him later. Assuming he survived whatever the hell this was.

Rowan steps back into the outside catering van's shadow, the smell of sausages and frying onions thick and dark in the air. The industrial estate sulks on the outskirts of Dyce, a sad collection of corrugated metal buildings with unpronounceable names and chunky logos, ringed in with chainlink fencing. Most aren't even open: just empty shells with 'FOR LEASE OR SALE' signs fastened to the gates.

'BANGERS AND BAPS' is painted along the back of the van in big black letters, not that anyone can see it. It's parked in a lay-by with nothing behind it but trees and weeds.

The Witch wanders across the road, hands in his pockets, chunky headphones sitting on top of his head, lips pursed in a tuneless whistle. Making noise for the sake of it, hauling his jagged aura of red and orange flames behind him. He pauses in front of the van's menu board and rubs his hands together. Grins. Then pushes the headphones back so they hang around his neck, and goes up to the counter. His accent is half American, half Scottish, his skin the colour of old newspapers. 'Yeah, can I get a bacon buttie *with* egg, and a thing of chips?'

A condemned man's last meal should be something a bit more special than that, shouldn't it?

Whoever's running the van is out of sight, but her voice is like the rumble of faraway thunder. 'You want tea, or a juice, or something?'

'Irn-Bru.'

He should've gone for fillet steak and a bottle of champagne.

'Coming right up.'

The plan is simple enough: follow him back where he came from, question him, then give him the chance to purify his soul, before delivering it to God. Easy.

Two minutes later, a little red Peugeot hatchback pulls into the lay-by, diesel engine grumbling and rattling to a halt. A large man with a dusting of grey hair around his pale forehead turns and says something to the pair of children in the back, then climbs out into the warm afternoon, leaving a black and green trail behind him. It barbs and swirls around his long black coat. Jabbing at the earth beneath his feet.

Rowan shrinks back against the side of the van. A Raptor. . . This isn't in the plan. This isn't in the plan at all.

He stops at the serving hatch and smiles. 'Aye, aye, Betty. Fit like the day, then?'

'Can't complain, Ian. Usual?'

'Aye, and a couple bags of crisps for the wains.' He turns and waves back at the Peugeot. The children wave back. A young boy and a little girl, her golden hair bobbing about an angelic little face.

'Oh, aren't they adorable?'

'That's the joy of grandchildren, you can spoil them rotten and no' have to worry about the consequences.' He slips his hand into his coat pocket, pulls out an old-fashioned iPod, and goes thumbing through the menu. 'You keen on *Steppenwolf*, Betty?'

'More of a Bruce Springsteen girl, myself.'

He pops the earbuds in, then puts the iPod back in his long black jacket. Like the wings of a crow. '"Born to be Wild" – can't beat it. Got a good rhythm.' He smiles at the Witch. 'How about you?'

A shrug. 'Dunno about old music.' He reaches up and

takes a tin from the counter. Clicks the tab on it and downs a deep draught of Irn-Bru.

Ian takes out a pair of black leather gloves and puts them on. 'Kinda my theme tune.' Then he turns and waves at the kids in the car again. Covers his eyes with his gloved hands, then throws them open. 'Peekaboo!'

The children giggle and do the same back.

Betty shuffles about inside the van, making the springs creak. 'Here you go, loon, one bacon-and-egg buttie, with chips. Sorry you've had a wait. Help yourself to sauce and that.'

The Witch steps forward, reaching for his food, a smile on his face.

One more go at peekaboo, only this time the children don't peek, they keep their eyes covered as Ian pulls a hammer from his long black coat and cracks the Witch over the back of the head with it.

The Witch stumbles, a cry caught in his throat, the tin of Irn-Bru erupting in a fountain of orange as it hits the ground. Then he's on his knees, holding himself up with one hand on the counter.

Ian drones out the opening words to 'Born to be Wild' then slams the hammer down on the Witch's wrist.

A squeal and he falls to the floor, curling up in a ball as Ian slams his boot into his back. Then he wraps his gloved hands into the Witch's hair and drags him around behind the van.

'What've you been told?'

Rowan peers around the edge of the van, using the big bottles of Calor gas as a blind.

The Witch is scuffing backwards through the dirt, ruined wrist clutched to his chest, the other hand up – pointing. Teeth bared. 'I'm *warning* you, Grandad, you don't know who you're—'

Ian kicks him in the face. 'It's Mr Falconer to you, sunshine.'

He rolls onto his front, bright red spattering from his mouth. 'Unngh. . .'

'And I know exactly who I'm messing with: Jake Ran Yingnu. You were supposed to do a job, Mr Ran.' Ian kicks him again. 'Did you *really* think twenty grand's worth of cannabis could disappear from your farm and no one would bat an eyelid?' Ian pops out the earbuds and stares down at him, head on one side, a bird of prey watching a wounded rabbit. 'Well?'

The Witch pushes himself up . . . then collapses forward again, forehead resting on the blood-stained earth, bum in the air, as if he's praying to Mecca. 'I didn't steal it! It wasn't me!'

'Think the McLeod brothers give a toss about that? That weed was in your care, you were *responsible* for it. And you let someone just waltz in and nick it in the middle of the night?' He backs up a couple of steps, then takes a run up and slams a boot into the Witch's ribs, hard enough to flip him over. 'How'd they find the place? How'd they get past the alarms? Who told them?'

'AAAAAAAGH. . .' Coughing. Wheezing. The Witch wraps his good arm around his chest, his teeth bloody tomb-stones in a scarlet mouth. 'It wasn't me, I swear, I didn't—'

'Place was meant to be secure. The McLeods *trusted* you.'

Tears roll down the Witch's cheeks, making clear trails in the dust. 'I didn't tell anyone! I did what I was supposed to do. IT WASN'T ME!'

Ian hunkers down beside him, the hammer's scuffed metal head resting on the dirt. 'You know what? I believe you. Wasn't your fault. You'd have to be sodding mental to screw with the McLeods like that, wouldn't you? And if you did, you wouldn't stick around afterwards: you'd be on the first flight out of here. Get as far away as you could before they came after you.'

The Witch's shoulders judder as sobs crack free from his bloody lips. 'I didn't . . . it wasn't me. . . I would . . . would *never*—'

'But it doesn't really matter what I think, does it? If Simon and Colin let you off with this, the next thing you know everyone thinks they've gone soft. Don't want that, do you?'

'Please. . .'

'Course you don't.' Ian sticks his earbuds back in, then frowns. 'Pfff. . . Missed the best bits.' He produces the iPod and pokes at it.

'Please, I'll . . . anything . . . anything you want, it's . . . it's yours. . .' The Witch pushes himself back along the dirty ground. 'I didn't do anything wrong!'

'Here we go.' Ian puts the iPod away again. Closes his eyes for a moment, nodding in time to the music. Then raises the hammer above his head and swings it down, right into the side of the Witch's knee. There's a wet cracking sound. A scream. Then he does it again. And again. Grabbing hold of the Witch's belt so he can't scramble away. Keeping the beat with his hammer as he sings along.

A metronome of blood and fear.

Born to be Wild.

Rowan watches until there's nothing left of the Witch's knees but pulp and shards of bone, then slips away.

Reuben pulled into the parking space right in front of a glossy edifice of yellow sandstone and emerald-green glass. Posters in the window encouraged people to bet on when the first goal would be scored against Celtic in the Scottish Cup Final on Saturday at Hampden Park, or who'd get red-carded, or injured, with photos of cheery actors holding wads of notes and glasses of champagne. From the look of things, being burned down was the best thing that had happened to the Turf 'n Track in years.

He hauled up the creaky handbrake, then turned to the poor sod in the back. 'You sit tight, Mr Fisher. My mate Terry's going to be right here watching you. Doesn't say much, but he's a nightmare with a Stanley knife.' Then the big man hopped out into the overcast afternoon. Looked back in at Logan. 'You: out.'

It wasn't as if he had much of an option. . .

He followed Reuben's broad back towards the Turf 'n Track's front door. 'Terry?'

'If the wee knob knows he's all alone in there, he'll get restless. Might kick up a fuss, bang on the sides of the van, try to get himself a wee bit of help. Terry'll be good company for him: make sure he does the right thing.'

The Turf 'n Track's door opened with a bleep, announcing their arrival into a clean, sparkling room with one wall of floor-to-ceiling flatscreen TVs. Another wall was covered in pages from the *Racing Post*, listing all the meetings, runners and riders. And all the way across the front: a long counter manned by three attractive young blonde women in green-and-yellow uniforms cut just low enough to show a bit of cleavage. All of them wearing enough slap to sink a Debenhams makeup counter.

Three men in suits sat at a breakfast bar thing in the middle of the room, watching the races, eating paninis, and sipping bottles of Corona with lime wedged in the neck.

Bit of a change from the old place.

Logan sniffed. The betting shop smelled of lemon air freshener instead of stale cigarettes, and the roof wasn't the colour of a smoker's lung. 'I liked it better when the floor was all sticky.'

Reuben lumbered up to the counter and slammed one big hand down in front of cashier number three.

448

She flinched. Recoiled back in her seat, then took a breath and straightened up and plastered a smile on her face. 'Welcome to the Turf 'n Track, Aberdeen's premier venue for—'

'Tell Creepy he's got visitors.'

The smile slipped a bit. 'Creepy. . .?'

'Colin McLeod. Or his brother the gimp, don't care. But you get him out here before I start sticking your punters through your fancy TVs, understand?'

She opened and closed her mouth a couple of times. Then leaned over to one side, obviously trying to make it look natural as she reached underneath the counter and jabbed at something. 'Please, sir, there's no—'

'Think I can't see you fingering the panic button?'

A blush crept across her cheeks, strong enough to bleed through the heavy layers of foundation. 'It's my first day. I didn't. . . Please don't hurt me?'

The door behind the counter marked 'Staff Only' opened and a man stepped into the room: broad-shouldered with a puddingy face, a chunk of ear missing one side, a pair of black wraparound shades hiding his eyes. He jerked his chin up. 'There a problem, Naomi?'

'It's not my fault, Mr McLeod, he came in and he's threatening people and it's my first day and I didn't—'

'All right. You go for a wee cup of tea. I'll deal with it.'

Reuben took a step back and cricked his head to one side. 'Well, well, well: look who the dogs dragged in.'

Simon McLeod rolled his shoulders, hands flexing in and out of fists. 'Reuben. Who let you off your leash?'

'You and me got a problem.'

Naomi squeezed past her employer and out through the back door.

Simon McLeod smiled. 'Think I give a—'

'Oh, you better, 'cos if you don't—'

'Actually,' Logan stepped up to the counter, 'we need to talk about certain . . . horticultural activities.'

The wraparound sunglasses turned in Logan's direction. Simon McLeod's nostrils flared as he sniffed the air. 'Who's that?'

'I'd show you my warrant card, but there's not much point, is there?'

A smile crawled its way across his face. 'Jessica, Fiona: Let the gentlemen through, then tell the punters we're shutting for an hour – fire drill. Then make yourselves scarce. Got some business to attend to.'

Simon McLeod's office was huge – the desk, coffee table and a pair of leather sofas spread out as if they didn't want anything to do with one another. Leaving plenty of room to walk between them without bumping into anything.

The magnolia walls were bare except for a Rottweiler's head mounted on a wooden plaque behind the desk, its fur patchy and singed. One ear missing, a bit like the office's owner. The name 'KILLER' was picked out in brass beneath it.

Simon McLeod settled into the chair behind the desk and folded his arms across his chest. 'So. . . What? You turn up with one of your bent cops and I'm supposed to be scared?'

Reuben cracked his knuckles. 'Had half a brain, you'd be terrified.'

'*Really?*' Simon took off his wraparound sunglasses. There was nothing underneath, just deep flesh-coloured dents where the eyes should have been. Even the eyelids were gone, leaving a network of twisted scars. 'You think *anything* you could do can scare me?'

Silence.

So what now?

Logan sat on the couch nearest the wall. It creaked and

450

squeaked under him – probably to make sure Simon would know exactly where he was.

Bloody Wee Hamish Bloody Mowat: *I have faith in you, Logan. It's in the common good, Logan. You don't want a drug war, do you, Logan?*

How the hell was he supposed to negotiate a peace treaty between rival drug cartels? Buy them tea and biscuits and ask them to play nice? He cleared his throat. 'This isn't a shakedown, I'm not a bent cop, and if we can come to an agreement it doesn't have to go any further.' Yeah, this was *definitely* a career high.

A smile crawled across Simon McLeod's face. 'Oh sure, because I'm going to say loads of incriminating things with you in the room. Anything in particular you want me to confess to while you're here? Kidnapping Shergar? Killing Lord Lucan? You've not caught Bible John yet, maybe that was me too? Course, I was only two at the time, but I've always been precocious.'

Logan stood and the couch creaked again. He shook his head at Reuben. 'Told you this was a waste of time. Go home and tell Wee Hamish, Simon McLeod isn't interested in a peaceful solution.'

Simon raised an eyebrow, tugging the scar tissue around his hollow eyes into new shapes. 'Wee Hamish? This isn't just Reuben acting the dick, throwing his weight around?'

'Who you calling a dick, you blind sack of—'

'Hoy!' Logan held up a hand. 'You're supposed to be facilitating, not making things worse.'

Reuben's shoulders went back and he stepped forward, his fists up. Then stopped, took a breath, and settled against the wall again.

Better.

Logan pointed at Simon, even though there was no way he could see it. 'Let's say, *hypothetically*, you've been going

451

around battering the living hell out of Oriental gentlemen with a claw-hammer. Your brother Colin's handy with a hammer, isn't he?'

Of course he was. Knees a speciality. People crippled while you wait.

Simon smiled. 'Those days are behind us, officer. Businessmen of our standing in the community would never get involved in anything like that.'

'Now suppose this was the opening salvo in a drugs war. Wee Hamish wouldn't like that. He'd think it was bad for Aberdeen. He'd think you should come to an agreement with your rivals that doesn't end up with any more injuries or deaths.'

'And if we didn't? Hypothetically.'

Reuben's voice was a dark rumble. 'You end your days as wee dollops of pig shite.'

The smile slid away from Simon's face. 'Well, you can tell Wee Hamish there's sod all we can do about it: no one knows who the other side is. That's why we're. . . That's why a local businessman might be interviewing your Oriental gentlemen.'

'You don't know who the new boys are?'

'Think they'd still be stealing from me if I did?' A shrug. 'Supposing I had anything these people wanted to steal. Hypothetically.'

Reuben folded his arms across his broad chest. 'Lucky for you I'm here then, ain't it? Got someone outside who knows.'

42

Reuben backed the battered Transit van into the loading bay behind the Turf 'n Track, stopping just shy of the breezeblock loading platform. He hopped down from the driver's side, lumbered around the back, then hauled open the rear doors.

Mr Fisher lay on his side, wriggling deeper into the Transit, feet scuffing on the plastic sheet. His whole body trembled, muffled sobs coming from beneath the blood-stained pillowcase.

Reuben reached inside and dragged him forward again. Hauled him upright. Then slammed a huge fist into his guts. 'Right, Mr Fisher. Here's how this works: you tell us everything, and you get off with a kicking. I think you're not cooperating, I start breaking things. I think you're *lying* to me, I carve you up like a chicken and feed you to the pigs one wee bit at a time. They eat everything: hair, skin, bone.'

He whipped off the pillowcase.

What the bloody hell was he playing at? Soon as Fisher saw their faces there was no way Reuben would let him live. Stupid fat sod: what was Logan supposed to do, stand back and let it happen?

Only Mr Fisher couldn't see a damn thing. Three strips of duct tape covered his eyes: one horizontal, two vertical, as if they were targets. Another strip covered his mouth. His black hair was long on one side and shaved on the other, a hollow tube stretching out his left earlobe, three silver hoops above it. . . Anthony Chung's friend: the one who worked in the bar. The one who tried to fight for Agnes Garfield's honour, and got kneed in the balls for his pains.

Reuben grabbed one corner of the gag and ripped it off, taking the stud in Dan Fisher's bottom lip with it.

'Aaaaagh. . . Bastard. . .' Blood dribbled down his chin.

Dan Fisher. Friend of Anthony Chung. Anthony who always had the best cannabis.

At least now it was obvious where he'd got it from.

Reuben hammered another fist into Fisher's stomach. Then stood back and waited until he'd stopped retching. 'Your starter for ten is: who's stealing weed from the McLeod brothers?'

A long string of spittle wobbled from his bleeding bottom lip. 'Oh God. . .'

Reuben sucked in a breath, then shook his head. 'Wrong answer.' A Stanley knife blade clicked out, then snicked through the cable-ties holding Dan Fisher's ankles together. Then he dragged one foot out until it was just hanging over the Transit's rear bumper.

'PLEASE! I DON'T—'

The van rocked as Reuben slammed all his weight down on Fisher's ankle. A muffled pop. And Fisher's foot didn't face the front any more.

Two seconds later the screaming started. Reuben gave him a count of three, then shut him up with another fist to the guts.

Logan grabbed his arm – it was solid, like a telegraph pole. 'That's *enough*.'

'Nah, we're just getting started.' He grabbed Fisher's other foot. 'Try that again, shall we? Same question.'

Fisher moaned and sobbed, snot shining on his top lip. 'Please. . . I just sell it on, I don't know who—'

The van rocked again and the other ankle made the same muffled popping noise.

'AAAAAAAAAAAAAAAAAAAAAGH. . .'

Reuben wiped his hands down the front of his boilersuit, then smiled at Logan. 'Not very bright, is he?'

'God sake. . .' Logan pushed past him and climbed up into the back of the van.

Fisher was back on his side, folding his knees up to his chest then out again – like a broken accordion. Mouth open in a silent scream.

Logan took hold of his shoulders and pinned him to the plastic sheeting, holding him still. Then leaned in until his mouth was an inch from Fisher's collection of earrings, and dropped his voice to a whisper. 'Listen up, you daft bastard: they're not kidding. This isn't the TV, there's no last-minute rescue coming. They're going to kill you if you don't tell them who's stealing their drugs.'

'I don't know, I don't know, I don't know. . .' A massive shuddering breath.

'You're going to *die*, do you get that? And it won't be quick. This'll be a happy memory for you by the time they've finished!'

'Please. . . It *hurts*. . .'

'That was just the warm-up, wait till he gets into his stride. Now who's stealing their bloody cannabis?'

Fisher's bottom lip trembled. 'It . . . Ton. It was Ton. Anthony Chung.'

Of course it was.

'You were Anthony Chung's best friend: everyone knows he always had loads of cannabis. You were selling it for him, weren't you? Passing it out through the bar. Even after he beat the crap out of you?'

'It was. . . I didn't have any choice.' Sweat sparkled on Fisher's face. 'Please, please, you've got to help me. . .'

'Who was he working with?'

Reuben's voice boomed out from the loading dock behind them. 'If you're gonnae bum him, get on with it so I can start on his kneecaps.'

'Will you shut up for two minutes?' Then back to Fisher. 'Who was Anthony working with, Dan? Who's in charge now he's dead?'

'I don't know, I don't—'

Logan took hold of Fisher's pierced ear and twisted.

'Aaaaaagh!'

'Do you *want* to end up carved into little pieces?'

The words came out riding on a wave of jagged sobs. 'I only dealt with Ton! He said . . . he said he knew someone who worked for these cannabis farms, and he could find out where they were, and all I did was sell it on, I never stole it, I swear on my mother's grave, I don't know. . .'

Reuben slammed the Transit van's back doors closed, shutting out the sound of Dan Fisher's sobs.

Simon McLeod slipped the wraparound sunglasses back over the holes where his eyes used to be. 'Come on then: who is it, and where do I find him?' A little smile escaped, then was quickly killed again. 'So I can meet up with him and sort this out nice and peaceful, like Wee Hamish wants.'

Aye, right.

Logan stuck his hands in his pockets. 'He's in the mortuary. He screwed his girlfriend over once too often and she staked him out on a kitchen floor, stabbed him three hundred and sixty-five times, then strangled him.'

Simon McLeod's eyebrows lowered a fraction of an inch. 'Hmm. . .'

'What?'

A sniff. 'Sounds like my kind of girl. But I still want the bastard's name.'

'So you can go after his family? No chance. They had nothing to do with this. The guy who stole your cannabis got himself tortured to death, and you didn't have to lift a finger.' Logan stuck his hands in his pockets. 'Wee Hamish wants you to stop the beatings. Not like they're doing you any good, is it? All that and you still didn't find out who was stealing from you.'

Simon shrugged. 'That's what happens when you ask the wrong people the right question. Hypothetically speaking.'

'No more beatings.'

A cloud of pale-blue exhaust growled out of the Transit's exhaust.

'Imagine there's a businessman who's invested a large sum of money to set up a number of indoor growing facilities and bringing over the specialists to manage them. Now imagine someone else comes along and steals from those farms. And that some of the businessman's key . . . horticultural staff are missing. If you were that businessman, wouldn't you think the gardeners were involved? Wouldn't you encourage them to keep their farms more secure?'

The Transit lurched forward a couple of feet, then stopped, engine still running.

'You weren't crippling the opposition, you were punishing your own people for being *stolen* from?'

'Call it a claw-hammer incentive scheme. Like the one your wee friend in there's going to join soon as he gets out of hospital. Well, unless Reuben feeds him to the pigs first.'

Logan turned. 'No one's getting fed to the pigs! And they're not getting their kneecaps pulped either. Fisher's done: his only contact was the guy who got killed, he doesn't know anything else. He gets a free pass.'

'*No one* steals from me.'

'He gets – a free – pass.'

The Transit van's horn blared.

'I'm serious, Simon. I find out something's happened to him, or the dead guy's family, and I come after you and your brother. And I ask Wee Hamish to do the same.'

A large hand thumped down on Logan's shoulder and squeezed. 'Trust me when I say: if you *ever* threaten me or mine again, I'll have you skinned alive. Understand? For Wee Hamish's sake, I'll leave the boy. But see if I get to the man in charge before you do? All bets are off.'

The Transit van rocked as Reuben ground his way through the gears. He pinned his mobile between his little round ear and his huge rounded shoulder. 'Yeah. . . No, don't think so. . . Hold on.' He held the phone out to Logan. 'Mr Mowat wants a word.'

'Hello?'

'*Logan, I hear it went well. Did you sort everything out with the McLeods?*'

'Simon says he wants to make peace, but you know what will happen if he gets his hands on whoever's running the rival operation.'

'*They're primitive people, Logan. They believe in Old Testament vengeance. But Reuben tells me you know who's stealing the McLeods' cannabis?*'

'I know who *was* stealing it. He's dead.'

Reuben stuck his foot down and the Transit lumbered across the lights on Westburn Drive. 'Lucky. Means Creepy can't get hold of him.'

'He was tortured to death by his girlfriend.'

'*Really? Now that* is *fascinating. And you're sure it was his girlfriend?*'

458

The lumpy concrete bulk of Aberdeen Royal Infirmary loomed above the surrounding buildings.

'Who else would it be?'

'Ask Reuben.' A pause. *'Now, would you do me a favour and put me on speakerphone?'*

Logan frowned at the mobile's shiny interface, then pressed the bit on the screen that looked like a loudhailer.

Wee Hamish's voice crackled out of the speaker, only just audible over the Transit's diesel drone. *'You know, it does my old heart proud to see the pair of you working together. Logan and Reuben: a team, looking after my city. It gives me a lot of comfort to know it'll be in good hands when I'm gone. Thank you both.'* Then Wee Hamish hung up.

Logan passed the phone back. 'He said to ask you who else would've tortured Anthony Chung to death.'

'Did he now. . .' Reuben took them right onto Westburn Road – next stop Accident and Emergency.

'What happened to making Wee Hamish proud?'

A grunt. 'Think you're getting off that lightly? You and me: we're not finished by a long shot.'

Brilliant. So much for bonding over a job well done. Well, half done. Kind of.

Maybe Samantha was right? Maybe the only way Reuben was ever going to go away and leave him alone was at the bottom of a shallow grave? Or banged up for a twenty stint in Barlinnie? Slightly more difficult to arrange, but at least no one would have to die. Who hadn't died already. . .

'Who tortured Anthony Chung?'

A smile twisted its way through Reuben's scars. 'Word is, the new kids on the block got themselves an enforcer who's a card-carrying psycho. Gets off on maximum pain.'

'You're saying he was done by *his own* enforcer? What kind of—'

'Think it'd be the first time one partner got greedy and the other one didn't like it?'

Fair point. But there was no way Agnes Garfield didn't kill Anthony Chung. Not with the magic circle on the floor, and the pricking knife she used on him, *and* the one she stabbed Dildo with. . .

It *had* to be her.

Didn't it?

Rowan huddles in the undergrowth on the wrong side of a chainlink fence. Don't breathe. Don't move.

The Raptor is gone, pootling away in his little Peugeot, his happy grandchildren in the back eating prawn cocktail crisps.

Why? Why would a Raptor punish witches like that? And not even ask any questions, just beat and pound away to an old song from the sixties. He hammered the Witch's knees until they looked like bone-flecked mince, then had a sausage in a bun and a cup of tea, laughing with Betty and chatting about going to the Algarve for the school holidays.

And all the while, the Witch lies twitching on the ground behind the Burger and Baps van, bleeding into the dirt.

He barely moves when the ambulance arrives. Not even when the paramedics stand over him in their green jumpsuits, staring and swearing at the mess where his knees should be.

Betty stands to one side, sipping on a mug of something, lying to a police officer. No, she didn't see anything. No, the man didn't order anything from her. The first time she knew anything was wrong was when she went to check the gas bottles, and found him lying there. She's round and small, too small for that deep rumbling voice, malevolent pulses of green and black oozing out of her like sound waves.

Rowan chews the skin around her left pinkie until the salty-copper tang of blood sparks at the end of her tongue.

It was her job to find and save the Witch, and instead he's forever out of her reach. His soul is forfeit.

She's failed.

The Transit van growled away, trailing a cloud of diesel exhaust behind it. Logan hauled Dan Fisher off the pavement and into one of the low-tech porters' chairs reserved for hospital use. Just an oversized dining-room chair with four slightly wonky wheels bolted onto the legs.

Fisher moaned behind the gag, beneath the stained pillowcase.

Logan removed them both.

Underneath, Fisher's face was pale and greasy. Shock.

A gentle slap on the cheek made him blink, his voice wet and creaky. 'Please, I don't know. . .'

'You're at A&E. Dan? Dan, can you hear me?'

The automatic doors into the hospital creaked open, and one of the two uniforms stationed at ARI stuck his head out. 'Guv? That you? You OK?'

'I don't know anything. . .'

Logan hunkered down beside the chair. 'Where is he, Dan? Anthony Chung's partner? Where do they keep the stuff? Where do you pick it up from?'

Fisher blinked at him, both pupils contracted to tiny pinholes in the watery blue iris. 'It hurts. . .'

'I know it does, Dan, but I need you to tell me how to find whoever's running Anthony Chung's operation.'

'I don't—'

Logan grabbed him by the collar. 'I saved your life, you little prick! If it wasn't for me, you'd be working your way through a pig's digestive system right now. So tell me where I can find him!'

461

'Guv?' The uniform put a hand on Logan's shoulder. 'Is everything OK?'

Fisher rocked his head to the side, until he was staring at the PC. 'I don't know, I. . . I just pick the stuff up when I get a text message. Different place every time.'

Logan pulled his face back around. 'But the same mobile number?' They could do a GSM trace, find out—

'No: codeword. "Moderator". . . Same codeword, different mobile.'

So much for that.

Logan stood. 'Better get him inside.'

'Yes, Guv.' The uniform grabbed the chair's handles and wrestled the wheelie-chair through the automatic doors and into A&E.

The doors hissed shut again, leaving Logan's reflection staring back at him from the glass. Would've been nice to head back to FHQ with enough information to break a drug ring. . . It might have distracted them from the complete cock-up at Ma Stewart's that morning.

43

Logan peered through the window to the intensive therapy unit. Dildo lay on a hospital bed, flat on his back, face hidden behind an oxygen mask plumbed into the wall.

A uniformed PC sat in a plastic chair outside the ward, head buried in a thick textbook, lips moving as he frowned his way down the page. Overhead lighting sparkled back from a fist-sized bald patch.

Logan stopped in front of him. 'Anything?'

'I can't understand a bloody word of this.' He held the book up: *Immanuel Kant's Critique of Pure Reason.* Nurse Claire strikes again. 'Apparently I can't prove the chair I'm sitting on exists, because I only *think* it exists because my bum tells me it does and I can't empirically trust my bum to tell the truth. . .'

'That what it says?'

'Far as I can tell, one of the great philosophical minds of the eighteenth century thinks my arse is a liar.'

'I wouldn't stand for that, if I were you.'

A short doctor with dark-purple bags under her eyes and a distinct list to the left, limped out of the ITU, let the door swing shut behind her, then leaned back and rested her head against it. Sighed at the ceiling tiles.

Logan cleared his throat. 'Is he. . .?'

She blinked, her eyes pinching around the edges, as if she'd just stood on something sharp. Then came a brittle smile. 'I'm sorry, it's been a long day. Can I help you?'

'Timothy Mair – the stabbing victim, is he. . .?'

'Ah, yes. No, he'll be fine. They stemmed the bleeding, and patched up the hole in his lung. We're keeping an eye out for secondary infections and oedema, but he'll be fine.' She stifled a yawn, then scrubbed a hand across her eyes. 'Sorry. Roll on July. . .'

'Thanks.' He made his way into the depths of the hospital. A pack of gurneys had gathered around the vending machines in the corridor outside. Ready to pounce. Two old men in matching brown plaid dressing gowns shuffled past, wheeling intravenous drips on stands and arguing about whether or not Aberdeen was going to get its backside skelped by Celtic in the cup final.

Logan kept going.

A pregnant woman with her left arm in a cast mashed her thumb against the button for the lifts. He joined her. Waiting till the thing creaked and groaned its way down from the fifth floor. *Ding* and the doors slid open. Inside, the floor was held together with strips of duct tape – the tape's silver surface scuffed and holey. They stepped inside.

Halfway up, the woman burst into silent tears.

'Are you OK?'

She didn't answer, just kept her face to the wall, until the lift juddered to a halt, then scuffed out and away.

The doors slid closed.

Logan shut his eyes as the lift rose again. It didn't matter how many photo exhibits they put on, or how many pretty paintings they hung on the corridor walls, Aberdeen Royal Infirmary was always going to be a sprawling concrete maze haunted by the sick and the dying.

Cheery stuff.

He took a deep breath as the doors opened again, and marched out and down the corridor. Head up. Pulling on a smile that *hopefully* didn't look that forced.

After all, he'd escaped the place, Samantha would too.

Eventually. . .

Logan pushed through into the ward.

Samantha sat up in bed as soon as he walked in. Her hair was pillar-box red, the tattoos on her arms standing out against her pale skin. 'Gah, I'm going mad in here.'

He pulled the visitor's chair around and sank into it. Didn't matter if his bum was lying to him or not, he was prepared to take its word for it. 'You would not *believe* the day I've had.'

'Cauliflower cheese again for lunch. How do you make cauliflower cheese beige? It's not physically possible.'

'Dildo got stabbed.'

'I know. But he's going to be OK, so. . .' A shrug. 'You going to read more *Witchfire* to me?'

'Can't.' Logan stuck his feet up on the bed. 'Got a meeting with Professional Standards.' He checked his watch. 'Started . . . ooh, just over an hour ago.'

Silence. Then Samantha folded her arms across her chest. Never a good sign. 'We need to talk.'

Here we go. 'Can't we just—'

'It's about time you got your finger out and got the flat refurbished. They finished the roof two years ago. You're lucky the architect's still speaking to you.'

'I just haven't had time, and—'

'I'm not going to be in here forever. Might be *nice* to have a home to go to. Don't get me wrong – I love my caravan – but. . . It's too close to the road, and it's a really busy roundabout. We'll need somewhere safer for Cthulhu to live.'

Brilliant: first Jackie, now Samantha. He was *not* stuck like a bug in amber. 'It's not—'

'Logan, it's been two years: finger-out time.'

He slumped further down into the chair. 'OK, OK, I'll see what I can— Sodding hell.'

Steel's theme tune sounded deep inside his jacket pocket. No prizes for guessing what she wanted. He dragged the thing out, fumbled it, and the mobile went clattering to the floor, spinning under the bed. Darth Vader's theme tune got louder.

'God's sake!' Logan wriggled out of the seat and peered under the bed. Bloody thing. . . He got down on his knees, and reached for it. The floor was cool to the touch, the smell of bleach and pine-scented disinfectant strong enough to make him blink. 'Come on you little sod. . .'

His fingers wrapped around the thing, just as the music died.

Samantha's head popped over the opposite edge of the bed, upside down, long scarlet hair sticking up like she'd been electrocuted. 'What does Her Wrinkliness want?'

He glanced back. 'She hung up. Probably wants a rant about me skipping out on Napier and his Professional Standards whinge. . .' Logan stared.

'What?' A hand appeared, brushed across her cheek. 'Have I got something on my face?'

There, hanging from the network of hydraulic rods and metal struts under the bed, was a knot of three small bones, held together with bright-red ribbon. The same shade as Samantha's hair.

Agnes Garfield's calling card.

She'd been there, in Samantha's room.

'Bastards. . .' He stood.

Samantha frowned at him. 'What?'

'Useless bloody halfwit bastards. . .' He wrenched open

the door, and stuck his head out into the corridor. 'GET YOUR ARSE IN HERE NOW!'

Back to the room.

She was lying face down on the bed, dangling over the edge, peering underneath. 'What? What's going on?'

'Supposed to be keeping you safe!'

Footsteps clattered out in the corridor, then a huge nurse came battering through the door. Arms like tree trunks, evil-twin goatee beard, little round glasses. 'What happened? Is everything OK?'

Logan jabbed a finger into the nurse's chest. 'You're supposed to be keeping an eye on her! What the bloody hell do you think you're playing at?'

'Sorry?' The nurse's forehead creased, fingers curling in and out in front of his chest as if he was playing on a tiny video game handset. 'OK, I'm going to have to ask you to calm down, or I'm going to have to call security.'

'THEN CALL THEM! If they'd been doing their bloody jobs this wouldn't happen. This is supposed to be a secure ward!'

'This *is* a secure ward.'

'Oh, it is, is it?' Logan grabbed him by the collar and hauled him over to the bed. 'Look underneath. Go on, LOOK!'

'OK, OK. . . Sheesh. . .' He dropped down on one knee. 'What am I looking for?'

'The bones, you halfwit!'

The nurse reached beneath the bed, fiddled with something, then stood. Agnes Garfield's talisman lay in the palm of his hand. 'Is this supposed to be some sort of joke?'

'A joke?' Logan snatched the bones and held them up, dangling them on the end of their ribbon. 'Where did they come from?'

'The only people who've been through here since I got

on shift are the nurses, the consultant, and the bloke who fixed the printer. And they've all got security badges.' He folded his massive arms and brought his chin up. 'So I think you owe me an apology.'

Logan poked him in the chest again. 'What about the catering staff? The people who came round with lunch? Or did they just magically teleport cauliflower cheese in from the canteen?'

The nurse took a step back. A frown pulling his features inwards, one hand reaching for the call button. 'Cauliflower cheese. . .?' He looked left, then right. 'Why would they bring food in here? I mean . . . it's the coma care ward. Everyone's on drips and tubes.'

Logan blinked. Turned to stare at the bed again.

Samantha lay flat on her back, arms over the covers. The breathing tube fixed to the hole in her throat hissed slowly in, and out. A feeding tube in her nose. Both eyes taped shut. Her hair was a faded lacklustre red with eighteen inches of brown roots. Skin the colour of yoghurt, tattoos standing out like graffiti on a church wall.

He cleared his throat. 'Yes. . . It's. . .'

'Are you feeling OK?'

'No. Of course.' Logan ran a hand over his eyes. Samantha was perfectly still, lying in the same position she'd lain in for the last two years. 'Look: when did they last clean the room? Agnes Garfield must've been in since then. We can pull the security-camera footage.'

The nurse shook his head.

'What?'

'The cleaners mop the floors, empty the bins, wipe down the surfaces, stuff like that. They don't sod about with all the hydraulic bits and bobs under the bed unless they're doing a deep clean, or, you know, something's happened.' A shrug. 'Could've been there for weeks.'

Three witch's finger bones, dangling away beneath Samantha's bed. Working their dark magic. Keeping him from finding Agnes Garfield.

Right.

Logan took a deep breath. Stared at the floor. 'Look, I'm sorry, I didn't mean to—'

'Yes, well. . .' The nurse nodded. 'I suppose, if I'm honest. If it was my girlfriend – if she was stuck in here, in a coma for a couple of years – I'd probably be squirrelly about it too.'

44

'I see. . .' Superintendent Napier steepled his fingers and peered over them at Logan. His hair glowed like the top of a Duracell battery, his long thin nose twitching as he smiled. 'And you feel this was sufficient reason to ignore our appointment?'

The Professional Standards office was quiet, just the buzz-click of an oscillating fan stirring the motes of dust drifting through a shaft of sunlight. The other two desks were clean and tidy, their owners disappearing as soon as Logan turned up. Leaving him alone with the Ginger Whinger.

'I was acting on information received at short notice. What did you want me to do, ignore evidence of a serious crime?'

'What I *want*, Acting Detective Inspector McRae, is for you to turn up when summoned at the appointed time. Not an hour and thirty-four minutes late.' He patted the ends of each pair of fingers in turn, forward then backwards, slow and methodical. 'And you're certain we'll find cannabis farms at these locations?'

A little sacrificial offering to confuse the issue.

'As I can be.'

Unless, of course, Wee Hamish Mowat, or his green-haired minion were lying to him.

'I see. . .' There was a pause, while Napier stared at Logan like a pathologist examining a dead body. 'And I *understand* you took the time to pop past Aberdeen Royal Infirmary.'

'I discovered one Daniel Fisher on my way to my appointment with you, someone had just shattered both his ankles. I escorted him to hospital, where he informed me Anthony Chung had been responsible for stealing cannabis from the McLeod brothers and set himself up as an independent wholesaler. Then I went to check on Dil— On Timothy Mair's condition. His doctor says he's got a punctured lung, but he should make a full recovery.' Logan nodded at the sheet of paper, sitting in the middle of Napier's desk. 'It's all in my report.'

'Ah yes, our unfortunate Trading Standards Officer. Funny you should mention that. . .'

Logan paused in the corridor outside his office, fingertips resting on the handle. There were voices inside, muffled by the closed door, but still recognizable.

Rennie: *'No, really, I've got—'*

Steel: *'Pin your lugs back, 'cos I'm no' saying this twice. You've got to make your mark in this world. You've got to drag your arse across the carpet of life like a dog with worms.'*

Worms?

Rennie: *'Yeah. . . I know it's a lovely thought, but—'*

Steel: *'Stand back, point at all them streaks and say, "That was me!" You see what I'm saying?'*

Rennie: *'Erm. . .?'*

Nice though it would be to leave them to it, Logan dragged the door open.

Steel stood behind the desk, fake cigarette jutting out between her teeth. She had her hands clamped around

Rennie's shoulders, kneading them like badly behaved bread. He sat in Logan's chair, eyes pinched, eyebrows up, hands flinching with every taloned squeeze. Mouthing the words, 'Help me.'

Logan dumped his report on that morning's fiasco in the middle of his desk. 'Sorry to interrupt your foreplay, but some of us have work to do.' He pointed at Rennie. 'You: bugger off and do something productive for a change.'

A pained smile broke across Rennie's face. 'Oh, thank God. . .' He scrambled out of the seat and bolted from the room, leaving the door swinging in his wake.

Logan pushed it shut. 'Worms?'

Steel had a quick dig at her underwire. 'You wanted me to mentor him: I'm mentoring him.'

'There's a difference between mentoring someone and traumatizing them.' Logan sank into the vacated chair and grabbed the first interview transcript from the pile in his inbox: DI Leith's meetings with the homebuyers who'd been to view the house where Anthony Chung had turned up tortured and dead.

Steel crossed her arms and leaned back against the windowsill. 'Let me guess, suspended without pay?'

Logan flicked through the transcript. 'Slap on the wrists. Apparently Napier thinks it was "irresponsible to involve a civilian in the attempted apprehension of murder suspect known to be violent".'

'Aye, well, the copper-topped Nosferatu's got a point.'

'What was I supposed to do, let her go?'

'Did that anyway.'

He got to the end of the transcript. There wasn't a single clue: no confession, nothing of any help at all. He pulled the next one from the stack. 'Are you actually here for a reason?'

Steel took another puff, making the end glow. 'Stroke of

genius, hauling a pair of cannabis farms out your backside like that. Wriggling off the hook. *Convenient.*'

'Yeah, well—'

'How long you been sitting on them?'

'It's not—'

'Supposed to be a team here, Laz.' The eCigarette stood to attention, the tip glowing an angry red. 'That means you don't get to park your arse on information! Did you think you'd raid them single-handed, shower yourself in glory, that it?'

'I only found out about them this morning, OK? Haven't had time to do anything about it.'

'Oh. . .' She frowned out of the window, scratching at the side of one boob. 'Well . . . look on the bright side. I'll tell people the info was yours if the raids come off OK.'

Logan stared at her. 'Raids?'

A cough. 'Thought you were playing silly buggers. So . . . I've got Leith raiding the house in Westhill, and Ding-Dong's doing the one in Blackburn. At least it'll keep them from twatting each other.'

'Thanks. Thanks a bloody heap.'

She stopped scratching and pointed at him. 'Well, you should've told me, shouldn't you? Instead of sneaking about.'

He folded forward until his forehead was resting on the badly typed transcript. 'God forbid *I* get any of the bloody credit. . .'

'Don't moan, it's your own fault. Now where are we with Agnes Garfield?'

'And how come Ding-Dong's not suspended? I should be the one raiding the place, it was my—'

Something bounced off the back of Logan's head. He straightened up. Steel was scrunching another sheet of A4 into a ball.

She lobbed it at him. Missed. 'Focus: Agnes Garfield.'

473

'Got patrol cars trawling Mastrick. So far, no sign.'

'She's sodded off, that's why. The one chance we've had to grab her, and *you* let her go.'

'Don't start. Got enough of that from Napier. We didn't have any choice – it was too short notice to set anything up. If your bloody firearms team hadn't sodded off with the keys to the armoury—'

'Blah, blah, blah.' Steel took one last puff on her fake cigarette, then pulled it from her mouth and twisted the end till it clicked. 'When our delightful colleagues from Strathclyde do their review of this morning's fiasco, try and no' make it look like we can't pee in a bucket without someone getting stabbed, eh?'

'It wasn't my fault!'

She pushed away from the windowsill and ambled towards the door, hands in her pockets. 'Might be an idea to sod off out of it for a bit. Let the dust settle. Maybe . . . oh, I don't know . . . have a bash at catching Agnes Garfield for a change?'

Logan did her the honour of a full two-finger salute.

'So,' Logan leaned back against the cell wall, 'Professor Marks: how's it going?'

What was left of the psychologist's hair stuck out in random directions from the circumference of his big bald pate; his eyes two dark holes in a pale face; two fingers covered in brown scabs where he'd been picking at them. 'I. . . I got them to call you because . . . because I want to cooperate.'

A bit late for that, given Goulding had already done them a profile, but what the hell. 'Have you now?'

'They keep putting loud people in the cells next to mine. Swearing and singing and shouting. . .'

Logan checked his notebook. 'And look at that: they've

got you down for the last slot in the Sheriff Court schedule.' It took a bit of effort, but he managed not to smile. 'Anyone would think they were doing it on purpose.'

'I'm going to release all my files on Agnes Garfield. If you need me to interpret them, I can do that too. Just *please* get me out of here.'

Logan didn't even blink.

Marks scrubbed a hand across his eyes. 'Look, it's. . . I know you say Agnes killed her boyfriend, but it's simply not possible. She worships him, and I don't mean that in a sloppy romantic clichéd way, I mean she *actually* worships him. As if he was a god. She believes he'll make everything better, that he holds the keys to everything she wants and needs out of life.'

'Yeah, well – he's lying on his back, in the mortuary, with three hundred and sixty-five stab wounds all over his body. And then she garrotted him.'

'Agnes is *not* a killer.'

'Really?' Logan folded his arms. 'Because I saw her stab a friend of mine this morning, through the chest, with a movie prop. He's in intensive care. She nearly killed *him*.'

Marks's scabby hands trembled up to his temples. 'She's. . .' A deep breath. 'If she's not taking her medication, the psychotic episodes will get worse. It'll be a terrifying time for her, she'll be operating in a world populated with monsters and witches, good and evil. And she genuinely believes she's on the side of good. Everything she does will be because she thinks she's saving people. It's not her fault.'

'What did you talk about: when she called after she went missing?'

'She came in to see me a couple of times. She was . . . excited. Jubilant even. She was making a difference, doing the Kirk's work.'

'And you didn't tell anyone. You just let her parents worry.'

475

'I couldn't, she made me promise. I have to respect my patients' wishes.'

Weaselly little shite.

'Did she tell you she'd killed someone?'

'She didn't kill anyone. She couldn't. Not unless Anthony Chung told her to.'

Which would make his torture and death one of the most half-witted suicides on record. Goulding was right: Professor Marks was an idiot.

Logan pointed at the mattress. 'Wait here. I'll go have a word with the PCSO. Maybe we can get you out of here without being hauled up in front of the Sheriff.'

A huge smile broke across Marks's face, tears glittered in his eyes. 'Thank you.'

'But that means you have to come up with something that can help us catch her, *before* she hurts anyone else.'

A nod. 'Yes, yes, of course.'

Logan stepped outside and closed the cell door behind him.

The PCSO stood in the corridor, head down, tongue poking out the side of her mouth as she thumbed away at her mobile phone. 'Told you we'd break him.'

'Remind me never to piss you off. . .' A frown. The sound of voices filtered down from the floor above – where the female cells were. Then a cheer echoed through the breeze-block staircase. 'What's all the ruckus?'

'Didn't you hear? We've got ourselves a bona fide celebrity in: assault.'

'Not that dick from the radio again, is it? The one who was on that reality TV singing thing?'

'Nope, a genuine Hollywood starlet. Half the dayshift are up there like a pack of randy goats, volunteering to give her a strip-search.'

For God's sake. . . Logan pointed at Professor Marks's cell.

'Get him processed and out of here. We're dropping the charges.'

'Thanks to *my* evil genius.'

'Yes, thanks to your evil genius.' Logan stuck his notebook in his pocket. 'And if you're tweeting about us having someone famous banged up, you can stop right now. This is a police station, not the *News of the World*.'

Pink spread across the PCSO's cheeks. 'Wouldn't dream of it.'

Yeah, right.

Logan headed up the bare concrete stairs to the next floor, where all the noise was coming from.

The corridor was jammed with uniformed and plainclothes officers, all staring straight ahead at something hidden by the press of bodies. Another cheer.

Logan tapped the nearest PC on the shoulder.

Guthrie turned and grinned at him, a Babybel mini-cheese half unwrapped from its red wax coating in his hand. His pale eyebrows shot up above two watery red-rimmed eyes. 'Isn't this great?' He bit the tiny cheese in half.

'What are you all doing?'

Guthrie nodded towards the crowd, chewing with his mouth open. 'She's posing for photos. Of course, half these idiots haven't a clue, they just think she's the woman who got her kit off in *Three Dead Men*, but she's done some excellent indie films.'

'And she's posing for *photographs*?' Logan dragged in a deep breath. 'GET BACK TO WORK, YOU BUNCH OF MORONS! YOU'RE SUPPOSED TO BE POLICE OFFICERS!'

He pushed his way into the crowd. 'You heard me: get out of it!'

Moans. Pouting. Grimaces. 'Aw, but, Guv. . .'

'Back to work! Go on!'

Slowly they drifted away, slouching and scuffing their

477

feet, until the only ones left were Logan, a shuffling PCSO with a porn star moustache, and Morgan Mitchell.

Her bright-red hair shone in the overhead light, turquoise eyes surrounded in layers of dark makeup, a *CSI New Orleans* T-shirt and blue jeans, high-heeled boots. She smiled at him. 'Inspector Logan, hi. Did you come for a photo?'

Logan glowered at the PCSO. 'You better have a bloody good explanation for this, Andy.'

'It. . . I thought. . . It. . .' He cleared his throat, then looked at Morgan. 'Erm. . .?'

'It was *my* idea. Thought the troops could do with a bit of a lift. And I don't mind, you know, long as no one tries getting to second base.'

'Andy, if your prisoner's not in her cell in thirty seconds, a bollocking from Professional Standards is going to be the least of your worries.'

'Yes, Guv. Sorry, Guv.' He wiped his hands down the front of his white short-sleeved shirt, then took hold of Morgan's arm. 'If you don't mind, Miss. . .?'

She went in without a fuss, grinning back at Logan as the door clanged shut, hiding her from view.

Andy shuffled his feet. 'It wasn't really a big deal, I mean she's not getting preferential treatment or nothing like that, it was just a couple of pictures for—'

'Shut up. What's she in for?'

'Yes. . .' He scurried off to a shelf on the wall and came back with a clipboard and a whiteboard marker. Then printed the words 'MORGAN MITCHELL ~ ASSAULT' on the little A5-sized board beside the cell door. 'Look, it really wasn't—'

'I'm pretty sure you've got something important to be getting on with, Andy. So I'm going to count to three.'

'But—'

'One.'

'It really—'

'Two.'

'Erm. . .' Andy stuck the clipboard under his arm and hurried away, shoes squeaking on the concrete floor.

Logan closed his eyes and pinched the bridge of his nose. It was like working in a sodding primary school.

Then he slid back the hatch in the cell door.

Morgan stood in the middle of the small space, arms out, nostrils flaring, rocking gently from side to side as she did a slow-motion pirouette. When she was facing back towards the door again, she lowered her arms and smiled at him through the little hatch. 'I like a man who knows how to take charge.'

'You think this is funny?'

She flipped the scarlet curls back from her face. 'You wouldn't arrest me, so I had to improvise.'

'By assaulting someone.'

'Thought you would've loved getting me in a pair of handcuffs.' She bit her bottom lip. 'I can be *very* naughty.'

'And this film you're doing next, is it worth getting a criminal record for?'

She just smiled at him.

Perfect. Logan stared back. 'Let me guess: tomorrow, just as you're about to go up in front of the Sheriff, whoever it was you assaulted is going to miraculously drop the charges. No criminal record. No problems getting in and out of the country.'

'*Witchfire* is a really important stepping stone for my career. I turn in a great performance here and next time *I'm* the one playing the lead in the Hollywood blockbuster. I'll get to pick and choose my projects. I'll get to work with legends.'

'Not if I do you for wasting police time, you won't.'

'You know, when Nichole and I found out we were going to be in *Witchfire*, the pair of us arranged to stay with this coven in Wyoming. They've got a compound way up in the hills, where "The Man" can't get at them. And we learned what it's like to be a witch in real life.'

'Wasting police time is an *offence*.'

'Did you know voodoo dolls have got nothing to do with voodoo? They originated in Europe: "Hubble, bubble, toil and trouble."'

'Who did you bribe to say you assaulted them?'

'You see, that's what it takes to turn in a really great performance – you have to throw yourself into the character, not just turn up and drone out your lines like an amateur. You have to inhabit the part: live it. That's what makes the difference between—'

Logan slammed the hatch shut. Bad enough they had genuine criminals out there without the cells being full of nutjobs getting themselves arrested for the fun of it.

Her voice came through, muffled from the other side. 'So . . . you want to take a raincheck on those handcuffs?'

45

Logan stuck his feet up on his desk, a cup of tea in one hand, his paperback copy of *Witchfire* in the other, while the speakerphone rang and rang and rang.

'*You've reached Lorna Chalmers. I can't come to the phone right now, but you can leave a message after the beep.*'

'It's half three: where the bloody hell are you?' He leaned over and stabbed the red button, hanging up.

No joy from her mobile, and no joy from the number for the flat she was renting on Jasmine Terrace either.

He tried Rennie instead. 'You heard from Chalmers yet?'

Rennie's voice boomed out from the speakers. '*Course not. Why should her holiness have to come into work like the rest of us plebs? Probably hung-over, kneeling on some dirty old man's bathroom floor, with her knickers round her ankles, vomiting lobster-and-chips all over the porcelain.*'

'Yes, very funny. Tell me, *Detective Sergeant*, have you found your missing tramp yet?'

A pause. '*Actually . . . it's a bit complicated. I—*'

'Then you're in no position to be a smartarse, are you? Get on to Control – I want the nearest patrol car sent round

481

Chalmers's flat. Unless she's dying of flu, I want her in here right now.'

'Gah. . .' Logan pulled a face, then spat the cold tea back into the mug. He moved it across to the other side of the desk, where it would be out of reach for next time.

He scanned down the page, looking for where he'd left off. Mrs Shepherd was just about to pull out someone's fingernails. . .

A knock on the door and PC Sim stuck her head in. 'Guv? Alpha-One-Three's just been on the blower: no sign of DS Chalmers at her flat.'

He put the book down again. Stared out of the window for a bit.

Sim cleared her throat. 'Guv?'

Wasn't like someone like Chalmers to just fall off the map, was it? An ambitious career-obsessed go-getter like her? No: she was the brown-nosing and hard-work type. The type who wouldn't take a sick day if her leg fell off.

Not unless she'd done something really stupid. . .

'Guv, do you need me, or can I—'

'Get your coat. We're going round.'

The trees on Jasmine Terrace trembled in the wind, dusty dark-green leaves hissing against each other. Sim stood in a lonely blade of sunlight, one hand holding onto her black bowler as she stared up at Chalmers's flat.

The other side of the road was a long terrace of traditional granite buildings, but Chalmers's place was part of a slightly more modern block, set back from the cobbles behind a rectangle of parched grass. Three storeys with a flat roof and Dutch-barn-style upper floor. Four units, with six flats in each. Only a five-minute walk from FHQ.

Logan stuck his hands in his pockets. 'Anything?'

482

'Nope.' Sim tried the intercom again. Waited for a bit. Then stepped back to watch the top-floor flat. 'Maybe she's not in?'

Maybe. . .

Logan pressed the 'Services' button, holding it down until someone got fed up of the noise and buzzed them in.

It was nice inside. Clean. He followed Sim up to the top floor.

The door to flat number five had a sticky label underneath the doorbell: 'Lorna Chalmers'.

Sim thumbed it and a grating *drrrrrrrrrrrrrrring!* sounded on the other side of the door followed by a long high-pitched yowl. She hunkered down, levered the letterbox open, and peered inside. 'Mail on the doormat. . . Oh, hello, puss. Who's a pretty boy or girl then?'

The yowling got louder.

'Guv?'

Logan squatted down beside her, sniffing at the letterbox. Something floral and plasticky, a hint of pine that could've been disinfectant? At least it didn't smell as if anything – or anyone – was rotting away in there. 'Try the neighbours, see if anyone's got a key.'

As soon as Sim was off knocking on doors, Logan pulled out his phone and called Control. 'Does DS Chalmers own a car?'

'*Hud oan. . .*' The nasal Aberdonian accent faded away, replaced by the sound of a rattling keyboard. '*Aye: it's a Mini, you want the number plate?*'

Logan jotted it down in his notebook. 'I want a lookout request on her and her vehicle. And get me a GSM trace on her mobile.'

More keyboard noises. '*Fit's she done?*'

'Hopefully, nothing stupid. Now put me on to DS Rennie.'

'*He's no' in the office, but give us a mintie. . .*'

A bleep, a pause, another bleep, then Rennie was on the line. *'Hello? Guv?'*

'Did Chalmers say anything to you last night?'

A sigh. *'How come it's always "Chalmers, this", "Chalmers, that" with—'*

'Anything about where she was going? Any ideas she had about where Agnes Garfield was?'

'You really think she'd tell me? God forbid she'd have to share the glory. Tell you, she's—'

'Did she talk about the case at all?'

Sim bounded back up the stairs, holding a Yale key aloft like the Olympic torch. 'Old lady in flat three had one. Says she hasn't seen Chalmers since yesterday morning.'

'All she ever did was ask questions. All take, take, take, and no—'

Logan took the phone from his ear and slapped a hand over the mouthpiece. 'Open it.'

'But we don't have a warrant, and. . .' Sim scrunched up one side of her face. 'Ah, got you: yes, I think I *can* smell gas. Someone inside might be in difficulty!' She stuck the key in the lock, twisted, then stepped inside.

Back on the phone, Logan followed her. 'What did she ask about?'

'Usual. Kept going on about the Anthony Chung murder. Said we must've missed something. As if! Wouldn't stop nagging me till I gave her the interview transcripts from when we spoke to the house buyers.'

The ones Logan had just read.

'And it's not like there's anything in there – none of them knew Anthony Chung or Agnes Garfield, and they've all got alibis. Complete waste of time.'

Logan bent down and picked up the mail from the mat. Mostly fliers from charities, a leaflet from the local Tory candidate – nothing like blinkered optimism – what looked like a council-tax bill, and two copies of the *Aberdeen Examiner*. Yesterday's and today's. 'Maybe the estate agent's left someone off the list?'

'Nah, got the guy who works there to show me the files. Everyone who's seen that place was on there.' A sniff. *'You want me to do anything?'*

'Yes: find your missing tramp.' Logan hung up on him and slid the phone back in his pocket.

Sim appeared from the flat's kitchen, carrying a ginger tabby in her arms. Its stripy tail lashed back and forth as it glowered at him. 'Poor thing must've been starved.'

'Any sign of a disturbance?'

She shook her head. 'Wish my place was this tidy.' The cat wriggled, legs sticking out at random angles. She let it down and it charged away into another room. 'Plates washed in the kitchen, bed's made, all the magazines are lined up on the coffee table.'

Logan followed the cat through to a small double bedroom. It disappeared under the bed. Sim was right: everything was tidy and ordered. Which was quite an achievement, given that Chalmers had only transferred down from Northern Constabulary a couple of weeks ago. Any normal person would still be living out of boxes.

Sim picked up a book from the bedside cabinet – a hardback copy of *Witchfire* with a red tasselled bookmark about halfway through. She flipped it open. 'Signed and everything.' Then she put it down again. 'Tell you, I had nightmares for weeks after reading that bit in the tower block.' A shudder. 'Baby oil. . .'

'Something's wrong.'

'Apparently he based the three old witches on real people. Think they tried to sue Hunter for putting them in the book, but it all got settled out of court.'

Logan turned slowly on the spot. There was nothing here.

Chalmers had just headed off to work like any other day, and never come back. And the only thing she'd definitely done was ask about the people who'd been to see the home where Anthony Chung died. *God forbid she'd have to share the glory. . .*

Sim tucked her hands into the armholes on her stab-proof vest. 'So. . .?'

'Time to go see a man about a house.'

'I really don't understand how we can be of any more assistance.' Mr Willox fiddled with the buttons on his desk phone, shoogling them from side to side. His grey hair was piled up into a combination comb-over and quiff on top of his wide head, a dark-blue suit and a thick purple tie making him look as if he'd just fallen through a portal from the early eighties.

Logan tapped a finger on the glass desk, leaving a smudge. 'Agnes Garfield and Anthony Chung got the keys to that property from somewhere.'

'Do you have any idea how much it's going to cost to clean the kitchen in the Abernethy house? And even if they *can* get all the stains out, who's going to want to buy a house where someone was tortured to death in the kitchen? It's not like we can make a feature out of it.'

'And you're sure everyone who viewed the place was on the list?'

He waved a hand at the lever-arch file on the desk. 'You've seen the paperwork. That's everyone.'

'So who else had access to the keys?'

'Well, I did, obviously; Jennifer on reception; Jake Smith, my partner; our trainee, Duncan Cocker; and a couple of people we use for viewing rural properties when it's simply not convenient to send someone out from the office.'

Cocker. Cocker. . .

Logan pulled out his notebook and went flipping back

through the days until he got to Monday when they were interviewing Anthony Chung's friends. 'Duncan Cocker – young, bit vague, sounds as if he just wandered off the set of some awful American teenage rom-com?'

A sigh. 'At Willox and Smith we pride ourselves on quality and service. Duncan's. . . He still has a lot to learn.'

Damn right he did. 'I need to see him.'

'Well,' Willox thumbed through a big desk diary, 'he's down to show a couple round a detached cottage with two bedrooms, sun porch, and excellent potential as an equestrian property, in twenty minutes, but you can—'

'I don't think you're really getting the seriousness of this.'

'We do have a business to run, and—'

'Get him in here *now*.'

Willox puffed out his cheeks, ran a hand across his comb-over quiff. 'I. . .' Then he leaned forward and pressed one of the shoogled buttons on his desk phone. 'Jennifer, can you ask Mr Cocker to step into my office please?'

Duncan Cocker shifted in his seat, licked his lips. Pulled on a twitchy smile. 'Nah: honest, I got no idea, you know?'

Logan sat back in Mr Willox's executive office chair and steepled his fingertips, the top two just under the tip of his nose. Doing his best Superintendent Napier impression. Staring at Duncan Cocker in silence.

'So, you. . .' A shrug. 'It's all OK, right?'

More silence.

He started to rise out of his seat, so Logan gave PC Sim the nod and she loomed over him, both hands on his shoulders, pushing him back down. 'Don't think so.'

'But I told you, I don't know, it's just, like, one of them coincidences?'

Sim patted him on the cheek. 'Tell me, Mr Cocker, do we look thick?'

Pause. 'No?'

'So why do you think it's OK to lie to us?'

'But I'm *totally* not lying, and—'

'Mr Cocker, it's not polite to call someone thick, is it?'

'I didn't say anyone was thick, it's like a—'

'Some people might take a lot of offence at that.'

He stared at Logan, hands up at chest height, as if miming the 'Please, sir, can I have some more?' bit from *Oliver Twist*. 'I didn't tell anyone about me knowing Ton, 'cos I didn't want to lose my job, and it wasn't like I had anything to do with it, yeah?'

Logan smiled at him. 'You have no idea how much trouble you're in, do you?'

'But. . .' A breath. Then he looked at the floor. 'Ton would kill me.'

'He'd have to join the queue. You see, the people he's been stealing from aren't the let-bygones-be-bygones type. They're more claw-hammer-to-the-knees kind of guys. And as soon as they know you helped Anthony Chung rip them off. . .' Logan sooked a breath in through his bared teeth. 'Well, they're going to be *very* interested in paying you a visit.'

'But I never—'

'Do you like your kneecaps, Duncan?'

Silence.

He wriggled in his seat, until Sim pinned him down again.

'The Inspector asked you a question, Mr Cocker.'

'I've. . .' A cough. 'I kinda let Ton have the keys to a couple places we're selling with vacant possession. You know, ones that haven't shifted for over a year? He does a bit of business there.'

'Until he ended up staked out and tortured to death in the Abernethy house.'

Cocker squeezed his knees together. 'Nothing to do with

me, I totally swear, I mean *totally*. I gave Ton the keys, he gave me a shed-load of weed. That's it.' He licked his lips and looked up at PC Sim. 'Er. . . All for personal consumption, yeah? I wasn't selling it or *nothing*.'

Logan tossed his notepad onto the desk, then followed it with a biro. 'Addresses.'

He made a little whimpering noise.

Bit his lip.

Then picked up the pen and scribbled down half a dozen of them. 'You got to promise not to tell Mr Willox, yeah? I mean, you know, it's my job and he might . . . with the keys and everything?'

Logan pointed at the notebook. 'Sign it at the bottom. And date it.'

Cocker did. 'And it don't have to go any further, right? The other cop swore it'd be OK – you don't have to drag me into it. She *promised*.'

Logan took his notebook back. 'Other cop?'

'You know, yesterday? The woman with the curly hair and the boobs? She totally promised.'

He sat forward. '*When* yesterday?'

'Afternoon. . . About half three, maybe four? I gave her the addresses, and that was it.'

The leads she was chasing down. The ones she said were dead-ends when she came through to volunteer for soup-kitchen duty.

Cocker cleared his throat. 'So, I can go now, right? Got to show a couple round a house. . .'

46

'*A right sodding disaster.*' On the other end of the phone, Steel sounded as if she was chewing on a mouthful of wasps.

Logan leaned against the roof of his rusty Fiat, notebook open in front of him. 'You're the one gave the job to Ding-Dong.'

'*Two injured officers. Armed standoff. Hostages. Bloody press everywhere. . .*'

'What did I tell you?'

'*Hostages! How can he screw up raiding a wee cannabis farm? Now it's all Waco comes to Blackburn.*'

'Should've let me do it then, shouldn't you? Now pay attention – I need you to get armed response units round to six houses. Have you got a pen?'

'*Leith managed to raid* his *without anyone getting shot. . .*' She paused. '*This isn't more cannabis farms, is it? Because we got in enough trouble last time.*'

Good question. 'No idea. Anthony Chung got keys to a bunch of properties from a friend who works for an estate agent's. Most of them are out in the sticks. That's why we could never find out where he and Agnes were staying – they just moved from house to house.'

'*Six addresses? You want me to get six addresses raided? What part of "Shotgun Hostage Drama in Suburban Cul-de-sac" did you no' understand?*'

'And you better get the SEB to go over them too, see if we can find anything else linking Agnes Garfield to—'

'*Pin back your lugs: I – don't – have – the – men. Got a sodding crisis going on here. If it's no' life or death, it'll have to wait.*'

'They might have DS Chalmers.'

Silence.

'Hello? Can you hear—'

'*You better be joking, Laz.*'

'She got the list yesterday afternoon and didn't tell anyone. For all we know, Agnes has her staked out on someone's floor right now.'

A barrage of foul language erupted from the earpiece. Then more wasp-chewing. '*Fine, I'll magic firearms teams up out of nowhere. Get them going round the properties. You happy now?*'

Ecstatic.

He gave her the addresses, then she slammed the phone down on him. Like it was *his* fault Chalmers was a glory-hungry overachiever.

Sim appeared on the other side of the car, her Airwave handset blinking away on her shoulder. 'Guv? Got Control on the line. They say there's an NPR hit on Chalmers's Mini going north on the Inverurie road at half nine last night.'

'Do they have her going back again?'

'Hold on. . .' Sim clicked the button on her handset and repeated the question. Then shook her head. 'She might have taken one of the back roads?'

Chalmers would still have come down King Street, or West North Street, or the beach Esplanade to get home, and the Number Plate Recognition system would have picked her up. And, more importantly, she would've fed her cat.

'What about the GSM trace?'

Sim checked. 'They say her mobile's not switched on.'

Logan drummed his fingers on the car roof. Heading north on the Inverurie road. That meant they wanted addresses on the list to the north-west of the city. . . And only three fit the bill.

'Guv?'

'Get in.'

They'd just have to do without a firearms team.

The Fiat bumped and ground its way down a dirt track, lined on either side with barbed-wire fences and thick knots of brambles, the ridge of grass in the middle scraping along the bottom of the car every time Sim hit a pothole. And as the track was pretty much all pothole, Logan had to stick his finger in his other ear to hear Rennie at all.

'What?'

The radio wasn't helping: '—*siege enters its second hour, Grampian Police have cordoned off Fintray Road, and are asking Blackburn residents to remain indoors. We spoke to Mrs Gilmore, who lives next door. . .*'

Mrs Gilmore sounded as if she'd just French-kissed a set of bagpipes. '*Aye, and then there was this big bang and a policeman went flying over the hedge into our roses. It's—*'

Logan switched it off. 'I didn't hear a word of that.'

Rennie took a deep breath and came back twice as loud. '*I said, the house at Rickarton is clear. Steel's got the other four-man team on their way to the place outside Stonehaven. But it's rush hour, so—*'

'What about the other two houses?'

'*Sorry, Guv. We're going as fast as we can.*'

Sim tapped Logan on the shoulder as the car rolled through yet another outbreak of gravel-edged pits in the track. 'There it is.'

House number two on the north-west of Aberdeen list was an ancient-looking farmhouse set back from the road, partially screened by a patchy beech hedge, the front garden a thicket of weeds. The walls were leper grey, the gable end streaked with rust from a buckled TV antenna. One chimney was missing a chunk off the corner and the slate roof was speckled with yellow lichen. Narrow dark windows glowered out at the surrounding fields. Behind it, a massive steading conversion was all fresh pointing and neat double glazing.

A bright-green Willox and Smith 'FOR SALE' sign was driven into the jungle of dockens and brambles.

'Get your team over to the next house and let me know if there's any sign of Chalmers.' Logan hung up and put his phone away.

Sim parked the car at the overgrown entrance to a small gravel drive. 'No sign of a Mini.'

Well, they weren't going to just leave it outside, were they?

He climbed out of the Fiat. The weeds in the driveway were partially flattened, as if a vehicle *had* been left there. . . Or they'd used it to reverse and turn around on the appalling track.

Sim joined him, pulling on her bowler. 'What do you think?'

'Someone's been here.' He pointed. 'See the trampled path through the weeds to the front door?'

'Unless it was sheep?'

She unhooked the pepper-spray from her utility belt and handed it over. Then snapped out her extendable baton. 'You want the front or the back?'

Thistles and nettles bound together around the side of the property. All spiky and stingy. Logan fiddled with the pepper-spray. 'Think I'll . . . take the front.'

Sim sagged slightly. 'Poop.' Then she straightened up and

waded her way through the undergrowth, elbows up at shoulder height, keeping her hands out of the danger zone.

Grass and broken dandelions squeaked under his shoes as he picked his way to the front door, hauling on a pair of blue nitrile gloves.

A scrunching crash sounded from the other side of the house, followed by, 'Oh . . . pooping, bum-pooping poop!'

Logan peered in through the front window. The glass was thick with dirt, but there was enough light to see a mildew-speckled front room, the wallpaper peeling away in one corner and stained with damp. No furniture, just marks in the swirly seventies-style carpet where it used to be. The other front window was pretty much the same.

He tried the key in the lock. Opened the door. And stepped into a dank corridor that smelled like mouldy bread.

The house was in a much worse state than the first one they'd tried – a bungalow with a DIY jungle gym out the front. No wonder they'd had trouble selling it.

A staircase led almost straight up, ladder-style to a small landing, but down here there was a bathroom clarted in rust and mould, the two empty front rooms, and a tiny kitchen. Half the units were missing their doors, the other half had them hanging off. Big black stains spread across the ceiling.

Talk about a fixer-upper.

There was another crunch, then more ridiculous pseudo-swearing, and finally Sim's face appeared at the kitchen window, cheeks flushed, mouth set into a hard line, a strand of sticky willy clinging to the brim of her bowler like a length of furry string.

Logan hauled open the back door and let her in.

She was covered in bits of greenery, sticky geordies all up her trousers, bits of bracken, green stains on her knees and elbows, scarlet scratches on the back of her hands and one cheek. She scowled at him. 'Not one word.'

The corners of his mouth twitched, but he got it under control. 'I've done downstairs. No sign of anyone.'

Back to the front hall.

The stairs creaked as they climbed, the balustrade wobbling every time it was touched. There was no way Anthony Chung and Agnes Garfield would have holed up here. Not with so many other, cleaner, less . . . diseasy properties to choose from.

At the top of the stairs was a small landing with a row of knee-high cupboards built into the angle of the roof, just visible in the gloom of a filthy Velux window. Two doors led off into what had to be attic bedrooms.

Sim stopped on the top step. 'Can you smell something?'

Logan stood where he was, sniffing. Whatever it was, it was sweet: floral. Not heavy enough to be cloying, but completely out of place in a tiny house that was rotting away inside.

He put one gloved hand on the doorknob to the first bedroom, turned, and let it swing open. Inside, a single bed sat against the back wall, the plaster on the coombed ceilings disintegrating, showing the lathe beneath.

Door number two. . . The knob turned, but the door stuck. He pushed harder and a ripping noise – like two bits of Velcro being separated – came from around the door frame. Duct tape.

And then the smell fell out of the room on top of them, curdling its way into Logan's throat and lungs, filling his nose with the stench of spoiled meat. His throat constricted, stomach lurching. 'Oh *Jesus*. . .'

The room was every bit as tiny as the first, but instead of the single bed, there was a Ring Knot marked out on the floorboards in black wax. The body was male, its stomach and chest bloated with gas, naked skin peppered with green and orange mould – covered in tiny purple slits, all the hair shaved off. Just like Anthony Chung.

Blood made dark pools on the floorboards, disappearing through the cracks. . . That must be what made the dark stains on the kitchen ceiling downstairs.

Sim slapped a hand over her mouth and nose. 'Jeepers!'

Logan hauled the door closed again. Took his phone out with trembling fingers. And called it in.

47

Insch's dark baritone growled out of the phone. *'What* exactly *are you playing at?'*

Logan perched on the end of the garden wall, one hand shielding his eyes from the pale golden sun. 'I'm kind of in the middle of something, so. . .?'

The Manky Mystery Machine sat on the overgrown gravel drive, its back doors hanging open while white-suited SEB techs humped boxes into the house. A cordon of blue-and-white 'POLICE' tape snaked in the breeze. Two patrol cars blocked the rutted track up to the property, Logan's rusty old Fiat parked behind them in the gateway to a field of luminous-yellow oilseed rape.

'Do you have any idea how much money it costs to keep a production like this running? Because—'

'Want to cut to the chase?'

A pause. *'You arrested Morgan Mitchell.'*

Logan stared up at the slate-coloured clouds. Sighed. 'I did *not* arrest her. She assaulted someone.'

'Let her out.'

'She *assaulted* someone.'

'Logan, it. . .' He took a deep breath. *'What if I get the other party to drop the charges?'*

497

'Don't think your star will be too happy with that – she did it on purpose so she could spend a night in the cells. I believe the term you used was, "Method-acting nutjobs"?'

'I'm haemorrhaging money here, Logan. I can't afford to have one of my main actresses banged up in Craiginches for a month!'

PC Sim clambered over the barbed-wire fence just beyond the end of the beech hedge, waved at him, then picked her way past the parked patrol cars.

'Ms Mitchell's up in front of the Sheriff tomorrow. I'll see if I can get you an early morning slot.'

'I'm serious, this is—'

'It's the best I can do. She assaulted someone, she got arrested. I'm not bypassing the whole criminal justice system as a favour for you or anyone else.'

Silence.

Sim stopped right in front of him, then picked the little round lumps of stickie geordies from her trouser legs.

'I didn't mean you should break the law.'

'I've got to go.' Logan hung up and stuck the phone away. 'Well?'

Sim sighed. 'You should see their house, it's *huge*. Great big kitchen and a built-in machine for making coffee and everything. I had a latte.'

Logan pinched the bridge of his nose. 'Do we have to have "the talk"?'

'Husband's in London on business, but I spoke to the wife and the daughter. Didn't see anything, didn't hear anything. The steading faces away from the house, and I checked the views from all the windows – you could hold an orgy in the front garden here and no one would know. As long as you kept the noise down. . . Ah.'

Logan opened his eyes again. 'What?'

Sim pointed down the track, where a Porsche Cayenne,

a Mercedes, and a dented pool car lumped and bumped their way through the potholes. 'Cavalry's here.'

Isobel peeled back her white SOC suit's hood. Her fringe stuck to her shiny forehead, cheeks glowing bright pink as she snapped off her gloves and puffed out a long breath. 'I'd estimate two, three days at most. In this heat it's difficult to be sure, but trapped up there with the door and window taped shut. . .' She lowered herself onto the bonnet of the patrol car, rubbing at her pregnant bulge. 'Pfff. . . MO appears identical to the Anthony Chung case.'

DI Leith groaned. A beige plaster stretched across the bridge of his nose, the skin already starting to darken around his eyes where Ding-Dong thumped him one. 'Like I haven't got enough on my plate. . .' He dug his hands into his pockets. 'Well, as Acting DI McRae found the body, I think he should be the one—'

'Oh no you don't.' Logan glanced back over his shoulder, where the duty undertakers were carrying a stainless-steel coffin out through the front door. 'This is all yours.' He turned and started down the track. 'I've got a missing police officer to find.'

Sim scurried up behind him. 'What now?'

'Go home. Your shift finished two and a half hours ago.'

'Peter's taking the kids to see that new Disney film. They'll come back full of caffeine and sugar.' She smiled. 'I'd rather be hunting down a murderer than deal with that.'

Logan got to the Fiat, pulled out his phone, and called Rennie. 'Any news?'

'Found some loose cannabis in the place out by Rhynie, but other than that: nothing.'

All three houses north-west of Aberdeen and still no sign of Chalmers. And no sign of Agnes Garfield either. . . The weaselly little git at Willox and Smith lied to them. 'Get over to the estate agent's in Kintore, I want a list of everything they've got for sale north of the city.'

'*But they'll be closed and—*'

'I don't care if you've got to arrest Willox for having a stupid haircut, get me that bloody list.'

Rennie opened the passenger door and slid into the Fiat Punto. Then curled his top lip. 'What smells in here?'

Logan stared at him. 'Did you get the list or not?'

A grin. 'Piece of the proverbial.' He held up an A4-sized magazine, with a photo of Bennachie on it and the words 'WILLOX & SMITH ~ THE PROPER PROPERTY PEOPLE'.

Logan took it and flicked through the photocopied pages.

'They do one every two weeks. It's separated into areas, and I got Mr Comb-over to mark everything that's been on the market for more than six months.'

Which looked like most of them.

He passed the property magazine to Sim in the back. 'Everything north-east of the city.'

'Yes, Guv.'

Rennie shoogled in his seat. 'Can't we just, you know . . . beat it out of Duncan Cocker?'

'He's lawyered up. According to Biohazard, everything's "no comment" now.'

'Little sod.'

Sim leaned through from the back. 'What kind of price range am I looking for?'

'Doesn't matter. Just has to be something liveable in, that's off the beaten track, and been vacant for a while. Goulding says Agnes Garfield likes ruins, so it'll probably have steadings, or outbuildings, something like that.'

'Right, vague it is. . .' She sat back again.

What else would Agnes Garfield want? Land? Nice garden? Central heating and double glazing?

Logan frowned. 'Any churches for sale?'

'Churches, churches. . . There's one in Peterhead?'

Too far away. 'Anything else?'

'Erm. . .' The silence was broken only by the sound of flipping pages. 'How about this: "Arquarthy Croft, Kirkton of Rayne. Excellent opportunity to purchase a development or renovation project in the heart of the Grampian countryside, within easy commuting distance of Aberdeen. This three-bedroom traditional farmhouse with extensive outbuildings and three acres of land believed suitable for equestrian use. . ." They always say that, don't they?'

'You're *supposed* to be looking for churches.'

'Didn't let me finish. ". . .believed suitable for equestrian use. Includes a derelict chapel with outline planning permission to create a four-bedroom family home with double garage. Four hundred and sixty thousand."'

'Ouch.' Rennie puckered up. 'Soon as it says "outline planning permission" you know you're about to be screwed.'

Logan drummed his fingers on the steering wheel. 'Anything else?'

Sim shook her head. 'That's your lot.'

Did a derelict chapel still count as consecrated ground?

Worth a try.

Logan turned the key in the ignition.

'—with gunmen in a four-hour standoff. Sources close to the operation say the suspected cannabis farmers are demanding a helicopter to take them, and their hostage, to Aberdeen Airport—'

Rennie peered through the windscreen as the wipers squealed their way back and forth across the pitted glass. 'Still don't see why we couldn't take the pool car.'

'—flight to Thailand. We spoke to Chief Constable—'

'Stop moaning.' Logan pulled the car into a small lane that disappeared into a forest of identical pine trees, all laid out in a grid, and killed the engine.

Sim clambered around till she was kneeling on the back seat, looking out the rear window. 'That's *definitely* it this time.'

Sodding estate agents and their crappy directions.

Rennie checked his watch. 'Maybe we should call for armed backup?'

'It'll take them at least half an hour to get here. What if Chalmers is staked out in the kitchen being tortured right now?'

'Yeah, but. . .' A shrug. 'And it's raining.'

Logan climbed out into the drizzle. 'Fine. Stay here then.'

Sim clambered out after him.

Arquarthy Croft sat on a small hill in the middle distance, surrounded by billowing golden fields of rapeseed. The house itself was in a rectangular patch of weeds and rhododendron bushes, dotted with about a dozen elderly trees, their branches heavy and drooping. The place was in slightly better shape than the last one, but not by much: a dirty grey northeast farmhouse with gable ends and dormer windows in the sagging slate roof. Off to one side sat a long L-shaped steading. The chunk furthest away from the house was little more than a ruin, the roof caved in, beams showing like ribs on a rotting body.

Sim pointed. 'Must be the chapel.'

Three stone walls, one with an arched window in it, the rest a pile of rubble.

Logan turned his jacket collar up against the rain. 'Right, we keep to the tree-line. Sneak up on them from the back of the property.'

She nodded, then handed him the pepper-spray. 'Just in case.'

Logan stuck it in his pocket, then hurried across the road,

over a barbed-wire fence, and into a field of rapeseed bordered by gnarled beech and oak. The thigh-high crop rustled against his trouser legs, filling the air with the smell of honey as he squeezed down the narrow gap between it and the drystane dyke. Soft earth squelched and sucked at his shoes.

Halfway along he stopped and hid behind a wall.

Sim hunkered down beside him and peered between the trees. 'Don't see any movement.'

'Probably inside getting stoned.'

Assuming they were even there at all.

From here the tumbledown end of the steading was directly between them and the house. Blocking the view.

'You ready?'

Rennie puffed and panted along the edge of the field, running hunched over as if he was in an American war film. He slithered to a halt and ducked down. 'Phoned Control and told them we needed armed backup.'

Great. So now—

Logan's phone bellowed out Steel's sinister theme tune. Right on cue. He pulled it out.

'What the sodding arseholes of cock *are you playing at?'*

'It's a precaution, OK? Nothing more.' He skimmed through his phone's menu and stuck the ringer on to vibrate only.

'Don't you bloody "precaution" me. I'm no' having another armed sodding standoff!'

Logan climbed over the drystane dyke, sticking to the edge of the next field – more rapeseed – making for the steading. He dropped his voice to a whisper. 'What do you want me to do: sit on my backside waiting for you to turn up with the gun brigade? That'll make great headlines, won't it: "Police waste time while female officer is tortured to death."'

'This is no' a game, Laz – your nutjob's killed three people. I'm no'—'

'And Chalmers is *not* going to be number four.'

'For God's sake! You're no' sodding Rambo, you can't just—'

'So stop wasting time shouting at me and get your firearms team organized.' He hung up on her and stuck the phone in his pocket. Managed a whole three steps before the thing started vibrating. Tough, she could leave a message. 'Everyone: phones on silent. Airwaves too.'

The barbed-wire fence at the end of the field was rusted and baggy, easy enough to climb over. On the other side a thicket of weeds and grass stretched away to the crumbled end of the steading. It grabbed at Logan's legs as he waded through to the building.

Sim picked her way through the fallen masonry and down the side, where the undergrowth gave way to a gravel yard, enclosed by the L-shaped steading on one side and a sea of nettles on the other. She stopped at a window and peered inside, keeping her voice down. 'Guv?'

He joined her at the window. A red-white-and-blue Mini sat on its own in a disused cattle court. Its driver's side wing was crumpled in, the windscreen a spider's web of cracked glass. The number plate matched: it was Chalmers's. 'Damn. . .'

At least now they knew they had the right place.

Rennie reached for the handle on the sliding wooden door.

Sim's eyes bugged, then she shoved him out of the way, sending him tumbling onto the gravel. 'Don't!'

'Ow!' He stared up at her, holding on to the elbow of his left arm. 'What the hell was *that* for?'

'Have you never raided a cannabis farm before?' She held out a hand and helped him up. 'Sometimes they wire door handles and window latches to the mains – booby-trap the place against rival gangs and the police. First place we did, DI McPherson ended up flat on his back all the way down the bottom of the drive. Hair sticking out in all directions, smoke coming out the lace-holes of his shoes. Had black fingernails for months after that.'

Rennie rubbed at his elbow. 'Jacket's got a hole in it now and everything.'

'Least you're not dead.' She glanced around the gravelled yard, then marched over to the nettles and picked up a length of blue plastic pipe – the kind they used to run water under the ground. She shoved it through the handle and hauled on the ends. The door creaked and groaned as she pulled it open.

Sim poked her head in through the gap, then out again. 'You're welcome.'

Logan stepped inside. A thick grey cable led from the inside of the handle to a plug set at chest-height on the wall. He snapped on a pair of nitrile gloves and flicked the switch off.

The Mini's airbags were flaccid droops of white, the steering wheel cover missing. Dark-red spots stood out on the plastic dashboard, like tiny jewels.

'Guv?' Rennie waved at them from the back of the cattle court.

A Ring Knot was painted across the dirt floor in black wax, a metal stake driven into the ground at each point of the pentagram. Dark stains littered the centre of the circle. No sign of the body.

Don't let it be Chalmers. Not after all this.

A sliding door in the side of the cattle court led deeper into the building. Sim did the same trick with the blue plastic pipe. 'Jeepers. . .'

Logan joined her. It was a long room, about the width of

505

a garage, with what had to be thousands of cannabis plants hanging upside-down from plastic washing line strung between the rafters. They'd discarded the bottom two-thirds of each plant – the leaves and the roots – leaving huge swollen buds clustered around a central stem, covered in frothy strands and speckled with purple. Why nick the whole thing when you could just grab the bit worth all the money?

Rennie reached out and rubbed one between his fingers. 'This lot must be worth a *fortune.*'

A row of oscillating fans kept the air moving, filling it with the sweet sweaty smell of marijuana.

The next room was full of the stuff too. No wonder the McLeod brothers wanted to cripple whoever was in charge: they'd stolen a hell of a lot of cannabis.

Sim flicked the switch on another plug wired to a door handle, then pulled it open, revealing grass and swollen rhododendrons, old trees and the side of the farmhouse. They'd run out of steading.

Logan gave the signal and they split up – Rennie and Sim going one way, while he went the other, keeping low and close to the farmhouse wall. The downstairs windows at the front and side of the house were blacked out – the other side of the glass streaked with paint.

So no one could see them sneaking about.

They met up at the back door. 'Suggestions?'

Rennie pointed at the low drystane dyke behind the house. 'We chuck one of those through the windows and dive in, Sweeney-style?'

Idiot.

Sim rolled her eyes. 'Batter the door in. It's a classic for a reason.'

'Or we could go for something less dramatic and just ring the bell.'

She wobbled the plastic pipe at him. 'Or maybe we try

the handle first?' It took a couple of goes, but eventually she got one end wedged over the doorknob then twisted.

Click, and the door swung open an inch.

Sim smiled. 'See, boys, that's the way the *professionals* do it.' She pushed on the pipe. 'Never send a man to do a—'

A loud boom tore through the wooden door, splinters ripping through the air like shrapnel. Sim flew backwards, arms and legs out in front of her, then slammed into the weed-flecked grass of the back garden and lay there, twitching.

48

A ball of smoke coiled up into the drizzle as Logan and Rennie dived to the ground. Then a moment of silence, broken only by Sim groaning.

The door lay half-open. A shotgun was fixed to the back, mounted in a makeshift metal frame, both barrels sawn off down to the wooden grip. Barking exploded from somewhere down the gloomy corridor. Then the scrabble of claws on tile and a gigantic Alsatian burst into view, going so fast it skidded into the wood cladding on its way around the corner. Big red mouth snapping around a million glittering teeth as it charged down the hallway at them.

'Gah!' Rennie lunged forward, grabbed the end of the blue pipe and hauled the door closed again.

THUD – the Alsatian slammed into the back of the door, barking and growling.

Logan scurried over to Sim, through the wet grass.

She lay on her back, both arms curled up and in, clawed hands covering her face.

He pulled them apart. . . Blood trickled down her left cheek, more from her forehead. Little slivers of wood stuck out of her skin like quills.

'Are you OK?'

'Oh . . . *poop!*'

Logan helped her to sit up while the dog hurled itself against the door.

So much for the element of surprise.

The front of her stab-proof vest was a mess – the Kevlar torn and peppered with splinters. Logan undid the straps and hauled it off her.

The black T-shirt underneath was soaked with sweat, but other than that, she was fine. He sat back on his heels. 'You lucky sod.'

'Ow. . .' She stuck a hand in the middle of her chest and pushed. 'Like being kicked by a cow. . .'

'Door must've taken most of the blast.'

'Jeepers. . .'

Rennie peered in through the hole in the door, then ducked back as the dog lunged, teeth snapping, at the gap. 'Aaagh! Good doggy, nice doggy.'

'Can you stand?' Logan pulled her to her feet.

'Ow. . .'

The whole bloody thing was a disaster.

'Will you shut that dog up?'

Rennie flattened himself along the side of the door. 'If you've got any good ideas. . .'

Sim grimaced, levering herself upright. Then stuck out her hand. 'Pepper-spray.'

Logan dug it out of his pocket and handed it over.

She lurched towards the door, snapping the cap off. 'Right, you hairy little poop.' The flat of her palm smacked into the wooden surface a couple of times and the dog went berserk, snapping at the opening. She gave it a faceful of spray.

Barking. Slavering. Barking. Silence. A high-pitched yelp burst out from the other side of the door. Then whining and yowling.

Sim shouldered the door open. No bang this time.

Inside, the place stank of wet dog, pepper, bleach, and something meaty: like oxtail soup.

The Alsatian was tearing around in a tight circle, back hunched, tail between its legs. Sim marched into the gloomy corridor, grabbed it by the scruff of the neck, and hauled open the nearest door. It was a filthy galley kitchen with yellow linoleum, a cracked sink, and a prehistoric electric cooker – a huge pot bubbling away on the stove. Sim hurled the dog inside and slammed the door on it.

'*Never* send a man to do a woman's job.'

Logan's shoes clacked on the chipped floor tiles. By the front door a flight of stairs led up to a small landing, doglegging around to the left. A white glow seeped out from beneath the other doors lining the corridor, making it look as if the place had been fitted with trendy mood lighting. He tried a handle, and it swung open on the surface of the sun. . .

Harsh light jabbed into his corneas, followed by a wash of heat that tried to squeeze the air from his lungs.

He stuck one hand up, shielding his eyes, and the room slowly faded into view. Two rows of lights hung from the ceiling, blazing down on a sea of chest-high cannabis plants, their dark-green five-fingered leaves gleaming. A walkway snaked between the aisles of growbags, lengths of black plastic tube looping from plant to plant. The walls were papered with tinfoil, bouncing the glaring light around the muggy room.

The other two downstairs rooms were the same, the only difference being the colour of the light bulbs.

Whoever it was, they'd gone from stealing the McLeods' to growing their own.

Back to the hallway.

'OK,' Logan pointed over his head, 'on three, we—'

A loud bang and chunks of plaster exploded out from the wall by his head.

510

Back into the nearest cannabis hothouse. Rennie went crashing through a stand of plants, Sim slithered to a halt on the other side of the door.

Slivers of tile erupted from the floor, then twice more as bullets turned them into shrapnel.

Logan dropped to his hands and knees and peered around the doorframe.

A man in boxer shorts and a long black bathrobe stood at the top of the stairs at the end of the corridor, a bottle of Jack Daniel's in one hand, a semi-automatic pistol in the other. White socks on his feet. A thick joint stuck out between his bared teeth, smoke curling through his patchy beard and long black hair. Eyes narrow and bloodshot. He wobbled from side to side, then raised the gun and squinted one eye shut.

It wasn't, was it? It *couldn't* be.

BOOM – the noise reverberated back and forth from the walls as another chunk of plaster erupted into dust. Nowhere near where they were hiding. Too drunk and stoned to hit the side of a bus.

Could it?

Logan had to shout over the ringing in his ears. 'Anthony? Anthony Chung?'

The gun wobbled around again, barked twice, tearing twin holes in the door opposite.

Rennie scrambled back through the cannabis plants, five-fingered leaves sticking in his hair. 'But Anthony Chung's dead!'

BOOM – another floor tile exploded.

'Yeah, well, as ghosts go, he's not taking it lying down, is he?'

'You said his dad ID'd the body!'

BOOM, BOOM – one in the doorframe, one in the wall.

His dad was obviously a lying bastard. Not only was

511

Anthony Chung very much alive, there wasn't a tribal tattoo on the left side of his neck.

Sim wiped a dribble of blood from her eyes. 'We can't just sit here like a bunch of lemons.'

BOOM – the ceiling got that one, dust drifting down and shining in the light from the open growing-room door.

Rennie licked his lips. 'We rush him. His aim's crap, right? We all run at him at the same time and. . .' He stared at Logan. 'What?'

'You're an idiot. We are *not* charging a man with a loaded—'

BOOM – another floor tile.

Click.

Logan stuck his head around the door again. Anthony Chung had one eye squeezed shut, holding the gun up in front of his face – moving it backwards and forward as if that would help get it in focus. The slide was racked all the way back, the round barrel protruding a good three inches, smoke curling from the hole.

He staggered back a step, then his eyebrows shot up and he dropped the Jack Daniels bottle. Reached for his dressing-gown pocket.

Logan charged, the shattered tiles gritty beneath his feet.

The bottle of bourbon hit the stair carpet and bounced, amber liquid spraying from the open neck.

Anthony Chung's hand disappeared into his pocket.

The bottom step creaked as Logan launched himself up the stairs, taking them two at a time, arms and legs pumping.

The hand reappeared with a huge chrome-plated semi-automatic.

Three more steps.

The gun came up, pointing right between Logan's eyes.

Too slow. . .

Anthony Chung grinned. 'Bye, bye.' And pulled the trigger.

49

Logan blinked. Stood there in silence. Then let out a huge breath, blood hammering in his ears. Oh thank *God*. 'Safety catch, you pillock.'

'No, is. . .' Anthony stared at the gun in his hand.

Then Logan slammed an elbow into his face, lifting him off his feet, sending him thumping back into the wall, arms out. The pistol clattered onto the tiles below.

In the interests of Health and Safety, Logan gave him a swift boot in the testicles as well. Anthony Chung curled up like a foetus, one hand clasped over his broken bloody nose the other wrapped around his battered bollocks.

Then Logan bent over and clutched his own knees, holding on while the room swirled around his head.

'Guv?' Sim patted him on the back. 'You OK?'

'Cuff him. Please.'

'Right, you little sod: Anthony Chung, I'm arresting you for the attempted murder of three police officers, possession of illegal firearms, and a horrible dog.' She dragged his hands behind his back and slapped the handcuffs on. 'And I am *seriously* hacked off about the shotgun behind the door too!'

Come on: still hadn't found Chalmers. Arse in gear.

Logan took another deep breath and straightened up. Then clambered up the stairs with Rennie panting along behind him.

The landing at the top was covered in red-and-brown swirly carpet, coming away from the edges. One door hung open on a bedroom with black sheets and a Ring Knot painted on the ceiling. Piles of clothes heaped up on the floor. A couple of open pizza boxes with grease stains on the cardboard marking out their ghosts.

Two more doors.

Rennie pointed at himself, then the one on the left.

Logan nodded and took the other, wrenched it open and froze on the threshold.

It was a bathroom, built in what looked like an extension, the ceiling covered in blooms of damp and mould. Yellowing tiles with dirty grey grout. A roll-top bath streaked with rust and full of water. And Agnes Garfield.

She was kneeling by the bath, holding something under the surface. Something face down that struggled and wriggled, two bare feet sticking out, ankles tied to the taps.

Chalmers.

'Let her go!'

Agnes looked up at him. Freckles stood out like bloodstains on her porcelain skin, her bright-red hair tied back in a ponytail, so much black makeup around her eyes that she looked like a corpse. She bared her teeth. 'I'm saving her soul.'

'Let – her – go!'

A shrug. 'As you wish. . .' Agnes stood, her hands out, palms up.

Chalmers' naked back rose to the surface, wrists bound behind her. The struggling got worse.

Sodding hell – with her ankles tied to the taps, and hands behind her back, there was no way she could get her nose or mouth above the waterline.

514

Logan lunged forward, elbowed Agnes out of the way and hauled Chalmers to the surface.

She coughed and spluttered, water streaming from her nose and swollen lips, eyes bloodshot and wide. 'Aaaaaaaaaagh!' Purple bruises covered one side of her face, tiny cuts on her shoulders and chest leaking scarlet trails into the dirty bath. Her head was completely shaved, covered in nicks and cuts and swollen scabs.

Something made a grating noise in the bathroom, behind him as Chalmers retched.

'You're OK! I've got you.'

And then Agnes's breath was warm on his cheek, her lips brushing his ear, voice little more than a whisper. 'What I do in its service lights a fire in God's name.'

Pain exploded across Logan's back, and he went lurching forward on top of Chalmers, sending her down beneath the surface again. Gurgling and twitching.

He rolled off and thumped to the floor.

Agnes stood over him, the lid from the cistern held in her hands like Moses with his tablet. She raised it above her head, clipping the bare light bulb and setting it swinging.

Then Rennie crashed into her, shoving her back into the cracked toilet. The cistern lid shattered on the edge of the cast-iron bath. 'Get off me!'

'Guv? You OK? Ow!'

'GET OFF ME!'

Logan scrambled to his knees and grabbed Chalmers by the shoulders. Hauled her back into the air as water slopped all over the floor and the light swung wildly from one side to the other, swirling the shadows around them like smoke.

Chalmers opened her bloodied mouth and screamed.

Gold and copper streaked the fields of rapeseed to either side of the farmhouse as the sun glowered through the thin gap between the heavy grey clouds and the horizon. Two ambulances and a handful of patrol cars blocked the road, their blue-and-whites strobing the lengthening shadows. Four members of the firearms team – too late to do any bloody good – sat on a wall in the sunshine, smoking cigarettes and laughing.

In the middle distance, a grubby once-white Transit van bounced and rolled its way up the track. The SEB, come to confiscate the cannabis.

Logan shifted his grip on the mobile. 'I'm kind of in the middle of something, Dave, so. . .?'

On the other end of the phone, Goulding sniffed. '*And I'm meant to be watching a production of* Kiss Me Kate, *but instead I'm stuck in the office going through the three hundred and sixty-two emails* you *dumped on me.*'

The fan mail. 'Ah. . .'

'*And as it's. . .*' A pause. '*Oh, for goodness' sake: it's gone half nine!*'

'Dave, it—'

'*I've been through about half of them, and allowing for the appalling spelling and grammar I've got twenty possible matches for whoever's torturing your victims and three potential necklacers. I'll get to the others tomorrow, but I've asked the computer science department to get hold of the server logs and—*'

'Actually . . . Dave . . . I was meaning to call you. We've just arrested Anthony Chung and Agnes Garfield.'

Silence.

'Dave?'

'*You told me Anthony Chung was dead!*'

'Yes, well . . . he got better. And she's definitely our killer, so you can ditch the rest of the emails.'

'*Do you have* any *idea how many hours I wasted on that profile, trying to get everything to fit because you told me—*'

'You were right about the trial by water. She was trying to drown DS Chalmers when we found her.'

'*I told* you *she'd never kill him.*'

'It's not my fault: Anthony Chung's father ID'd the body, I just. . . Hold on a minute.' Logan stuck his hand over the mouthpiece as a short paramedic stomped to a halt in front of him. Her hair was swept up in a droopy ponytail, jowls wobbling around a soured mouth. Like someone's disappointed mum.

She jabbed a finger towards the ambulance. 'If she doesn't start cooperating, I'm going to sedate her.'

Back to the phone. 'Dave, I've got to go.' He hung up, and followed the paramedic's big wobbly bum to the ambulance, then around the side to the open doors.

Chalmers was sitting on the tailgate, coughing, each breath rattling as if something was loose inside her chest. 'I don't want to go to hospital. . .' The silver blanket crinkled as she drew it tighter around her bare shoulders, reflecting back the swirling blue-and-white lights. Grey and purple bruises seeping out into the skin of her shaved head.

The paramedic let out a long sigh. Then rolled her eyes at Logan. 'Tell her.'

'You need stitches and antibiotics. You're going to hospital.'

Chalmers took another hit on the oxygen mask. Did some more coughing.

Logan patted the paramedic on the shoulder. 'Give us a minute.'

'I mean it: I'll sedate her if I have to!' Then turned and stomped off towards the firearms team.

'You're lucky you're still alive.'

Chalmers nodded. 'She was at the soup kitchen. Agnes. . . Right there, lurking in the shadows, watching everyone. Followed her. . .' More coughing. 'Lost her round the back of the Bon Accord Centre.'

'Why the hell didn't you call it in?'

'So I went round the addresses again: all the ones I got

517

from Duncan Cocker. There was no one there in the afternoon, but I thought. . .' A shrug, making the blanket crackle.

'You thought you'd catch her yourself and take all the glory. Well, that worked out well, didn't it?'

Growling and scrabbling came from the front door as a pair of dog handlers hauled the Alsatian outside on the end of a long pole, both of them struggling to keep the noose tight around its neck.

Chalmers wouldn't look him in the eye. 'Bumped into Agnes at a house near Fyvie. Literally.' Chalmers fiddled with the oxygen mask, twisting the soft plastic back and forth. 'And when I woke up, I was tied up in a grubby little kitchen. . .' She wiped a hand across her eyes. 'I didn't tell her anything. . .'

'You wouldn't have been in that situation if you'd called for backup.' Logan took a step back, pulse thumping in his neck, heat spreading behind his temples. 'Because of you, PC Sim nearly died. Rennie nearly got electrocuted. And I was *this* close,' he held up his hand, thumb and forefinger almost touching, voice getting louder with every word, 'to being shot in the face!'

'I just wanted. . . It wasn't meant to work out like this.'

'Really? Well *that's* OK then, isn't it? Everything's forgiven!' He poked her in the shoulder and the space blanket crackled. 'You listen up and you listen good: I'm the one who'd have to tell Sim's husband and kids she died because you couldn't face sharing the bloody credit!'

Tears spilled down Chalmers's cheeks. 'It wasn't my fault. . .'

'Hope you're proud of yourself.' He turned his back and walked away.

Thursday

50

The wub-wub-wub of a floor polisher dragged Logan back above the cold green waves and thumped him down in the visitor's chair in Samantha's room.

'Gagh. . .' Someone had sneaked in at some point during the night and replaced his spine with sharp rocks and broken glass. He creaked himself upright. Yawned. Stretched. Slumped. Then shuffled through to the bathroom, rubbing the grit out of his eyes.

The face in the mirror peered back at him with two beautiful black eyes.

Then frowned: there was something he was meant to do. . .?

Nope, no idea.

Time for a pee and a wash.

Samantha didn't move as he pulled his shoes back on, just lay there like a corpse, all wires and tubes and lank brown hair.

He cleared his throat. Forced a smile. 'Probably going to be a long day today. Do you fancy pizza or something for. . .'

What was the point?

Something heavy settled on his shoulders, trying to crush him down into the grey terrazzo floor.

And then his phone went – 'If I Only Had a Brain'.

Logan hauled it out. 'Do you have any idea what time it is?'

'Nearly half seven, Guv.'

It was? He checked his watch. Sodding hell. 'Why didn't anyone say?'

'They've turned up another body at the farm. Looks like the poor sod was stabbed all over, throttled, then buried in the ruined chapel. Dr Graham says the bones in that cook pot in the kitchen are definitely human too: scapula, skull, five ribs, and an ulna. Apparently they're a bit on the ancient side. PM's at ten if you fancy it?'

So Agnes Garfield was planting corpses in her very own garden of bones.

'Not really.' He hauled his tie back with one hand and tightened it. 'But I think I know who your bones in the pot belong to: one Nicholas Alexander Balfour.'

'Ah, right: the spiritualist bloke from the graveyard. Cool. Wondered where he'd got to. Anyway, I spoke to Guthrie – he's heard back from SOCA's American Justice Department goons. Anthony Chung's got form for dealing and a couple of DUIs, but you want to know what's really *interesting?'*

Logan held the phone against his chest, then leaned over and kissed Samantha on the forehead. Her skin was cool and clammy against his lips. 'Got to go. I'll see you later, OK?'

Back to the phone.

'Guv? You there?'

'Go on then: what's really interesting?'

'Turns out his dad's linked to about two dozen hydroponic cannabis farms in San Francisco. They couldn't prove anything, but everyone knew it was him.'

Like father, like son. 'Thanks. Tell Steel I'll be there in twenty.'

Rain pattered against the window of Steel's office, making shining ribbons that glittered their way down the glass. She sat back with her feet up on her desk, fake cigarette dangling out the side of her mouth. 'So she's a nutbag then?'

Dr Goulding shrugged, then crossed his legs the other way. 'Let's just say she's a deeply disturbed young woman.'

Steel looked up at Logan. 'That's Liverpudlian for "nutbag".'

'She's as much a victim of Anthony Chung's drug baron fantasy as anyone she hurt for him. He cast himself in the role of Moderator, the man in charge of the Fingermen in *Witchfire*. Kept her off her medication and on high-concentration THC cannabis. She believed everything he told her.' Goulding held his hands out – *nothing up my sleeves*. 'I've started her on Risperidone, so we should see an improvement in her mental state before too long. In the meantime, I've arranged for a Mental Health Officer to see her later this morning. Agnes needs to be transferred to a secure psychiatric facility where she can be taken care of, *not* locked in a prison cell.'

Steel puffed on her fake cigarette. 'Tell that to the four poor sods she tortured to death.'

'Yes, well. . .'

She hauled open a bottom drawer, and pulled out a box the size of a thermos flask. 'Laz: you caught her, and Anthony Chung; rescued Chalmers; and didn't get anyone killed. Here.' She chucked it to him. 'You can have your present after all.'

Logan caught the box. Whatever it was, it was wrapped in brown paper. 'Do I want to know?'

Steel grinned at him. 'Open it.'

OK. . .

He peeled back the paper, exposing a plain cardboard box. Lifted the lid and stared. It looked like a plastic vagina, stuck on top of a thermal travel mug. 'What the sodding hell is *this*?'

'It's a Fleshlight: you stick your Wee Willie Winkie in it and jiggle it about. You've been a right miserable tosser since your girlfriend ended up in the hospital, do you good to relieve a bit of tension now and then.'

Oh dear God.

'For the tape, I'm showing Mr Chung exhibit six, a semi-automatic handgun of Eastern European origin.' Logan held up the ugly black weapon in its clear plastic evidence pouch. 'Mr Chung, would you like to tell us where you got this?'

Anthony Chung grinned. 'Dude, it's—'

His lawyer put a hand on his arm. 'My client has no comment to make.'

Again.

'Mr Blake, your client's prints are all over it, and we have three police officers as witnesses, do you really think a jury will—'

'My *client* has no comment to make.'

A knock on the door, then PC Guthrie stuck his head into the room. 'Guv?'

Logan sat back in his seat, closed his eyes. Gritted his teeth. 'Interview suspended at . . . nine forty AM. DI McRae leaving the room.'

Outside, Guthrie shifted from foot to foot, glancing up and down the corridor as Logan closed the interview-room door.

'This better be important.'

Guthrie dropped his voice to a whisper. 'It's Insch. He's downstairs going ballistic. Something about an early court date for his Hollywood starlet? Says he's been calling you all morning.'

Oh. . . crap. Logan sagged against the wall. He was supposed to get Morgan Mitchell up in front of the Sheriff first thing. Knew he'd forgotten something. 'OK, OK, I'll sort it.' He pointed back, over his shoulder at the interview-room. 'Go tell them we're taking a fifteen-minute break. Give them a bit more time to work on their lies.'

The cell block was a lot quieter than yesterday. Today the only sound came from the PCSO office radio, oozing out hits of the nineties. Which probably counted as cruel and unusual punishment under the European Convention on Human Rights, but what the hell.

No sign of Kathy in the lower cell block, so he tried the one upstairs instead.

She was bootfaced, dragging a mop back and forth across the concrete floor. A bucket of dirty water sat beside an open cell, filling the air with the pine-fresh stench of disinfectant. '. . .but no, it's *Muggins* here who has to clean it up. . .'

Logan stayed well out of mop-range. 'Having fun?'

She glowered at him. 'Why is it that as soon as anyone pukes their guts all over the place, everyone disappears?'

Maybe not then. 'I need to get Morgan Mitchell bumped up the court schedule.'

'What am I, their mother? Lazy bunch of—'

'Kathy: court schedule.'

She jabbed the mop into the grey water, sending a little wave slopping out and onto the concrete. 'I'm *busy*.'

'OK. . .' He put his hands up. 'I'll wait.'

He backed off a couple of paces, stuck his hands in his pockets, rocked on his heels. Then pulled out his phone and switched it back on. There was a pause then it bleeped at him: eight new voicemails and a dozen text messages. All from Insch. He deleted the lot.

Kathy scrubbed the mop across a stubborn spot. 'Not even my sodding job!'

It looked as if most of the cells in the women's section were empty. According to the boards by the doors, only three still had their occupants: an Amy Brooke – shoplifting; Morgan Mitchell – assault; and Agnes Garfield – four counts murder.

Logan slid the hatch back.

Agnes was sitting on the edge of the blue plastic mattress, her knees together, feet together, arms at her sides, hands folded in her lap. Still as a stone. Then she turned her head to face him. The heavy black eye makeup made streaks down her cheeks, like ravens' wings.

A blink. Then she opened her mouth. Closed it. Swallowed. Then tried again. 'I'm . . . sorry.'

Bit late for that. 'It's not your fault. You're ill.'

'I never touched your girlfriend, I just. . . She's very pretty, lying there, all peaceful. . .' A little smile. 'I was so jealous. Sleeping for years and years, waiting for her prince to kiss her and wake her up.'

'That why you hung bones beneath her bed, so she wouldn't wake up?'

Agnes frowned at him, as if he'd just said something incredibly stupid. 'Why would I do that? The bones were meant to protect me from you. Tenet Nine: "The Lord helps those that help themselves."' She licked her lips. 'But they weren't working. I tried everything I could think of, but you kept looking for me, so. . . I'm sorry I cut your brakes.'

'That was *you*? I could've died!'

Agnes nodded. 'I've been . . . *confused*.' She looked down at her fingers, twisted them into a knot. 'Is your police officer friend all right?'

'You shaved her head, stabbed her, and tried to drown her. What do you think?'

A pause. 'Are you going to kill me?'

What? 'No, I'm. . . Why would we kill you?'

'I hurt so many people. I thought they were witches. We. . .' Her red hair fell forward, covering her eyes. 'I thought I was doing the Lord's work. Purifying them with the trial by blood. Making them confess. Saving their souls. . .'

So Reuben was right: *Word is, the new kids on the block have an enforcer who's a card-carrying psycho. Gets off on maximum pain.*

'It was you, wasn't it? The enforcer.'

The words came out as a low murmur. 'The Kirk is my mother and father. It is my rod and my staff. My shield and my sword. What I do in its service lights a fire in God's name.'

'The witches worked for a rival drug gang, I get that, but what did Roy Forman do? Did he see something he shouldn't? Was Anthony dealing at the soup kitchen and he found out? Is that why you burned him?'

Agnes peered up at Logan from behind her curtain of hair. 'Burned?'

'Necklaced. Staked to the ground with a tyre wedged over—'

'No!' She shook her head. 'The trial by fire is *barbaric*. A stain on the Kirk.'

'But he was—'

'Rowan would never do that.' She shuddered. 'Not ever.'

Logan stared at her. 'You didn't burn Roy Forman?'

Sodding hell.

Steel scowled at him, mouth pulled down, making the wrinkles stand out. 'Well, of course she'd say that, wouldn't she?'

'Why? She's got nothing to gain – she's already admitted to torturing three people to death, robbing graves, and trying to drown Chalmers. She knows she's going to spend the

527

next twenty to thirty years in a secure psychiatric ward. What's one more death?'

'Arrrgh. . .' Steel slapped both hands over her face then folded over until her head rested on her desk. The words came out all muffled. 'You're no' *seriously* suggesting we've still got some mentalist out there burning people?'

He pulled out his phone and got Control to put him on to PC Sim.

Not answering her Airwave handset. Try her house instead.

She picked up on the seventh ring. *'Oh, come on, can't I even have* one *day off? I got shot yesterday!'*

'You've read *Witchfire—*'

'Yes, I'm feeling much better, thanks for asking. The stitches itch a bit where a shotgun went off in my face, *and my whole chest is one big bruise, but other than that. . .'*

'Do you want me to send Steel over to kiss it better?'

A pause. *'Urgh. . . I think I just threw up a bit in my mouth.'*

Steel peered up at him between her fingers. 'What am I kissing now?'

'The necklacing – trial by fire – does Rowan ever do it?'

'No. That's all *Mrs Shepherd. Rowan doesn't believe in witches so the whole burning people thing sickens her. . . Why?'*

Of course it did. 'Thanks. Enjoy your time off, OK?' He hung up.

If Rowan wouldn't do it, Agnes Garfield wouldn't either. . . But maybe a method-acting nut-bag would. The kind of person who'd go all the way to Iowa to learn about witchcraft. The kind of person who thought they had to live the role in order to play the character. The kind of person who could turn up at a soup kitchen and abduct someone like Roy Forman.

Logan's phone blared at him as he hurried down the stairs to the cell block. Unknown number. He pulled it out. 'McRae?'

'*You the one put an ASAP request on DNA samples from a body? John Doe, torture victim?*'

'Ou Tuesday.' Logan pushed through the doors at the bottom. 'This is what counts as ASAP now, is it?'

'*Sarcasm. Helpful. You try getting anything done when they reorganize your department every three sodding minutes, then lump you with a sodding software* upgrade *that throws false positive and negatives the whole time!*' A pause, filled with what sounded like angry breathing. Then a slow hissing noise. And finally he was back. '*We've a ninety-nine percent match with a Mai Shi-tu, arrested half a dozen times for possession, housebreaking. Low-level drug dealer from Glasgow.*'

The double doors onto the rear podium burst open and Rennie swaggered in, then stuck his arms up, fingers making the victory signs. Like a young, blond, Richard Nixon. 'Who's the daddy? Oh yes!'

'Yeah, well, that would've been really useful information yesterday when it actually mattered.'

'*There's no need to be a dick about it, it's not like—*'

'Next time we say ASAP, we *mean* ASAP.' Logan hung up on him.

A hunched figure hurpled in behind Rennie, leaning heavily on a walking stick, his left leg encased in a filthy cast from the knee down. His face was covered in scabs and scratches, his hair plastered to his head by the rain.

Rennie waved at Logan. Grinned. Then turned and swept an arm towards his limping friend. 'Ladies, and gentlemen, the one, the *only*, Mr Henry Scott!'

Henry Scott stopped where he was, licking his chapped lips, eyes shifting left and right. 'I'm sorry. . .?'

Rennie beamed at Logan again. 'See: told you I could do it. Found him in Kincorth, hiding in a derelict building.'

'I didn't do anything. . .'

The smile slipped from Rennie's face. 'I know you didn't,

Henry.' He patted him on the shoulder. 'I tracked down your sister, she's been worried about you. Wants you to go live with her and the family in Perth. Help you get better.' Then Rennie backed off a pace and sniffed the hand he'd just patted Henry Scott with. He shuddered. 'But first, we need to get you a bath . . .'

Logan stayed where he was while Rennie led Henry Scott away. As soon as they were out of sight, the sound of Rennie whistling 'We Are the Champions' echoed up the stairwell.

He slid the hatch open on cell number three.

Morgan Mitchell lay on her back on the mattress, staring up at the advert for Crimestoppers painted on the ceiling. She raised her head and frowned at him. Then sat up. 'Well, well.' A smile. 'You going to give me a seeing-to with the rubber hoses now?'

'It was you.'

She stood and padded her way across to the door. 'Of course, we could start with some light spanking, if you're not ready for the heavy stuff yet.'

'Agnes Garfield didn't necklace Roy Forman, you did.'

'Little old me?' She bit her bottom lip. 'Now that *would* deserve a sound thrashing. That's what you Brits call it, right?'

'You were there on Friday, with Nichole Fyfe, when he went missing. What did you do: slip him a bottle of supermarket whisky so he'd go with you? So you'd know how it felt to do that to someone?'

A laugh. 'Seriously?'

'This is a joke to you?'

Her eyes narrowed. 'Better believe my *art* is not a joke.'

'You burned a man to death so you could play a part in a film.'

Morgan took a step back from the door. 'I didn't do anything of the kind. I didn't hurt anyone. Yes, I was at the soup kitchen, but I was with Nichole the whole time, helping the homeless. And you can't prove a damn thing.'

'Oh *believe* me, we'll—'

'I did three seasons on *CSI New Orleans*, do you really think I wouldn't know how to clean a crime scene?' A little shrug, then the smile was back. 'You know, if I'd done this terrible thing.'

He stared at her.

'You've got nothing, Inspector. If you *had* something: you'd be charging me.' She spun around on one foot, as if she was on a dance floor. Then settled back onto the mattress, one knee up, an arm behind her head. 'Now, be a good cop and take a hike. I've got atmosphere to soak up.'

51

Insch paced up and down outside FHQ in the rain, grumbling into a mobile phone, an umbrella thrumming over his shiny bald head.

Logan turned up his collar and hurried out through the automatic doors from reception, hopping his way between the puddles. He stopped just short of Insch. 'You knew, didn't you.' It wasn't a question.

Insch curled his lip, the sagging skin on his neck stretching like a tortoise. 'I'll call you back.' He stuck the phone in his pocket. 'So you *finally* deign to speak to me.'

'Why didn't you say anything?'

'You'll be happy to know, I've been speaking to Ma Stewart. We're making her the authorized supplier for authentic *Witchfire* merchandise. It's high quality, it's locally produced, and it helps support Aberdeen's elderly community.'

'Morgan Mitchell.'

'I have . . . spoken with the person she's alleged to have assaulted. Turns out it was all a misunderstanding. He slipped and fell. Banged his head. And when she helped him up, he confused the order of events. He's apologized and withdrawn the charges.'

Logan stared at him. 'What about Roy Forman?'

Insch dug a bag of carrot sticks from his pocket and stuffed one into his mouth, crunching and frowning at the same time. 'The Hardgate Hobo? What about him?'

'She killed him. She lured him away with a bottle of booze, drove him out to the middle of nowhere, and burned him. All for your bloody film!'

'Don't be an idiot. The gentleman she *allegedly* assaulted has dropped the charges. Now let her get back to work.'

Back to work. . .?

Logan jabbed a finger in Insch's chest. 'You *knew*!'

'I have no idea what—'

'Don't, OK? Just. . .' He marched away half a dozen paces, then back again. 'Roy Forman died, *screaming* in agony.'

The only sound was the rain, making drum-rolls on Insch's umbrella. 'Morgan Mitchell – didn't – kill – anyone.'

'She was there the night he was abducted. She *says* she was with Nichole Fyfe, but what do you want to bet Nichole was so stoned you could've paraded half the circus up and down in front of her and she wouldn't have noticed?'

Insch's face was growing darker, the muscles along his jaw rippling. 'And I'm telling you—'

'All that bollocks about "You can't just turn up and drone out your lines, you've got to inhabit the part. You've got to live it." She killed Roy Forman just so she'd know what it felt like.'

He clenched his eyes shut, two trembling fingers pressed against the folds of skin at his neck – taking his pulse. A thick vein throbbed on his forehead. 'Morgan wouldn't—'

'You said it yourself.' Logan poked him in the chest. 'She's a method-acting nutjob. She thinks this performance is going to catapult her to superstar—'

'NO!' Spittle flew from Insch's mouth, accompanied by little flecks of chewed carrot. 'MORGAN MITCHELL DIDN'T KILL ANYONE!'

Logan took a step back. 'She did it, and she thinks we can't touch her.'

'She. . .' Air hissed in and out of his nose, like a broken bellows. 'I've sunk everything I've got into this *bloody* film. We can't afford to go back and reshoot every single scene Mrs Shepherd—'

'What the hell happened to you?' Logan turned on his heel and marched back towards the station. 'You used to be a police officer.'

'Look, Inspector McRae, if you're just going to sit there and scowl at my client, I don't see any point in continuing this interview.' Anthony Chung's lawyer gathered together his paperwork.

'Maybe if your *client* said something other than "no comment", Mr Blake, we'd actually get somewhere.'

Sitting on the other side of the table, Anthony Chung just smiled at him.

Fine.

'Constable Buchan: do the honours.'

'Interview suspended at ten fifty-two.' She reached forward and switched the audio and video off.

Blake stood, but his client stayed where he was.

Anthony's American accent was beginning to fray around the edges, a hint of Scottish creeping in. 'You go. I want to have a word, with The Man. Off the record.'

'I have to advise you not to say anything to the inspector—'

'I'm cool.' The smile became a grin. 'They know I didn't kill anyone.'

'Don't tell him anything.' The lawyer pointed a chewed finger at Logan. 'If I even *think* you've tried to coerce my client, I'll have you suspended quicker than you can say "misconduct".'

'Constable Buchan, escort Mr Blake to the canteen. And make sure he doesn't steal any spoons.'

As soon as the door closed again, Anthony sat forward in his seat. 'Is she OK? Rowan?'

'Bit late to worry about that now, isn't it? After what you made her do?'

'She was so . . . *happy*, yeah? All these years her mom's treated her like she's a little kid or something: telling her where she can go, who she can speak to, who she can love.' Anthony shook his head. 'You know she slit her wrists when the old bitch said she couldn't see me any more? The pills weren't working, she was miserable the whole time. So yeah: I made her happy.'

'Is there a point to this, Anthony? Or are you just showing off as usual.'

'She was like a zombie on the pills, she hated it. Lumbering through the weeks like she wasn't even there.' He wriggled forward in his seat. 'You never love someone enough that you'll do *anything* for them? And I'm not talking about a box of candy and some flowers, or dinner and a movie, I mean change the whole world just 'cos it makes them glow?'

'You made her *kill* people.'

'Yeah, you're all outraged and shit, but I've never seen her that alive before. You know? She's living the dream.' He smiled. 'And you can't do her for the murders – she wasn't in her right mind. It's not her fault.'

'No, it's not.' Logan stood. 'It's yours. And do you know what? As we're off the record: you're going down for at least eight years, and the people you stole from? They'll have someone inside waiting for you.' He held up his hands. 'I'm not trying to threaten you, or pressure you into making a deal, I'm just letting you know you're well and truly screwed. You're responsible for every one of those deaths, *and* the poor sods who got crippled. You won't last a month.'

Anthony picked at a chip on the tabletop. 'I. . .' He licked his lips. Looked up at the camera, sitting dead high up on the wall. 'I did it all for her.'

'You tell the guys in the shower block that. The ones with the homemade knives.'

A little chunk of Formica peeled away beneath his fingernails. 'I need you to look after my mom and dad.'

Logan leaned back against the door and folded his arms.

'I mean, when the McLeods find out it was me stealing from them, they're going to go after him, aren't they?' Anthony gave a little laugh. 'Course they are. They'll think he told me where the other farms were, but he didn't. I followed him to work one day, saw who he spoke to. Then I followed them. Took a couple of weeks, but I worked out how the operation fits together.'

'Your dad works for the McLeods?'

Of course he did. Simon McLeod said he'd paid a fortune getting the best in the business over to grow for him, and according to the US Justice Department, Raymond Chung had form for growing cannabis in San Francisco.

Logan groaned. 'Is that why your father told us the body we found was yours? He wanted his masters to think you were dead, so they wouldn't go after you?'

Anthony stopped picking. 'I *never* stole from Dad's farm. Simon and Creepy Colin McLeod – you wouldn't believe how bad they'll mess you up if they think you're not looking after their merchandise. That's why I never touched the weed Dad was growing.'

'Let me guess: everyone else was fair game?'

'He had nothing to do with the thefts, it was all me.'

'What a *great* son you are. Very thoughtful.'

'He doesn't deserve to get fed to the pigs.' Anthony drew himself up. Shoulders back. 'You get him and Mom into witness protection, and I'll *totally* tell you where all the

McLeods' farms are. You can shut down the whole operation. That's got to be worth something, right?'

Rennie whistled. 'And he's giving us everything? The McLeods are going to *love* that.'

Logan kept going up the stairs. 'Every time he targeted a new farm, he'd ID one of the drones and get Agnes to pay them a visit. Told her they were witches so she'd torture the details out of them. Then they go in, avoid the booby traps, and steal all the cannabis they could fit in their truck.'

'They're going to rip him a new one the minute he sets foot in Craiginches, aren't they?'

'Of course they are. That's why I've got him going in as a vulnerable prisoner.' Logan pulled a sheet of paper from his pocket and handed it over. 'You're always moaning that you never get the credit for anything, so I'm giving you the happy job of going out there and telling Mr and Mrs Chung their little boy's not dead after all. And then take the two of them into custody. It's—' The phone blared. Logan pulled it out. 'McRae.'

'Is this ASAP enough for you?' It was the forensic lab guy he'd given a hard time to earlier.

Logan stuck the phone against his chest and shooed Rennie away. 'Don't just stand there.'

He waited until Rennie scurried off before going back to his mobile. 'Look, I'm sorry about—'

'We got a DNA match off your necklacing victim. And before you get all sarcastic again, I know the samples went in on Sunday, but the one we matched it to didn't hit the system till yesterday evening.'

All the moisture disappeared from Logan's mouth. 'Yesterday evening?'

Please. . .

'A Morgan Mitchell.'

He grinned. Maybe there was a God after all.

*   *   *

537

She kicked and screamed, teeth bared, snapping at the arm of the uniform dragging her off the set. Scarlet hair flashing in the movie spotlights.

Zander Clark slumped in his director's chair, hands over his head.

The rest of the cast and crew just stared.

Insch marched over, throwing his arms in the air, shouting.

And Logan stood there, in the middle of Soundstage Three. 'Morgan Mitchell, I'm detaining you under Section Fourteen of the Criminal Procedure – Scotland – Act 1995, because I suspect you of having committed an offence punishable by imprisonment, namely the murder by burning of one Roy Forman. . .'

Chalmers sat propped up on a barricade of scratchy NHS pillows. The bruising down the left side of her face was aubergine dark, yellows and greens just visible at the edges. An IV line disappeared into a shunt in the back of one hand, little square patches of gauze and cotton wool poking out above the neckline of her hospital gown. A faint dusting of grey coloured the skin of her shaved head, between the tie-dye bruises and scabs.

The other three beds in the ward were occupied: one woman lying flat on her back, snoring; another reading a crime novel the size of a breezeblock; one more lying on her side, shoulders quivering as she cried.

'No, I'm fine. Never better.' Chalmers fiddled with the nurse call button, turning it round and back again in her hand. Never quite pressing it.

'Really?'

She blinked. Pulled on a smile that didn't go anywhere near her pink, watery eyes. 'It's not as bad as it looks. . .'

'You got stabbed twenty times with a pricking blade, and then she tried to drown you.'

Chalmers stared at the call button. 'I'm fine.'

The hospital's background hum droned on, broken by the snores and choked-back tears from the other beds.

Logan laced his fingers together. 'They're going to invalid you out.'

She shook her head. 'I'm. . .' Then wiped a hand across her eyes. 'You got over it, didn't you. You told me. I just need to do what you did: see a psychologist. Try that "talking therapy" thing. I can get over this.'

The ward door banged open and she flinched.

An old lady in a black T-shirt and red tabard reversed into the room, pulling a trolley with tea things on it.

'I'll be fine.'

'You're not getting the choice. You take the early retirement or they instigate disciplinary proceedings. A little ambition's a good thing, but loose cannons only work on TV and in books. People nearly died, just so you could further your career.'

Chalmers sat upright. 'But I can—'

'You're done.'

'Pffff. . .' Logan eased back into the visitor's chair. 'My back is *killing* me.' He wriggled from side to side, pushing the bruises until they snarled.

Someone had tidied Samantha's bedside cabinets, lining up the Lucozade bottles like soldiers on parade, the stack of unread magazines perfectly centred on the veneer surface, the copy of *Witchfire* perched on top of them like a brick.

'So, she pleaded for a bit, then she cried, and then she called for the nurse.' He levered his shoes off and let them thump to the floor. Wiggled his toes. One of them poked through the hole in his right sock. He stuck both feet up on the bed and stifled a yawn. 'So how was your day?'

No reply, just the hiss of the ventilator.

'Yeah, me too. Did I tell you Morgan Mitchell's still denying everything? Doesn't matter – we've impounded the car she was driving Friday night. It's going to have traces of Roy Forman in it. And accelerant.'

A knock on the door, and Nurse Claire popped her head in, eyebrows up as if she'd just sat on something sharp. She slipped into the room, with one hand behind her back, the other holding a finger up to her lips.

Logan smiled. 'Before you say anything: I need to buy more socks. I know.'

She bumped the door closed with her bum. 'If anyone finds out, I'll be for it, so this is just between us, OK?'

Oh. . . If this was going to be an offer of sex, she was in for a bit of disappointment. 'Actually, I'm—'

'Tada!' Claire pulled her other hand from behind her back. There was a shoebox in it with little holes poked in the side. 'Very much *not* allowed in the hospital.'

She placed it on the bed and removed the lid. 'She's ten weeks old.'

A pair of beautiful blue eyes peered up at him from a little stripy bundle of fluff with impossibly large hairy ears. It opened its mouth in a silent meow.

'Her name's Misty, but you can call her Cthulhu, if you like.'

A kitten and a sex toy, all in one day. 'But—'

Claire patted him on the arm. 'You're very welcome. And I've got a starter pack from the vets for you at the nurses' station. Just make sure you take her home before anyone sees her.' Claire checked her watch. 'Better get back to work.'

And she was gone.

OK. So now he had a cat to look after.

Couldn't deny that she was cute. . .

He reached in and took Misty / Cthulhu from the shoebox and settled into the chair again. She was like a little rigid

540

ball of fur, tiny needle-sharp claws scrambling for purchase on his shirt. Not the cuddling type then.

He plonked the kitten down on the bed instead and helped himself to one of the bottles of Lucozade, twisted the top off and took a swig. It was warm, but drinkable.

'I know what you're thinking, Cthulhu: how did Morgan know where to burn Roy Forman's body? Turns out that when they were bonding with the coven in Wyoming, Nichole told her all about her misspent youth in Aberdeen, including where she and her dog-murdering boyfriend used to burn the cars they'd nicked.'

Cthulhu padded her way up and down the covers, sniffing things.

Logan frowned at her. 'No offence, but I feel like a bit of a pillock talking to a cat. I don't care what Goulding says.'

Samantha sighed. 'Well, it's not her fault she can't answer back, is it?'

'I suppose.' Another scoof of Lucozade. 'I phoned the architects, by the way. He's getting the builders organized again. Should start sometime in the next couple of weeks.'

'Halle-bleeding-luiah.' She sat up in bed and picked Cthulhu up, one hand cupped beneath the pale fuzzy tummy. 'Don't you listen to stinky old Daddy, you're perfectly lovely to talk to.'

A burp rattled Logan's diaphragm. 'Oops, pardon *me*.'

He sagged back into the chair.

'Been a weird kind of a day. . . After all the sodding about, and the drug raids, and catching Roy Forman's killer, the ACC says that DI's job in Peterhead's mine if I want it.'

Samantha stared at him, her voice jagged and brittle. 'Congratulations.'

'What, and spend half my life either stuck on the A90, or never seeing you? Told him I'd wait till something permanent came up in Aberdeen.'

Cthulhu did her silent mew again.

Samantha looked as if she was trying to hide a smile by nuzzling her nose into the space between the kitten's ears. 'What about Wee Hamish's cheque?'

'Think I'm going to give it to the guys who run the soup kitchen down the Green. Roy Forman would've liked that, wouldn't he?'

'No idea. Never met him.' Cthulhu wriggled and meeped, until she was allowed back down onto the covers. Then Samantha reached for the copy of *Witchfire* on the bedside cabinet. 'Come on, *Jackanory* Boy: make with the story.'

Logan loosened his tie and settled back in his seat. Opened the book. Smiled. Girlfriend, kitten, and a pat on the back. Maybe things were going to be OK after all. 'Right, here we go:

"Above the tower block, the slate-coloured clouds crackled with lightning, followed a heartbeat later by a chest-tightening bellow of thunder. . ."'

And then, just to round off a perfect day, Cthulhu peed on the end of the bed.

STUART MACBRIDE

A *SUNDAY TIMES* NO.1 BESTSELLER

MULTIPLE AWARD-WINNING AUTHOR

**READ ON TO FIND OUT MORE ABOUT
STUART MACBRIDE'S BESTSELLING NOVELS**

'The Logan McRae series is set in Aberdeen, the Granite City, Oil Capital of Europe, perched on the east coast of Scotland. They always say, "write what you know" so I did – using Aberdeen as the backdrop for a series of horrific crimes, murders, serial killers, with much eating of chips and drinking of beer.

Of these, the only ones I have any direct experience of are beer and chips, but some nice local police officers helped me fill in the rest.'

Stuart MacBride

Winter in Aberdeen: murder, mayhem and terrible weather

It's DS Logan McRae's first day back on the job after a year off on the sick, and it couldn't get much worse. Three-year-old David Reid's body is discovered in a ditch: strangled, mutilated and a long time dead. And he's only the first. There's a serial killer stalking the Granite City and the local media are baying for blood.

Soon the dead are piling up in the morgue almost as fast as the snow on the streets, and Logan knows time is running out. More children are going missing. More are going to die. If Logan isn't careful, he could end up joining them.

It's summertime in the Granite City: the sun is shining, the sky is blue and people are dying...

It starts with Rosie Williams, a prostitute, stripped naked and beaten to death down by the docks – the heart of Aberdeen's red light district. For DS Logan McRae it's a bad start to another bad day.

Rosie won't be the only one making an unscheduled trip to the morgue. Across the city six people are burning to death in a petrol-soaked squat, the doors and windows screwed shut from the outside.

And despite Logan's best efforts, it's not long before another prostitute turns up on the slab...

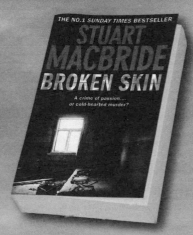

The Granite City's seedy side is about to be exposed...

A serial rapist is leaving a string of tortured women behind him, but while DS Logan McRae's girlfriend, PC Jackie 'Ball Breaker' Watson, is out acting as bait, he's trying to identify a blood-drenched body dumped outside Accident and Emergency.

Logan's investigations suggest someone in the local bondage community has developed a taste for violent death, and he soon finds himself dragged into the twilight world of pornographers, sex-shops and S&M.

Meanwhile, the prime suspect in the rape case turns out to be Aberdeen Football Club's star striker. Logan thinks they've got it horribly wrong, but Jackie is convinced the footballer's guilty and she's hell-bent on a conviction at any cost...

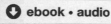

Panic strikes the Granite City...

When an offshore container turns up at Aberdeen Harbour full of human meat, it kicks off the largest manhunt in the Granite City's history.

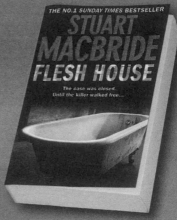

Twenty years ago 'The Flesher' was butchering people all over the UK – turning victims into oven-ready joints – until Grampian's finest put him away. But eleven years later he was out on appeal. Now he's missing and people are dying again.

When members of the original investigation start to disappear, Detective Sergeant Logan McRae realizes the case might not be as clear cut as everyone thinks...

Twenty years of secrets and lies are being dragged into the light. And the only thing that's certain is Aberdeen will never be the same again.

'You can't be an eyewitness if I cut out your eyes...'

Someone's preying on Aberdeen's growing Polish population. The pattern is always the same: men abandoned on building sites, barely alive, their eyes gouged out and the sockets burned.

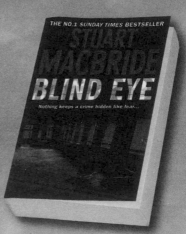

With the victims too scared to talk, and the only witness a paedophile who's on the run, Grampian Police is getting nowhere fast. The attacks are brutal, they keep on happening, and soon DS Logan McRae will have to decide how far he's prepared to bend the rules to get a result.

The Granite City is on the brink of gang warfare; the investigating team are dogged by allegations of corruption; and Logan's about to come to the attention of Aberdeen's most notorious crime lord...

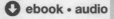

ebook • audio

Everyone deserves a second chance

Richard Knox has done his time and seen the error of his ways. He wants to leave his dark past behind, so why shouldn't he be allowed to live wherever he wants?

Detective Sergeant Logan McRae isn't thrilled about having to help a violent rapist settle into Aberdeen. Even worse, he's stuck with the man who put Knox behind bars, DSI Danby, supposedly around to 'keep an eye on things'.

Only things are about to go very, very wrong.

Edinburgh gangster Malk the Knife wants a slice of Aberdeen's latest development boom. Local crime lord Wee Hamish Mowat has ominous plans for Logan's future. And Knox's past isn't finished with him yet...

'You will raise money for the safe return of Alison and Jenny McGregor. You have fourteen days, or Jenny will be killed.'

Aberdeen's own mother-daughter singing sensation are through to the semi-finals of TV smash-hit *Britain's Next Big Star*. But their reality-TV dream has turned into a real-life nightmare. The ransom demand appears in all the papers, on the TV, and the internet, telling the nation to dig deep if they want to keep Alison and Jenny alive. Time is running

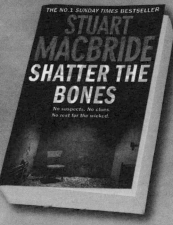

out, but DS Logan McRae and his colleagues have nothing to go on: the kidnappers haven't left a single piece of forensic evidence and there are no witnesses.

It looks as if the price of fame just got a lot higher...

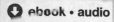
ebook · audio

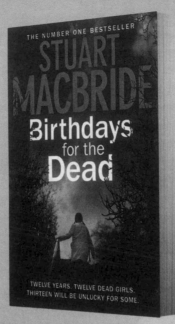

THE NUMBER ONE BESTSELLER

STUART MACBRIDE

Birthdays
for the
Dead

TWELVE YEARS. TWELVE DEAD GIRLS.
THIRTEEN WILL BE UNLUCKY FOR SOME.

Detective Constable Ash Henderson has a dark secret...

Five years ago his daughter, Rebecca, disappeared on the eve of her thirteenth birthday. A year later the first card arrived: homemade, with a Polaroid stuck to the front. Rebecca, strapped to a chair, gagged and terrified. Every year another card – each one worse than the last.

The tabloids call him 'The Birthday Boy'. He's been snatching girls for years, always just before their thirteenth birthday, killing them slowly, then torturing their families with his homemade cards.

But Ash hasn't told anyone what really happened to Rebecca – they all think she ran away – because if anyone finds out, he'll be taken off the investigation. And he's sacrificed too much to give up before his daughter's murderer gets what he deserves...